Also by
Terrence Damon Spencer

Strong

The beginning of a series

and

The REP

PREMISES

TERRENCE DAMON SPENCER

PUBLISHING

Published by Dreams To Paper Publishing
P.O. Box 9241, Pueblo, Colorado 81008

This is the work of fiction. The events described are imaginary.
The settings and characters are fictitious and not intended to represent
specific places or persons. Any actual persons, living or deceased in
comparison are only a pure, coincidental
resemblance.

All brand names and product names used in this book are trademarks,
registered trademarks, or trade names of their respective holders.
Dreams to Paper Publishing is not associated with any product or
vendor in this book.

Graphics and cover by Dreams To Paper Publishing
Cover design by Dreams To Paper Publishing
Copy Editing by Erica N. Guerra
Author's Photograph: Tabitha Spencer

ISBN Paperback: 978-0-9981456-7-9
ISBN eBook: 978-0-9981456-6-2
ISBN Hard Cover: 978-0-9981456-8-6

CHAPTER 1

SAFE TRAVELS

(A late Tuesday December Afternoon)

The intense record setting blizzard denies travelers a clear path to their destinations and bullies them from the snow covered pavements. Many travelers who have ignored the weatherman's warning, "To only travel if absolutely necessary", now find themselves abandoning their vehicles on the sides of highways and interstates. Their only option is to seek refuge to nearby hotels from the relentless, early December snow pounding. Howling sixty-seven mile an hour winds create scattered snow drifts like icy ocean waves through Gastonia, North Carolina. Most businesses and schools have been given the warning to shut down since the conditions were soon to become worse.

Lloyd Burgess, a sixty-four-year-old black gentleman, and manager of Quick Time gas station, is about to check out his last customer before shutting down his store. His thick, short cut afro and well-trimmed beard rival the whiteness of the outside snow; like thick frosting on a chocolate Christmas cookie, his granddaughter often told him.

He exhales sharply through puckered lips then fans himself with a notebook next to the register. He could barely tolerate the rising heat in his store. *You gone boil me to death one day messing with that damn thermostat, Saundra.*

Tired of hearing how she had things to do, and how her daycare provider was about to close, Lloyd sent his cashier, Saundra, home early when she was supposed to help him close the store. *Lies.* He had already overheard her talking on her phone with her mother, telling her the diapers were at the bottom of the orange and pink bag. No matter. He had shut this store down a million times alone in the past. What is one more day? However, this was no regular day.

He wipes the beads of sweat forming on his forehead, then rolls up the sleeves of his dark gray Oxford shirt to mid forearm. A black inked detailed tattoo (a military issued rifle turned upside down with the muzzle in a set of combat boots, a Kevlar helmet balanced on the stock, with the words "Honor the Fallen" written beneath it) showed on his forearm as he reached for his collar. He clears his throat as he unbuttons the second and third button then checks the thermostat behind him just as his last customer, an old colleague from the steel mill he once worked with, walks up to the counter.

Lloyd rapidly presses the down button until the temperature drops from eighty-five to seventy-two, then turns to address the customer with a smile. "Hey Milton! How the hell are you today, sir? Did you find everything okay?" Lloyd asks, pulling the customer's windshield wiper fluid, powdered donuts, and cherry coke closer to the register to scan.

The man's flannel jacket and John Deere hat is seasoned with melting snow. "Hey—Hey! Yeah, I think I got what I need." His fatty neck and jaw jiggles briefly as he fishes around in his back pocket for his wallet. "I'd be doing a whole lot better if this damn snow would go away. God's taking a big, white crap on us, and I don't like it."

Lloyd laughs. "You staying healthy?" He scans the donuts.

"I'm trying too..." He chuckles as Lloyd places the powder covered delights in a bag. "Though them sugary thangs prove I'm lyin' through my teeth, huh? Momma won't have it, though. That junk food and all. So I'll gulp those down like a pelican before I get to her house." He tosses a ten dollar bill on the counter before getting his total.

Lloyd flashes him a surprised eye. "Gonna go pay a visit to your Mom in *this*?"

"Yeah. I gotta get through Charolette quick. I know Momma will have a dang fit if she's snowed in with no one there with her." He clears his throat. A nasty sound of mucus and spit loosening, gurgling, enough to make anyone gag. But he held it in his mouth.

Lloyd knows by the sound of it that he needed to spit, so he reaches for a paper funnel next to the register. Before he could offer it to him, he swallows it down with the frown of a man taking a spicy shot of whiskey.

Lloyd cringes, quickly remembering where he had left off in the conversation to take his mind from it. "Sounds like fun."

"You don't know my Momma. Fun ain't nowhere in the agenda; I promise you. Bunch of undone jobs I gotta tend to, fixing the dishwasher, patching a broken windah. Heh, not to mention a whole heap'a snow I have to plow. So, no, sir... No fun at all."

Lloyd chuckles. "Well, if she's anything like I remember you were, you got your hands full with more than just the work." They both chuckle before Lloyd asks, "Is this gonna be everything?"

"Yes sir, Mr. Burgess. Should have everything I need right here...oh wait!" He grabs a bag of barbeque chips and tosses it to the counter.

Lloyd shakes his head, laughing in his throat. "Alright. Well, you know this window washer fluid is buy one get one half off?"

"No, I should be okay with just this."

"Now, I wouldn't feel right if you walked outta here without what's owed to ya; gone ahead and grab yourself one more on me. You may need it with this mess going on out there. Better to have it than to not when ya need it."

"You may be right."

4

As Milton steps away from the counter to retrieve his extra item, Lloyd notices a beat-up, red Suburban backing up into the front parking space. From the looks of it, with its dented rear bumper and broken out rear window, sealed with what looked like trash bags and duct tape, the truck has seen its share of accidents and fender benders.

He throws his hands on the counter and groans with frustration. "Come on now." He says, drumming his well-groomed fingernails on the counter. "Look at this mess. I'm gonna have to flash this closed sign to keep people from pulling up here. I don't know why people ain't just staying home. Look at it out there! What the hell could be so important that you need to come to a gas station in the middle of a *got*dang blizzard?"

"Well, how about gas? That's important." Milton laughs.

"They didn't pull up to no pump, so..."

"Yeah, it looks like I won't be your last customer today." Milton says, returning to the counter. "You better shut it down and turn off that sign if you're gonna make it home."

"Yeah. Yeah, I sure as hell don't wanna be stuck here either. I got a television, a few beers and a remote waiting on me."

Lloyd finishes bagging up the items with one eye on the Suburban. He hands Milton his bag and drops the change in his palm.

"Be careful out there. Drive safe!" Lloyd says, closing the drawer to his register. "And be careful going out that door. Storm blew that door open and ripped the arm off of my hydraulic door closer. Gotta get a new one."

Milton plants his free hand on top of his hat to hold it down. The electronic bell chimes as he exits the store. A cold gust of wind, accompanied by snow, blows wildly inside giving Lloyd a quick chill through his thin clothing.

"Woo Wee!" yells Milton. His quick reflexes grabs the door, before it could swing open too wide, and pulls it closed. He then turns back to the window and mouths the words, "Have a Merry Christmas," then gives Lloyd a quick smile and a wave before disappearing into the parking lot.

Lloyd takes a look outside at the Suburban, just sitting there at idle. He could faintly hear the gulping sound from the dual exhaust just before another gust of wind thunders against his store windows, bringing a blinding blanket of snow with it. *What in* the *hell are they doing out there?* He impatiently waves at the truck through the store window. *Better get'cho asses in here before I lock these doors.*

He gives the SUV one more irritated glance as he stares over the shoulder of a plastic snow man through the window before flipping off the light switch to his blue and red neon *OPEN* sign. He then, plunges his right hand deep into his pocket, withdrawing a single key. *You wanna sit out there gone 'head and* sit *out there, then, but these doors fixen to be locked.*

As he rounds the corner from behind the counter, the key slips from his grasp and lands behind the wire potato chip display stand.

"Jesus Christ, Lloyd." He mutters.

He reaches blindly behind the stand and partly under the counter. He grimaces as his fingertips touch thick dust and an unknown squishy chunk of God-knows-what, before feeling its smooth metal surface surrounded in gritty dirt. He snags the prize, catching some of the gunk under his clean nails.

"Got'chu!" He grins.

The front door chimes as it blows open. Startled, he jumps to his feet, nearly knocking over the potato chip stand, to see who had entered. He whips his head around, panning every corner of the store. No one.

The wind is blowing so hard it forces the door back open, allowing more snow inside. He rushes over, leaning into the door with everything his one hundred and fifty-four-pound body could muster, finally closing it tightly.

He takes a second to catch his breath while planting the side of his foot against the door. "Hello?" he yells. "I'm about to lock up, so make your presence known before I secure this hatch."

He gets no reply. Just the thundering wind against the door. He checks the ceiling mirror and pans the store once more. Nothing. Satisfied, he aims his key into the keyhole but stops halfway when he notices the red Suburban is gone. Nothing outside except his truck, and an empty lot of snow drifts and disappearing tire tracks.

Lloyd hunches his shoulders. *Must've left after seeing me turn my sign off.* He jams the key in and gives it a good hard turn, then repeats the same thing in the second keyhole, locking himself in.

He backs away from the door, dusting off the snow from his arms and shoulders, when he bumps into someone behind him.

Startled, he spins around raising his fist to a short petite woman cradling a six pack of Shepard's beer. The bottom half of her face is covered by a black scarf wrapped around her neck, and a knitted cap pulled down on her head, barely above her eyes. The only visible part of her face is her dark brown eyes and milky white skin.

"Sweet Jesus!" he exclaims dropping his fist to clutch the center of his chest. "Young lady..." he swallows deep, then catches his breath. "Where on earth did you come from? The store is closed now."

"I'm so sorry, sir." she muffled through the scarf with a giggle. "I was back by the beverages. Your sign said *open* when I came in. You're pretty much the only store, that is, thank God."

"Well, I yelled, 'Hello'. Ya didn't hear me?"

"I'm sorry, I didn't hear anything. This scarf over my ears is kinda thick and my hearing is bad as it is." She places the beer on the counter. "Can I just pay for this? I don't want anything else."

He takes in a deep breath to calm his still racing heart, then checks the door once more.

"Okay. I can only take cash. I just shut my credit card machine down, so, I hope that's okay." He says, making his way around to the back of the counter once again, suddenly catching her strong fragrance of marijuana. "And you know that's three-two beer. Not regular."

"Yeah, I have cash." She says. "This is gonna have to do. With this weather, all the liquor stores are closed. May as well have some fun when you're gonna be snowed in, right?"

He flashes a partial smile at the corner of his mouth but doesn't take his eyes off of the young lady, who in turn, doesn't remove hers from him. She doesn't seem like a threat to him, yet he still gives her the once over inspection. She doesn't stand awkwardly as if she were concealing a weapon. Her coat is closed, and both hands are laid on the case of beer she wanted to purchase.

"Is that what brought you out in this weather? Beer?" He asks.

"I know. I am just trying to get home from a friend's house. I wish I had some liquor, to be honest with you. But like I said..."

He checks outside to the parking lot once more. "Did you walk? I don't see no car out there waiting for you."

"Yes sir. I refuse to be stuck at her house in this weather. Her Dad is a piece of shit perv and he makes me uncomfortable. I'd prefer to be home and in my own bed."

He scans her beer. *Calm down Lloyd. She ain't no gun wielding psychopath.*

"Well, if you have a ways to go, I'd be happy to give you a ride, young lady. That weather is something else right now and I'm quite confident my truck can get you where you need. I don't think you can see two feet in front of you out there, and this storm ain't something to be testing your luck with, especially walking with a case of beer."

"No, I'll be okay, sir. Thank you."

"Okay. Well, is that gonna be all for you, sweetie?"

"Yeah, this should be it." she says, her innocent stare shifting to the contents of his register as he opened it. "Oh, and I'll take some gum. And a pack of Winston 100's—and also the condoms behind you."

"Damn. What happened to that being it?" He chuckles. "You want the box or the soft pack." He says, turning his back to her to locate the cigarettes and condoms hanging on the wall behind him.

"The soft pack, please."

"Not a problem. Like I've said, I'm about to leave soon. Are you sure you—" He stops in mid-turn seeing in the store window, the reflection of the woman he was talking with, and now a tall man beside her, aiming a gun at the back of his head.

Lloyd immediately drops the box of condoms and raises his hands slowly to just shoulder height. "Now, don't go doing

10

anything stupid." His heart kicks into overdrive as he gradually turns to face them. Suddenly he is staring down the barrel of a nickel-plated, snub nose .38 revolver, held by a tall, thin, bald white male. His face is partially covered by a bright-red scarf (in the same fashion as the girl, now standing behind him). His aim is shaky.

"Shut up and back away from the register, nigger! And you better not move. Stay just like you are." The man sits on the counter, swinging his legs over it and to the other side, while keeping the barrel trained on Lloyd. "Where's your safe?!" he demands, shoving the gun closer to his face.

Lloyd flinches with trembling hands. His lower jaw quivering and unable to answer. The man smirked at the wide-eyed fear on Lloyd's face as if he were drawing power from it.

The man raises his gun, pushing it closer to Lloyd's face. "I said, 'Where's the goddamn *safe*!?'" he exclaims, cocking the hammer back with his thumb, then aiming, slowly raising the barrel to the old man's forehead.

Years of therapy, to cure his post-traumatic stress disorder, could not have prepared Lloyd for what he was facing at this moment. Brief flashbacks of the Vietnam War, and gruesome acts surface the anxiety-filled, alcoholic, paranoid veteran he thought he had under control. His breaths stutter, hands tremble and his eyes shut tight as the old demons of war invade his mind.

"Don't you fucking have a heart attack on me, old dude. Not before you give us what we came here for." He nudges his forehead with the barrel. "Hey! I'm not screwing around."

Lloyd clinches two shaky fists beside his head and takes in deep breaths to calm himself. Slowly, he opens his eyes taking notice of the cheap swastika tattoo between the thumb and index finger of the man's gun hand.

"I-I don't have a safe."

The man looks over to the girl, "What the hell are you waiting for?"

As if released from a deep, gazing trance, the girl removes a small, black, plastic grocery bag and makes her way around the counter. She looks up at Lloyd, with sorry in her eyes then begins scooping handfuls of cash and dumping it in the bag.

The man pistol-whips him, knocking him back against the wall, where he drops to the floor and crushes a box of Christmas decorations that he was going to put up the next day. "I know there's a damn safe in here somewhere!"

"Holy shit, there's gotta be at least five-hundred in this drawer. This is good. Get what we came here for and let's go! Fuck that safe." The girl says while tying a knot in the bag handles.

"No, he's got more." He kicks Lloyd's legs then yells down to him. "I know you have a safe in here old man! Where the hell is it!? Stop jacking around or I swear to God..."

"I told you. Ain't no safe here! Just take that and go, please. It's all that's in here." he pleads.

"Damn it, Dean, let's go!" The girl screams.

12

Dean drops his aim and turns to her with a disgusted and disappointed look in his eyes. "*What* the *fuck* did you just do?"

"Let's go!" she yells again.

He throws his hands up. "You just gave him my Goddamn name! I can't believe you just *fucking* did that. Are you serious?"

"It doesn't matter now. Get the keys and let's go! Now!"

Lloyd takes advantage of their quarrel and locates the glowing red panic button, just underneath the counter. It's a little more than arm's length away but he has to do something. He scoots a little closer, then stretches out his arm, his hand still shaking, his index finger extends, finally hitting its target firmly.

"Hey—hey—hey!" The girl yells quickly pointing down to Lloyd.

Dean spins around, acting on impulse to Lloyd still holding the button down. He takes aim with his pistol and fires. The .38 caliber slug finds its exit at the back of his skull and lodges into the wall behind him.

The girl's jaw dropped just as fast as her beer and bag of money hit the floor. The site of Lloyd's lifeless body falling limp to the floor was something she'd never seen, nor ever wanted to see in her lifetime. "No! No—No—No! What did you do!?" Tears well in her eyes quickly, as she nearly collapses from her sudden weakened state.

"Shut the fuck up, Steph!" he exclaims, now jamming his hands deep into Lloyd's pockets. "Pick up the money and get to the truck!"

13

He removes Lloyd's wallet, keys, and the gold watch from his wrist. (Dean tosses her the keys, silently delegating her the next step of their escape.) Dean can hear the keys jiggling from her shaking hands as she aims multiple keys to the inside deadbolt keyhole until finally unlocking it.

"Get a fucking move on!" Yells Dean.

When she unlocks the final bolt, the door blows open with such force, if she had not stepped aside to pick up the sack of money she set down, it would have taken her face with it. The door crashes to the other side and smashes the breakaway glass, crumbling down to the tiled floor.

Steph nearly slips on the glass pieces as she grabs the stolen belongings and races out of the door.

Dean stands over Lloyd, who's arm and finger are still extended from his last act of desperation. He kneels to see what it was Lloyd's finger may have been pointing too. To his horror, he notices the flashing red, candylike button underneath the counter.

"Fuck!" he stumbles back in a hurry, then scrambles to his feet and races out the door, just as Steph pulls around in the red Suburban and slides to a stop.

He yanks open the door. "Move—I'm driving!"

He pushes her over to the passenger side. "That asshole pushed a panic button, so cops are coming. The snow is gonna

14

hold them up, so we got some time to get the fuck out of here. You got that money?"

Steph holds up her quivering hand, dangling the plastic bag.

Dean slams on the accelerator. The throaty sound of the exhaust roared as they passed a man nearby, shoveling packed snow from around his tires, on the side of the road. He watches as the back end of the red Suburban fishtails and slides its way down the unplowed street until it disappeared into the blinding chaos.

CHAPTER 2

TRESSPASSERS

Steph's feet are planted firmly on the suburban floor mat, her nails digging into the armrest with her body pressed deep into the weathered, cloth bucket seat. "Slow down!" she yells. "You don't have control of the truck and it's fucking sliding. You're gonna wreck us!"

"I'm in four-wheel, shut up!"

"You can still wipe out in four-wheel. You *don't* have to drive like this. Nobody is fucking chasing us, so just please—please, slow the fuck down!"

Dean glances at her briefly, drumming his fingers on the steering wheel. Gradually, he lets off the accelerator.

As the truck slows, he gains more control and Steph releases her death grip from the armrest. She takes in a few shuddering deep breaths, finding it near impossible to calm herself now that she is an accomplice to a murder. From the corner of her eye, she watches Dean leaning forward on the steering wheel with his fingers hooked on top of it. His lips are puckered in an unhappy firmness with a touch of squinting anger in his eyes. Neither of them say another word for the next few miles.

❦ ❦ ❦ ❦

Still shaken up and frustrated, Steph unwraps the pack of cigarettes she took from the store, but not before wiping the spot of blood from the thin plastic wrapping. "You didn't have to kill him." She says breaking their silence. "We were supposed to just go in there and scare the shit out of him. That's all." She cracks her window, lights a cigarette, then takes a long drag. "Scare the shit out of him, and make a little money in the process, *that's* all!"

"What did you expect me to do? You told that jig my name, Steph. Then you screamed all crazy and shit. I thought he pulled a gun—so I shot him."

With her hands still shaking, Steph takes puff after puff until her cigarette is nearly gone within a couple of minutes. She crams the finished butt through the partially opened window, while holding in her last drag of smoke. "Where are we going?" She asks calmly, blowing the rest of the smoke through the window.

"What do you mean, 'Where are we going?' We have to finish the job."

17

"You're shit'n me, right? We just killed the dude, we're in a stolen truck and we're *going* to his house now? Are you fucking nuts? Abort mission, man!"

"We were paid good money," He glances at her. "We hit the house as planned, search it and then get the fuck outta Dodge."

"That was the plan, but now it's gonna be even harder to find anything-since you *killed* him;" she mutters; "he was supposed to be with us for this part. But you had to get greedy with the whole freak'n 'Where's your safe!?'"

"We just have to look around, so we aren't risking being caught any faster because it won't take long. Relax. Besides, it's just *one* dude, and he lives alone. How big can his house be?"

🦋 🦋 🦋 🦋

(6:23 PM)

Approximately thirty-minutes before nightfall, Dean and Steph pull in front of an old, white, two-story, Victorian-style home that is barely visible in the subsiding storm. Hints of the front porch are visible from under the huge snow drifts formed around it, as if the home were sinking in a sea of white waves. A forest of snow-capped trees frame the backyard, and on the sides, random pines and bushes outline its flanks. It was one of only a few houses on the long road in Harrisburg, North Carolina.

A living room curtain of the brown house across the road is gradually pulled back, while the homeowner observes the Suburban approaching.

"Wow, that's pretty big for just one dude to live in." Steph says, rolling her window down to get a clearer view. The snow blows in, cooling the comfortable warmth they had sat in for nearly an hour. "Now what?"

Dean parks the SUV in front of the house, then cuts the engine. "Let's make this quick."

Steph takes notice of the distance in the deep snow, then flashes a defiant gaze back at him. "Hell no, you could've pulled up closer to the front door! Don't you think?"

"What, and get stuck? Quit your bitching and let's go! And not the front door either. Head to the back." he orders.

"Fuck, that's even further."

Dean wastes no time jumping out into the snow, leaving Steph with no option but to do the same. The snow is deep, coming up to her crotch. She has to lift her knees high if she is to gain any ground and catch up to the taller Dean, who has no problem stepping through like an elk, the snow barely coming above his knees.

Steph, shivering, stands closer to Dean for warmth, as he fumbles around for the right key to the old paint and wood chipped door. She notices the forest tree line behind them, and how still it looks despite the harsh, blowing wind. The dark, thin trees shoot up to the sky. The overcast covers their true height.

Even though it was bright and white outside, the forest had a dark look and feel to it. She then notices the tiny path into it...dark and narrow. She couldn't shake the sensation...the feeling that something was out there looking back at them through the trees.

Dean drops the keys.

"Damn it!" he exclaims startling Steph from her gaze, as he kneels into the snow.

"What?"

"I dropped the damn keys in the snow."

"Oh my God—are you serious?" She says, cold and nervous, as she bounces on her toes. "This is a bad sign. I think we should just go. It's gonna be dark soon. Like, *real* soon."

Dean ignores her and removes his right glove to fish around in the deep snow. "Got'em!" he brags, dangling them in her face.

The hinges of the screen door squeal, along with the sound of the rusted storm door spring, stretching across the middle, as he opens it. Once again, he fumbles with the keys, trying one after the other, until the fifth key finally turns the deadbolt lock. The door doesn't open. Dean leans into it with his shoulder and breaks the door free from the thick, dried paint that sealed it.

"That's funny." He says.

"What's wrong?"

"It's like this door hasn't been opened in a while."

The door creeks and pops open with bits of paint and dust falling to the floor. He peeks inside. Immediately, the combined smell of mold and mildew saturate his nose with a musty odor.

"Pew, Damn it! That's bad," he chokes, "I can barely see a damn thing in here. We're going to have a hard time in about thirty-minutes."

Steph wastes no time entering, shoving her partner inside to escape the cold. She then grabs ahold of the door to close it, but it snatches away from her grasp and slams shut. For a moment she pauses, staring at the doorknob in wonder of what just happened. *Had to be the wind from the storm.*

"Shit, that's horrible. You would think he'd clean this place once." Dean scanned the kitchen, only able to see what the fading light, through the window above the sink, would provide. Part of the kitchen counter, an old wood table, and chair are barely visible. The darkness of the room makes it even harder for him to ignore the overwhelming smell, "You don't smell it?!" He asks, almost begging the question for a confirmation it wasn't just him.

Steph breaks her stare with a grimacing frown. "Geez that is funky, but it *is* an old house."

While stomping the snow from their boots and dusting themselves off, Dean notices a faint echo from the noise they are creating. The type of echo made when someone moves into their new home...a home that's empty, with nothing to absorb the sound.

"Shh–Shh," He taps Steph, still swatting the snow from her crotch and pants, on the shoulder."

21

She pauses to listen. "What?"

He feels along the wall next to the door, and flips the light switch, revealing a near-empty and spacey kitchen. The only furniture – a small, dusty, old table, two kitchen chairs, and an old yellow refrigerator that was partially hidden behind the door when they entered. There are two other doorless entries to the kitchen—one directly in front of them, and the other to the right, framing the pitch darkness on the other side. They both stood, puzzled.

"What the hell is this." he says.

"You sure this is the right house?"

"The keys worked, *didn't* they?" He snaps.

"Are you sure that old guy lives here?" Steph opens the yellow cabinets; each one is bare and dusty inside. "I mean, I'm no rocket scientist, but it looks pretty fucking empty in here to me," she says leaving them all open.

Dean takes interest in the yellow, and near-antique refrigerator to their left, pulling the silver handle to the freezer up top. Empty. He then opens the refrigerator door below. The interior light doesn't come on and the inside is practically bare— housing all but one blue Tupperware bowl on the top rack. The temperature inside is slightly warmer than the kitchen. He flicks the refrigerator bulb with his middle finger a couple of times.

"It's probably not plugged in." Steph says, noticing the loose cord dangling from a bent nail in the wall, and reaches for it.

22

"Don't worry about it. Leave it alone!" Dean orders before she could grab it.

Curious, Dean reaches for the bowl just as the refrigerator starts running. The light inside flickers, then steadies to a low watt glow.

He draws back his hand as if he were avoiding a steel trap. "You fuck'n..." he mutters angrily.

Steph, standing behind him, facing the opposite direction, looks around the empty kitchen as he grabs and opens the container. He peels back the lid, breaking the vacuum seal. Immediately, he could hear crackling-like an amplified bowl of Rice Krispies cereal. He snatches off the lid to find it full of rotting meat, teaming with maggots.

"Shit!" he yells, dropping the bowl.

The light in the fridge flickers out.

Steph spins around. "What? What's wrong *now*?" She looks over his shoulder.

"God damn maggots, man!" he hisses as he quickly jumps to his feet and frantically wipes his hands on his pants.

The kitchen light blows out with a flash. And in that instance, unbeknownst to them, a dark manlike figure appeared in the doorway, leading to the hall behind them.

"This is just not working out for shit!" Steph says.

"Get your phone."

Steph impatiently removes her gloves, then her cell phone, from her coat pocket, and activates her flashlight app. Within seconds of the app being used, her phone beeps.

"Fuck, I thought I charged this thing." She aims the beam of light toward the spilled contents in front of Dean. "Maggots?" she laughs. "Looks like a bowl of rice to me, you idiot."

Dean takes another look. Molded brown rice, and square chunks of what looks like meat, dumped in front of him, but no maggots. *Man, I must be losing my shit.* He kicks the container away, splattering the contents against the wall, near the outlet where the cord dangled. He grabs the cord with a confusing frown on his face, then plugs it in. The light comes on once again, but this time, a little brighter than before.

"You should have kicked your meth habit like you did that bowl, and maybe you wouldn't be seeing shit," she laughs.

"Fuck off! I swear, that damn bowl had... Nevermind. Let's do this and get the hell out of here."

"Whatever!" She turns her attention to the doorless doorway in front of them, which she soon finds out, leads into a dark hallway. "There has to be another light switch around here somewhere. We should just leave that fridge open until we find something." She says panning her light down the hall to her left, leading to a room at the end, then to her right-where she could see a portion of the foyer staircase. She decides to take her chances venturing down the hall to her right, ignoring the door she passes in the middle of the hall on her left. The wooden

24

floorboards groan with every step. The end of it brings her to the entrance of the foyer. With the front door to her left, she pans her light to the right, revealing an empty living room with a large fireplace. "And you're positively *sure* we have the right place?"

"Yeah, why?" Dean says, following in behind her. The floorboards scream even louder under his heavier step.

She turns toward the front door noticing an entrance to the dining room to her left. Also, empty. "Well, look for yourself."

They both stand in the dining room entrance, puzzled. The bright-glowing, white scenery outside, provides them with very little light through the bare, curtainless windows. The old wood flooring pops and creaks as they enter it. Her phone beeps again.

"Kill your light and save the battery. We can see for now and may need it later."

"Where's your phone?" she says, putting hers back into her pocket.

"Out in the truck."

Steph lets out a disapproving sigh, then flips one of three light switches on the wall. Then the other two. Nothing.

"That's not gonna work," he says, pointing at the ceiling, "No lightbulbs. There's gotta be one somewhere though. Just check the other rooms and grab one."

Dean follows behind her to the living room. "Shit there's no lightbulbs in here either. Looks like, when they moved out, they took more than just the furniture." he says, raising to his toes to knock down an old dusty cobweb.

"Come on," says Steph, leading him to the base of the large foyer staircase that ran up along the wall and ended in still darkness above. The little bit of light from the refrigerator shines dimly through the other doorless entrance of the kitchen, that leads into the living room. But it wasn't enough to light the way.

Steph activates her flashlight app once again, and points the wide beam into the room, revealing the beautifully finished, yet dusty wooden flight of stairs. The risers, tread, banister, and rail all shared the same dark stain. She gently places her hand upon the top of the brilliantly hand-carved newel, in the shape of a large acorn, detailed with tiny leaves swirling to the tip.

She aims her light to show their path, but the darkness seems to swallow her light. They both hesitate to climb.

"Now that's freaking creepy. You first," says Steph.

"Yeah, right. You're the one with the flashlight," he takes a step down and behind her.

"Wow, what a man *you* are, dude. What a man." She jabbed sarcastically.

They both edge the stairs, dragging their shoulders against the wall, wide-eyed and hearts beating heavy. The stairs grumble with every step, each sounding louder than the last.

Dean sticks close behind her, looking down at the dimly lit foyer. He doesn't dare mention to her the chill he felt at his back.

The feeling of something behind him, watching. *No. After that last comment she had made, I'll save myself the embarrassment. Man up bro. Man up.*

"Stop pushing me." she says, pulling her shoulder away from his firm grip.

He pulls his hand back; he was unaware he had been touching her. "Well, hurry up then." he demands attempting to save face.

"What? You scared? You know, you could've gone first."

They stop near the top three steps, pausing before stepping onto the landing. Her dimming flashlight barely gives them the clear path they need as she takes the final step, and aims it down the dark hallway.

The dying light outside gives just enough light to show her one door to her right, which was open, and the closed door, across the hall. They were the closest doors to them.

They continue down the hall toward the room to the right with extreme caution. Dean still follows closely at her back. She peeks in while she eases the door the rest of the way open, the door drags on its hinges as she steps inside. The room was empty like the others, and gave off a feeling inside that brought chills up her spine. A large multi-paned window in front of them brings in the wintery glow outside, yet, the room itself seemed to give off its own blackness. The walls and wood floor are straight and plain, with an even darker stain than the staircase.

She spots the light fixture up above—out of its three light sockets, only one contained a bulb. Dean leaves her side to look out of the bedroom window.

Steph locates the light switch and flips it on... nothing happens.

"Shit! Are you serious? Did the guy living here have something against lights?"

"Maybe it's a fuse box? I don't know. But we don't have time for all of that. I think we should give up on finding a light and find this stash." he says, watching the sun through an overcast sky disappear on the horizon.

Steph removes the lightbulb and shakes it, groaning after hearing the sound of the broken filament rattling around inside.

"We can make this quick if we split up." Dean says, turning to face her.

"Are you kidding? There's nothing here—look around."

"We don't have enough time for any bullshit-debate, Steph!" he yells, "It's here, hidden. Otherwise, we wouldn't have gotten paid to look for it. We need to cover as much ground as possible before we lose what little light we have. Check for faulty walls, hidden compartments, loose bricks, wood; whatever. And do it quick! Okay? You take the downstairs. I gotta piss." He unzips his pants near a corner by the bedroom closet.

"Go to the bathroom, you fucking pig!" she exclaims.

"Shut up! What does it matter? No one lives here, *obviously.*"

His sigh of relief, and the sound of his trickling pee, disgusts her. She throws her hands up as if surrendering, and backs out from the room.

The house is darker now. The handrail and balusters framing the landing are barely visible down the hall. *Dean wasn't joking. It's getting dark, quick.* She peers down into the foyer before creeping down the stairs. About halfway to the bottom her phone beeps, then powers off.

She smacks it with her hand as if it were a flashlight with a loose battery. "Damn it!" she exclaims, angrily shoving it back into her jacket pocket.

Dean lets out another sigh of relief, then widens his stance to avoid the growing puddle of pee between his black combat boots. Behind him, the bedroom door was gradually, yet silently closing. He thought he saw it move and flinched a bit, but shook it off and continued relieving himself. Then, with great force and speed, the door slams shut.

He jumped, quickly looking behind him, then yells, "Fuck! What the hell's your problem!" he yells to Steph. He continues draining himself in the corner, unaware of the closet door opening beside him.

Steph, still on the stairs, also jumped from the sound created by the sudden impact of the slamming door; she turns and looks up, "Asshole!"

She continues her descent, down the now, even darker staircase, questioning herself. *Why am I doing this again? Why the hell did we separate in this creepy-ass house. Isn't that the last thing you are supposed to do in a scary movie? You're an idiot for getting yourself into this, Steph.*

She couldn't believe what she was doing. Walking down the creepy, creaking steps of a creepy house. She found herself trembling, the closer to the foyer she became, her heart thumping hard against her sternum. The only thing driving her was the desire to get this all over with quickly. Consequently, the only way to do that is to do what Dean said they needed to. And fast.

Finally, she reaches the bottom step and into the foyer. With the refrigerator still providing some light for guidance, she creeps along, on the balls of her feet, to the hallway and stops at the door she had passed before. *Probably the basement.* As she reaches for the door handle, she cringes at the thought of going down there alone. Almost as fast as she touched the handle, she grimaces, and removes her hand from the door, as if it were coated with fecal matter. *I'll try that door last.*

As she passes the entrance to the kitchen, she noticed something odd. The cabinets, she was sure she left open, are now closed. She stands, puzzled, in the doorway, panning the dimly lit kitchen, then continued to the door at the end of the hall. She peers through its multi-paned window on her tiptoes. *Mudroom.*

With little hesitation, she opens the door and begins checking the cabinets, one after the next coming up empty handed. She tries one last cabinet, above the washer and dryer hookups, and reaches deep inside.

"Yes!" she hisses, pulling out a beat-up, silver flashlight.

She shakes it, rattling the loosely-fitted, 'D' size batteries inside. A flick of the switch, and a few taps on the bottom of the dusty device, gives her a bright beam of light. She had hoped the light would ease her fear of the surrounding darkness, but instead it casts dancing shadows in every corner. Inanimate objects seemed to have a life of their own as she wields the light about. *Calm down, calm down. Let's get this shit over with, Steph.* She takes a deep breath. *I guess the kitchen is just as good of a place as any to start.*

Through the kitchen window, she admires the view of spooky snowcapped trees framing the backyard. The snowstorm had finally subsided, leaving a beautiful scene of a winter wonderland.

She notices something small that moved swiftly through the forest and stopped at the base of a tree. It's too dark to make out what it is, but there is definitely something hiding—peeking out from behind a thin tree trunk.

The floor groans behind her, yet she doesn't turn around. "Dean, come here and look at this. I swear there's something in the woods right there." she says, keeping her eyes trained on, what seemed like, a small child.

There's no answer from Dean. She aims her flashlight through the window, but the bright glare, reflects back at her. She drops the light to her side and peers through the window again, it's gone.

"Dean!" she whispers more forcefully.

Still no answer.

Frustrated, she leaves the kitchen and into the hallway, shining her light down the length of it, into the foyer, but the basement door was now wide open, and blocking a part of her view.

"Dean, you there? I swear if you're trying to scare me—this is the wrong time."

She pauses, waiting for an answer or noise. She then eases toward the basement door, extending her hand timidly for the doorknob. She grabs the cold metal, knob and pulls the door open wider to make her way around it. The high-pitch squeal of the hinges drown out her voice as she yells for her partner again.

"Hey, are you down there?" she stares down at the wood-planked steps leading into a dark abyss.

"Yes." he whispers.

She aims her new light down, cutting through the darkness with ease. No one is there. Just dusty steps and a brick wall at the bottom of them.

"Why are you down there in the dark? How the hell can you see?" There is no answer. "Come on up. This place is starting to freak me the fuck out, man."

The batteries shift in the shaft of her new tool and the light goes out.

"You come down here," he whispers, "I got something to show you."

She takes one step down, then stops. Something doesn't feel right to her; besides, the voice didn't respond like the aggressive sounding man she was used too. She backs up to the top, then shakes her flashlight which flickers, yet doesn't stay on.

She groans. "Dean?"

There's no answer.

The wood stairs creak, slowly, one after the other, closer, and closer... then stop. Her breath quickens and heart beats heavily as she steps back, still looking down into the pitch-blackness below, and grabs the basement door behind her. Whatever it is making the stairs creak, felt like it was only a few steps away from her. Slow, wheezing type breaths grew closer to her as she stood... horror-struck.

Then, something whispered, with a raspy voice, "it's so cold." It was so close that she could feel his speaking breath near her lips. Her eyes gape open. Panic-stricken, she falls back to the wall, hitting her head. "So... cold."

Her shock and shortness of breath robs her the ability to scream. She kicks the door closed, grabs the flashlight, then races for the foyer, tripping at the base of the stairs. Her flashlight bounces off the base of the stairs, flickers on, then skittered across the floor, stopping with the beam aiming down the hall.

"Dean!" she screams, looking toward the upstairs.

The flashlight dims out just as the basement door bursts open.

Slow, heavy footsteps approach. Suddenly, cold air rushes across her body tightening her skin. She lets out the breath she was holding from the paralyzing fear. It floats in front of her, making her panic; taking high-pitched, quivering breaths, she scrambles on all fours up the steps.

Reaching the landing, she pauses on her hands and knees to look behind her.

Tears well in her eyes as she stands, using the wall for a crutch. She looks behind her and down the upstairs hallway, wondering why Dean hasn't come to her aid, but it's too dark to see anything.

Steph turns her attention back downstairs, when movement in a shadowy corner near the front door, catches her eye. She, still breathing heavily, focuses in on the source of the movement.

"Is that you, Dean? Stop fucking around, man!"

Suddenly, the roaring engine of a truck and its heavy plow, dragging across pavement and through the snow, approaches outside. Its blinding lights blaze through the front door window and brightens the entire foyer—revealing to her an empty corner... the same corner she knows she saw movement. The truck's rumbling fades in the distance, along with its lights, bringing things back to darkness.

34

From the stairs, she backs up carefully, and enters the hall. But each one of her steps is matched with an ascending step. She stops for a moment, yet the footsteps keep climbing, then increase in speed.

Steph turns down the hall blindly, dragging her hands along the wall until she comes across the door leading to the bedroom she is sure Dean is still in. She grabs the knob, jerking and pulling, but it won't open.

"*Open* the *fucking door*, Dean!" She shoves her shoulder into the door multiple times, yanking and kicking frantically at it.

When the approaching footsteps reach the top of the stairs, she charges the door one last time, breaking through and falling to the floor inside. Immediately, back on her hands and knees, she scrambles to slam the door shut.

The footsteps stop. There would be, practically, dead, silence if it weren't for her rapid, quivering breaths. She presses her feet firmly against the base of the door when, suddenly, the doorknob slowly turns, chirping and squealing to the left then, even slower, dragging and grinding to the right. She presses her feet even harder against the wood, then... the doorknob stops. For a moment, there is nothing, until violent pounding behind the door begins, shaking the walls around her and echoing throughout the room. She places her hands firmly over her ears to protect them from the deafening sound.

She knows her tiny legs aren't strong enough to hold out whatever was delivering multiple, extremely heavy impacts to the door. *This door must be stuck in the same way the back door was when we entered.* She can hear something pushing, gradually forcing its weight against the center of the door.

The mysterious thing, behind the door, starts to ram with force. With each blow, the screws holding the hinges to the frame loosen and begin to strip from their settings. She slowly stands to her feet, watching in horror, as the door's structure begins to crumble before her.

She takes a step backwards.

There's no escape besides the window behind her. No one else knows she is there besides Dean. *Where is he!*

She takes another step back, breathing through her curled fingers she is holding in front of her mouth. The only weapon she had to defend herself with on the floor downstairs with dead batteries.

She takes another step back, tripping and falling over the lap of Dean, whom is on the floor and leaning against the wall near the window. His eyes are wide open and pupil's pure white—the look of terror is frozen on his face.

She grabs him by the jacket with both hands.

"Dean—Dean!"

His head tilts back with a thud against the wall, and his jaw clicks open with a sound like splintering ice cubes. A last, frosty breath floats from his lips, expanding and thinning out into nothing.

She releases him from her grasp, with wide eyed terror in her eyes. His dead body slumps to one side then he tips over, face down, onto the floor... *thud!*

"Oh my God,"—she places her shaky hands over her lips, "Oh no—Dean..." she whispers.

The door continues to bow inward, and the wood splinters with each blow to it. The sound of the door cracking, and the smaller wood fragments soaring toward her, makes her feel overwhelmed with fear. She screams loudly in distress, then cries in defeat, cowering next to Dean's lifeless body... her only defense to whatever it is on the other side of that door.

She suddenly notices the gun. The revolver, still tainted with the blood of the store owner, held loosely at Dean's fingertips. She wastes no time retrieving it, frantically checking it with her violently shaking hands for bullets. Trembling with fear, she aims at the weakening door, which finally bursts open. Two bright-shining lights shoot through, blinding her.

"Police!" A man shouts. "Drop your weapon! DROP IT NOW!"

Outside, the quiet calmness after the storm is broken by the sound of multiple gunshots going off inside the house of 2300 Brookshire Lane.

CHAPTER 3

ROSES ARE RED

Friday, June 14th, (3:57 PM)

The strong, pungent smell of mildewed towels under the kitchen sink would be unbearable to most, but is nothing Owen hasn't dealt with before. A couple quick turns of his wrench tightens the slip nut at the top of the leaking trap pipe—literally starting and finishing his job all at once.

He removes himself from his damp, cramped surroundings and stands, tall over old Ms. Freemont as he dusts off his blue work uniform.

Her old, white, and slightly weathered cheeks glow red when she catches a glimpse of his smooth, brown, glistening, muscular chest, wet from the dripping water underneath the sink, through a partially unbuttoned shirt.

He removes his gloves, but then fishes around inside of the left one, squeezing at the ring finger until his gold band slips out into his palm.

"Gets caught in there sometimes," he says, smiling. He then turns on the faucet and checks under the sink once more. "That'll do it. It's dry as a bone now," he says, shutting it off again. "Looks like you had *another* loose nut Ms. Freemont."

She chuckles. "Sweetie, I've had a loose nut for over forty-five years," her eyes gesture towards her husband, watching television in his recliner. "If a wrench could've fixed *that* one, I would have hit him over the head with it years ago."

They both laugh as Owen tosses his tool in his bright-red, metal Craftsman toolbox, then flips the two latches shut.

"Okay, Ms. Freemont, that should keep things going for a while. I'm just not sure how that nut keeps working itself loose. I swear I put some Loctite on there and everything last time. But, if you have any other problems, don't hesitate to give me a call, okay?"

"Okay. But I'll only give you a call if you'd stop calling me 'Ms. Freemont'. Try, Barbara, instead. I mean, good God, you make me feel like I'm ancient."

"Agreed," he smiles, "but, you're definitely not ancient. You barely look old enough to be a grandma."

She laughs. "I should be calling you old—with that poor eyesight of yours. Now what do I owe you?" she says opening her checkbook and clicking her pen.

"No, I couldn't possibly charge you for that, ma'am. Please, keep your money. It was my pleasure."

She keeps writing. "So now it's '*ma'am*?'" She shakes her head, "You're going to take this money, young man, whether you like it or not." She rips the check free. "You can't run a business and take care of your young ones if you're constantly giving old gals like me a break. Now take it. You're one of the best... if not *the* best handyman here in Charlotte. Own it, young man."

Owen sighs and accepts. Deep down he knows she is right. There is no way that he can afford to turn down the money she was giving for his service. Business isn't exactly booming, with so many competitive handymen in the area. And right now, this is his only source of income. *Just take it. You need groceries.*

He reaches for the check with a slow hand, "Thank you, Ms.—I mean, Barbara." He tucks the check into his back pocket.

She holds a shushing finger to her lips. "I put a little extra on there for you. So, don't say nothing about the total around Mr. Free..." she quickly clamps her lips shut.

Mr. Freemont comes shuffling into the kitchen in his house shoes, as if he were cross country skiing. He makes his way over to the cabinet, and throws them both a frowning glance, before reaching for a drinking glass inside.

"You two done jaw-jacking in here, or can I get a damn glass of water now? Gonna have me die of thirst out there—been wait'n so long."

"I could only hope! Get ya dang water, Louis, and don't you dare start!" She exclaims, leading Owen to the front door by his arm.

"Thank you so much, Barbara, you've always been so kind to me."

"That's only cuz you've been so good to us. Now, talk nothing more about it."

She pulls him in for a quick hug, then sends him on his way down the walkway. He places his tools in the back of his tan Dodge pick-up truck, with the words "HANDYMAN MOSELY" stenciled on the door in large italic yellow letters, along with his phone number. He gives her s single waive before pulling off.

❦ ❦ ❦ ❦

(4:17 PM)

Owen exits a gas station clutching two wrapped, single long-stem roses in his right hand, when he notices a woman from the opposite side of the pump smiling at him. He ignores her obvious attempt to gain his attention, pops open his gas cap cover and begins fueling his truck. As he waits for his tank to fill, he unwraps the flowers and tosses the plastic wrapping in the trash next to the pump.

The woman notices his wedding band and roses, then sucks her teeth.

His phone chimes—it's a text from Rose.

It reads, "Why don't you just let them stay with us tonight?"

He huffs, then jams the phone back into his pocket.

Suddenly annoyed, he glares at the gas pump's digital display as it reaches fifty-two cents shy of the forty dollars he'd prepaid. The small change wasn't worth the trip back inside and the long wait in line, so he squeezes the handle, forcing in every drop he could.

The tank overflows, spilling gas down onto his boot. Every glistening-gold drop that followed was like slow motion to him, as he drifted off into thought. He started daydreaming of the day he was on his first date with Theresa, and she had accidentally spilled her soda on his brand-new tennis shoes.

A limited-edition pair of original Nike Air Jordan 1's with the retro high band. Most men would have lost it instantly, seeing the sticky substance ruining the laces, leather and soaking into the tongue. The hazel gray eyes, Owen was lost in all evening became desperate as Theresa frantically looked for a napkin to bend down and wipe them off. He caught her by the arms and stood her up before she could reach them, planting a deep warm kiss, for the first time, on the juicy lips he had imagined kissing all night.

HONK—HONK!

He's startled from his dream by an old woman staring at him behind the wheel of an old classic Buick Skylark, waiting behind him.

She sticks her head out of the window. "Well, are ya done or ya just gonna sit there and block the damn pump?"

He replaces the nozzle and cap without a word, then jumps in his truck. Gently, he places the roses on the seat beside him and starts the truck, throwing the shifter in drive mode. Just before driving off, he catches a glimpse in his rear view, of the old woman tossing her hands up impatiently.

🦋 🦋 🦋 🦋

Owen creeps down a narrow cemetery path at five miles per hour. His brakes grind as he stops; gazing out of the driver side window to the sea of headstones. The clouds gradually mask the sun, followed by a light rain falling to his windshield. With a heavy heart, he gently picks up one of the roses lying on the passenger seat, takes a deep breath, then steps out of the truck.

He hikes the grassy incline, weaving through the different headstones, until he reaches one that is covered at the base by an assortment of fresh and old flowers. His eyes well up with tears as he moves a few of them to the side, revealing the name of Theresa Lynn Mosley. Carefully, he places his rose on the top of the stone, drops his chin to his chest and falls to his knees.

❦ ❦ ❦ ❦

The sun peeks through parted clouds once again, shining its light for the last time before nightfall. Owen stops his truck in front of a large, red colonial style home, honks his horn, then waits. He notices someone peeking through the curtains from the living room, yet no one emerges from the front door. The curtain is thrown closed.

After waiting for a few minutes, he grows increasingly impatient and decides to find out what the matter is. *Why do we have to go through this every day, damn! Just send the damn kids out already.* He snatches the keys from the ignition and climbs out.

Before ringing the doorbell, he takes a deep, calming breath, then presses the glowing white button. After a short time, he could hear the faint thundering of approaching steps—before the door is yanked open with such force it created a vacuum like pressure that gently, and ever so slightly, pulls him forward.

A middle-aged black woman scowls at him as she stands in the opening, holding the door as if she'd like nothing more than to slam it back in his face. Her hair is pulled back tightly into a short ponytail. Her thin wine-colored cashmere sweater matches the Hilary Duff glasses she stared at him through, with intense anger and disappointment.

She purses her lips and grabs the door firmly. "Did you *not* get my text?"

"No, I'm sorry, Rose. I didn't."

She stands back allowing six-year-old, Jacob Mosely, to pass as he secures his Pokémon backpack on his shoulders. She places her hand on his head. Her fingers nearly disappear into his thick, black, curly hair before kissing him on his cheek. With his eyes and skin color, he was the spitting image of his father in children's clothing.

"Bye Gamma, love you!" Jacob says, smiling when he sees his father. "Hey Dad!"

Owen kisses him on the forehead. "Go get in, the door is open."

"Kay."

Owen refuses eye contact with Rose, hanging his head and looking down at the base of the door. He can feel the heat from Rose's gaze. She doesn't bat an eye. The last time he stared back at her she took a couple of swings at his face, and it took the full strength of Al, her husband and Grandfather to the kids, to keep her from him.

Fourteen-year-old, Kyra Mosely, approaches, her head down, and hugging an empty and near-deflated teal backpack to her chest. Her long dark-brown hair is braided back into thick cornrows and fluffed out at the back around her shoulders. Owen notices something different about her demeanor and her lack of eye contact, quickly glancing at him with her mother's hazel-gray eyes. Not the usual greeting with a smile. Instead, she shares the same disapproving expression as her Grandmother, whom she kisses on the cheek.

She squeezes by Owen, without a word. Avoiding any physical contact—as if he were some filthy homeless man, who reeked of feces, begging for change in a store parking lot.

"Hi, baby, how was the last day of school?" Owen asks.

She keeps walking without a word—joining her brother in the backseat and slamming the door shut.

Owen turns to address Rose, but the door slams loudly in his face. Any closer and he would've had the permanent smell of her wood door in his nose. He hangs his head once again.

The closer he gets to the truck he can see Kyra, her eyes fixed forward while attempting to sink back into her seat as if she were trying to keep him from her field of vision.

"Kyra, you could ride up here in the front seat, with me. There's plenty room." he says, climbing in.

"No, I'm good." She rolls her eyes.

"Can I, Can I!?" Jacob yells.

"Yeah, I don't see why not." Owen says.

"I do," Kyra frowns. "you can't have a car seat in the front seat, *Dad*, he's too young."

Her tone and angry soul piercing eyes punched him painfully deep, in the chest. He's never heard her speak to him like this before. *What the hell. Did I miss a birthday? Something at her school I should have been too? Is she finally going through her womanly change?*

46

"Aw, man!" Jacob says, balling his lip.

"Yeah, she's right, Jacob." He turns to key to the ignition. "I forgot that. I'm sorry."

"If Mom were here, she'd remember." Kyra grumbles. "And why does it smell like gas?"

Owen holds his tongue while placing the truck into drive. He glances back at her through the rearview mirror, as she stares angrily through her window. Discreetly, he turns his attention to the passenger seat and contemplates the fate of the single rose he had intended on giving her. Then, with the quick slight-of-hand skills of an amateur magician, he covers it with his clipboard.

🦋 🦋 🦋 🦋

The highway is still slightly congested, with stop-and-go rush hour traffic. Periodically, Owen checks the rearview mirror, looking back at his troubled daughter gently cradling a folded piece of tissue in her hand. Jacob is fast asleep.

"Are you okay back there?" he asks.

No reply, instead, she shakes her head and rolls her eyes so high her pupils nearly disappear into her forehead.

"Excuse me, young lady, I asked you a question."

"Yes! Okay?! I'm fine!" She roars.

"Did I do something to you?"

Traffic begins to move.

She sucks her teeth. "No."

"Well, can you tell me why you look and seem so upset with me right now? Your attitude seems to be directed at me." He says, still looking at her in the mirror, hoping to get some sort of eye contact.

She's grimacing while watching a little boy in the car next to them who is rummaging through his nose with his index finger. The boy shows no shame, smiling at her as he continues stretching the insides of his nostrils.

Owen, slams on the brakes, nearly hitting the stopped car in front of them.

"Jesus, Dad!" Kyra screams. "You gonna kill us too?!"

Owen's heart sinks—not from the close call with the car, but from his daughter's outburst.

"What do you mean by that, Kyra? What is *that* supposed to mean?"

Jacob is awakened from his nap, rubbing his eyes, and wiping the drool from the corners of his mouth.

"Nothing," she says. "Just drive, Dad! Please, just drive."

The traffic is already moving again, and the cars behind them begin impatiently honking their horns. Kyra's eyes well with tears, but she wipes them before one can fall. One loud drawn-out horn blows which breaks Owen from his stare. He closes the large gap between him and the car in front.

48

"Can we get Oreos when we get home? Gamma already fed us. But she didn't have dessert."

"Sure, little man. I don't see why not."

❦ ❦ ❦ ❦

As soon as Owen pulls his truck into the driveway of their large, modern colonial style home (accented with dark-gray and white trim), Kyra jumps out before the truck could come to a complete stop. Before Owen could fix his mouth to yell at her, she was already halfway to the front step.

Smiling, she stops at the door, drops her bookbag, and kneels in front of the brass-platted mail slot. She raises the flap slowly, giggling as she looks inside the dimly lit foyer, then drops it closed with a clank. Slowly, she raises it again, looks inside a little longer, and then drops it again. Once more, even slower this time, the small hinges squeal as she peers inside. She pokes out a pouting bottom lip just as a large, beige, and black spotted paw lunges out and swipes playfully in the opening. Kyra jumps back and giggles.

Owen approaches from behind, carrying Jacob slumped over his shoulder in one arm, and fumbling his keys with the other. His heart grows heavy every time he passes the FOR SALE sign on the front lawn. When he opens the door, a large beige African Serval cat, the size of a medium sized dog, is standing in the opening like an Egyptian statue. Her large ears are perked up and her tail happily thrashes, sweeping about the floor.

"Hi, Jinx!" Kyra says, kneeling down to pet her. "Where's Ducky? Go get Ducky." Jinx gallops to the living room and Kyra follows, dropping her bag in the middle of the foyer.

Owen squats down and picks up today's mail, some having been chewed on corners. He sets Jacob down on the living room couch and begins sorting through the stack. *Nothing but junk mail and bills.* He lets out a huge, sighing breath when he sees the URGENT stamps on both the electric and insurance bill, then tosses them on the foyer console table.

The red digital display on his phone phone shows one voicemail waiting. Eager, he presses the play button in hopes that it is a call from his real estate agent informing him of an offer for the home.

The house had been up for sale since Theresa's death and he'd hoped this would end his financial struggle.

"Hey, big brother, it's Marley," Owen lets out a disappointed sigh. He can already hear the slur in his little brother's words. "I really wish you would give me your cell phone number so I can get in contact with you. I mean, who has a home phone nowadays, Big Bro. Anyways, I was calling to see if you've changed your mind on giving me some work. Theresa's passing is a big loss and I know you could use the extra hand. Times are hard for you... I know, Big Bro, so you gotta let me help. At least until you sell that big-ass house." There's a pause, the sound of ice cubes hitting the bottom of a glass, and then he chuckled. "Hey... But what you need to do is sell that big-ass cheetah Theresa left you with before she eats yawls' ass. I bet you can get some good money for her. Call me."

Overwhelmed with defeat, Owen pinches the bridge of his nose and closes his eyes. *Why—why—why can't you stop that God damn drinking, Bro. I got enough problems already. I sure as hell can't include your mess.* Even though he's under the influence, he knows Marley is right. He *could* use the help. But he can't risk another episode even close to when Marley showed up late to a customer's home with the smell of Peach Crown Royal on his breath. When the customer didn't want him working in their home in his condition, he referred to them as "racist hillbillies". Owen lost some good-paying customers that day. And with having very few clients now, the risk was too great to allow him in.

He's startled by the deep, mechanical belching sound of Ducky, carried firmly in the mouth of Jinx behind him. The Navy-themed, stuffed duck—muscular, and completed with its own sailor hat, stogie and five-o'clock shadow—is dropped to the floor where it belches again upon impact.

🦋 🦋 🦋 🦋

(6:33 PM)

Owen is in the kitchen reading the back of a box of Hamburger Helper, while Kyra, sitting at the kitchen table, is on the home phone chatting away with her friend, Nekia from school. He unpacks the ground beef and places it in the preheated skillet, then waves at Kyra to get her attention. She rolls her eyes slightly and turns away.

"Sweetie, can you keep an eye on this ground beef while I go unload my power tools from the truck?"

"Hold on, Nekia" she covers the phone, then looks to the box on the counter. "Gross, Hamburger Helper... *again*? Sick."

"Well, it's what we have right now. Besides, the last time we had that was a week or so ago."

"No, let's try two days ago, *Dad*. We had the beef stroganoff one, remember? Gawd!"

"Oh, that's right. Well, this one is 'Mexican Crunchy Taco'. You'll like it."

Kyra places the phone back to her ear. "What are you guys having for dinner?" She frowns. "Really, I love meatloaf and mashed potatoes!" She places the phone on her chest again. "Can I go to Nekia's house for dinner?"

"No! No, you can't. You will stay here and eat dinner with your brother and me, as planned." She scowls at him, as he makes a gesture pointing two fingers to his eyes, then to the sizzling skillet, before walking off to the front door.

"Ugh. I hate it here," She whispers into the receiver. "I wish I lived with my grandparents."

Hearing that, Owen pauses by the screen door, opens it, then closes it as if he'd left. He can hear her sniffling quietly.

"No—No I can't. I wish she was still here cuz I hate him; I hate it here. It's not the same without her and he acts like nothing happened. *He* should be dead and not her."

His heart shatters. He struggles to keep his bearing and not march back into the kitchen to make her hang up the phone. He knows that any action taken would result in things getting worse between them.

Sadness and anger grow inside him as he steps outside, gently closing the screen door behind him.

🦋 🦋 🦋 🦋

Though they live in a better part of the neighborhood, Owen still took precautions and locked his more expensive tools away every night. The neighborhood may be nice, but he knew these types of neighborhoods were targets for criminals looking for high-end items. Besides, his truck screamed "EXPENSIVE TOOLS INSIDE!" with the decals all over it. He wraps the cords and places his power tools neatly in a large, tan tool bag before heading to the garage.

He approaches the security panel next to the garage door. Immediately, the high school picture that Theresa used to show him proudly and repeatedly, dressed in her High School soccer uniform, pops in his head. Thirty-six was her jersey number when she played for Panther Creek High School. She constantly reminisced of her high school days and winning the game against their rival team, sending her team up state. From that point on, thirty-six was her lucky number. She often told him, that victory, set the pace for her continued success.

Owen enters 3-6-3-6 on the security display panel. The large white (16 by 8 foot garage door) slowly opens, revealing half of the garage packed with storage boxes, and the other with a covered vehicle. The license plate on the bumper of the black BMW, partially showing from under the car cover, reads: "36AllDY".

Owen tosses his tools on the work bench, raising a small cloud of dirt and dust. In the windowpane in front of him, is a selfie-style picture of Theresa. The captured moment of her looking at the camera as she licks the top of a strawberry ice cream cone, in a seductive manner, is one of his many favorite pictures of her. Owen removes the photo and, with his thumb, wipes away the dust that had settled on it. He recalls that night at the carnival, while looking closer at the ring on her hand holding the cone. He'd missed how happy they were at that time and how great things were going financially. He felt they could rule the world. It was the perfect time to pop the question.

She commented in the past about how cliché purposing with a diamond ring was and how a real man, her soul mate, would know what she wanted.

Just before she took this picture, high above the ground on a Ferris wheel, he reached into his pocket and removed a silver spider turquois ring; her favorite stone. Owen smiles when thinking about how excited she was, and how he thought they would die and fall to their deaths with her flailing about and screaming like she did. She had eventually calmed down when she saw him clutching the safety bar, grimacing in fear. She looked at him with shimmering, teary, gray eyes and kissed him deeply.

🦋 🦋 🦋 🦋

The loud piercing beep of the smoke detector interrupts his fondest memory. *The meat! Damn it, Kyra!* He drops the picture and takes off in a sprint, nearly tripping over the storage boxes on the garage floor. He bursts through the back door into a kitchen filled with smoke, and witnesses Kyra fanning the skillet with a dish-towel.

"What the hell happened?!" He exclaims.

"I don't know, the meat burned!" She whined, with an attitude, as Owen grabs the skillet from the oven and tosses it in the sink, running cold water over it.

"It's not my fault!" she screams.

"Whose fault is it then, Kyra!?" Owen yells, then he calms himself immediately, taking in a deep breath. "Kyra, you were supposed to watch the meat like I'd asked. A simple job... one you've done before." He cranks the faucet handle closed. "You're just too *damn* distracted by that *damn* phone; I'm sure of it. Your mother would have..."

Kyra looks up at him wide eyed, her mouth dropped open. Without a word, she runs off, up the stairs to her bedroom, and slams the door shut.

He throws a wooden spoon across the kitchen, splattering food on the wall. "Damn it, man." He leans back against the sink. "Now what?" he mutters to himself.

❦ ❦ ❦ ❦

(7:21 PM)

Later, Owen walks in the kitchen with two brown paper bags that were just delivered to his front door. Jacob is kneeling in a chair at the kitchen table, with a fork in one hand and a butterknife in the other, sword fighting against himself.

"Go upstairs and get your sister, please. Tell her I have Chinese food, if she wants it."

Jacob drops his fencing weapons to the table, "Kay"

Owen removes each oyster pail from the bag and places them neatly in the center of the table. The smell of the sesame chicken has his mouth watering. He admires the small spread of food while crushing the paper bag into a small ball.

Jacob returns and hops back into his seat, grabs his fork and reaches for the oyster pail full of white rice.

Owen watches him, then steps out into the foyer to look upstairs. It's quiet. "Where's your sister?"

56

"Upstairs. I told her but she said she, 'doesn't want your stank'n Chinese food'. She told me not to say."

He frowns "Thank you, Jacob."

Owen takes a deep breath and ascends the staircase to Kyra's bedroom. Through the closed door, he can hear her listening to Justin Bieber at a low volume. He hesitates for a moment, preparing himself for the verbal assault, then knocks.

"Sweetie, you have to eat something. Why don't you come down and have dinner with us?" There's no answer, so he tries the door, but it's locked. He knocks once more. "Kyra, open the door, baby. You know I don't like it when you guys lock your bedroom doors."

Her door vibrates from thunderous music—now cranked up to full volume. He balls his fists and prepares to pound on the door, but instead, drops his hands to either side of his body. *Fine.*

He rejoins Jacob in the kitchen. "Okay, little man, it looks like it's just you and me for dinner this evening. But it's kind of late now, so as soon as you are done, off to bed, okay?"

"Kay. Can I watch cartoons?"

"No, Jacob, you can watch them in the morning. Now, eat son."

He groans. "Ugh, I don't *ever* get to watch cartoons."

"Come on, man, don't start. You know what the rules are." He smirks, "How about I make it up to you and get you some donuts in the morning."

Jacob perks up. "The chocolate crunchy ones and a cake one?"

Owen nods affectionately, "If that's what you want."

❦ ❦ ❦ ❦

(1:34 am)

A tiny gray spider dangles above Jacob's bed, its eight legs extended and fanned out wide. Slowly, it begins sliding down its silk thread towards Jacob; he is fast asleep in his quiet, moonlit room, cuddling an old-toy Voltron robot in his arms. He rolls to his other side, accidentally hitting the button on the robot's chest.

"FORM BLAZING SWORD!" The robot yells, waking him.

Jacob opens his eyes a little, immediately noticing his opened door and flickering lights in the hallway.

Jacob's curiosity takes him from underneath his covers and onto the carpet, grabbing his robot protector by the leg before venturing out into the hall. Finding a very slight tinge of bravery in his Sesame Street pajamas.

Cautiously, he walks past his father's bedroom, peeking inside to verify he was asleep. Satisfied by the faint snoring in the dark room, he makes his way to the top of the stairs, and then peers over the banister and down into the foyer. All of the lights are off, but the television light, from the living room, illuminates the foyer like a strobe light. The volume is low.

There's a scream and dramatic music playing, followed by more aggressive flickering lights. He's not afraid, but grows more curious than before. The further he gets down the stairs, the clearer the sounds become. *Sounds like a scary movie.*

The more intrigued he became, the wider his smile grows. His father would never allow him a night of horror movies—nothing even close to that nature. 'Goosebumps' was even shut down as soon as Owen discovered him watching it. No. Harry Potter was the closest thing to a scary movie he had ever seen. And even for *that,* he needed to beg for permission.

His steps, on light, six-year-old feet, are stealthy as he closes in on the living room. On the screen, a woman is running through the forest, constantly looking back as she trips and falls about to try and evade her unseen pursuer.

He holds his robot close to his chest, as he watches with intense wide-eyes. Whatever was chasing her, seemed to be getting closer and closer. The music silenced as she began walking—the sound of leaves and sticks rustling and crunching under each step.

Suddenly, the face of a decaying, zombified man appears from around a tree in the dark. His teeth are long and exposed from deteriorating gums and rotting lips. He lunges out at the unsuspecting woman, startling Jacob, who screams backing away from the tv, when all of a sudden he is grabbed by the shoulders. He screams even louder, dropping his robot to the floor.

"FORM BLAZING SWORD!" It yells.

From behind, his mouth is covered, muffling his whimpering.

"Shhh! Shut up, or Dad will hear you. You turd! What are you doing up anyways?" Kyra says, releasing him.

Jacob's heart is racing, but he is relieved it is just Kyra.

"I saw the tv from my room. What are *you* doing up?" he demands.

"Minding my business, like you should be, *Baby Jay*. Go back to bed." She orders in a whisper while pointing to the stairs.

"Don't call me that! I hate that."

"Shhh! Geez. If you're gonna stay up, then sit down, and shut up." She orders, now pointing to the couch. "And I am *not* watching any cartoons, so if this stuff scares you, you better go back to bed, *now*."

"No, I'm gonna stay *right* here, with you."

Kyra's angry expression turns to wide-eyed shock when she notices a spider crawling around on Jacob's shoulder.

"Ew—ew," quickly she grabs a throw pillow from the couch.

"Wha..." She swats Jacob on the side of the head, knocking him to the floor. "What the heck, Kyra?"

"Where'd it go—Where'd it go!?" She says, frantically searching the floor, with the pillow raised to strike again.

"What was it?"

"A big, gross spider."

Jacob grabs his robot from the floor and scrambles onto the couch. "Where is it!?"

She drops her defense. "I think it got away. Shit!"

Jacob gasps. "You said a curse."

"Oh, shut up! If you're gonna stay down here, you can't be a little tattle-tale... or I'll tell Dad I caught you down here watching Adult Swim."

"Whatever."

"I'm going to the kitchen to get some spray. *Don't* touch that controller."

As Kyra disappears into the kitchen, Jacob slips underneath the blue blanket draped over the back of the couch.

🦋 🦋 🦋 🦋

(Saturday 7:17 am)

Owen awakens to Jinx's deep purring at his bedside. Her nose gently nuzzling his cheek and jaw. When he opens his eyes, she is face to face with him, trilling to greet him.

"Hey girl! You hungry?" She trills even louder from his petting. "Okay, move back so I can get up."

"Maow, Maow!"

Her deep yowls let him know she is ready for breakfast. Jacob used to laugh because he thought she was saying *now*. Now that she had succeeded at getting him up, she would not stop meowing until her hunger was satisfied.

Owen climbs out of bed, steps into his black corduroy slippers, then saunters down the hallway toward Jacob's room with Jinx close behind him.

Owen yawns deeply as he pushes Jacob's door open. "Hey, son, you want some eggs?"

He frowns at the empty bed. The sheets are ruffled and hanging off the side onto the floor. He looks further inside the empty room. *Maybe he's with Kyra.* He shuffles down the hallway to her room with Jinx still following closely, like a cat siren, meowing every few seconds. He pushes Kyra's door open. Empty.

"Kyra... Jacob!?" He calls out, making his way to the foyer a little faster, then down the stairs.

He hears the faint muttering from the television downstairs, followed by a familiar jingle from a local car dealership's commercial.

He lets out a silent sigh of relief when he finds them both wrapped under blankets and asleep on the couch.

Jacob's arm is hanging off the side, with a death grip on the arm of his robot, barely touching the floor, and, Kyra, with her toes at the back of his head. She's wrapped in a comforter cocoon, with a plate of half-eaten Chinese food on the coffee table in front of her.

He gently pulls the blanket down from her face, when one of two teabags hits the floor. The other remains on her forehead. *What the hell.*

"Kyra. What's this on your head?"

"Huh?" She peels her eyes open, wiggles her arms free and swipes her forehead, catching the other teabag in her hand. "What the...?" She kicks her brother, startling him from his sleep, making him drop his robot to the floor. "Wake up, turd. What did you put on me?"

He sits up rubbing his eyes. "What? I didn't do nothing."

"Did you put this on your sister's head?"

Jacob hesitates. "Yeah."

"Oh my God!" Kyra exclaims.

"Why, Jacob?" Owen asks.

"I don't know."

"Yes, you do. Answer my question." Owen kneels down next to him. "Have you been watching the late-night cartoons when I told you *not* to?"

"No."

"Jacob...?"

Jacob sighs. "Just a little."

Kyra throws the teabag at her brother, hitting him in the neck. "He's been watching that Adult Swim."

"Stop it, Kyra!" Owen orders.

"Jacob Mosley. Man, I've told you repeatedly not to turn that garbage on, didn't I?"

"Ya, but..."

"Ya, 'but' what, Jacob?" Owen asks

"But I wanted Kyra to be nicer to you. Jungle Jim said he had a bad night out with his date. She was mean. He said when she passed out asleep, he teabagged her forehead. She woke up nicer then..."

Owen's eyes buck open. "Hey—hey, nevermind! I'm sorry I asked."

Kyra bicycle kicks her legs from under the comforter, nearly kicking Jacob in the head, to escape. "Oh my God—Oh my God—Oh my God! Are you serious, you turd!?" She stomps away to the bathroom, wiping her head and slams the door shut behind her.

Owen chews at his bottom lip, looking away from Jacob, then purses his lips to suppress the humor that his son may detect on his face. It's taking all he could muster to remain stern and reenforce the rules.

"That decides it, Jacob," he says, taking in a deep breath through his nose. "I'm gonna put a parental block on the cable. I should have done it a long time ago."

"Aww. But Dad!"

"Don't, 'Aww, Dad' me, you knew better."

Jacob hangs his head. "Kay."

"Go wash your hands for breakfast, and apologize to your sister when she comes out?"

"Kay." He perks up, "are you gonna get donuts?"

"Do you think you deserve donuts after what you did?"

He slumps forward, hanging his head again. "No. Well, can I have Captain Smash Cereal?"

"I should make you oatmeal for what you did to your sister."

"Ugh! Why do you buy that stuff, Dad? You don't even eat it!"

"Cuz it's cheap and good for you?" He stands and kisses Jacob on the forehead. "I think you have enough in there for one more bowl of cereal. After that, no more Captain Smash, okay?"

"Awe man. Never?"

"Not 'never'. Just for now. Go wash your hands."

"Maybe, one day, we can actually get Captain Crunch," Jacob says, running off. He squeezes past Kyra coming out of the bathroom, wiping her face with a damp cloth.

"Kyra, try to stay off of the phone today, please. I have a couple phone calls I'm expecting today. Very important."

With a contempt expression, Kyra rolls her eyes. "You wouldn't have to worry about missing a call if you didn't have that ancient *home phone* service. You don't even have call waiting? Why didn't you just give them your cell number?" She lowers her voice mocking him. "*Oh, cuz I have a cheaper phone service, Kyra. And a lot of times I don't get a good signal in parts of the house. I don't have much money.*"

"You know how things are right now, Kyra. Why are you giving me such a hard time? Take it easy. I *am* trying my best."

She pushes past him, throws the damp towel on the couch, and strides up the steps to her room.

"Maow!"

Owen looks down at Jinx, who is staring up at him. "You gonna give me a hard time too?"

CHAPTER 4

WHEN IT RAINS...

(1:16 PM)

Owen had just finished washing his face, and is now leaning on the bathroom sink with both hands, his arms locked out by the elbows. *Lord, please forgive me. I can't do this without you... I need you back, Theresa. The kids, they...* As if experiencing an absence seizure, he is nearly hypnotized staring down into the slow draining water, swirling into the darkness of a silver ring. He finally blinks from the welling tears that tickle his eyelashes; he closes his mouth before the pooling drool drips from his bottom lip.

As he stands upright; a warm tear falls from his face and onto the porcelain edge of the sink. A deep breath helps clear his mind and refocuses him on the day. He snatches his toothbrush from its cupholder, and squirts a generous amount of toothpaste onto the bristles.

His grip on the handle is extra tight. Vigorously, he brushes back and forth, working up a thick lather, while staring into his own guilty, remorseful eyes in the mirror. The lather drips from his lips in soapy glops. He stops. More tears well as he gently removes the brush from his mouth.

In his sudden silence, he could hear mumbling coming from Kyra's room. From the tone in her voice and the giggling that followed, it was none other than, Nekia, she was speaking too.

"Kyra! Get—" His sudden outburst spat toothpaste on the mirror. Frustrated, he spits out the rest and rinses his mouth, then dries hurriedly with the face towel.

Kyra is lying in bed, chatting away on the home phone, with Jinx curled up next to her, when Owen arrives at her door scowling at her.

"Kyra, I asked you, *please*, don't tie up the phone. Please, get off. Whatever you have to tell your friend can wait, sweetie."

She mutters something in the phone, then addresses her father. "Yeah. But, only if you stop calling me, 'sweetie'."

Her words continue to chip away at his—already, broken heart, and it shows in the faint, painful sadness in his eyes. He swallows, what would have been an angry outburst, and responds in a calm voice.

"If that's what you want. Hurry and get off, please."

"Okay already, geez." She puts her mouth to the phone, "I have to go. Yeah, I'll call you later. Bye!" She then slams the phone down on the soft bed.

Owen holds out his hand. Kyra rolls her eyes again, then tosses the phone to him.

"Thank you." Owen says stepping away from the door.

"Dad!" Kyra roars.

Her screech shot up his back like ice cold claws. He steps back into the room. "What?"

"Can I get a cell phone?"

"I can barely afford the one I have now for my business."

"I looked into it; it's not going to cost you that much more per month. Only like, twenty dollars. Then you don't have to worry about me being on the phone all the time."

"I said, no. It's not in the budget right now."

Kyra frowns. "I'm the *only* girl that doesn't have a phone at my age. All my friends have one. Even Mariah's Dad got her one. Nekia and..."

"Mariah's Dad is, also, a successful attorney," he smirks "When we get back on our feet, everything will be okay, we will see about getting you a phone then. You'll be okay for now. Trust me."

"No, I won't." She says through clenched teeth. "*Mom* trusted you... and look where it got her."

"Okay, that's enough! You need to stop."

"No! If Mom was here, we wouldn't have to worry about financial difficulties. Maybe you should get a *real* job. Then, we won't have to sell the house."

"What makes you think this isn't a '*real job*'? I'm *only one-person*, young lady. I'm doing what I know how to do. Besides, I'm doing the best that I can. Maybe someday things will look up. Your mother is gone, and I wish to God she wasn't. I wish there was something I could do to bring her back."

"But, it's *your* fault she's not here. Isn't that right, *Dad!*?" she bared her teeth at him. "Yours! Grandma told me—she told me everything."

Owen's heart drops and he swallows deep—the spit feeling like a large jawbreaker going down. He's thunderstruck for the moment, as his daughter gives him the coldest, most hateful stare. A stare that translated, if she had telekinesis, she would have torn his body in two, right where he stood.

He grips the frame of the door and hangs his head. "Baby, I *didn't...*"

"Get out of my room!" she shouts, turning away from him while crossing her arms over her chest.

Owen hesitates, but backs away slowly. He knows in his heart, that this is a discussion that he should probably save for another day. He closes the door, gently, placing his hand on it as he listens to the muffled cries on the other side. *She hates me. And I'm not sure I blame her one bit.*

Suddenly, the home phone rings downstairs. On the third ring, Jacob fumbles the cordless receiver from its stand. "Mosley residence," he answers, "umm, my dad is busy upstairs. Can I take a message?"

Owen comes thundering down the staircase. "Hey-Hey, who is that?"

"I don't know. Some lady?"

"Give me the phone." He whispers. "Go play—Go play."

Jacob runs off and up the stairs.

"This is Owen Mosely."

"Hi, Mr. Mosley, it's Penny, with Munden Real Estate. How are you?"

"Oh, hey, Penny. I'm okay. How are you?" Owen answers, with delight in his tone.

"I'm great... and *you'll* soon be doing even better than okay with the news I have for you."

His heart picks up pace. "Why, what's going on?"

"Well," she hesitates, "I received an offer on your home earlier today. I was going to call you this morning, but I wanted to be sure that the buyer was serious."

"Oh my God! Thank goodness!" He exclaims, taking the conversation to the kitchen table and dropping into a chair. "What are they offering?"

"Well, I have the details. I'll explain everything fully, and you tell me what you think."

"I'm listening..."

"Are you sitting down?" She asks, with a smile in her voice.

"Yes!" He impatiently responds.

"Alright. So, you've received an offer, but not for the full, eight-hundred thousand that you're asking for. The buyer wants to give you a cash offer, for six-hundred and fifty thousand dollars."

"I'll take it!" he exclaims.

"Okay, but not so fast," she laughs, "there are a few things that the buyer wants that, we should go over."

"Uh—oh!"

"No... no, 'uh oh'! It's pretty basic with these types of things. First, they want four percent of the sales price returned to them, at closing, to go towards Closing Cost Assistance, a home warranty..."

"What? A home warranty. What's that?" Owen interrupts.

"I'll explain more about that later. Nothing to worry about. What you *do* need to worry about, is they want to close within thirty days."

"Holy shit, thirty days!?" Owen exclaims. "I'd have to be packed up and gone by then?"

"Yeah, I'm sorry. Now, you don't have to agree to everything. You can tell me, 'no', and why, then I'll present it to their agent and see what happens. Want to do that?"

Owen sighs, looking toward the stack of unpaid bills on the console and listening to the sound of Jacob playing upstairs in his room. Then there's Kyra. The money could make things better for them, for sure. However, the thought of giving up his home— the home that Theresa and he had worked so hard in obtaining... their dream home–going to some stranger, saddened him deeply. But, the reality of it is, he needs the money and can't afford the home with his current income.

"No," he says. "Let's do it. I *need* to do it. You'd think that I would know more about this business, since my wife was a real estate agent, but I've just heard bits and pieces in conversations. She dealt with big properties like these."

"Okay. I have a few more things to go over with you, then I'll call the buyer's agent to give them the thumbs up. Okay?"

"Okay, sounds good."

"Don't sound so sad, Mr. Mosely. With that amount of money, you can find a place in no time. Hell, you could *buy* a place in no time."

"That's not it. There's more to this move than just the money. I'm leaving a lot behind. However, unfortunately, it needs to be done." He takes another quick breath and perks up. "This *is* good news though. It's what my family needs."

❦ ❦ ❦ ❦

Owen walks through the front door, balancing three pizza boxes in one arm—a pepperoni for himself, one cheese, for Jacob, and the other with pineapple, Kyra's favorite. He places the boxes on the table, with a two-liter bottle of root beer soda.

He steps back into the foyer, "who wants some pizza!?" He yells, upstairs.

"Oh, me!" Jacob yells, springing from his bed, then carefully stepping through his, tactfully placed, Army men on the floor. It doesn't take him long before he is seated at the kitchen table, swinging his feet, with a huge smile on his face. "Did you get a cheese, Dad? Did you get a cheese!?"

"The box on the top. But go wash your hands first, little man." Owen orders. "And actually *use* the soap this time."

"Kay."

"Have you seen your sister?"

"She's in her room."

Owen prepares all of their plates, with two slices a piece, and four cubes of ice in each of the three, large yellow cups. He, then, lights a sea breeze scented, turquoise candle with a yellow lighter, and places it next to the picture of Theresa above the fireplace. Dinner time was always special to her. She would always preach about how 'family should be together during that time and it was the most important meal of the day'. Lighting the candle was his way of making her present and paying respect.

Jacob emerges from the bathroom with a smile. Wiping his hands on his shirt, then skipping his way to his spot at the kitchen table.

"Did you use soap? And wipe the seat?" Owen asks.

"I didn't go pee. I used soap though," Jacob raises his hands above his head. "See, smell my hands."

"No, I trust you. Eat up. I'm gonna go check on your sister."

Before he could finish, Jacob had already began stuffing his face full of cheese pizza, his eyes widen with delight.

Owen stands in front of Kyra's room—his fist hoovering an inch from the door, hesitating to knock, while anticipating the angry response he would receive. He knocks on the door gently. She doesn't answer, so he tries once more—with just a touch more force. She still doesn't answer.

Owen turns the doorknob, and eases it open. Kyra is lying in bed facing, away from him, submerged up to her shoulders in a salmon-colored comforter.

Assuming she is asleep, he enters silently.

Hearing the floor groan under his feet, Kyra opens her eyes partially, watching him through a reflection of a silver, handheld mirror propped up on her vanity.

He places her plate of pizza and a cup of soda next to the lamp on her nightstand, then covers her food with a thin, paper napkin. He watches her for a moment, wishing he could dump every thought about what happened into her mind, before she was set on completely rejecting him... if only it was possible.

He backs away, without a word, and closes the door gently.

Jacob's tiny fingers peel a piece of peperoni free of the thick cheese, humming as he feeds it to Jinx—waiting beside him.

Owen sees this coming in from behind them. "Jacob no!" he exclaims. "Jinx isn't supposed to eat food like that—you can get her sick. That's people food. And that's *my* pizza!"

"Why? We eat it. Why doesn't it get *us* sick then?"

"Animals eat different stuff than we do, so you can't give her that, okay?"

"Kay. Cheese neither?"

"No, Buddy. No cheese."

"Kay. Where's Kyra?"

"She's asleep."

Jacob licks his fingers, peels some cheese from his pizza, then tilts his head back, dangling the stretchy goo above his mouth. "No, she's not. She's still mad at you." He says dropping it into his mouth.

"Jacob, I know I taught you better manners than that. Sit in your chair right, and don't eat your pizza like that."

"But I always eat my pizza like that. It's fun. You used to do it with me."

"What did I say!?" He roars.

Jacob obeys, but not without a brief, defiant glare. He drops down into his seat, flicking the rest of the cheese off his finger and onto the plate. "Why aren't you fun no more, Daddy? You used to be fun." He takes another bite. "Is it cuz Momma's gone?"

Owen drops his hands below the table, and clasps his fingers between his knees. He's hungry, but for whatever reason, after Jacob's question, can't bring himself to eat. *Everything's changed for sure. And I don't know how to handle it. I don't know what to do.* He looks up to Theresa's picture next to the flickering candle—then back to Jacob, his mouth open and chewing away, playfully, with the fronts of his teeth.

Jacob stops immediately when he notices his father's gaze, hangs his head, and chews slowly.

"Chorry," he says through the wad of food.

Owen flashes a faint smile, picks up his slice of pizza and takes a large bite.

"Jacob."

When Jacob breaks the stare from his plate, Owen begins masticating his food in the same manner. Gobs of cheese, bread and peperoni dance around, as they are mashed by the fronts of his teeth.

Jacob throws his head back, giggling uncontrollably, then locks eyes with his father, as they both chew like cavemen. Jacob tops his father by showing his chewed food, rolling it around with his tongue.

Owen laughs, "Oh, okay. Okay, I give up."

Through the balusters above the foyer, Kyra watches quietly, with a disapproving glare.

🦋 🦋 🦋 🦋

Later, Owen notices Jacob is lightly chewing on a piece of crust, hanging from the corner of his mouth.

"You full?"

Jacob rubs his stomach, "Uh huh. My belly is tight."

"Well, if you feel like it, you can go up to your room and play." He says clearing Jacob's plate. "But, no cartoons for you right now. At least, not until I put a parental block on the cable." Jacob races off, just as Jinx strolls into the kitchen. "Hey, before you go up, blow out Mommy's candle, please."

"Kay!"

Jinx rubs against Owen's leg nearly tripping him up.

"I forgot, it's dinner time for you too, huh?"

He removes a plate from the refrigerator, filled with strips of baked chicken, then dangles it above Jinx's head. She wastes no time springing up on her hind legs and standing—nearly to Owen's shoulders. She swats at the morsel, knocking it from his hand and to the floor, and devouring it quickly.

🦋 🦋 🦋 🦋

Jacob shoves his large, Tonka dump truck across his bedroom floor, plowing through a platoon of Green toy Army men on the other side. He, then, rushes to the other side to aid the wounded.

"Oh no, what happened fellas?" he asks, picking them up and standing them upright again. "Looks like you guys got hit by a Kamikaze truck, loaded with explosives." He picks up his light-blue toy two-way radio. "Sir, we are under attack, send in air-support, now!" Next to Jacob, is a fleet of paper airplanes he'd created. He picks up two, and throws them in the direction of the rival red Army men, positioned in the front of a pile of neatly stacked stuffed animals. The paper planes land in the middle of enemy territory, doing minimal damage. "Sir, we need something stronger. The airstrike just isn't enough."

He looks around to see what he has available, anything to *really* cause damage to the enemy, red Army. He fishes through his toybox, shoebox and under his bed, but nothing will do. He pans the room, coming across the cartoon military poster on his wall—full of machine gun fire, explosions and a GI holding a flamethrower to a bunker full of Nazi's.

He reaches deep into his pocket, removing the yellow lighter he had swiped from the fireplace, when blowing out his mother's candle; he, then, turns his attention to his fleet of paper airplanes.

❧ ❧ ❧ ❧

Kyra finishes off the last slice of her, now, cold pizza, and washes it down with the rest of the soda, raising the cup until the ice slides down to her lips. Even though she's still a bit thirsty, she refuses to leave her room—avoiding the risk of facing her father; so, she sucks on one of the few remaining ice cubes.

She climbs out of bed to retrieve the folded piece of tissue paper, still delicately sitting on her desk. The dainty tissue paper gift was given to her, the day she left her grandparent's home.

Carefully, she peels open the methodically wrapped paper, revealing a white monarch butterfly. Her grandfather caught it for her collection during his trip in Hawaii. He told her, the Chinese believe, that a white butterfly symbolizes the soul of a departed loved one.

"*Danaus Plexippus,*" She mutters in awe.

She thought of her mother, while softly tracing the edge of its delicate wings, with the tips of her middle fingers.

She places it on the bed, taking extra-special care in handling the incredibly fragile specimen, then reaches under her bed for a paper towel roll. She rips off a sheet, laying it flat under the light of her desk lamp. With a pink spray bottle filled with water, she spritzes the towel lightly, and places the butterfly, dead center.

She could almost hear her mother, whispering to her, the day she taught her this. "*You can damage the wings if you don't soften them first. It also makes for a good wing spread. Now, you can pin it to your display box.*"

Carefully, she folds the moist paper towel over the butterfly, and places it in a small Tupperware container.

With the container tucked under her arm, she carefully cracks open her door, just enough to peek into the hallway. She pauses, for a moment, to listen. Jacob is playing quietly in his bedroom, and she can hear the television going downstairs. Quietly, she makes her way down the hall to the top of the staircase. She leans over the rail, satisfied at the sight of her father asleep on the couch—his head tilted back and mouth wide open.

With each step, she pauses from the groaning wood under the carpeted steps, while gripping the banister rail firmly. Eventually, she makes her way down to the bottom step. And despite the noise, Owen barely moves.

She moves swiftly through the foyer, then slides, in a pink pair of no-show socks, across the kitchen floor—where she stops in front of her tall stainless-steel destination.

A heavy, rapid pounding at the front door startles both, her, and her father—startling him from his sleep. He sits up straight, dazed and confused. Then lets out a long grunt before coming to his feet.

As he shuffles through the living room toward the front door, wiping the sleep from his eyes and face. He notices Kyra standing in the kitchen—hugging her container to her chest. He points to the door with a confused expression. She hunches her shoulders, with just as much confusion in her eyes.

He flips on the porch light, and yanks the door open wide. His neighbors, Mr. and Mrs. Jensen, stand before him with a crazed and eager look in their eyes.

Both reach for Owen's arms, frantically, to pull him outside.

"Your house—your house..." Screams Mrs. Jensen, leading him outside by the arm. Then, she points to the upstairs with her free hand.

"We called 911!" Exclaims Mr. Jensen. "Your house! It's on—"

Owen's eyes buck open, "WHAT!?" Yells Owen.

To his horror, smoke is coming from Jacob's bedroom window. The orange light, from the flickering, dancing flames, grows larger by the second. The fire alarm blares.

Owen pushes them away as he runs back inside. "Kyra, get out, now!" He takes off up the steps, three at a time, "Jacob!"

When he gets to the hallway, Jacob is running toward him, spilling water from a green toy-bucket he is carrying. Thick, black smoke spills from the top of his open doorway, and into the hall. An anxious, painful look of regret radiates from his eyes.

"I'm sorry Daddy, sorry!" He screams.

"Get out, now! Go!" He rushes over to Jacob's room. The inside is filled with black smoke. The neatly-stacked stuffed animals are swallowed by roaring flames; soon, flames are spreading to the curtains beside the ignited plush toys. Owen grabs the bucket from Jacob and throws it on the fire, but it was like spitting in a volcano. "Jacob, what did you do!? Get out of here, now, son!"

He spins around to get more water, but sees Kyra standing in the hallway, she is frozen from shock. "Damn it, Kyra, I said, 'get out of here'! Take your brother, and go!" He orders. She doesn't respond. "Kyra! Now! Take your brother outside, and get far away from the house. Across the street! Move!"

She suddenly snaps to, and obeys.

Owen tries to step into the room, but by now the heat was too unbearable. Soon, the entire room is consumed by flames.

"Jinx!" Kyra yells. She spots her father's cell phone on the console and grabs it. The large cat leaps from the couch, and follows them outside to the front curb.

Owen attempts to salvage what he can. First, he grabs his wedding photo album, then his wallet and medications.

With his arms full, he watched as the fire began to claim the hallway; instead of running, Owen freezes right where he stood. Through the blazing wall, he could see, what looked like, black smoke in the shape of a woman. It, then, disappeared in the flickering flames.

Despite his deadly surroundings, he stands in awe for a brief moment, then suddenly realizes that if he doesn't leave now, he will never leave.

🦋 🦋 🦋 🦋

The entire home is consumed.

Tears stream down Owen's face, as he watches the last hope of finding stability for his family, burn to the ground. The kids observe from a safe distance in their grandparent's car, while the fire fighters do what they can to put out the flames.

Some neighborhood children, and adults, witness a man, that once had it all together, fall apart—dropping to his knees and crying out loud. He buries his face in his hands, and slumps forward into the grass.

"I'm sorry Daddy," Jacob cries, watching him from the rear window. "I didn't mean too!"

"Jacob, turn around, and sit-down, sweetie." Rose orders.

"No!" He snaps, then opens the rear driver-side door and runs to Owen. Jacob nearly falls onto him, as he wraps his arms around his dad's neck, from behind.

With her nose running, and cheeks wet from tears, Kyra watches them from the car.

"You two are gonna stay with me, for a little bit, baby." Rose says, reaching over the driver's seat to comfort her—rubbing her back. "Everything is gonna be just fine, don't you worry." She sighs, "You two have been through so much, already. I'm gonna save you from this. Okay?"

CHAPTER 5

...IT POURS

(Late August)

A sliver of sunlight burns through the black living room curtains of Marley's one-bedroom apartment, tracing down the wall, like a slow-moving, white laser, as the sun climbs. If it weren't for the ticking of the large, black with gold-trimmed clock on the dining room wall, and Owen's gentle snoring on the couch, the apartment would be completely silent.

Gradually, the light travels down until it reaches Owen's lower brow. He grimaces from the focused beam, and crams his face into the back couch cushion, then yanks the blanket over his head.

It does not take long for him to drift back into a deep sleep; almost as though perfectly timed, with his rediscovered slumber, the three locks on the apartment door disengage one at a time. The door creaks open, and slams shut shortly thereafter, jolting Owen from his sleep. He tenses from the sound of keys being tossed, and skidding across the kitchen counter.

Owen grunts and moans, realizing it's Marley, returning home from yet another long night out. He hums a tune, as he passes Owen, on his way to the bedroom. Then silence.

Owen takes in a deep breath, hoping the silence meant his brother had passed out on the bed. *Thank God. Maybe I can get in another hour, or two, of sleep 'cause I'm exahus....* Owen begins to drift back to sleep when Marley's stereo system blares, vibrating the walls and floor with the Funkadelic tunes of "Flashlight".

Owen angrily explodes from underneath his blanket, then storms toward the bedroom, his fists balled tight.

Marley has his back to him, rocking back and forth to the beat, as he pours Peach Crown Royal in a short glass, using his dresser as a personal bar. He is dressed in black slacks, a purple, silk dress shirt, matching the color of his glistening Gator shoes. His reflection in the dresser reveals a silver cross dangling from a thin chain, in the middle of his exposed chest. His beard is short, trimmed tight, and faded back to his ears on both sides, albeit, long and uneven at the chin; his head invariably maintained— clean shaven and smooth.

Despite his brother's shared financial hardships, Owen admired how he, somehow, always finds a way to keep looking so clean and polished. However, there were *no* feelings of admiration, not this morning.

Owen enters the room, furiously marching over to the stereo, and pushes the power button.

Shocked, Marley spins around. "The fugh..."

Owen doesn't say a word. He just wipes his face, returns to the couch, and retreats under the covers.

Marley watches him from his bedroom door, smiles, then tosses back the contents of his glass in one, painful-looking swallow. "You okay, bro?" He asks, his words slurring. "You wanna a drink?"

"It's almost six o'clock in the morning, Marley. No, I *don't* want a drink, man. I just wanna sleep. I got a lot I need to do, in a couple of hours."

"What? What you got to do, King-O? It's Friday, and you got no calls to go to? The kids are at their grandparents, and you got no money. You should've come out with me, like I asked, instead of sitting up in here—moping all night. Have a little fun."

Owen slowly turns his head from the pillow, and gives him a squinting glare. Owen is sure he knows where this conversation is headed. It's not often Marley calls him by that name, but when he does, it means there is an argument brewing.

It started one day, when Marley overheard their mother telling Owen that 'he would rule the world one day'. Marley didn't feel she shared the same confidence in him, even to this day. As children, when chores needed to be done, and done *right*, she would call on Owen. *'King-O'* is Marley's way of rubbing their childhood in his face. Reminding him that Marley knows Owen was... is—their mother's favorite. Making Owen feel guilty, yet, self-pitying his own mother-son relationship, at the same time. Just one word... one name... did that in an instant. *Oh shit, not now... What the hell is he in his feelings about, now? Bad timing, little bro.*

"Marley, I don't have time for this. Can I just get some sleep?" He pleads.

"Why you always avoid talking to me? Huh?" He approaches the back of the couch. "Like I'm not worth your time, or good enough to talk too. Like I'm stupid. You don't even return my calls, man."

"Marley, please, man! We can talk about this when it's not so damn early."

"And you always putting me off. Like now! You only called me because you needed a place to stay." Marley takes a seat at the corner of the couch, nearly sitting on Owen's feet. He places his empty glass on the coffee table, and lays back.

"My fucking house burned down, and almost took us with it! What did you *expect* me to do? And I don't *always* put you off, I just have a lot going on, brotha. It's nothing against you, you know that. I swear."

"Yeah, you always busy. Just like Momma." He closes his eyes. "Momma never had time for me, either. She spent more time with you, and watching tv." His slurred words drifted apart, and his eyes grew heavy. "She didn't even have time to whoop my ass when..."

Owen felt Marley's weight against his feet getting heavier. "Marley?" he nudges him with the toes at his back. "Marley?"

"Huh?"

"Dude, *please* go to bed."

Marley doesn't budge, drifting off into a drunken sleep, and pinning his brother's feet behind him. Disgusted, Owen accepts the discomfort in trade for the silence, and buries himself, once again, under the blanket.

🦋 🦋 🦋 🦋

Owen is seated at his brother's tiny kitchen table, with a small pile of bills scattered out in front of him. His jaw muscles flex, with his cell phone pressed firmly against his ear, aggravated while listening to the instrumental hold music of the song, *Don't worry, Be happy.*

Finally, after nearly, fifteen minutes of waiting, the phone rings.

"It's a beautiful day at Morgan's Insurance, this is Jessica. How can I help you?"

Owen sighs with frustration. "Jessica? I was on hold waiting for Michelle. She was gonna transfer me?"

"Okay. Transfer you, where, sir?"

"To the Claims Department."

"This *is* the Claims Department, sir. How can I be of service?"

"I'm trying to find out the status of my claim. I was supposed to receive a call back a couple days ago."

"Alright, I'd be happy to assist you with that, sir. Can I have your first and last name, please? And, the account number associated with the claim."

"I gave this all to her already. How many times do I need to keep giving my account information, before someone can help me?"

"I apologize, Sir; however, this is a different department, and I needthat information to pull up your account. So, if you'd please, I need that information in order to verify your account."

"Owen Mosely. 4434470"

"Thank you, Mr. Mosely. One moment, while I pull up your information." She says, drumming away on her keyboard. "It shows here, Mr. Mosely, that your insurance has lapsed."

"What does that mean?"

"It means, we wouldn't be able to honor your claim, sir."

"You're kidding me, right?" He snaps.

"I'm afraid not, Mr. Mosley. You haven't paid on your account, so, it caused the status to go into a lapse. It also looks like we have contacted your agent, in request for payment, if your claim is to go through."

"So, you're telling me, if I make a payment to the account, I could get my claim to go through?"

"Yes, it looks that way."

"How long do I have?"

"Looks like you have two days, Mr. Mosely. Not that much time."

Owen sighs and takes the phone away from his ear in disgust, then returns it. "How much is my payment?"

"Well, with the late fee, it comes out to three hundred fifty-seven dollars and sixty-five cents."

"Good Lord. I don't have that kind of money right now."

"I'm sorry Mr. Mosley. It's the only way the claim will get processed. And, if you wait too long, your account will close."

They both are silent for a moment, while Penny types her notes.

Owen quickly ponders options in his head, of what he could possibly sell. Immediately, he thinks of his wife's car, that was safe in the garage during the fire. *Would I be able to sell that in two days?* His only other option is to speak with Rose. The very thought of having to ask her for money, made his stomach turn. He anticipates the look on her face, or the tone in her voice, after he asks. *That conversation probably wouldn't go over so well.*

"Mr. Mosley?"

"Yes," He says, startled from his thoughts. "I'm sorry."

"No worries, sir. Is there anything else I can do for you?"

"You got three hundred and sixty dollars I can borrow?" He chuckles.

"No, sir, I'm sorry." She responds, with a smile in her voice.

"No, I'm kidding. I'll see what I can do, and call you back, hopefully, before the deadline."

"I hope so, Mr. Mosley. Good luck, sir."

"Thank you!"

After hanging up his call, Owen pauses for a moment, holding back the tears that are welling in his eyes. He scrolls down through his contacts until he gets to Rose. His index finger hovers over the call button for a moment, then presses it.

The phone rings, and his heart thumps to a new quicker beat. He can barely breathe steadily, as he anticipates where the conversation will lead. The phone rings a few more times. Just as he was about to hang up, the line is picked up.

No one answers. He waits for the greeting while hearing Jacob playing in the background.

"Hello?" Owen says.

"Yes." Rose replies with disdain.

Owen's heart pounds, even harder, feeling her animosity through the phone. He swallows, then takes a deep breath. Suddenly, Marley enters the living room, while brushing his teeth.

"Rose, I need your help."

Marley swiftly spins around, wide eyed, with toothpaste dripping from the corners of his lips.

"There's nothing I can do for you, Owen. There's nothing I *want* to do for you."

"It's not just for me. It's for the kids, too. I have no money, and the insurance claim won't go through unless I make a payment in two days. It's almost four hundred dollars. I don't have that type of money right now. I need your help so I can get the kids stable, again." He pleads.

"You shouldn't concern yourself with money right now, or with the kids. You need to get your stuff together. How dare you call me and ask for favors."

"I know, I'm sorry; but..."

"Sorry!?" she yells, "sorry for what, Owen? Because of you I have nothing. Theresa is gone, and it's *your* fault. And you have the nerve to call and ask *me*, of all people, for a favor?" She moves away from the children, and into the kitchen. "And you almost get my grandchildren killed in a house fire. What were you thinking? What were you doing? How *dare you* call me and ask for a favor. If you were in front of me, I'd slap you in your *damn* face, Owen; how dare you call me."

94

Marley mouths the words, "What were you thinking?"

"Rose, I want to spend some time with the kids this weekend. Do you mind if I pick them up and take them to the park?"

"Yes, I do mind. It's time I start taking some action with this situation. I refuse to allow you to do anything else to this family. You'll be hearing from my attorney, soon. I'll be going for custody of the kids."

"What!? Why would you do this to me, Rose!?" He exclaims, squeezing his phone tightly. "After everything I've lost."

Rose takes a deep breath. "Ask yourself that question again, and think about it. Everything you did, you did to yourself." The line disconnects.

Owen, near tears, winds his arm up to throw his phone across the room, but Marley catches his wrist.

"Don't do it, bro, you'll regret it."

Owen snatches his arm away, and stands to confront him—fists clenched tight. They would be chest-to-chest with their noses touching, if it weren't for Owen's two-inch difference in height over his brother.

Marley takes a step back, and extends his arms out on either side. "I'm not your problem, bro. I'm here to help. Back up!"

Owen breaths deep, but exhales with a slight whimper, trying to hold back the inevitable nervous breakdown he felt erupting inside of him. He can hold back for now, but the rage builds inside of him. He clenches his fists even tighter and leaves the apartment quickly, leaving the door wide open behind him.

Marley gives chase, but stops at the door. "Where you going, bro? Hey!"

Owen doesn't look back.

Marley watches as he disappears into the door leading to the stairwell.

❦ ❦ ❦ ❦

Owen's utility truck comes to a screeching halt in front of a local liquor store, startling a middle-aged woman walking past. He slams the driver-side door, and marches inside.

"Good evening!" The store clerk says, from behind the counter.

Owen ignores her and beelines for the hard liquor. He wastes no time grabbing the first thing he could get his hands on. His blind choice - Seagram's 7.

The young woman behind the counter hesitates to acknowledge him, after noticing his hostile nature and bloodshot eyes. She scans the bottle.

"That will be seventeen dollars and thirty cents." She says timidly, while bagging the bottle.

Owen tosses a twenty-dollar bill onto the counter, and snatches the paper bag, leaving the store without a word, or his change.

❦ ❦ ❦ ❦

(11:57 PM)

A distraught and intoxicated Owen, has the accelerator of his utility truck nearly floored, blowing past the speed limit down a dark highway. The dark silhouettes of trees cradle the damp road, against the moonlit sky in front of him.

His attention and steering are on autopilot, while thoughts of his last argument with Theresa, a spilled bottle of pills on her bedside and a funeral, all blaze through his mind.

He rounds a curve, when the high beams of an oncoming vehicle nearly blind him. He veers to the right to avoid the vehicle, and on to the shoulder of the road, tracing the edge of a deep ditch. He jerks the wheel to the left back onto the highway, swerving back and forth until he regains control. Despite his close call, he doesn't let off of the accelerator. Instead, he snatches his bottle from the passenger seat, and takes a quick swig of the honey-colored liquor, just before his passenger side tire blows out.

He drops the bottle, and grips the wheel with both hands, locking his arms out in front. "Shit!" The steering wheel jerks violently in his hands as he struggles to maintain control; finally, he lets off the accelerator, for the first time since he left the store.

The truck eventually comes to a sliding halt, in front of a fifty-five mile per hour speed limit sign. He drops his head to the steering wheel. His deep, panicky breaths slow as he hugs the wheel firmly against his forearms, pressing his forehead to the horn. His eyes become filled with rage, just before letting out a loud cry in frustration.

Minutes go by. A number of different vehicles pass, as Owen stares at his shoes through the steering wheel, pondering the certainty of his situation - failing to see any light at the end of the proverbial tunnel.

Sitting up in his seat, he wipes his face free of tears. His expression of pain and desperation fades to a deadpan, lifeless gaze.

In the driver side mirror, he notices the headlights of an approaching vehicle in the distance. He opens the glove compartment and gently removes a picture of himself, Theresa, and his children; the moment was captured when Kyra was only ten and Jacob was only two - maybe three-years-old. Theresa had the corny idea, for all of them to wear the same colors - black bottoms with white tops. He forces the slightest of smiles, kisses the photo gently and crushes it in his fist. *I'm sorry.* He drops the crumpled picture, and slowly, steps out of the truck and into the road, facing the approaching speeding vehicle. He raises his chin and breathes in deeply. The sound of a semi's horn sends his heart racing, but he stands his ground, raising his chin even higher, clenching his fists tight. He turns his head from the high beams flashed in his eyes, and notices something... someone sitting in the front seat of his truck, watching him. A familiar, dark silhouette of a woman he still loves. He gasps.

"Theresa?"

The semi's horn blares, just as he finds the strength to dive out of its way and into a puddle of mud, beside his truck. Quickly, he scrambles to his feet, using the truck's running boards and smearing muddy handprints on the side door. He gets his footing, and presses his face in the driver side window. The front seat is empty. But... on the passenger seat is his photo. Uncrumpled and pressed flat.

🦋 🦋 🦋 🦋

(9:46am)

Marley pulls open the curtains to the living room, letting in a blinding beam of sunshine. The bright rays penetrate the thin blanket covering Owen's face, waking him. He squints, licking and smacking his lips to create enough saliva to moisten his dry mouth.

"Wake up, Negro! I got some good news for you." Marley orders, fanning a sheet of paper in front of him.

Owen groans and rolls over, burying his face into the cushion. "Not right now, I'm sleeping, man." He mumbles. "Why can't you ever let me sleep."

"Had a little bit too drink last night, I see... and got your muddy boots all over my damn carpet," Marley says. "But whatever, 'cause what I have for you here... you should be able to pay for new carpet for me, in no time."

Owen slowly peeks from under the blanket. Marley is standing over him, with a great big cheesy smile on his face. He raises the paper for Owen to see.

"What's that?"

"What this is, big brother - is proof that God is good. I got a buyer for that BMW, man. Said they'd take it off of your hands for fifteen thousand."

"What? How much did you list it for?"

"I put it online for twenty. But—"

"Twenty!?" Owen roars. "I asked you to put it up for thirty, Marley. That can sell for at least twenty-five, easy."

"Man, nobody was biting on that car for *that* much," Marley says, dropping the paper down on him. "Besides, you need money *now,* and you need to help with some things around here. I suggest you get that money because you don't have time to be wasting trying to get top dollar."

After looking over the paper, Owen shakes his head, disagreeing with his brother. "I can't. I can't, man. It's Theresa's car."

"What? You can't what, Owen... let *go?* You have to let go, man!" Marley roars. "You can't sit around here with no income. Your kids can't wait on clothes and a new place to stay. That old bitch can't *wait* to snatch your kids away from you, and this is her opportunity," Marley kneels down closer to Owen. "I love you, man, but Theresa is not coming back. You can't hold onto that. Big bro, you have to do something. And you need to act now. When your hangover goes away, I suggest you give him a call."

Owen contemplates the situation for a while, staring at the sheet of paper. He knows Marley is right. Marley usually has a pretty level-head on his shoulders when he is sober.

"Okay," he tosses the paper on the coffee table. "I'll call him."

"Alright! Yes! And when you get paid, make sure you cut me off a chunk for two month's rent. And a little bit for setting up this deal," Marley says, walking off to the bathroom. "And can I borrow a little bit for my—"

"I'll give you two month's rent, Marley. Full rent. That's it. That way, you don't have to worry about it at all. I should be out of your hair by that time."

"Two month's rent is good. I can handle that," He turns to the kitchen. "Maybe some food, too? 'Cause yo big-ass can eat like Daddy used to."

"Deal! Now, can I go back to sleep, please?" Owen pleads.

"Yeah. By the way, you may want to check the countertop. I've been putting your mail up there, for a few days now. Seems to be stacking up."

"It's nothing but bills, I bet. I'll get to them when I can."

"One of them says something about an attorney's office, or something. Hopefully, no one is trying to sue your ass. You may want to check it ASAP, big bro."

Owen groans, throws the blanket off of him and stomps his way into the kitchen, snatching the stack of mail from the countertop. It's wrapped tightly in a dirty, stretched out rubber band that snaps before he could peel it off.

He sifts through the stack, tossing bill after bill, junk mail after junk mail, next to the sink, before finally coming to the letter from a *Creston Law Offices*. His stomach swarms with butterflies, as he anticipates the reasons they could be contacting him. He's sure it's about the kids, custody, or something else he had neglected to do during these hard times. He rips the envelope open. His eyes growing wider with every word he reads. His worried and fed-up expression turns into excitement and surprise.

"Marley-Marley!" He yells, dropping the remaining mail onto the kitchen floor.

CHAPTER 6

HOME SWEET HOME

(Two weeks later)

With a large manila envelope in hand, Owen exits the building of Creston Law Offices, sporting a blue suit and tie, a spring in his step and a smile a mile wide. He eagerly jumps into the front seat of his utility truck, and begins dialing Marley on his cell phone.

"I did it, little brother!" Owen says. "I just signed the paperwork, so it's all legal."

"Man, that's beautiful. I'm so happy for you," Marley says. "That couldn't have come at a more perfect time."

"I know, that's right!"

"God is good, isn't he?"

"Yes, he is, man." Owen sits back in his seat, glowing. "I got a home. Me and the kids. We have a second chance at this."

"Technically, I would say it's your third."

"Whatever. I don't even care right now. Let's just hope I don't have any reasons, in the future, to earn a fourth chance."

"I'd love to be a fly on the wall, when you tell Rose. I'm surprised you kept it from her this long. I figured you would've thrown it in her face the first chance you got."

"I didn't want to count my chickens and jinx myself. Bad luck seems to be following me around a lot, lately," Owen says. "Rose has a lot of money, and a lot of friends. I just felt like somehow, she would find a way to fuck things up for me, so I don't get the babies. Now that I have all of the paperwork signed, there's *nothing* she can do."

"Right on. Speaking of Jinx, what did you ever do with that evil-ass leopard?"

"I didn't sell her, if that's what you're wondering. Rose actually allowed her to stay at her place for a while, but the kids told me she put her up in a kennel, since she was fucking up her furniture. They said her growling at night terrified her. She never did that at our house though. She must be freaked out by her new environment or something."

"That's one evil pussy," Marley laughs. "Okay, now my other question is, did you find out who left you the property?"

"Yeah. Theresa developed a lot of friends working for that real estate agency for so long. Some man named, Lloyd Burgess, was someone she helped buy this house, and he was so grateful – he left it to her in his will some time ago. Must not have had any family, for him to just leave it to her like that."

"So, when you gonna move in, and how far away do I have to drive to come see my older bro, now?"

"It's just a few miles away, man, nothing you can't handle. Harrisburg." Owen says, then smiles sinisterly, "you gonna help me move, right?"

Marley's smile changes to a peeved, vacant expression. "Not to be an asshole bro, but you don't have that much stuff to move."

"I got that stuff from the garage, in storage, and some stuff that was donated to us. That's about it. But, if you can't help me, I understand. Me and the kids can do it."

"You think I'm gonna leave you and the kids hanging like that?"

Owen smiles. "No, no I don't."

❦ ❦ ❦ ❦

The brakes to Owen's small, ten-foot moving truck rental, squeal as he pulls to the side of the road, finally stopping when the front tires bump and drag against the concrete curb - a cracked, and crumbled curb, in front of an old white, weather beaten and faint-grey trimmed, Victorian style home. Besides a little lean in the foundation, the home looked solid. The grass around the front is somewhat patchy, but it's not something Owen felt he couldn't fix.

Kyra is in the passenger seat, fast asleep, alongside Jacob – in the middle seat, sleeping quietly, with his head in her lap.

Marley, driving his brother's company truck, packed with other loose belongings, and some furniture donations - from previous neighbors and friends, pulls up behind him. Amongst the belongings is Jinx, yowling impatiently, in her large, portable kennel.

"Kyra, Jacob, we're here," Owen says, with a soft voice. He shakes them both gently by the shoulder. "Wake up."

Owen eagerly jumps out, leaving them in the vehicle. He yanks the keys from his pocket, as he strides up the walkway to the front steps. The middle of the three steps, flexed when he stepped on it. The old, white paint, covering the steps, was chipped and weathered, exposing hints of its, previous, grey color underneath. *Just a few pieces of wood, and I'll fix those right up.* The rest of the outside seemed freshly painted, but not by a professional. The paint was thickly applied, the glass, in the center of the door and windows, had traces of brush streaks - where no painter's tape had been used. However, it was not something Owen hadn't expected – (being how old the house is).

Kyra peels her eyes open, the look of disgust melting over her face. "Gross!" She exclaims, scowling down at her little brother - who is drooling on her new pair of jeans. She can feel that the cool, pooled saliva had soaked through the fabric, and onto her skin. She uses the hood of his purple pullover, nearly choking him, as she aggressively wipes the mess. She then, shoves his head off her thigh, making his head smack onto the seat.

"Ugh—what the heck, you butt!" Jacob mumbles.

"Look what you did to my clothes; you sick, little midget—" Before she could finish her verbal assault, she notices her father unlocking the front door to their new home. Her mouth falls open in disbelief. "No freaking way."

"What?" Jacob asks, popping up from the seat to see.

"Oh my God, is this seriously our house?" She rolls down her window. "Dad! Please tell me you're just picking up something from here."

Owen throws her a disapproving frown, then wipes a clean spot in the front door window, to look inside.

"Nope, that's your new home, little lady," Marley says, startling Kyra, as he approaches the blindside of the window. "Now, it doesn't look like much, but give your Dad a break, okay? You know he has skills, with those hands of his. He'll have that place together, in no time. Don't go making all kinds of negative, okay?"

"But, Uncle Marley, look at it. That's just asking for trouble. Even the yard looks creepy."

Marley looks. "Damn! You ain't lying." He chuckles. "Yeah. It is a little creepy. But you'll get used to it. Ain't nothing to be afraid of. It's probably not as creepy inside as it looks outside," he then opens her truck door. "Come on. Let's go give him a hand."

Kyra sucks her teeth.

Jacob quickly crawls over her, "I hope there are kids in the neighborhood. There was nobody to play with at the other house." He jumps out, and races all the way to his father's side, leaving the slow-moving Kyra behind.

As her and Marley make their way up the walkway to the porch stairs, Kyra gives the house another once over. The loose boards of the porch steps shift and creak, as she and Uncle Marley climb them. Her eyes scan the front side of the house, until they stop at one of the dark windows on the second floor. A feeling came over her, as if something were staring back down at her through the parted, thin, white-shear curtains.

With excitement in his eyes, and a smile on his face, Owen unfastens all the locks quickly. The door is stiff and won't budge, so he drives his shoulder into it, over and over, yanking and twisting at the doorknob. For a moment, he gives up, inspecting the door frame and dented metal doorknob.

"Damn, that paint is thick and nasty." Says Marley, "I hope all your doors ain't like this."

"Yeah. We're just gonna have to break it free. I need your help, man," Marley steps up, and gently pushes Jacob aside. "Be careful not to lean into the glass. Push at the top of the door. On the count of three." Owen says, which prompts Marley to place his hands on the door, above Owen's head. "One, two, three!" They both shove the door as hard as possible, breaking the paint seal, forcing both men to stumble recklessly into the foyer. Inside, multiple doors randomly slam shut upon their entry. The sound catches them both off guard, freezing them where they stood, as the dust, they'd disturbed, settles in the air around them.

Marley clears his throat, "Was that supposed to happen?" Asks Marley.

"Was *what* supposed to happen?" Owen asks.

"You didn't hear that? The doors slamming shut'n shit?"

"Air vacuum." Owen says. "I mean, coming in as hard as we did would cause that. There's probably another open window in here, somewhere."

"Yeah, right."

As they dust themselves, Owen steps further inside to explore, with Marley and Jacob close behind. Each one of their steps creates a symphony of grunting floorboards that echo throughout the empty home.

"Man, this is beautiful," Owen says, admiring the dusty, old woodwork. "The floor design is almost like our old house, but a lot older."

"Yeah, much older," mocks Marley.

Owen flips the light switch, to shed some light on the poorly lit surroundings, but nothing.

"Hmph." He grunts.

"What?" Asks Marley.

"You see that? No lightbulb," he reaches up to the empty light socket.

Marley walks into the kitchen. "Yeah, looks like there's none in here, either. I guess we know what your first home investment is gonna be."

"Hey, if I give you some money, would you mind going to the store and grabbing some? It's gonna get dark pretty soon, and the last thing we need, is to be moving around in a dark home that we don't even know yet."

"Sure thing, big bro."

"Can I go with?" Kyra asks eagerly, and still standing outside the doorway.

"Yeah, but please, hurry back." Owen shoves his hands into his pocket and removes a ten-dollar bill. "I don't have anyone, but little Jacob here, to help me move our things. So, please just get those and come right back."

Marley snatches the money, and gives a thumbs up on the way out.

※ ※ ※ ※

Upstairs, Jacob's urge to explore his new home is interrupted by a desperate need to pee. He rushes to the bathroom, located just passed the landing of the staircase, and

110

pushes open the creaky door - peering inside. A crisp chill creeps over him with the faint smell of must.

The walls of the bathroom are seafoam green with a white base. Matching tiles, in a checker-like fashion, make up the entire floor. A beautiful, vintage pedestal sink sits in the center of the wall to his left, with a mirror cabinet above. Straight ahead of him, is a white Victorian-era tub. The shower curtain liner, that hung from an oval shaped rod, seemed to glow against the little bit of light, penetrating through the small window behind it. The poor-lighting made corners questionable and dark.

Holding his crotch with one hand, he flips the light switch repeatedly, before noticing the three empty light sockets above the sink. *Dangit.*

He eagerly bounces on his toes as his need to relieve himself increases. Swallowing his fear of the unknown, he steps inside to the toilet, his back to the rest of the room. With near-blind aim, an explosive yellow stream misses the center of the porcelain bowl, and splatters to the back of the lid and seat before he could control it to the center of the water.

For a moment, he is relieved—until, through the sound of his pee splashing in the water, he notices a faint sound of clicking – a rapid clicking, coming from somewhere behind him.

Without losing his aim, he slowly peeks over his right shoulder, stretching his neck as far as it would let him. The clicking stops, and he sees the bathroom is empty. No sign of what could have been causing the noise. He returns his focus to the toilet, unable to shake the feeling of unease and the tingling at his back, as if eyes were watching him.

He looks over his left shoulder, focusing on a dark corner next to the tub. "Come on," he whispers, hoping to rush the process that eventually slows to a fading trickle. He shakes twice, like Dad says. No more. Then, zips up quickly.

Owen is walking up the stairs, carrying two medium-sized, cardboard boxes, when Jacob plows into him, knocking a box of his clothes to the floor.

"Dammit, Jacob! What did I tell you about running, man?" He says, gathering the spilled items. "What if this had been glass or something?"

Jacob, out of breath, looks at his father. "I heard something. In the bathroom."

"What?"

"It sounded like breathing, and some clicking."

"It's probably the pipes, son. If you and your sister don't stop freaking yourselves out..." He shakes his head. "I don't know what I'm gonna do with you two. Can you, please, run to the car, and bring in what you can? There's some small bags in there you can get."

Jacob looks to the bathroom door, as his father starts down the hall to his room. "Kay."

🦋 🦋 🦋 🦋

Across the road in a similar style of home, a neighbor watches the Mosley's, through partially opened blinds.

Marley steps out of the utility truck, with two green, plastic bags full of brand-new lightbulbs from the dollar store. The wind begins to blow, hard, kicking up dirt and blowing it into his face. He turns away, before it could get into his eyes, catching a brief glimpse of the window across the street, as the blinds abruptly shut.

"The fuck—" Marley raises his bag and waives at the home, then turns up the corner of his lips. "You got some nosey neighbors out here, Kyra."

Owen comes out to greet them. "Oh man, just in time. It's starting to get dark in there. Thanks." Owen says, grabbing one of the bags. "Can you throw a couple of these in the kitchen socket, and the living room, Marley?"

"Yeah, sure thing... but," Marley says, checking his watch. "I need to get going. I got someone coming up here to pick me up in a few."

Owen drops his head, shaking it in disbelief, then places his hands on his hips. "I thought you were going to help out."

"Man, I did. I've been with you most of the day. You know I can't do work during the night. I got shit to do, big bro."

"Kyra, can you please take these bulbs, and go check yours and your brother's rooms to see if you need any? If you need them, put *one* in for me, and bring back the rest."

Kyra sighs. "Which room?"

"Whichever room your brother hasn't picked. I think he's already moved some of his things in one of them."

"Ugh, seriously, Dad?" She roars. "You let a *six-year-old* pick his own room before me?"

"Well, I didn't *let* him do anything. You weren't here, and I'm busy moving stuff in... that I'm *obviously* not gonna get any more help with," Owen says, scowling at Marley. "Maybe you can talk Jacob into picking the other room."

"Oh, my *Gawd*, this is not happening!" She says, "I wish we could've just stayed with Grandma."

"Well, that's not happening, young lady, so, go now, please."

Kyra snatches the bag and storms upstairs but stops midway. "Where's Jinx?"

"She's tied to a pole in the backyard. She wouldn't do anything but pace at the backdoor, so I left her out there. It's a new place, so she's gotta warm up to it. Now, please go do as I asked, before we are lost in darkness."

She sucks her teeth, and stomps up the rest of the stairs.

🦋 🦋 🦋 🦋

With his head pressed against the glass, Jacob watches the tops of the trees that outline the backyard, sway at the mercy of

114

the strong wind. Fall leaves swirl about the lawn near Jinx, tied to a laundry line pole. She's motionless. Her attention is fixed on the dark path opening into the forest. Jacob knocks on the window to get her attention, when, suddenly, his bedroom door bursts open.

Kyra storms in with clenched fists. "Who said you can have this room? I'm the oldest, so *I* get to pick first!" She yells.

"Who says?"

"*Dad* said, you little shit. So, move your stuff to the other room, now!" She orders.

"No!"

"Yes, I'm serious, Jacob. Now!"

"I don't have too, Dad said!"

🦋 🦋 🦋 🦋

Owen watches as Marley's ride speeds off down the street, blaring its bass filled music, and kicking up the dead leaves on the street behind it.

He hears Jacob scream, at the top of his lungs, upstairs. Without hesitation, he sprints through the foyer and up the dusty staircase, quickly arriving at the doorway of Jacob's room. Jacob is laying on top of his blue suitcase; Kyra is pulling at the handle, dragging it, along with Jacob, attached like a leech, across the floor.

"Leave it alone, it's mine—it's my room!" Jacob yells.

"Stop—Stop—Stop! Stop, you two," Owen demands, breaking up the tug-of-war. Kyra swats her father's hand from her shoulder. "Just what the hell is going on? You two are in this house, for just a few minutes, and you're already at each other's throats?"

"*He*, doesn't get to pick the room first, Dad, I do!" Kyra exclaims. "And he won't move his stuff to the other one."

"I don't *wanna* move rooms, I like *this* one. And you were gone with Uncle Marley, so you lost out, and this one is *mine*."

Kyra growls and balls her fists again.

"Sweetie, did you even *look* at the other room before staking claim on this one?" She doesn't answer. Instead, she rolls her tear-filled eyes. "You should really take a look at it, Kyra. You may like it, who knows?"

"You're *always* against me," she roars. "I wish Mom was here. Then, I'd have someone on *my* side, for once. You *always* take his."

"Baby, that's not true, I—"

Without another word, she angrily pushes past Owen, to the bathroom across the hall, then slams and locks the door behind her.

Jacob stands his suitcase upright. "Is this gonna be her room, Dad?"

"She'll be alright, son. She's just having a hard time right now," Owen places his hand on Jacob's head. "But for now, just hold off on bringing the rest of your stuff up here. We need to get something in your stomach, before it gets too late."

🦋 🦋 🦋 🦋

Kyra quietly sobs on the bathroom floor, with her back against the tub, and her face buried between her knees. Gently, she strokes the smooth tiles with the tips of her fingers, while remembering how things were when her mother was still alive. Her memory takes her back, as early in her life as she could remember, then up until the last day she had seen her.

It was the night before her death, when she came into Kyra's room, and laid beside her. After Theresa lightly kissed her twice on the forehead, Kyra felt a warm tear land on the side of her neck. By the time she turned over to see her mother, the door was closing, and the light from the hallway shut off.

"Jacob, that's not where that goes!" Owen yells from downstairs.

Hearing the commotion, Kyra takes in a deep breath and stands, allowing a tickling tear to trickle down the bridge of her nose, where it lingers at the tip. Quietly, she approaches the bathroom door; with her sleeve, she wipes away the evidence of her weeping, then places an ear to the door. The sound of her father and brother, rustling around downstairs, gives her the opportunity to investigate the unclaimed room, without interference or pressure.

She squints her teary eyes, as she steps out into the bright hallway. The entire house is completely lit up with brand new lightbulbs. The house looked different with so much light. Dirty and dusty still, but not as dark and creepy, like before. If only the musty smell would go away.

She reaches the end of the hallway and stands at the entrance of the other bedroom. Her eyes light up, upon entry, and an awed expression spreads over her face, as she approaches the all-white, loft style bed with a built-in desk underneath. Carved into the bed's wood frame are small butterflies and flowers. She feels how smooth the grooves in the designs are, admiring its beauty and detail. She keeps running her fingers along the frame, smiling until she reaches the end. She turns around and stands in front of her window; she has a clear view of the front yard, and the house across the road. *Sold.*

🦋 🦋 🦋 🦋

The wind picks up speed, blowing hard through the kitchen window above the sink, and knocks over one of the small potted plants that Owen had placed on the ledge. Dirt and pottery fragments scatter in the kitchen sink. Quickly, Owen closes the window and latches it shut, but soon takes notice that Jinx is no longer tied to the pole in the backyard.

"Kyra, did you bring Jinx in?" He yells, upstairs to her.

"No! Why?"

"Jacob, did you?"

"Huh?" He yells, from his room.

"Did you let Jinx off her leash? Or is she upstairs, with you?"

"No!"

"Shit!" Owen mutters, hurrying towards the backdoor.

Kyra comes running down the stairs, a worried look in her eyes. "Is she gone? Did you lose her!?" She exclaims.

He doesn't answer, scanning the empty backyard with wide eyes. He cups his hands around his mouth. "Jinx! Jinx—come here, girl!" He yells.

"Oh my God! I can't believe you! Where is she Dad—where is she!?" Kyra exclaims.

Owen approaches the pole he thought she was secured to, and finds the leash lying in the grass, still intact and unbroken. He picks it up to inspect it further, then looks toward the opening in the tree line.

Disgusted, Kyra backs away, shaking her head. "You lost her. You lost Jinx." She says softly, but with swelling anger.

Owen finally turns to address her, but before he can get a word out, she runs back into the house.

He throws the leash back to the grass. *Shit.*

He curls his hands around his mouth. *"Jinx!"*

Resting his hands on his hips, he steps closer to the tree line, hoping to catch a glimpse of her exploring the forest. But there is no sign of her. *Damn. She could be anywhere in there.*

As the wind rustles through the trees, there is a sound accompanying it. He could faintly hear it - the distant sound of a long, drawn-out, high-pitched whistle in the air.

CHAPTER 7

WELCOMING PARTY

(Friday, Early October)

Jacob explodes out from the center of a pile of leaves Kyra had loaded on top of him, roaring at the top of his tiny lungs, and curling his fingers, in front of himself, like the claws of a monster.

She laughs, then dumps more leaves on his head. "You're gonna be such an even *bigger* dork when you get older."

"No! I'll be cooler than you." He laughs, then roars even louder.

"I seriously doubt that." Kyra smiles, then shovels an even bigger scoop of leaves to dump on him, burying her now, *giggling* brother completely.

❧ ❧ ❧ ❧

Inside, Owen, wearing a pair of long blue sport shorts and a white tank top, arranges the furniture. He positions the couch and loveseat in an L-shaped fashion, safely away from the dusty, charcoal-stained fireplace, then takes a step back to confirm the distance.

The doorbell rings.

Owen slowly leans back to get a view through the foyer, attempting to make out the blurred figure, through the thick, glass panel on the other side of his door. *Whoever it is, is too short to be Marley. Damn. Maybe Rose found another reason to come over and cuss me out. Nah, that can't be her.*

The doorbell rings again, followed by a firm knock.

"Hello?" A woman says, peering into the blurred glass through cupped hands.

"One moment," Owen says with a confused frown.

The woman steps back as he unlocks the door. Owen can see her distorted image, as she fixes her hair, adjusts her clothing, then picks something up from the floor of the porch.

After unlatching a series of locks, he finally opens the door. A fair-complected, middle-aged woman, with shoulder length dark- almost black- hair and gray highlights, smiles at him, initially; but then, begins shamelessly gawking at him, with her bright-blue eyes, as if he were a sweet desert-in the form of a six-foot-tall Venti Mocha Cookie Crumble. She brushes the few strands of hair, that blew into her eyes, behind her ear, while balancing a chocolate cake, in front of her, in the other hand.

"Hello. I'm sorry to bother you, but I thought I'd introduce myself, and welcome you to the neighborhood." She says, offering the cake by raising it under his nose.

Owen jolts his head back, to avoid a near-collision with the creamy frosting. "Oh, thank you! Thank you, very much." He takes it with both hands.

"It's a double chocolate cake." She licks the bit of frosting from her thumb. "I hope you like it. I wasn't sure what flavor you might like, so I just thought most people like chocolate. It's kind of a neutral flavor. But, in my opinion, one can't go wrong with a little chocolate in their lives." From the corner of her eye, she catches some movement in the upstairs window, but by the time she looks up, the curtain is closing.

"Oh, well thank you again for thinking of us, Mrs....?"

"Miss, it's Miss Michaels. Lorna Michaels," she shakes his hand with a limp wrist, gripping with the tips of her fingers, as if she were waiting for him to kiss her hand. "Used to be Mrs. Michaels, but my husband passed some time ago. He's the reason I live here. Had some unfinished business here in town, but died before he could get it together. Yep, I just live right there, across the street from you."

"It's nice to meet you, *Miss* Michaels. I'm Owen Mosley, and my two children are Kyra and Jacob," just then, both children come sprinting in from the back door without closing it, then up the staircase behind Owen, with Jacob in front. "Guys, you need to take a shower before dinner," Owen yells. "I'm not kidding!"

"You have some lovely children, Mr. Mosley." Lorna says.

"Please, call me Owen. And excuse my children for being rude. They're at that age."

"No, no worries. Children will be children. And please, you can call me Lorna. That 'Miss' stuff just makes me feel all old, lonely and miserable."

"You're not the first person to tell me that," he smiles.

"Is it just you, and the three babies, then?"

"Just me, and the *two* you just saw. Lord knows I don't need another."

The screen door in the kitchen creaks.

Owen turns his attention behind him to see what it was. As he did, Lorna looks up to the bedroom window upstairs again, then back to Owen. Her eyes drop to his waist side. "Oh, my lord!" She exclaims, backing away.

Owen gasps with delight, and his eyes buck open, as Jinx approaches and circles his legs, rubbing against him.

"Jinx, where the hell have you been?" Owen says, kneeling, and scratching her behind the ear. "I'm sorry. She got away from us a few days ago and we haven't seen her since. The kids must've left the back door open and she was able to get back in. I thought we'd lost her for good."

Jinx finally sits in front of him, with her ears perked, and eyes fixed on the unknown guest.

"My, she is beautiful. And look at those eyes. One green and the other, what is that—gray?" Lorna says, leaning in to pet her.

Jinx growls deeper than she ever had, making Lorna draw her hand back quickly-as if she were avoiding the falling blade of a guillotine.

"Hey—hey, stop that. What's wrong with you?" Owen roars, gently stroking the top of her head. "Man, I'm so sorry. She's never done that before. She has to be hungry. And, no, actually both of her eyes are green."

"Not to be rude, but I'm fairly sure of my colors. Been looking at them for forty-eight years," she chuckles. "What kind of cat is she?"

"She's an African Serval. Kind of like the Great Dane of domestic cats. She belonged to my wife, before she passed."

"Oh no, I'm so sorry to hear that."

"Thank you."

🦋 🦋 🦋 🦋

"Hurry up, in the bathroom, Jacob!" Kyra yells, lightly kicking the bottom of the door, while cradling shampoo, body wash and a rainbow-colored loofah in both arms.

"I'll be out when I'm done using the toilet."

125

"You better not be pooping, you little shit!"

"Yep," Jacob giggles, dangling his feet. "And I'm gonna tell Dad you're cursing, again."

She kicks the bottom of the door harder, in disgust.

🦋 🦋 🦋 🦋

"Well, I'd better get going, it sounds like you have your hands full," says Lorna, looking toward the upstairs. "I'm sure you have a lot to do, but if you ever need anything, feel free to let me know. I'm just right across the street, here; I'm home most of the day so, anytime." Owen attempts to close the door, but Lorna isn't quite out of the way for him to do so. He mentally sighs. "Not that you'd really need anything from me. Seeing you're a handyman, and all. I may have to call you to come fix some things at my house." She grins, with a hint of seduction.

"Uh, okay. Well, that's my number on the side of the truck. Feel free to give me a call if you need anything. I definitely could use the work."

"Oh, I will." Lorna says, backing away.

"And thank you again, for the cake."

"You are *very* welcome. And don't worry about the cake plate. Just give that back whenever you're done."

Owen's sighs and rolls his eyes as he shuts the door. When he turns around, Jinx is staring at him, sitting oddly motionless, like an Egyptian statue. He notices her demeanor is different than it had been before. He can feel it. He sets the cake down on the floor and looks closer; he is suddenly amazed at the green and grayish colored eyes glaring intently back at him.

He reaches for Jinx's face to look closer, but Kyra kicks the bathroom door again, even harder than before, startling him.

Owen jumps to his feet. "What's going on up there!?"

Jinx retreats to the living room and climbs onto the couch where she lies down, locking eyes with Owen once again.

"Jacob won't get out of the bathroom!"

"Jacob Mosley, hurry up and finish your business, or you won't get any chocolate cake after dinner!"

"Chocolate cake!?" He giggles.

Moments later, Jacob emerges from the bathroom, menacingly smiling up at his sister.

"Well, it's about time, Baby Jacob."

"Yeah, now you have to smell my poop in your steamy hot shower." He giggles.

Kyra bumps him with her hip and knocks him to the floor. Before he could retaliate, she slips inside the bathroom, and slams the door shut with the heel of her foot. A look of pure repugnance replaces her devious smirk, as the foul essence of her brother's ploy enters her nose. She dumps her things in the sink, quickly covering her mouth and nose with both hands, and peers into the toilet full of little lumpy brown turds.

"Ugh, gross! Don't you know how to flush!? Ugh, you're such a gross little-ass, Baby Jacob! Did you even wipe your butt?" She turns her head while pushing the lever with the tip of her index finger.

Jacob collects himself from the floor. "Stop calling me that! I'm not a baby!"

❀ ❀ ❀ ❀

In the basement, under a soft white lightbulb, Owen cleans, and then hangs his tools on the wall over his new wooden workstation. He squeezes the trigger to his power drill repeatedly but is getting no response. He places the dead tool on the counter, and grabs his flashlight, shining it under the counter, through dusty cobwebs and dangling lifeless insect caucuses, until he locates an electrical outlet. With one hand, he blindly reaches back up on the counter for the charger cord, when his light catches the corner of something gray and square, far back against the wall. He gives up his blind search for the cord, and brushes away the cobwebs, until he reaches, what looks to be, a dusty, old, long toolbox.

He tries to lift it with one hand, but it has considerable weight; so he grunts and pulls, dragging it inch-by-inch, until he could get it with both hands from under the counter and out into the open.

He places it on the counter and wastes no time flipping open the rusted latches on both sides. He pulls at the handle, but it's rusted shut. No matter how hard he yanked, the box would not open to reveal the possible treasures inside.

With a flathead screwdriver, he begins prying at the corroded seal around the opening, tapping at the back of the handle with his hammer, until it finally breaks open. He drops his tools to the counter, then positions the box under the light, pausing before slowly opening it. He lets the heavy lid fall open. A disappointed look replaces the curious one, as he glides his fingers across the top of hundreds of old keys. Different kinds. Different sizes. Some old, some rusted, and some newer.

A loud thud, directly above his head, sends dust and debris down over him. He angrily dusts off his head and shirt. "I thought I told you two to go to bed!" He yells to the ceiling. "Kyra, Jacob? You hear!?"

There is no reply. No sound of footsteps rushing away from his angry tone. The basement door slams shut. His heart skips a beat, but he quickly becomes furious.

Certain his children had disobeyed him, he approaches the bottom of the basement stairway and begins climbing with purpose - when the light that glowed around the basement door, shuts off.

He stops four steps away from the top. "Hey! Kyra? Jacob? I know I told you both to go to bed, didn't I?" Again, no reply. He takes one step up and the door unlatches, then opens slowly, binding and creaking, until it stops halfway.

❦ ❦ ❦ ❦

With his teeth brushed, and Transformer robot pajamas on, Jacob perches at his curtain-less window, seated in a small, multi-colored wooden chair that only a six-year-old could fit in and would find comfortable. He watches the relentless wind, wildly blowing the bare trees in their moonlit backyard. The rattling, poorly-insulated window allows the cold wind from outside to waft inside. Jacob shudders, quickly retrieving his green pullover that was draped over the back of his chair.

As he slides his arms inside and pulls the hood over his short, dark, curly hair, he peers outside once again. From the dark path in the tree line, a small, white ball is carried into the yard by a breeze. It stops, nearly dead-center of the lawn. Despite the more than gentle wind blowing, it holds still, barely moving in the wavering blades of grass.

Jinx, coming up from behind, startles him, and places her front paws on the windowpane, joining his curious gaze outside.

"Geez, girl—you scared the crap outta me." He whispers, stroking the soft, yet slightly course fur on her neck while briefly admiring the black lines and spots that make up the design of her coat.

He turns his interest back to the ball in the yard, but it is no longer there.

Jinx lets out a few deep-muttered meows and hops down from the window. Jacob watches as she disappears from his room and into the hallway. His door entrance is dimly lit by the moonlight shining through the window behind him - casting his outstretched shadow on the floor in front of him.

There is a noise behind him at the window. He spins around to see what it was. He gasps. Immediately horrified by the white ball pressed firmly against the window, he falls backward from his chair and screams. "Dad!"

It began to slowly grow in size, pressing harder against the glass, and gradually blocking the glowing, moonlit sky behind it. The fragile glass begins to crack, little-by-little. Jacob was finding it hard to breathe, nearly holding his breath in fear, as he stays on the floor, wide-eyed and frozen in disbelief. The sphere expands and flattens itself further across the failing window.

"Dad!" He screams once more.

Suddenly, the lights come on. Jacob scrambles to his feet and bolts to the bedroom door, slamming into his father's waist, hugging him tightly.

"Hey—hey, calm down, son. What in the hell are you screaming about?"

Jacob points to the window. "There! Right there!"

"What? What's right where?"

Jacob's eyes widen. He watches, as his father leaves his side to inspect the, now, unbroken window with the clear view of the backyard.

"It was a big, white ball, Dad. It was trying to get in my window. It was *right* there, pushing on the glass! It kept getting bigger and bigger! I think it was trying to get me."

After inspecting the window more, Owen notices the full moon in the middle of the sky. A harvest moon, huge and glowing like the large, white ball Jacob described. The biggest moon he had probably ever seen. He smiles.

"Time for bed, son." He says, turning to pick him up.

"But, Dad, it was—"

"Don't 'but, *Dad*', me. I know we've had a lot going on within the past week. And you, like your old man, need some rest." He gently places him in bed. "I guess I'm not the only one imagining things around here today, huh?"

"I didn't *imagine* it!" Jacob roars.

"Watch your tone," he orders, picking up the toy Voltron from the floor. "Here's your robot. If anything else happens, you know he has your back. Now, can you please get some sleep? For me?"

Jacob sighs with frustration as Owen pulls the blanket up to his shoulders, then tucks him in, with a kiss to the forehead.

"Night."

"Mm!" Jacob grumbles through tightly sealed and puckered lips.

Owen nods his head and smiles, shutting off the light and closing the door.

"Hey!" yells Jacob.

Owen pops back in, kneels, and flips the switch on the soccer ball night light. "Sorry. Good night, son."

As soon as the door closes, Jacob sits up and crawls across the bed to his window, slowly peeking one eye around the window frame. Hesitantly peering outside at the grassy, tree-framed scenery, illuminated by the large moon, he notices the tranquility; even the wind had calmed.

🦋 🦋 🦋 🦋

High up in her bed, Kyra sleeps peacefully, dreaming of her mother standing in a field of thistles, while wielding a butterfly net.

Kyra watches from just outside the flowers, as her mother swings the net gently downward onto the butterflies. Everything around her has a sunny glow to it, including her mother.

"Got it!" Theresa yelled.

She holds the net firmly to keep the elegant winged-beauty from escaping and bounds through the field in slow motion towards a, much younger, Kyra - who's standing in the grass holding a pop-up habitat cage.

"It's a Monarch." Theresa says.

"It's beautiful."

Theresa presses the net gently to the grass. "Look. Can you tell me the gender?"

Kyra kneels next to her. Then with her finger, she points to the wings. "It's a boy."

Theresa smiles. "That's right. What made you come to that?"

"The two dots on each of his wings."

"What part of his wings?"

"The hindwings."

"Right," Theresa smiles and caresses Kyra's chin. "You're getting rather good at this, aren't you? Open the cage, and let's see if we can get a few more."

"Can I catch the next one!?" Kyra says excitedly.

"Of course, my love," she hands her the net. "Just make sure you're careful. Use a gentle, downward sweep. They're very delicate creatures."

"You're gonna kill it anyways, right?"

"Well, we aren't going to smash it," she laughs, "but you can't put it on display if the wings are all bent or damaged. There's a better way to do it in the Kill Jar."

"Don't call it that! I hate that name," Kyra sighs. "Can we call it something else?"

134

"What do you suggest, my love. You can name it whatever you want."

"Hmmm, how about—"

Kyra's dream is interrupted by the sound of her bedroom door creaking open, an inch or two, allowing the light from the hallway to cut through the darkness of her room like a thin spotlight. Assuming it was her Dad peeking in on her, or Jinx coming inside, she quickly falls back to sleep, snuggling back into her blanket.

Cold air creeps in and kisses the back of her neck. She shivers, pulling her blanket further up onto her shoulders while rolling over and nuzzling back into her warm pillow. The light coming through the top of her partially-opened door pierces through her closed eyes. She squints and shifts away from it, then gradually drifts back into sleep again, when there is a loud bump. She sits up quickly, her sleepy-eyes are wide open, but her vision is blurred. Her heart skips a beat, and her breath quickens, when she notices her door is swinging completely open, and rebounds off of the wall as if something had just flung it open.

The hall lights shut off right before her eyes. As she tries to gain focus, she draws her feet closer to her chest, feeling vulnerable in front of the dark depth of the hallway.

The complete silence scares her. She draws her blanket closer, covering her mouth and nose, barely seeing above it. She scoots back to the wall, away from the edge of the bed.

From the corner of her eye, she catches something shift to her left, in the dark corner of her room. She gasps, quickly spinning in that direction. The closet door opens silently, then stops. She doesn't make a sound, holding her breath and trembling under her blanket. The door moves open again, even wider.

Feeling trapped with nowhere to go, she braves her fear and whispers, "Jacob?"

She got no answer.

Stuck at the top of her bed, she looks to the hallway, then back to the closet door. She lets out a quiet, shuddering breath as she creeps to the edge of the mattress. Her father's room was next to hers, and she could get there quickly.

She builds up the courage to lean closer to the edge of the bed and looks down to the floor, but it's too dark to see. At that moment there's scratching; it's an aggressive scratching - coming from inside the closet. She gasps with a short, high-pitched squeal, covering her mouth and sitting back against the wall once again.

The scratching continues with more aggression. It's as if something were digging frantically at the floorboards, or scraping against the wall.

All she can think of is getting out of her room, as fast as possible, and to the safety of her father's. Once more, she gathers the courage and cautiously leans forward, measuring the distance between her and the floor. She thought of climbing down the ladder, but it was way too close to the closet.

She had no choice. It was now or never. She lays down on her chest and slowly throws one leg over the side of the bedrail, while reaching and feeling with her big toe for the top of her desk below.

The scratching abruptly stops, and so does she, freezing in place, with her legs dangling.

The hinges of the closet door give a short squeal. Kyra quickly attempts to pull herself back up onto the bed, just as Jinx leaps onto it in front of her; in her mouth, she is holding an old, spooky-looking, pale-faced stuffed animal with large blue eyes. The face is so white, it practically glows in the dark, like a ghost. Kyra screams and loses her grip, falling on top of her laundry basket, full of dirty clothes, and knocking over her butterfly display kit, before tumbling to the floor.

🦋 🦋 🦋 🦋

Owen, Kyra and Jacob are all huddled in Kyra's room, staring inside the closet at a small hole in the back wall. Owen looks down at the doll that Kyra brought to his attention. Dirty and charcoal gray, having the body of a teddy bear, but the face of a sad porcelain doll with a dingy complexion and frowning, sickly-blue lips. Owen stared with a frown of his own into its huge, ocean-blue, gemlike eyes, then back to the hole in the wall, aiming at it with his flashlight.

"You say she pulled this out of *there*?" He asks, kneeling to inspect the hole closer.

"Yeah. She scared the hell outta me."

Jacob gasps. "You cursed."

She glances at him. "It's in the bible, so it's not a curse. Grandpa said."

"Nuh-uh."

"Yeah-huh, so shut up." She orders.

"Both of you, stop it, please," Owen says, standing up. "I don't see anything else in there - no rat turds or nothing."

"Rat turds!?" Screams Kyra. "We have *rats?*"

"I said, *no* rat turds. There's nothing to worry about. Whoever lived here before made that hole. It's not chewed. I'm just gonna have to patch it up later. Something else to add to the list of things I need to do with this house." He clicks off his flashlight. "Ya'll go get ready for the day."

Before leaving the room, Owen notices her butterfly display kit on the floor. He kneels to pick it up, triggering Kyra's Kill Jar to roll to his feet. A scotch tape label on the side of the jar, written in Kyra's handwriting, reads, "Owen".

CHAPTER 8

SOCIALIZING

The next day (5:34 AM)

Owen, wrapped in a cocoon of bedsheets, is in a deep sleep. The sheer, mint-green window curtains glow, from the outside morning light, in his dimly lit room. The Wind Tunnel floor fan roars on high by his bedroom door, gently blowing the bottom of the window curtains and bedskirt. He wouldn't be able to rest without that comforting sound. The still calmness of the house, and lack of air flow, makes it nearly impossible for him to get a good night's rest. The dark and quiet at night, left him questioning every creak and pop of the house settling. Was someone in the house? Was *something* in the house? He knew it was just old wood, wind, and pipes, nevertheless, he still went without sleep because of it.

The fan shuts off. It's spinning blades slow to a stop. Eventually, Owen awakens; he immediately notices the change in the air and his dead fan. He climbs out of bed; he's wearing all but boxers and a white t-shirt and rubbing the morning crust from the corners of his eyes, then kneels next to the fan. He checks the cord, tracing it to the wall outlet. It's still plugged in. He checks the back of it. The speed-selector is pointing to high. He switches it from off to on, repeatedly, but nothing.

"Shit." He wipes his face with both hands, looking over to his digital clock on the nightstand. Nothing but a blank, black screen where bright-green digital numbers should be. "Damn fuse." He mutters to himself.

Before checking the fuse box, he heads to his master bathroom, nearly stumbling over some unpacked boxes, next to the dresser, that he procrastinated to unpack.

He sorts through his medicine cabinet, collecting pill bottle after pill bottle, dumping the required dosage of each into his palm until there is a small collection of candylike medications. He chokes them down, without the recommended eight ounces of water - immediately gagging and feeling the discomfort of the chalky tablets and sticky capsules cramming down his dry throat. He cranks the water to full blast, and cups his hand under the faucet to drink, accidentally knocking an open bottle of pills to the floor.

With his face wet and dripping at the chin, he gazes down at the blue pills that are scattered beside his foot. His eyes tear up,

140

and his hands clench into tightly closed fists, that begin to shake, as a sudden rage builds within him. A tear slides down the bridge of his nose and hangs at the tip, ready to drip, when he explodes with anger, slamming both fists on the porcelain sink and knocking the rest of the pill bottles to the floor. The numerous pills scatter about under the sink creating a pharmaceutical horror.

Owen drops to his knees to gather them. His hands quiver, unable to hold some of the smaller pills long enough to place them back into their bottles.

Suddenly, there's a pounding he could hear from in the distance - like an echo of him slamming his fists onto the sink. He sits up to listen, dropping the contents in his hands to the floor. One after the other, thumps keep going with a steady beat, shaking the floor, and causing the pills around him to vibrate with each impact.

He jumps to his feet and races through his bedroom, ripping open the door and stepping out into the hallway. The house grows silent. He waits for it to happen again, staring down the dark hall toward the stair landing. *Where the hell was that coming from? Was it the kids?* He's startled by the sudden roaring whirl of the floor fan cutting back on. His heart kicks into overdrive and his breath quickens. The alarm clock now blinks the bright-green digital display of twelve AM.

With a sigh of relief, he turns to reenter his bedroom when the pounding starts again. Owen, wide-eyed and startled, jumps and staggers back into the hall. The pounding grows louder than before. *Downstairs! Front door.*

Owen sprints down the hall at top speed, stopping at the top of the staircase. The pounding continues, but no one is at the front door. "Hey! Who is that!?" He screams, leaning over the banister. The pounding abruptly stops – as if obeying a command. *What the fuck is going on!*

Kyra flings open her bedroom door, rubbing her eyes. "Why are you screaming!?" She roars.

"Did you hear that? That loud–" He turns his attention downstairs again, still seeing nothing. No one at the front door, and everything is as quiet as before.

Jacob opens his door, yawning, with his blanket around his shoulders and head.

Kyra crosses her arms in front of her. "Hear what? All I heard was you screaming like you're crazy and woke us up."

He looks to Jacob, who hunches his shoulders. Kyra backs into her room, annoyed, and slams her door shut.

❀ ❀ ❀ ❀

(8:48 AM)

"Give them to me!" Jacob orders.

"No, I want some!" says Kyra, smiling.

142

"You don't even like them!" He stands on the chair at the dinner table and reaches for the box of Space Crunch cereal; she snatches it away and pours it into the bowl in front of her.

Jacob is nearly in tears and screams, "I'm gonna tell Dad!"

"Gonna tell me what?" Owen says, walking into the kitchen.

"Kyra took the cereal. She doesn't even *like* Space Crunch, and she took the last of it!"

"So what!? Your name's not written on it." She says. She licks her lips as she pours the 2% milk slowly. "Mmm," she teases.

Jacob plops down in his chair, folds his arms and scowls at her. When Owen turns his back to them to retrieve a container of orange juice, she takes a spoon full and places it in her mouth, closing her eyes and making a face to Jacob, like it was the best thing she'd ever eaten.

"I hate you!" Jacob yells.

"Hey—hey knock it off." Owen orders, as he sits at the table. "Jacob, go look in the cabinet—there should be another full box in there. I just bought it the other day, and your sister knows it. She's picking on you."

Jacob wipes the tears that nearly fell from his eyes, climbs down from his chair, and then sticks his pointed tongue out at her. She returns the gesture with a cheek full of overly sweet and unwanted cereal.

"Also, Jacob, what did I tell you about sneaking downstairs and watching that cartoon channel in the middle of the night?"

"Um, not to."

"That's right, so why do you keep doing it?"

"I can't sleep sometimes. It was too noisy and cold last night." He says, seating himself once again, and disappearing behind the brand-new, bright-red with yellow writing box of cereal he placed on the table.

Owen pushes it to the side. "I'm talking to you, son. What was noisy?"

"The clicking sound and the whistling outside."

"What clicking sound? I didn't hear anything." Kyra says.

"It was in the hallway at first. Then by my bed. Then in the hallway again. It kept waking me up. It got kinda cold in my room, so I came downstairs and..."

"...and you turned on that dang cartoon channel."

Jacob hangs his head. "Yeah."

Owen shakes his head. "And what you heard was probably something in the basement, echoing through the vents. Like the furnace clicking on and off."

"Or rats!" Interrupts Kyra. "Ugh," disgusted, Kyra spits the partially chewed cereal into her bowl. "I just don't see how you eat that crap. It's nothing but sugar."

"Kyra, watch your mouth." Owen orders.

"What? I just said *crap*. That's not a bad word."

144

"A bad word, in this house, is whatever I say it is, young lady."

"Whatever." She mutters, as she leaves the table; she goes to the kitchen sink, and dumps the cereal in the garbage disposal, then turns to the counter and opens a loaf of whole wheat bread from the cupboard.

"What are you doing?" Owen asks.

"I want toast and peanut butter."

"Look, that was a perfectly good bowl of cereal before you regurgitated it. Your brother could have eaten it. We can't afford to be wasting food around here. Business is slow right now, and I don't make much money as it is."

"Okay-okay! Geez!" She exclaims. "Everything is about what *he* wants. You buy *him* cereal, where's *mine*? He has dorky new shoes, that light up. You don't buy stuff *I like*; you're always on *his* side." She pushes the loaf of bread away and throws one slice on the counter in anger. "Wow! *And* the bread is frozen! Oh, my God!"

"What? Frozen?"

"I'm so done right now." She says, storming off. "I wish Mom was here!"

"Deja boo." Jacob says with an overly-full mouth of cereal, the milk dripping from the corners of his lips.

"Déjà vu, son."

"That's what I *d*aid."

Owen handles the frozen piece of bread; curious and puzzled, he checks the entire loaf, which is hard and cold as well.

"Daddy can I go outside and play in the back?"

"Yeah. Pick up those toys in the living room, then you can. Just stay where I can see you from the kitchen window."

❦ ❦ ❦ ❦

A brand-new set of red Army action figures are lined up, side-by-side, on the slanted handle of an old, rusted wheelbarrow. One-by-one, they are picked off by rocks, like little bullets, slung in their direction from Jacob's wrist rocket slingshot.

"Should we call in air support, Sir?" Jacob says to a set of green Army men next to him. "No need for that. I think we can handle the last few, even though they're in an elevated position."

Jacob takes aim at the last of his inanimate enemies, drawing back intensely on the yellow, hyper-velocity rubber band of his deadly device, then releases. He misses his target. The small rock deflects off the metal wheelbarrow and launches up into the air. It soars through the backyard, landing at the dark tree line behind it.

Out of ammunition, he decides to retrieve more rocks, and reset his fallen enemies, back to their original position, for another attack. With each step, the soles of his shoes flicker, like mini strobe lights, dancing back-and-forth from red to blue. With each recovered item in the yard, he finds himself closer to the tree line, stopping at the edge of its shaded, worn path.

Despite the bare tree branches, and the bright sun shining down on him, the forest remained nearly as dark and mysterious as it did at night. There is a creepy calmness about it, as if it were... waiting for him. The distant sound of a whistle rang out through the trees, all around him. When the whistling finally stopped, it traveled away, like a fading echo - high in the dark branches.

Jacob stands in place, motionless yet unafraid, when something from inside the forest catches his eye. At the base of, one of the many tall trees, there is a white sphere, just like the one that was trying to press its way into his room. It sat oddly near the tree as if it were peeking around the trunk at him. But even still, he does not feel afraid; his curiosity will not allow him to back away. Instead, he takes a step forward into the thick dead leaves and branches that lay before him. They crackle and snap under his forty-four-pound frame, when suddenly, the ground gives from beneath him.

Jacob can barely let out a scream as he plunges into the pit, catching himself, at the edge of the hole, by an exposed root. He claws and grabs frantically at the sticks and leaves with his free hand, while his feet dig and kick trying to find footing in the loose, damp soil, crumbling around him. He screams, but the soft surroundings absorb his cries for help.

The brittle root begins to fail, ripping from the soil. He slowly begins slipping into the dark, dirty abyss, reaching up one last time, with what little strength he had left, when he's startled by someone looking down at him. The light above them made it hard to see their face; it is just a silhouette of a small boy, who reaches out quickly to grab Jacob's free hand.

With the boy's help, a little grunting, and a lot of pulling, Jacob is able to climb his way to safety. They collapse to the ground at the edge of the hole.

For a moment, Jacob can only lay in the soil, exhausted and out of breath.

The boy stands above him and smiles.

His hair is just as dark as Jacob's, but not as curly. He has a similar peanut butter complexion, with dark brown eyes, and wearing an off-white t-shirt, now soiled from his heroism. He could almost pass as Jacob's brother.

Jacob returns the smile. "Thanks." He gurgles, then clears his throat.

The boy nods.

"Jacob!" Owen roars from inside the kitchen, loud enough for Jacob to hear him through the back screen door. "Jacob, come pick these toys up in this living room, like I told you to, man. Now!"

He climbs to his feet. "I gotta go," He says, dusting himself off. He extends his hand. "Thank you. Thanks a lot."

They shake hands and Jacob sprints off through the backyard, his shoe lights flickering, but not as bright as before, with them caked with mud.

"Jacob Mosley," Owen says, stopping him at the door. "Man, what in the world were you doing out there? Look at your clothes, man." Owen inspects him, turning him around until Jacob is facing the backyard. Jacob thought he'd get one more look at the boy, but he was already gone.

🦋 🦋 🦋 🦋

Later in the afternoon, a navy-blue Ford Taurus pulls up behind Owen's utility truck. Through slightly tinted windows, the driver shuffles through paperwork on a clip board, then shoves it all in an old, leather flapover briefcase.

A short, round, dumpy woman emerges - wearing a men's light-blue collared shirt tucked into her brown khaki pants. She reaches deep into her pocket, and removes her identification card, attached to a black lanyard, then places it around her neck, flipping her picture forward. She takes a quick look at the Mosley residence, and with a deep calming breath, places a tan fedora hat, with a chocolate-colored band, snug on her head. Her short, flat, brown hair curls inward at the bottom, hugging her chubby, blemished face.

After laying on the doorbell a few times, she begins to knock. Her knuckles graze the door, just as Jacob opens it. He doesn't greet her. Instead, he stares curiously.

"Well, hello," she says. "You must be, little Jacob Mosley?"

"Uh huh."

"My, what a handsome young man you are. My name is Kat. Is your father home, sweetie?"

"Yeah, hold on," he replies, skipping towards the kitchen and yelling down the hall to the open basement door. "Daddy, some man is at the front door!"

She grimaced.

Moments later, Owen emerges from the basement, cleaning his hands with a towel, then stuffs it in his back pocket.

"Hi. Can I help you?"

"Yes. Mr. Mosley? Owen Mosley?"

"Again, yes. May I help you?" He asks again, but with more concern.

"My name is Kat Dillon. I'm with the Department of Social Services. Would you mind if I come in?"

Owen's heart drops. With a wide-eyed expression, he steps to the side to allow her room to enter, then fastens the door closed behind her.

"May I ask what this is all about?"

"Is Kyra here also?" She asks.

Owen conceals his frustration, knowing of the things the people in her position can do... how misleading they can be.

"Yes ma'am, she is. Could you please tell me what's going on?"

"Do you mind if we sit? I'll explain in just a moment." She says with a forced smile.

Owen directs her toward the living room, where they take a seat on the couch. Kat removes some paperwork from her briefcase and places it on the coffee table in front of her.

"Mr. Mosley, I was called to visit your home because our department has some concerns that they would like for me to investigate." She says, grabbing part of the paperwork and flipping through a couple of stapled pages.

"Concerns? What concerns?"

"Someone called us to report that... well, in a nutshell... the children aren't being properly taken care of, Mr. Mosely."

Owen stands. "What!? Who?" He reaches for the paperwork and she quickly yanks her hand away. Owen suddenly notices the "*fear*" in her eyes, or rather, her *acting* in fear, so he cautiously slides away to his side of the couch and takes a deep breath. "Am I gonna need an attorney for this?"

She gazes at him, as if she were in fear of another attack, but he felt as though she knew she was in no danger. He took it as a warning to be conscious of his every move. *Here we go with this shit. Just keep your distance, Owen, and find out what crap is being stirred in the pot.*

Her "frightened" expression disappeared as quickly as it appeared.

"Feel free to consult whomever you'd like Mr. Mosley. Again, I am just here to conduct an investigation. If everything is in order, be assured, you won't be seeing me again."

"And you can't tell me who called you?"

"It *was* an *anonymous* call, Sir. No, I cannot."

Annoyed, Owen stands and places his hands on his hips, calming himself as he walks toward the fireplace. When he turns around to address the situation, Kat is hugging her briefcase tightly to her chest, her eyes wide with fear, and her mouth gapped open.

Owen brushes his hand over his face. "Jesus," he whispers. "Ms. Dillon, feel free to look around. My kids are well taken care of. I don't have the most, *nor* the best. But I provide a living for my babies the best way that I can right now."

She cautiously places the briefcase onto her lap, then shoves her files back inside.

"I'd prefer to speak to your children first. There should be no need for me to inspect your home, Mr. Mosley. Provided, they let me know that everything is okay."

Owen nods his head. "Alright. Okay. I can get them for you. Would you like something to drink? Water?"

"No, I'm fine. Thank you."

Owen, still peeved at the social worker's false displays of fear and concern, heads toward the base of the stairs.

"Kyra and Jacob, come down here please!"

With her head on a swivel and her chin held high, she scans the room while resting her hands on the briefcase that occupies her lap. Her eyebrows raise periodically, increasingly annoying her host, who is watching nearby.

"We just moved in, not long ago. I'm pretty good with tools, so I'll have the placed fixed up in about a year, or less. I also own my own business – 'Handyman Mosley'."

"Does that bring in good money for you? You and the children?"

"I'm working on that right now. I have a little bit of money from donations, the selling of my car, and some, possible, new clients coming up."

"So, for the time being, you're living on borrowed and limited funds? No real *steady* income coming in. No medical care? What about school? Where do the children go to school?"

"Currently, they are being homeschooled by their grandmother, who is more than qualified to teach. As far as good money and medical care, not at the moment," he takes a quick breath. "Look, I... *we* just lost everything. We *really* don't need this in our lives. All we want to do is rebuild and be happy."

She doesn't respond to him; she just stares at him down her nose, like an arrogant queen in men's clothing.

"I'd like to speak to the children, if you don't mind, Mr. Mosley."

He impatiently drums his fingers on the wood banister. "What if I do mind? What if I asked you to leave?"

"Then, this could get a lot uglier than you'd like, sir. A lot uglier than it needs to be. Please don't go down that road."

"Kids!" He yells even louder.

"Do the children have their own rooms?" She asks.

He ponders for a moment, gazing at the manwoman, with tensing jaw muscles. When she stands and turns her back to him to get the full three-hundred-and-sixty-degree view, Owen slips her a middle finger. "Yes, they—"

Suddenly, Kyra and Jacob come thundering down the steps. Kyra stops mid-step, scowling down at her father, who quickly withdraws his one finger salute upon noticing her.

"What are you doing?" Asks Kyra.

"Nothing—come down here for a minute, please. I need for you to meet someone."

Kyra rolls her eyes, and begins lazily bouncing down the steps. Jacob immediately approaches Kat with an innocent smile and his hand extended.

"Nice to meet you again, sir."

"Nice to meet *you* again, young man. But I'm afraid it's, *Ma'am*, not sir." She pets his head. "If you two wouldn't mind, could you show me your rooms?"

"Sure!" Says Jacob, eagerly leading the way back up the steps.

Owen watches as they ascend the staircase while continuing to introduce themselves, but Kyra's gaze lingers on him joined by the faintest of sinister smiles.

The phone rings.

"Hello." Owen answers.

"Hey, big bruh; it's Marley. How *do* you?"

"Marley. Hey, man, don't ask," he says, slightly louder than a whisper. "I got a visitor right now."

"Oh, shit! You on your period?" He laughs.

"Come on, man. I'm serious."

"Sorry. What's her name?"

"It's not what you think. But her name is Kat, and she's upstairs with the kids right now."

"What? With the kids?" Marley exclaims with concern. "You got the woman upstairs with the *kids*? You know that's a big no–no, bro. Did you even hit it yet?"

"Marley–Marley, slow down, little brotha. Not that type of visitor. This woman is with the Department of Social Services."

Marley pauses.

"Oh. Oh no, man. That's not good. You don't need that kinda shit in your life."

"Yeah, tell me about it. She's upstairs talking to the kids right now. Just when I thought things were getting good for us, then *she* shows up."

"Man, and she's up there interrogating the kids? Them fuckers are sneaky man. She's gonna end up twisting their words. Be careful what you say and do. Just smile, obey and get her the fuck out! Do you know why she's there?"

"No. I have no idea, at all. She just showed up here on my doorstep saying she was 'conducting an investigation' that stemmed from an 'anonymous phone call'."

"That's dirty. Who you think it was?"

"Well, who else do you *think* it would be? Rose... no doubt, trying to get custody of the kids from me. I'm just gonna have to play it cool and see what happens. I'm not gonna let her screw things up."

"I bet she's got connections up there."

"Yea. That scares me too. Anyways, what's up, man?"

"Nothing. Can't a little brotha call and check up on the big one?"

"Yeah, whatever, Marley. You forget that I know you."

"Well, I was gonna ask you for a little favor, but I see now is probably not the right time for you."

"No time is good for your mess. But, man, come on. What's going on?"

156

Marley pauses. "Do you still have any of that money left over?"

Owen rolls his eyes. "Why Marley?"

"This is for you, King-O, not for me. I know you need tags and insurance on that truck. And with money being as tight as it is for you right now, I think I have a way out. I have a friend who has their hands in all kinds of things."

"I'm listening..."

🦋 🦋 🦋 🦋

Close to an hour later, Kat and the children emerge from Jacob's room. Downstairs, Owen is petting Jinx on the couch, eagerly awaiting the outcome of her visit, and to finally get rid of this social worker.

Butterflies invade his stomach as he stands to greet them. Kyra stops midway down the steps to watch over the handrail; she has a partly-devious smirk on her face. Jacob darts out from around Kat.

"Dad, can I have a snack?"

"Not right now, Jacob." Says Owen.

"But it's midafternoon. I always have a snack midafternoon."

Owen rolls his eyes. "Okay. Three cookies and an apple. Nothing more, Jacob. You understand?"

"Kay!" He runs off to the kitchen.

Kat approaches him but keeps her distance as she secures her notes and paperwork in her briefcase. "Alright, Mr. Mosley. I think I have everything I need."

"Good. As you can see, my children are well taken care of, and there's nothing to worry about."

"Well, I wouldn't go that far, just yet. I do have some concerns that we may need to address... some things that were brought to my attention. And you may want to do something about the temperature in Jacob's room. It's freezing in there."

"What '*things*?'"

"It's really nothing to worry about. However, I'd be careful having a house full of young girls here, but Kyra seems incredibly happy that you're planning to have a birthday party for her." Owen looks up at Kyra, still smiling but now refusing any eye contact with him. "Well, we will be in touch, Mr. Mosley."

Kat heads out of the door, and down the porch steps, with a muddled Owen behind her. He stops at the top of the stairs.

"But don't I have a right to know what it is you're concerned about? What was said upstairs?"

She keeps going without stopping or turning to address him. "Like I said, we will be in touch, Mr. Mosely."

Now in fear and frustrated, he watches her throw her things on the passenger seat and drive off. He lightly, yet firmly, punches a wooden beam next to him.

CHAPTER 9

TREE AMIGOS

(3:17 AM)

The coils from the space heater glow bright-orange near the foot of Jacob's bed. He's asleep, curled up tightly under his Star Wars blanket, with his hand being the only part of him exposed from underneath.

The warm heater's glow fades for a moment, as if it were going to shut off, but powers up again, bright, and back to normal just as the door opens, groaning slowly on its hinges.

The blackness outside the door had a life of its own, creeping in and spreading to the ceiling, walls, and floor. Gradually making its way over to Jacob's bed. If he were awake, he would hear the faint chattering just outside his door that crept in with the darkness.

The heater shuts off completely. The orange glow fades out, allowing only the faint glow of the soccer ball nightlight to shine dimly near the door. Jacob's covers peel back gently, by an unseen force, then stops once Jacob's face is uncovered. He winces from the cold, drawing his hands and knees closer to his chest for warmth, then he snatches the blanket back over him.

The darkness retreats into the hallway. The space heater kicks back on, and returns the orange glow to the room, and warmth to Jacob.

❦ ❦ ❦ ❦

(5:43 AM)

A hue of light-blue on the horizon kisses the darker night sky that precedes it, a sign of dawn approaching. As the sun rises, the light shimmers against the thin layer of frost in the corners of Jacob's windows.

Tick.

A small pebble hits the bottom of the wood window trim, chipping a layer of the icy coating.

Jacob fidgets while deep under his covers; his trusty soccer ball nightlight flickers off as the light shines through the window onto it.

Tick.

Another pebble hits the window – just a little harder, startling Jacob from his sleep. He pops up from under the quilted cloth-face of a snarling Chewbacca. Squinty-eyed, he looks around his room to locate the noise.

Tap.

A third rock, even bigger, finds the glass; hitting it even harder and leaving a small, dusty impact mark behind.

Jacob crawls down to the foot of his bed and peers out of the window, and looks down into the backyard.

Using his fingernail, he scrapes away at the frost to get a clearer view at something moving in the tree line. Jacob smiles, seeing the boy that saved him, waving. He waves back. The boy then waves again, but this time, beckoning him to come outside. He looks back at his alarm clock. It's nearly six o'clock. He hesitates for a moment, then looks back down to the trees, except the boy is already gone.

For a moment, Jacob thinks of the trouble he could get into, for leaving without his father's permission, and so early in the morning. But then, he thinks about himself finally having a friend to play with, and this could be his only chance at it. Maybe if he hurries, he could catch him before he gets too far. *If I leave now, I could be back before Dad wakes up.*

He leaps out of bed and tiptoes over to his bedroom door, listening through the partial opening for any early birds roaming the house. It's quiet, so he swiftly and quietly heads over to his dresser, removing a pair of pants and a clean t-shirt that he quickly puts on. Finally, he tightens the Velcro straps of his LED sneakers, and snatches his green pullover from the chair.

With his Voltron robot under his arm, he takes one slow step out into the hallway, immediately lighting everything up like a squad car on a crime scene. He gasps, covering his shoes with his pullover to muffle the flickering light display, then pauses. Kyra's door, down the hall, creaks open and out steps Jinx. Her eyes reflecting like emerald-and-gray diamond gems.

Jacob raises his finger to his lips. "Shhh".

Satisfied that no one else had awaken, he makes his way to the stairs, on his toes while using the wall for balance, being extra careful not to trigger the sensors in the heels of his shoes. He then straddles the banister and slides down, butt first. The speed of his descent is more than he could handle—only having one hand to brake, while the other dangled his heavy robot. His tiny rear end slams hard against the bottom post. He grimaces from the sudden agony and chews on his bottom lip to keep from whining.

In pain, he dismounts slowly, but lands hard to the floor causing his shoe lights to activate again. Without hesitation, but holding his rear with his free hand, he runs as fast as he could through the kitchen, where he slips out through the back door undetected.

Racing through the backyard, he lights up the scenery like the rapid-flashing gumballs of a police vehicle, in high pursuit; he then stops abruptly at the tree line. He looks up at the trees that tower above him, their leaves rustling gently in the wind, then into the woods that held the dark of the night inside.

Suddenly, a branch snaps - just ten or so feet in front of him. But it's too dark to see what's inside.

"Hey!" He yells, a little louder than a whisper.

There's no response, so he carefully steps inside of the forest, minding the hole he nearly fell into the other day. His shoes guide his every step - casting colorful, dancing shadows in the short distance.

"Hey, where are you?" He whispers.

No answer.

Deeper into the woods he goes, in the direction he thinks the noise came from. He looks behind himself to make sure his home is still in view - just in case he needs to make a hasty retreat.

He gasps, startled by a tapping noise just above him. All he can see is the dark silhouette of the trees, neighboring the twilight sky overhead, so he stomps his feet to get his shoes glowing once again. The colorful strobe light effect reveals a large tree in front of him. He stomps again and again, as his eyes scan up the tree, until his vision comes to a large dark structure above him.

Tap-Tap-Tap.

The sound came from above him. His eyes widen and his heart picks up speed. "Hey kid. You up there?" Nothing. *He had to have heard me that time. Why don't he answer me?* The structure begins to creak, as if something with considerable weight was walking about inside. His imagination takes control of his thoughts. *Maybe something is up there, and it eats little kids. Maybe it got that boy.*

He looks behind himself, suddenly realizing he is a little deeper within the woods than he'd wanted to be. He can no longer see the house, from where he's standing. He takes a deep breath and a step back, while looking above, once more.

Tap-Tap-Tap

He had enough; he spins around, and bolts through the woods, as fast as his legs could carry him, looking back periodically to make sure nothing was following. From in front of him, he's met with a bright beam of light. He screams at the top of his lungs and falls to the ground; panicking, he scurries backward while using his hand to block the blinding light.

"Jacob!" His Father yells, aiming the flashlight away from him. "Jacob, what the *hell* are you doing out here, boy?"

At that moment, Jacob couldn't decide whether he was frightened or relieved to hear his father's booming voice. But, either way, it was better than being torn apart by whatever it was in that thing above him.

Owen drops the flashlight and stands him up, holding him firmly by the arms. "What, in the hell, possessed you to come out here, this early!? In the dark. *And* without my permission? Do you know how scared I was—looking all over the house for you?" Owen then hugs him.

"I-I was following my friend."

"I don't care what it was you *thought* you were doing, Jacob." He breaks his embrace and looks Jacob in the eyes. "You know better than to do what you did. It's a good thing I saw your shoes flashing from your bedroom window, or I would've called the police."

"I'm sorry, Dad. I'm sorry." Jacob says, shaken, trembling in his father's grasp.

"Okay. You know, I should spank your butt," Owen says, picking up the flashlight. "Don't ever do that again. You hear?"

"Yeah."

As Owen leads him away by his hand, Jacob looks back to the dark forest as they start to enter the yard.

"What in the hell?" Owen shines his light in the large hole. "You see that," he says in a calmer voice, "thank God you didn't fall into that. I'm gonna have to get something to fill it up. Until then, you stay clear of this part of the yard. Hear?"

Jacob doesn't answer. His focus is at the base of another tree. Feeling something or someone, staring back at him.

"Jacob!?"

He's startled from his gaze. "Huh?"

"Did you hear what I just told you?"

"Yes."

"Good. Now since you wanna wake up early and play "little explorer", you can go explore that dirty bedroom of yours, after you wash up and get dressed for the day. G'on in and go upstairs."

🦋 🦋 🦋 🦋

(Later that day)

Owen left home to do a repair job on a client's washer and dryer set, leaving Kyra responsible for watching her little brother. She lay comfortably on the couch, facing away from the staircase, while watching *Twilight,* with a bowl of Spicy Sweet Chili Doritos beside her.

Upstairs, Jacob does as his father asked, cleaning his bedroom in a manner that most six-year-olds would. He plays with, just about, every toy before placing it in its proper location, all the while chewing away loudly on a small white sack of gummy bears, leftover from a visit to his grandparents. Periodically, he peers out of his bedroom window towards the forest, wondering if the boy would ever show again.

He takes a handful of gummy bears and crams them into his mouth but doesn't chew. Instead, he licks and rotates each one in his mouth, then sucks away the moisture. One-by-one he removes each gooey, sticky bear and presses them to the window he's looking out of. First the yellow, then red, orange and finally the green, pressing it firmly to the glass with his thumb, while chewing and swallowing the rest.

In the blurred distance, he sees something moving. It's *him...* the boy he saw earlier. Once again, he's motioning, with one hand, to Jacob to come outside, his other hand hidden behind his back.

Remembering what his father said, and in fear of what happened earlier that morning, Jacob shakes his head 'no'. From the corner of his eye, he can see the red gummy bear slowly sliding down the glass, and soon, drops from the window.

The boy then moves his other arm, from behind his back, and dangles Jacob's toy Voltron by the leg.

Jacob's jaw drops. He immediately glances over to his empty bed, where he normally keeps it, then around the room to see if he'd accidentally left it somewhere. *On the floor maybe...* He flattens himself on the floor, peering under his bed. Nothing. His heart sinks as he realizes he must've dropped it when he was in the forest earlier.

"Stupid." He whispers, thunking himself on the forehead with his fist.

As he returns to the window, his anger swells inside as he thinks of the abuse this boy could be putting his metal comrade through; Jacob imagines the boy throwing him against a tree or slamming him in the dirt. He could be doing anything to him. He can't stand the thought of all the different possibilities. And regardless of the consequences, Jacob knew there was no way he was going to leave his best toy to this unknown kid.

❦ ❦ ❦ ❦

Jacob, wearing his older sneakers, stays low, slithering down the stairs and away from his sister's view. He wastes no time with his escape, knowing the loud, action scene on the television will drown out the sound of the creaky spring on the screen door.

To his surprise, the boy is still there, unlike before when he retreated so promptly. He waves, then disappears into the forest. Jacob takes in a deep breath, then follows.

The boy is quick, jumping over large branches and the trunk of a collapsed tree. With everything he has, Jacob tries to keep up, but stumbles over a small log. He quickly recovers to continue his pursuit.

"Hey-hey wait! That's mine! Gimme my robot!"

Jacob stops to catch his breath, slumping over with his hands on his knees. As his heavy breathing slows, he listens, panning the woods around him, but the boy had disappeared. Not even the sound of him running through the brush could be heard, nor the wind blowing through the trees above. Nothing.

When he looks above, to the tops of the trees, he realizes he is, once again, standing under the dark structure of a large tree.

"Hey!" Jacob says softly. There's no answer.

He begins walking around the base of the tree, grasping quickly that it's a large treehouse that he is standing under. In awe, he drags his fingers along the bark, while admiring the building above, when he comes across a ladder on the other side of the trunk. It led high up, into a square, dark entrance in the center of the treehouse. The sudden sound of moving, battery-powered robotic joints, coming from the opening, both angered and frightened Jacob.

"Form blazing sword!"

He hesitates, nervously licking his lips as he ponders his next move. He takes another deep breath, then releases a sharp exhale. He wipes his hands on his pants and looks up, once more, before climbing.

The ladder wobbled at first but held firm, as he starts his slow climb, staring up at the entrance as he ascends. Just before making it to the top, he stops.

"Hey. Hey, kid." He says. Still no answer.

He is just about to take his next step, looking down to check his footing, when he realizes how high up he has gotten. He grew dizzy and quickly hugs his body close to the ladder, closing his eyes tightly. As he stands there, the wood step of the ladder pressed firmly to his cheek, he remembers what his father said when he climbed high-up for the first time. His friends were far-up in the tree, and he was barely above the ground, trembling. He said, *"I got real dizzy. But they kept teasing - calling me chicken, and all sorts of names, 'cause I was afraid of heights. So, I closed my eyes and imagined I was flying up, like I do in my dreams. I'm not afraid of heights in my dreams. And I like to fly in them. So, I pretended I was dreaming, looked up, and kept on going like I was soring, high above."*

Jacob turns his head upwards and prepares himself mentally for the rest of the climb. He *has* to save his stolen comrade. He then, opens his squinting eyes and is met with the cold, deadpan gaze of the boy - looking back down at him from the entrance. His heart flutters. The boy smiles and suddenly slips out of sight.

Having enough of this chase, Jacob braves the last few steps and slowly emerges from the floor of the treehouse into, what looks like, a hall connecting a room to his left and another to his right. The treehouse, from this view, seemed to wrap around the entire tree.

🦋 🦋 🦋 🦋

Kyra, crunching away on the last of her bowl of chips, is immersed in the last scene of her television show, while Jinx cleans her paws on the floor in front of her.

Unknown to her, the basement door gradually opens. The sound of its creaking hinges is drowned out by the loud action scenes of her movie. Jinx lays on her side and watches, as the door slows to a stop before the doorknob could touch the wall. She rolls to her stomach, whipping her tail back and forth in anticipation, and focusing on the dark opening of the basement.

For a moment, nothing happens. Then, something at the bottom of the doorway slowly brings itself into view; the small, gray paw of a stuffed animal, an ear next, then, eventually, part of its pale, porcelain face, with one sad, blue eye peeking around the corner. It is the toy Jinx had dug from the wall in Kyra's room; it shimmies, as if something were holding it and teasing the cat to come play.

Jinx's eyes dilate and her ears fan back. The doll continues its shaky-dance at the doorway and coming out just a little further to entice the cat even more. Jinx tucks her back paws underneath her belly, preparing to pounce.

Kyra swipes away at the bottom of the bowl with her fingertips to gather the last of the crumbs into a pile, then dumps them into her mouth while tapping the bottom of the bowl for the remains.

The basement door slams shut, shocking her. She loses her grip of the bowl which tumbles to her lap and onto the floor. Immediately, she notices Jinx is no longer in front of her. Kyra looks behind the couch, then scans the room. *Had to be Jacob.*

"Baby Jay, you better be up in your room cleaning." She yells upstairs.

Her attention is captured easily again by the new cell phone commercial on the television. While picking up the bowl, her eyes gleam at the sight of the "store representative", who's holding up the "latest in cell phone technology".

"No more dropped calls. The durable screen guarantees no more cracks or unaffordable repairs," the representative says, "and you'll never have to worry about repeating the words, 'Can you hear me—Can you hear me—Can you hear me?'" As Kyra dusts off the spilled crumbs from her shirt and couch, the volume from the television begins to rise. The cell phone commercial glitches and loops, repeating the store rep's last few words.

"...can you hear me—can you hear me?"

The surround sound's power indicator clicks on, suddenly amplifying every word to its maximum volume, through tiny speakers and eight-inch subwoofers that surround her.

"...can you hear me—can you hear me!"

Kyra panics, scrambling in search of the remotes, digging into and under the couch cushions, then shaking out the blanket she was under. She finally finds them on the floor to the side of the couch. *How the hell—*

The sound becomes unbearable. She fumbles the remotes, and frantically presses the volume buttons on both, but to no avail. Kyra tries the power buttons, but still, no response. She smacks the remote controls in her palm repeatedly and tries again. Nothing. Frightened and frustrated, she drops them to the floor and covers her ears.

Suddenly, there is a pounding coming from the foyer, near the steps and front entrance. It grows louder, joining the glitching commercial, and simultaneously shaking the floor beneath her. Kyra's eyes are wide with fear and her hands tremble over her ears. She screams. The instance she does, the power shuts off and the television blacks out.

Kyra is almost in tears, and her thumping heart feels as though it's lodged at the base of her throat. She slowly lowers her quivering hands. Her wheezing breath is now the only sound in the house.

🦋 🦋 🦋 🦋

Jacob cautiously wanders down the short, narrow hallway, until he reaches what seems to be the front room of the treehouse. The smell of old, damp wood fills his nostrils. Even though rays of the afternoon sunlight shine through a small, four paned window onto the floor, the room holds a darkness to it— similar to the forest. Not far from the stretched-out, square shapes of light on the floor, in a dark, dusty corner of the room, sits his robot. Eagerly, he rounds the corner to retrieve it, but trips over a large object, scraping his leg and stumbling to the floor. His painful cry startles a group of resting birds, which flutter away, outside the window.

Breathing in through clenched teeth, he holds his leg in the dim light and raises his pant leg slowly. The skin is peeled back on a tiny wound and has only a little blood, but to a six-year-old, it was like the end of the world and hurt like hell.

He groans in pain, rubbing the skin around the small abrasion, when the wood floor creaks to his right. Quickly, he spins toward the origin of the noise, and sees an empty wall with the window centered. There is nothing there but a dirty brown blanket, lying flat on the floor, just outside of the window's light.

He scoots to the wall behind him; he starts to stand, using the wall for support, as if his leg had been broken, shifting all of his weight onto his good one. His robot is within reach, but before

173

he can bend down to retrieve it, wood groans from near the window, once again. Jacob swallows hard, staring at the blanket that is somehow, now in the middle of the floor, illuminated by the light from the window.

Jacob, wounded and trapped, trembling and wide-eyed, backs flat against the wall. His nostrils flare with every breath, and each exhale is accompanied by a low-toned whimper. *I just wanna go home. I just wanna go home.*

The bundled blanket begins to move, little-by-little, forming a small hump in the center; it continues to grow and raise, higher and higher, like a large, ghostly shadow silhouetted against the light behind it, eclipsing the window as it spreads out wider on either side.

As it raises, Jacob slides down the wall onto the floor next to his toy, wheezing louder as the dusty, brown mass moved closer. He tried to scream, as it towered above—engulfing him in the shadow it cast—but he could only manage a high-pitched whine, tossing his hands up in front of himself.

Jacob closes his eyes and buries his head into his arms. "Go away—go away—go away..." he mutters, as the floating blanket is nearly on top of him.

Peeking between the small forearms of his defense, he is about to scream in terror, when suddenly, the blanket falls to the floor; out jumps the little boy clapping his hands loudly. He carries on like a pantomime, laughing in silence. He points repeatedly at Jacob and claps even louder, entertained by his own prank.

Angry, but feeling a touch of relief, Jacob swipes the tears from his eyes and watches the boy celebrate his own success.

"That wasn't funny!" Jacob roars.

The boy stops and points at him again, covering his smile with the other hand.

Jacob has had enough; he grabs his toy and storms passed the boy. Immediately, the strange child grabs a wooden stick and taps it on the edge of the window frame three times.

Tap-Tap-Tap

The familiar sound stops Jacob, just before he drops through the floor onto the ladder below. The boy does it again, then taps a praying hand gesture, in an apologetic fashion, to his lips.

🦋 🦋 🦋 🦋

Kyra is in the kitchen, with the home phone pressed to her face and her back against the refrigerator.

"Sweetie, it could've been Jacob that slammed that door, or maybe your father?" Rose says, on the other end.

"But he's gone. Jacob is cleaning his room, but—"

"Well, there you go. Your brother. All that bumping had to be him jumping around upstairs."

"You don't understand. It all happened at once. It just doesn't seem right here... something's wrong. Can I just come to your house and stay for a bit?"

"Oh, baby. You know your grandfather and I would love nothing more in the world than for the both of you to come stay with us forever... but we can't," she takes a deep breath, "at least not right now."

"I'm over the age of twelve; I should be able to say where I can go, right? Isn't that the law?"

"It's not that simple, sweetie. What about your brother. You don't want to just leave him there. He's not over twelve."

"It's just not fair. Nothing is." She sniffles.

"I'm here for you. You know that. Just stay strong for me, okay? Somehow, someway, I will make this right for all of us."

Kyra wipes her tears with the back of her hand. "Okay."

"There are no ghosts in your house, sweetie, I promise you that. You're just a victim of an odd moment." She pauses. "You know what I do when I'm upset? I take a long, hot bath and drown my worries in it. When I'm done, I drain them all away."

🦋 🦋 🦋 🦋

Kyra jams the plug into the drain of the tub and blasts the water to fill it. With no bubble bath on hand, she pours a little bit of her vanilla-scented shampoo in for some bubbles. The smell and sound of the water brings her to her comfort zone. *Maybe it was Jacob. He was probably clowning around, making all kinds of noise, and not doing what Dad told him.*

She drags her fingers through the water a few times to mix the shampoo evenly, then heads to Jacob's room, while she lets the tub continue to fill.

She stands just outside of his door—that's cracked open just a hair. "Hey, I'm gonna take a bath, so if you need me, I'll be in there. Okay?" She gets no answer, so she gently pushes the door open wider. His room looks nearly the same way it did when her father told him to clean it. There's movement under the white bedsheets. "You're not supposed to be napping, dork. You're gonna get it when Dad gets home. You better hurry and finish."

The movement under the sheet stops, and the covered head turns slowly in her direction. She doesn't wait long for his reply, rolling her eyes and slamming the door shut.

🦋 🦋 🦋 🦋

Behind the closed bathroom door, Kyra is submerged up to her chin in warm water and small tickly bubbles. She hooks her thumbs together, and fans her fingers out to form an underwater butterfly. She flaps its wings, imagining it flying high-up through clouds as she raises her hands above the soap suds, then back underneath. It was a game her and her mother played, during bath time, when she was little. She smiled as she imagined Theresa on the other end of the tub, doing the same hand gestures, as they cuddled their feet together under the water.

It felt so real, as if her mother were there with her and tickling her toes with her own. She closed her eyes for a moment and tilted her head back, resting against the back of the tub.

A cool, gentle draft skims over the tub, making a sizzling sound, as hundreds of bubbles all pop virtually at once. She opens her eyes and notices the bathroom door is open, about an inch or two. Another draft blows in—kissing her moist skin.

"Jacob!" She yells, sitting up and feeling the chill that suddenly took over her face and shoulders. "Jacob, can you come close the bathroom door for me?" No answer. "Please."

A cooler, not-so-gentle breeze shoots through the door opening, pushing it open another inch or two. She quickly drops down into the water to warm herself, then pulls the shower curtain around the tub to block the breeze.

She peeks around the curtain. "Jacob?" The door closes gently. "*Thank* you!"

She sits back in the tub, now seeing a blurry view of the bathroom through the sheet of plastic around her. The warmth of the water comforts her again, but she's disappointed at the sight of her bubbles that are nearly gone. She closes her eyes once again, attempting to bring herself back to the relaxing state she was in before, sinking deeper, until the water is up to her chin.

She allows herself to be at the mercy of the water, letting her arms float to the surface. Soon, her legs raise, and her toes emerge under the faucet, while she drifts off with thoughts of her mother, until the cool air glazes over her toes and exposed arms, once again. She opens her eyes slowly. To her sudden horror, she discovers the curtain pulled back, and the bathroom door wide open. Kyra sits up quickly—making the water splash—and firmly grabs the rolled sides of the Victorian tub.

"Jacob?" She says shakenly, lowering herself in the water, enough to just peek over the side.

The light flickers for a moment, then shuts off completely. The light shines down through the diamond-patterned window blocks above her, like a dim spotlight into the tub.

She turns her head slowly toward the sound of clicking, coming from the dark corner to her left. She can see nothing, but all her senses warn her that she is not alone.

She doesn't blink; her eyes stay fixed on the corner as she turns her body, sliding back to the other side of the tub and away from the sound. The back of her head bumps the faucet, but she stays low. Her new position in the tub made it difficult to see the corner, especially with the light from the window now in front of her.

"J-Jacob? Stop it."

There's no such thing as ghosts. She thought, repeating what her grandmother told her. She wanted to believe it was Jacob in the corner—that maybe it was some sick prank he was pulling for calling him names and treating him like a baby. Yet deep down, everything within her told her... this isn't Jacob she is facing.

Breaking her paralyzing fear and shivering from the intensifying cold, she reaches over the side of the tub to grab her towel, still refusing to revert her eyes from the corner.

She drapes the towel in front of her as she stands, tucking the corner of it under her quivering chin. Before she could climb out, something bumps the front of the cast-iron tub, with such force that the water ripples toward her.

Kyra nearly slips inside the tub while trying to escape, but manages to climb out, stepping on her towel, then tumbles to the floor. The clicking-chatter in the corner grew closer and louder. She gathers herself and runs to the light switch, quickly flipping it on and revealing the lonesome laundry basket in the corner, overflowing with used towels.

She wraps herself tighter in the towel and inspects the rest of the bathroom from the doorway.

"Where's your brother!?" Owen yells, standing behind her.

Kyra screams.

🦋 🦋 🦋 🦋

"So, were you always not able to talk?" Jacob asks.

The boy nods '*yes*', then crawls over to the wooden toy box that Jacob tripped over before. Despite the dusty and dirty surroundings, the toybox was clean, finished, and well taken care of. Clean—like when his dad would clean the wood furniture with the orange smelling spray and cloth. The boy reaches behind it, and removes a notebook-sized chalkboard, with a piece of white chalk attached to the wood frame by a string.

He writes in large, capital letters, "DENNIS", then points to himself with his thumb.

"Oh, your name is Dennis?"

He nods.

"I'm Jacob, Jacob Mosley."

Dennis begins writing again, then holds it up. It reads, "Were you scared the other day?"

"The other day? Oh, when I was following you. No, Why?"

Jacob waits patiently, as he erases each response with his forearm and writes again. "You looked scared. You dropped your toy."

Dennis stands and walks to the corner to Jacob's robot, picking it up. With a smile, he places it on Jacob's lap.

"Thanks!" Jacob says, blowing the dirt off it. "It's my favorite toy." He stands it on the floor in front of him. "Do you live around here?"

Dennis nods his head, then points out of the window towards Jacob's house. Jacob rises on his knees, barely able to see out of the window; yet, he could see the roof of his own home, surprised that it's as close as it is. It seemed like he'd been running through the forest forever. He stood, taking notice of the home closely to his—just across the road.

"Oh, you live by me. I just moved here." Jacob dusts himself off and looks around the room, dragging his fingers along the wall. "This tree house is awesome. Do you play here a lot?"

Dennis nods his head.

"Man, that must suck balls that you can't talk."

Dennis just hunches his shoulders, not giving Jacob much more of a response.

"My dad says I can 'talk enough for ten people sometimes'. So, I can talk for you, with no problem, if you need me to some time."

Dennis smiles, then reaches deep into his pocket, pulling out a long, white string with the ends tied together. With a smile he sits on the floor and begins lacing it between his fingers.

"What are you doing?" Jacob asks, getting closer to him in order to see better.

Dennis twirls and scoops the string with different fingers, his eyes almost crossed as he focuses. To Jacob, it looked like his hands had become tangled in a stringy mess. Dennis spreads his fingers and stretches the string tight.

Jacob's face lights up. "Whoa! That's that big tower in Italy, huh? I saw it on Bugs Bunny."

Dennis smiles, then untangles the string to begin another string figure.

182

Jacob watches intently to see what his new friend will develop next. This one takes a little longer. Dennis lightly bites on his bottom lip as he weaves his finger art. Finally, he spreads his fingers apart, showing a large spider web.

"Wow, that's cool. I wish I could do that. You're gonna have to teach me how to do it, Dennis. That's pretty awesome."

Dennis smiles and unravels the string from his fingers, then offers it to Jacob.

"Jacob! Jacob, you up there!?" Owen screams from outside.

Jacob's eyes buck open. He tenses up and draws his hand back.

"Oh crap, that's my dad. I have to go." He whispers.

"Jacob!" He screams, even louder.

The two boys wave at each other as Jacob disappears through the floor and down the ladder.

As Jacob drops from the treehouse and down the ladder, Owen storms over toward him, his jaw muscles tensing. As soon as he touches the ground Owen swats him on the butt firmly, stunning Jacob.

"What did I tell you about taking off without my permission!?" Owen bellows, as he points in Jacob's face. "Something could've happened to you."

"I—"

"You know what? Don't say anything! Just go to the house, now, Jacob!" He orders. "Move!"

Jacob rubs his stinging bottom while cradling his robot with the other arm, then runs away.

Owen follows, then briefly looks up at the treehouse, with an eerie feeling that someone was looking back down at him; but, the glare from the sun bouncing off the window, prevents him from confirming his inkling.

❦ ❦ ❦ ❦

In the middle of downtown Raleigh, North Carolina, in a six-story building, Kat Dillon sits and listens attentively while centered in front of the desk of her supervisor, Sheila.

"...just makes things more difficult. Are we going to move forward with this case or not?" Sheila asks.

Kat flips through her notes. "Court is scheduled with the Stephen family for next month. Considering Mr. Stephen's questionable past, and the mother not being anywhere in the picture, the guardian ad litem and I both agree that the children should be placed with a relative."

Sheila nods her head in agreement, digging through the file a little deeper, as she sifts through the copy of Kat's notes. She then closes the file, and separates the magnetic bridge of her reading glasses, dropping them around her neck. With both hands, she tucks her white, shoulder-length hair behind her ears.

Kat hands her another file.

"Is this the new case we got the anonymous call about?"

"That's the Mosely family file. Yes."

"Have you had a chance to speak with the parent?" Sheila asks, opening the file and reconnecting her two-part spectacles.

"Yes, Ma'am - I did. I paid the family a visit in their new home. Seems they've had a lot of unfortunate happenings in the past couple of years. The issues seem to mostly stem from the father's negligence."

"Explain."

"Well, the daughter, Kyra, seems to have quite a bit of animosity towards her father. Almost immediately, she complained about him being gone all the time, and how, 'if he had only been watching her brother', their previous house wouldn't have burned down. She said it was his fault her mother died, but then wouldn't explain why she felt that way. From what I gathered after interviewing both children, they spend quite a bit of time without adult supervision.

"That's going to take a little more investigating. We can document your interview with the children, but without proof, or physically witnessing what was said, we can't create a case. It looks like Kyra is fifteen years old, so technically, she can be left alone for a certain amount of time, according to state law—but not at night. Did they mention being left alone at night, possibly?"

"No, ma'am."

"Has Kyra displayed any reason for you to think she isn't fit to be watching her brother for long periods of time? Any instability because of recent occurrences? And if the father is gone all the time, how long is he gone for?"

"I'm not sure."

"Well, I suggest you get a little more information before we start a case on this family. It sounds like you may need to pay them another visit. We are not gonna move on this parent unless you can find me something more solid to go on. We need definite proof that these children are in some sort of current danger. If you can get Kyra, or his son, to talk a little more... maybe even catch him in the act of leaving at night... something."

"I understand. I'll get right on it."

CHAPTER 10

AN OFFERING

(6:35 AM)

Stretching his arms and dragging down the hallway in his sleeping clothes, Owen pushes open Jacob's bedroom door. Choking at the end of his widemouthed yawn, he drops his head with disappointment. Jacob's bed is, once again, empty, and his nightlight is unplugged and on the floor. He inspects it briefly, then plugs it back in.

Owen saunters toward the stairs, when the mumbling of the television in the living room confirms his suspicions.

Jacob is curled in the fetal position, jammed in the corner of the couch and shivering. His knees are tucked close to his chest, with the fallen blanket on the floor next to him.

Owen sighs. "Jacob Mosley..." he mutters to himself.

Grabbing the blanket from the floor, Owen slips it over Jacob, stretching the fabric over his shoulders and tucking it behind his ridged body, where he feels the remote in the crease of a cushion.

Foul language and adultlike humor from the claymation cartoon behind Owen, assaults his ears. He aims the remote with a disgusted frown, pressing hard on the power button, until the pink color of his thumbnail turns white.

The cool, wood floor sends chills through his feet, as he makes his way toward the kitchen; he passes by the basement door at the same moment that Kyra bursts through it. Owen spins around, with his fists up, to guard—planting his feet in a boxer's stance.

"Fugh—" he drops his guard with a sigh of relief. "Jesus, Kyra! You about gave me a damn heart attack! What are you doing up so early?"

She clutches a small, clear box close to her chest and frowns. "Is it against the law to get up early?"

"No, but what were you doing in the basement? What do you have?"

"My display pins," she snaps, and shoves them out in view. "God! You said I could get them from your toolbox. *You* put them there. It's not *my* fault you put them in the basement!" She rolls her eyes and makes a beeline toward the stairs.

"Hey, I was only asking. I'm sorry," He watches as she disappears at the landing. "You want some breakfast? I'll make some pancakes, and maybe some eggs, if you want." He shouts up to her.

Kyra's stomping, that ends with the door slamming, gave him his answer.

🦋 🦋 🦋 🦋

Two cast iron skillets are on the stove; one is sizzling with round breakfast sausage, and the other buttered, while Owen whisks a large bowl of pancake batter until it was creamy smooth. Jacob covers a bowl of cheesy scrambled eggs with an empty plate, then watches as his father pours the first of many future pancakes into the skillet.

"I get that one. Remember?" Says Jacob, pointing into the steaming pan.

"Watch out, Jacob, don't burn yourself." Owen smiles. "I know, man. Those were the best ones for me too, when I was about your age... all buttery, and crunchy on the edges."

"Yep!" Jacob smiles, then climbs on the counter to open a cabinet.

"Hey-Hey get down, man. What... are you on a mission to hurt yourself this morning? I got hot stuff all over the place, and I don't want you to get burned. Get down, man."

"Where's my ABC plate?"

"Hold on, I'll find it. Now get down, like I said."

Jacob jumps down with a sad look on his face, then throws himself in his seat. Owen checks the dish rack in the sink and removes a white plate with the complete alphabet, in colorful lettering, around the edge. In the center of the plate, Bert, Ernie, and Grover are surrounding Oscar the Grouch. The plate reminds Owen of more innocent times—when Jacob used to watch respectable, prerecorded television shows, and Sesame Street was one of his favorite things. The plate was the first thing Jacob could remember his mother giving him.

"Found it."

Jacob perks up as Owen places the plate in front of him.

Kyra enters the kitchen without acknowledging anyone and sits down at the dinner table. Gently, she lifts the plate off the large bowl.

"Cheesy eggs." Jacob blurts out and smiles, knowing that's her favorite.

"Yeah... *so!?*" She snaps.

"So, those are your favorite."

She looks up at her father standing at the stove with his back to her. She squints and places the plate back down. "Only when *Mom* used to make them."

190

Jacob immediately looks over to Owen, who is clearly trying to ignore her comment, stirring the batter, far past its recommended creamy consistency, even more.

Kyra grabs the bottle of syrup and pretends to read the contents on the back.

Owen stops his stirring and places the bowl on the counter. "Son, why am I always finding you downstairs in the morning? Is your bed not good enough for you?"

"No, well... yeah, it is. It's just..."

"It's just, what?"

"It's just, I can't sleep sometimes."

"Is it too cold? If the space heater isn't working, you can sleep in my room until I get that room insulated better."

"No. I keep having a dream. Well, I think it's a dream, or something. This man walks up and down our hallway at night. Sometimes he stops at my room and stares at me."

"That's kind of a weird dream to be having," says Kyra.

"That still doesn't explain why you're downstairs when you should be in bed," Owen says. "Just because you had a dream?"

"I get really cold when he stares at me. It didn't just happen once." He picks up his plate. "Even with my blanket on, it gets cold. So, I wake up and go downstairs, where it's warmer." He then picks up his spoon, smiling at his shiny, inverted and concave reflection while baring his clenched teeth. While bringing the spoon closer, he begins rapidly clicking his teeth together, which immediate catches Kyra's attention.

"Are you cold?" Asks Owen, while he pours the batter into a skillet.

"No. He just kept doing that." He clicks his teeth some more. "Like that, but faster. Real fast—like those wind-up teeth in cartoons."

Owen looks deeper over his shoulder, to Kyra, noticing the growing fear in her expression as Jacob continues his teeth-chattering.

"Stop it!" She yells, placing the bottle on the table, a little harder than necessary, and making Jacob jump in his seat.

"Kyra—" Owen exclaims.

"Well, he's so annoying with his noises."

"But you don't have to—" Owen catches himself, looking into her sad eyes as she seemingly waits for him to take Jacob's side.

Jacob takes a drink of milk from his glass, then licks the milk mustache from his lips. "Oh yeah, and I think he keeps unplugging my nightlight, too."

"Okay, enough about the man," Owen snaps. "If you come downstairs again and I see that mess you've been watching on the television, I'm gonna spank your butt, hear?"

Jacob hangs his head. "Kay."

"You're gonna make me put a block on that television, little man, and I don't want to have to do that. I should be able to trust you when I tell you to do something."

Owen throws Kyra a quick glance, then tosses one of the cooked pancakes onto a serving plate.

❦ ❦ ❦ ❦

(12:37 PM)

One, lonely, green army man action figure is launched—by Jacob using his wrist rocket—from the open treehouse window, soaring high into the air and near the tops of the trees surrounding them. Its parachute deploys perfectly, and the two boys watch, as it slowly descends to the ground.

"Cool, huh?" says Jacob. "Ok, my throw, I go." He drops the slingshot next to Dennis and leaves the treehouse to retrieve the action figure outside. Once there, he folds the parachute and strings behind the army man then climbs back into the treehouse where Dennis is waiting patiently. Jacob drops to his knees next to him, out of breath. "Okay your turn. Then you have to get it."

Dennis picks up the slingshot, but fumbles with the army man a few times before Jacob helps him wrap it in the leather slingshot strap. Dennis pulls back hard and aims high into the trees.

"Remember to stay away from the—"

Before Jacob could finish, Dennis launches it into the air, even higher.

"Wow, that's super high." Jacob says.

Again, the parachute deploys perfectly, and they both watch, as it slowly floats down through the trees, miraculously missing every branch along the way. Jacob has a huge smile on his face, but Dennis is nearly expressionless, with not so much as a hint of a smirk.

A gentle breeze starts to blow, and drifts the parachuter closer to the tree branches. Jacob's smile disappears. It floats above the pointed tip of a branch, but it shifts slightly to the right—though not enough to miss it completely.

"No!" yelled Jacob.

Dennis turns to him, then back to the dangling toy blowing in the wind. He grabs his chalk board. "I'm sorry."

Jacob sighs. "It's okay. I know you didn't mean to."

Dennis nods.

"But *now* what are we going to do?"

Dennis thinks for a moment, then reaches into his pocket, and pulls out the string he had shown Jacob before. He writes on his chalkboard. "I could teach you."

Jacob nods anxiously, then sits down in front of him.

194

Dennis extends his hand, offering the string inside. He nods his head for Jacob to take it and, with little hesitation, he did.

Dennis takes ahold of Jacob's hands to guide him, slowly lacing the string over his thumbs, then between each of his fingers. Before long, Jacob could see nothing but a tangled mess between his fingers when Dennis sits back and, for the first time, smiles at Jacob.

"What?"

Dennis makes a motion with his hands—spreading his fingers and widening his arms.

For a moment Jacob was confused, then understands what he was asking him to do. He spreads his fingers and hands apart.

Confused at what he had created with the string, Jacob looks to Dennis.

Dennis scribbles quickly on his chalkboard. "Cat's Cradle."

"Cool... but not as cool as the stuff you did the other day. Can you show me some of that?"

Dennis nods and grabs Jacob's hands once again, undoing the laces until the string is only wrapped around his pinkies and thumbs. Dennis's eyes nearly cross, as he focuses on every finger and every lace that he commanded Jacob's hands to move. Again, he smiles, sits back and motions for him to spread his fingers and hands.

"Wow, what's this?"

"Jacob's ladder." He writes.

"Like my name? There's a ladder named after me?"

Dennis nods.

Jacob inspects the stringy design closely while Dennis begins writing on his chalkboard again. "You keep the string and practice. Okay?"

"Kay." Jacob shoves the string in his pocket. "But I wish we had more toys. I mean like, *actual* toys."

Dennis smiles and crawls over to the toybox. He places his hand on the lid and looks back at Jacob. When he opens it, it's full of toys, with colors so bright, they seemed to glow. Small trucks, cars, balls, and many other things, filled the inside of the old, wooden box to the brim.

"Whoa! I didn't know that stuff was in there." Jacob springs to his feet and races over. "Are these yours? How come you didn't show me this before?"

Dennis shrugs his shoulders.

They both smile at each other, then dig deep into the box.

They play energetically, racing toy trucks from one part of the treehouse to the other. Then, Dennis played with a toy guitar, while Jacob fiddled with solving the blue side of a Rubik's Cube. Then, they play fencing, with plastic swords, until Dennis fell to the floor, exhausted.

Dennis leans back on his hands, watching Jacob stab and swipe at an invisible opponent with his toy sword. He then grabs

196

his chalkboard and writes. "I wish we could play forever. Don't you?"

"Hell yeah!" Yells Jacob, thrusting the tip of his weapon into the wall.

❀ ❀ ❀ ❀

(1:47 AM)

The waxing gibbous moon is mostly hidden behind an overcast of clouds. No moonlight will be shining through the window, into Jacob's room tonight; the only provided luminescence is the soft-glow of his soccer ball nightlight, next to a closed bedroom door.

Jacob—exhausted from a long afternoon of playtime with his new friend—is sound asleep. His legs are sprawled out and drool seeps from the corner of his mouth, soaking into his pillow.

The soccer ball nightlight flickers off and on, buzzing as it grows in brightness, to a point where it's bright enough to illuminate his entire room—even more than the main ceiling light could. It gradually dims back to its soft, four-watt glow, when the doorknob slowly turns. The rusty, vintage latch squeals as it gradually retracts into the edge of the door. The door pops loose, jolting Jacob from his sleep. His eyes dart open and he sits up, panning the room with sleepy eyes and blurred vision. Seeing nothing strange, he crawls to the foot of his bed and peers down into the backyard from his window. It is pitch-black. The only thing he could see was the, somewhat visible, reflection of his face in the glass, with the distant image of the door and nightlight behind him.

Attempting to focus in on any portion of the backyard, he catches the nightlight dimming gently in the reflection. He continues to watch the partially illuminated door, as it eases open without a sound. His eyes grow wide and his breathing quickens, fogging the glass with his rapid warm breath. The instant the hinges bind and drag, he scrambles to the head of his bed and dives underneath his covers.

Jacob freezes at the sound of the chattering teeth in the door's opening. *Go away! Leave me alone!* The squealing hinges stop, only making the lonely sound of the chattering more terrifying.

With quick, shuddering breaths, he focuses on what he can see through the sheets, which is just the low-glow of the nightlight that is suddenly interrupted by something passing quickly in front of it. He jumps, whimpering softly through longer, drawn out breaths.

The nightlight shuts off suddenly, followed by the sound of it falling. The hard-plastic bounces and skips across the hardwood floor, stopping at his bedside. The room fell silent. Jacob waited, trembling under his dark environment that grew colder by the second.

The floor creaked. Jacob gasped hearing it and snatches his pillow in front of him. The footsteps grew closer, and his heart raced faster. He could feel it was near—whatever *it* was—almost in front of him, by how the air changed. He hugs his pillow tighter and buries his face into it; swiftly, his blanket is ripped off from on top of his head. He closes his eyes and lets out a loud shriek that is quickly muzzled by a hand.

"Shhh-shhh—shhh. Shut up—Shut up, Jesus." Kyra whispers. His muffled screams abruptly stop after hearing the familiar sound of his sister's voice. "God, you scream like a little girl."

Jacob, near tears and out of breath, swats her hand away. "Wha—what you doing in my room?" he gasps a deep, calming breath. "I thought—"

"You thought what?" she interrupts. "You thought I was *him*?"

He scoots away from her and hugs his pillow once again. "No."

"Don't lie Jacob. I know you hear it too, or you wouldn't have said what you did at the table." She looks back at the door. "The clicking... you hear the clicking, too. In the hallway, don't you?"

He looks at the hallway, then down to his nightlight, on the floor next to the bed, oddly wrapped with string—the same string Dennis gave him. The nightlight was mummified in it. He hadn't removed it from his pullover pocket, that's still draped over the back of his chair at the foot of his bed.

He throws Kyra a quick glance, then stares down at his toes. "Yes. Sometimes."

"Did you hear it tonight?"

"Yeah." He looks up at her. "You heard it too? That's why you're in here?"

They both look over to the dark hallway from his bed.

"Scoot over." She says, nudging him over, and climbs in the bed next to him.

CHAPTER 11

MALL RATS

(10:34 AM)

Owen is sitting at the kitchen table, shuffling through receipts and bills while attempting to figure out this week's budget, when the sound from the television disturbs his focus. He leans back in his chair, teetering on the back legs, to see into the living room. Kyra lazily aims the remote at the television, while surfing through channels, as Jacob—on the other side of the couch—twirls a throw pillow in the air, catching it, repeatedly.

As Owen is fixing his lips to yell at them for the sudden interruption, he notices the disappointed and bored expressions on their faces. He chokes down his anger, purses his lips and tosses his papers to the side.

"I think we need a break from this house," he says, as he walks into the living room and stands by the television. He folds his arms and smiles. "What do you guys think?" Neither of them answers. "I was thinking we could go to the mall... maybe?" They still don't respond, but he can see the subtle smirk on Jacob's face. "Well, if anyone wants to go to the mall with me, I'll be leaving in about twenty minutes. So be ready. If not, I guess I'll just have to go by myself."

As Owen walks away and up the stairs, Kyra and Jacob look at each other. Kyra grimaces at the smile on his face. Jacob quickly and apologetically wipes it away.

🦋 🦋 🦋 🦋

(11:00 AM)

Owen jogs down the steps in a ballcap, jeans and pullover to an empty living room, and the television shut off. He looks through the kitchen window to the backyard, then back to the living room. Thinking he may have missed them when passing their bedrooms, he jogs back up the stairs, stopping at the top.

"Hey, are you guys coming with me, or no?" He yells.

He's saddened at the sight of Jacob's closed door, and Kyra's gradually closing and then shutting tight. *Did I do something wrong? What in the hell was it now?* The silence hits his heart like a sledgehammer as he waits, hoping for some kind of response.

202

Hanging his head, he spins around and slowly makes his way back downstairs. As he grabs his keys from the kitchen table, once more, he looks upstairs in hopes that one of the children, at least Jacob, would hurry to catch him before he left. But nothing.

He ambles over to the front door hanging his head. He feels alone, unloved, and betrayed. It was as if someone stuck a giant needle in his back and sucked out all the happiness he had left inside. The growing need to cry tingles behind his eyes, as he opens the front door. He lifts his head, pulling the door shut behind him; to his surprise, Jacob is jumping with both feet, leaping from one sidewalk square to the next, and sees Kyra leaning against the truck, with her arms folded, partially rolling her eyes upon seeing him.

"You said *twenty* minutes? It's been like *thirty*." She snaps.

He takes in a deep breath of relief, and tilts his head back, while batting his eyes to rid them of the sad tears that had formed. New tears of joy and solace follow, so he quickly turns to the door and pretends he's checking the lock. He wipes his cheek a few times with the soft, cotton fabric that covers his shoulder, and clears his throat.

"Jacob, you couldn't grab a clean pair of pants, son?" He says, turning to them as if he wasn't just on an emotional rollercoaster. He pulls the bill of his cap lower to cover his eyes. His heart beats strong, instantly healing from his previous thoughts, as he rounded the front of the truck.

"I'm not responsible," says Kyra, "he wanted to get ready on his own, so I left him alone."

Owen unlocks the doors with his key fob. "Its fine. You look good, son, despite the dirty pants," he opens the back door. Kyra gets in the front with her, recently predictable, troubled demeanor. "Seatbelts," he smirks.

🦋 🦋 🦋 🦋

Concord Mills Mall is crawling with shoppers—like stirred ants in a large colony—nearly bumping into one another on the way to their next purchases.

In the center of the chaos, Jacob holds on tight to the pole of his golden carousel horse—waving, as he passes his father and sister, who stand just outside the portable fencing that surrounds it. He throws his head back, noticing the mirrors above him, and smiles at his spinning, brightly-colored reflection.

"You sure you don't want to go for a ride, Kyra?" Asks Owen.

She rolls her eyes. "I wouldn't get caught dead on that thing. So, yeah—no!".

Jacob leans out from his horse, as the carousel comes around to the staff member controlling the ride. Stretching out as far as his hip restraint allows him, he yells, "Go faster—Go faster!"

The staff member flashes a phony smile, then continues sipping her soda from a straw.

As Jacob passes her, he notices a bald black man dressed in a red, flannel shirt and black pants; his hands are shoved deep underneath his armpits as he leers at Jacob. As the carousel grew closer, the man's smile grows wider and creepier. His facial expression reminds Jacob of the Joker from Batman; however, his smile is framed by a scraggly, salt-and-pepper goatee instead of red lipstick. Jacob's smile quickly disappears when he sees the man's jaw quivering violently.

Owen notices his son staring curiously into a section of empty seats. Even as Jacob passes it, he twists his body in order to continue his gaze. Soon, the man drops of out sight on the opposite side of the carousel. When Jacob comes back around, he looks again for the man, ignoring his family as he passes. The man is gone. He notices no sign of him—not even him walking away from the seats where he sat.

Jacob feels the ride shift, as it begins to slow, taking him for one more trip around, before eventually stopping on the opposite side of where his father and sister waited.

Immediately, he fumbles with his safety strap, pulling and tugging at it. He nearly screamed—startled by the hand of the staff member who lunges out to unbuckle him.

"Okay, rides over. You need help getting down, little man?" She says.

"No. And I'm not little."

He stares at her, while blindly finding his footing, with one foot still pointed-down in the faux stirrup. He grips the bar tightly, while sliding off the side of the horse's red armor and, with his eyes still locked on the staff member, puffs out his chest and straightens his shirt.

"Oh, well excuse me, big guy." She smiles. "Where are your parents?"

Just then, Owen appears by the fencing near them. Jacob points to him, then jumps off the carousel platform to reunite with his father.

"Your sister didn't want to take her turn. I have another ticket if you want to go again."

"No, I'm good." He says, jumping from one black square to the next, until he's right beside his father. "Can we get some ice-cream or something?" He balances himself inside one of the black squares, being careful not to fall into the surrounding white ones.

"Yeah, we can, but before we do anything else, I need to go pee. Like now!" says Owen.

"TMI. Why can't you just say you need to go to the bathroom? Why the details!?" Roars Kyra.

"What makes you think that's a lot of detail. Everybody pees."

"I pee." Says Jacob, holding onto his father's forearm for balance.

206

Owen raises his eyebrows. "Are you trying to say we have *potty* mouths?"

Kyra grimaced at his attempt at humor. "Yeah, just stop."

"I thought it was funny." Says Jacob.

"Well, you didn't laugh," Kyra says. "Can we just go to the bathroom already?"

"Yeah, let's go." Owen says, reaching for his son's hand.

Jacob grabs his wrist for balance, but then pushes it away. "I'm good—I'm good." He then leaps from the black square he was in to another adjacent to it like a game of hopscotch.

"What in the world are you doing?" Says Owen. "You've been doing this since before we left the house. You're gonna fall."

"Trying not to get eaten. If I touch the white squares, the alligators will get me."

"I'm gonna die if you don't hurry up."

"I can keep up."

🦋 🦋 🦋 🦋

Owen holds the bathroom door open for Jacob, but soon realizes he isn't right behind him now, like he was just a few steps ago. When he looks back, he sees that Jacob had stopped, standing on a square with his feet close together—like a diver on the tip of a diving board. He has a worried look on his face as he looks down at the change in floor pattern.

"What's wrong? Come on." Says Owen.

"No more black squares."

Owen notices that there are a few rows of white squares in front of him that no longer have the scattered black ones for his son to evade his imaginary attackers.

"Jacob! Come on man. I don't have time for this."

"But—"

"Now!" He orders.

"Wait—Wait, I got it, Dad," He reaches his arms up like a toddler wanting to be picked up. "Can you be a big gust of wind?"

Owen hesitates. "Only if you'll be done with this game afterwards."

"Kay."

Down the hall and sitting in the mall's food court, Kyra observes her father tip-toeing like a ballerina toward Jacob in a zigzag motion—his arms outstretched like an airplane.

"Oh...my God." She mutters.

Owen circles Jacob once, before getting behind him and scooping him up, into the air, by his waist. He circles with him one time over the white, square lake, before bumping open the bathroom door with Jacob's butt, then setting him inside.

Jacob's smile spread wide. "Thanks, Dad; they almost got me." He says, walking over to the short urinal.

"You're safe now. They won't get you in here. Ugh, especially with the smell. You would think they would keep the mall bathroom cleaner than this."

"Looks clean."

"Looks can be deceiving," Owen says, stepping into a stall. "You gonna be okay out there? I'll be quick."

"Yeah."

As Jacob pees, he looks at his curved reflection in the moistened, chrome flush valve. He widens his eyes and bares his teeth, making one funny face after another. He leans forward, closer to the chrome, and giggles when his nose seems larger than the rest of his face.

"What's so funny?" Asks Owen.

"Nothing. Just looking at my face in the pipe."

A dark, thin, shivering blur develops next to the reflection of his face—taking shape behind him. He spins around and discovers an empty bathroom and a large sink mirror. He looks back into the chromatic reflection and the blur is still there, but closer. Curious, he zips his pants and steps away to peek around the stalls, but no one is there.

"I'm almost done," says Owen, "make sure you wash your hands and flush that urinal, okay?"

"Yeah."

Jacob wipes the damp flush valve with his sleeve, and looks into the drier reflection again, before forcefully pulling down on the handle to flush. *No black figure. No blur. No matter.* He continues on, like nothing has happened, shuffling his feet toward the sink—the sound of powerful flushing still behind him.

His little hands can barely reach the sensor to turn on the water, but he manages; the faucet sprays out warm water to his fingertips. Jacob rubs his flat palms together, to get them wet, then reaches for the soap nozzle next to the faucet. It was a chore to reach the sensor, but the soap dispenser is even more of a task. He manages to pull himself up on the edge of the sink, balancing on his belly while squirting the pink foam onto his hand.

When finished, he climbs down, wiping his hands on the sides of his pullover, when he notices the string hanging from his pocket. Grabbing it by the end, he pulls the string out until it's dangling long and straight in front of him, then places it on the sink in a swirly mess. Being careful not to get it completely wet, he continues drying his hands, then scoops the string back into his palm.

Before he can shove it back into his pocket, he notices something odd about the tip of the string. It is moving. Moving like the head of an earthworm. He poked at it with his finger, but it lay still. Jacob begins to think that something is wrong in his head and wonders why he is seeing things like he is.

He gives it one more look. It was slight, but the tip of the string moves, once again. Immediately, Jacob tries to drop it to the floor, but it wraps around his wrist, then quickly slithers up and around his entire arm. He frantically raises the sleeve of his pullover, but it is too quick for him to grab. It all happens so fast, that he doesn't have time to scream. The string pierces his neck like a needle. Jacob begins gagging and clawing at his neck to grab the string, but by this time, it had imbedded itself into his skin, his pupils gradually turn pearly-white.

Owen flushes the toilet, stepping out of the stall, with a look of satisfaction on his face, as he begins washing his hands at the sink.

"Jacob?" He looks behind him to the urinals, then dries his hands on the sides of his pullover, squatting down to see under the bathroom stalls. "Jacob!"

He quickly springs to his feet, snatching the bathroom door open, where he instantly has a clear view of Kyra, standing next to a small group of boys—all carrying skateboards. But no Jacob next to her.

His pace quickens to a light jog. He sees Kyra mutter something to the boys and they quickly disburse.

She crosses her arms in defense, preparing for his verbal attack.

"Where's your brother!?"

She quickly unfolds her arms. "What? What do you mean? He was with you!"

"He was just in the bathroom with me, washing his hands. You didn't see him come out? He would've walked right passed you!"

"No, I—"

"Damnit, Kyra! Stay here in case he comes back!" He says with a low, but stern voice. Then, with his adrenaline pumping and heart pounding, he begins searching frantically through the food court, raising on his toes to see above the crowds of people surrounding him.

"Jacob!" He screams, startling those around him.

Some stop and look around, unaware of who they are looking for, while others step away from him, as if he were mad.

"Sir—Sir, what's the problem? What's going on?" A mall cop says, flanking Owen to his right.

"My son. My son wandered off."

Owen gently shoves him to the side and continues his desperate search.

"Hey, give me a description and maybe I—"

Owen doesn't listen and almost trips over the mall cops' feet. "Jacob!"

The cop quickly follows while activating his shoulder mic. "Southeast section of the mall, possible lost child and terribly upset father, on a rampage searching for him. I need eyes on cameras." He releases the button and reaches for Owen, once more. "Sir—Sir, please slow down, and let's get control of the situation. We may be able to help."

Owen spots a play area at one end of the mall. The commotion going on there sends him plowing, shoving, dipping and side-stepping shoppers, until he reaches the side of a dinosaur slide. He pushes a couple huddled over someone.

"Move, don't touch him! He's having a seizure. Roll him on his side!" A woman yells. "Where are his parents. Find his parents and call 911!"

Owen parts two people aside and his heart sinks when he discovers Jacob—violently shaking on his back. His eyes rolled upward to where his pupils were barely visible. *God no!* He quickly drops to his knees, beside him, on the fake grassy-turf. "Jacob," he mutters, touching his shoulders. Almost immediately, his body begins to calm.

"Are you his Father!?" A woman yells to the horrified and nonresponsive father. Shaking his shoulder. "Sir—Sir, are you his dad?"

🦋 🦋 🦋 🦋

Owen waits impatiently by himself on one side of the hospital waiting area, while Kyra and her grandparents sit on the opposite side of the room, furthest from him. Periodically, Rose glances in his direction with a hateful gaze .

Pretending as if he doesn't notice, Owen leans into his knees with his elbows, and flattens his hands to his face.

After what seems like hours—however, only thirty minutes— the doctor, a very clean-cut Hispanic male, arrives with a smile, yet puzzled expression. Owen jumps to his feet, wiping his sweaty palms on his jeans. He's soon joined by the grandparents and Kyra from the side.

"Is he okay?" Owen asks.

"He's fine. He has no fever; blood sugar is fine. He's not on any medications, correct?"

"No. He's not on any medications." Says Rose, partially stepping in front of Owen.

"Well, other things like bright flickering lights, certain types of music, lack of sleep, emotional stress... can all cause a seizure. Nonetheless, for me to come to any type of conclusion, I will have to draw some blood, with your permission."

Owen gives a slight, consenting nod.

Rose frowns. "What do you think is in his blood," she looks over to Owen, then back to the doctor. "I mean, what could possibly be in his blood that can cause something like this?"

"Ma'am, there could be a number of things that can cause it. But the only way we are going to know for sure, is after reviewing the blood work. After I have the nurse draw his blood, we are going to patch him up and send him home with you, sir. But I suggest keeping an eye on him until we get some results. Maybe sleep next to him for a few nights."

Rose huffs and rolls her eyes. "Good luck with that."

Owen swallows his desired retort, closing his eyes briefly, "How fast can you give us some answers?" Asks Owen.

"Usually, the lab gets me info within twenty-four to forty-eight hours. But I promise you, you will know as *soon* as I know. You have my word. Now, if none of you have any more questions for me..."

Owen shakes his head, followed by Rose.

"Okay, then. We will keep in touch." The doctor leaves the waiting area.

Kyra, hugging her grandfather's waist, is led by him back to where they were waiting. But Rose glared at Owen with such anger, he could almost feel the heat emitting from her eyes.

"Why?" She says with shaking turned up palms. "Why are you doing this to them. To us?"

"Rose, I'm not doing any of this intentionally. Please. He's my son. I wouldn't do anything to hurt him."

She shakes her head with disbelief. Her wide, pain-stricken eyes well with tears. "Just give them to us. We will take *good* care of them. You can move on and do whatever it is you need to do or be. You can hang out with your friends without worry. We just want—"

"No, Rose!" He snaps.

Al grabs their belongings and quickly approaches the escalating situation, just as Rose reaches for Owen's pullover. She grabs it tightly by the hood and raises her hand. Owen slips from her grip, but she still has ahold of the cord on his hood. He dodges and deflects her attempts at slapping his face, without retaliation, using his forearms to guard.

"Rose, no!" Al grabs her by the wrists, taking most of his strength to separate her from her assault. "You definitely don't need to be doing this. Calm yourself!" He says firmly, without yelling, through tense lips.

Once free, Owen steps back with puckered lips and teary eyes, then looks over to Kyra, retreating away from the chaos with tears of her own.

"Just give them to us, damn it! Stop killing my family, you son-of-a-bitch!" Rose screams through her husband, standing in front of her.

"Baby, no! Come on. Let's go. Let's go, now. We all could use some rest."

Rose bursts into tears, "I don't need rest. I want my fucking grandchildren!"

Al gently restraints her, then whispers into her ear, just as Kat Dillon appeared in the hallway with a clipboard hugged to her chest.

Rose drops her desire to fight as quickly as she started it, and without another word. Al circles around her, then rests his hands on her shoulders from behind to guide her to the exit.

216

❦ ❦ ❦ ❦

Jacob cringes from the pain of the needle, biting his lip and whimpering through his nose, as the last of the sample tubes fills with his blood.

"All of that's coming out of me?"

The nurse chuckles. "Yes, it is. You're full of this stuff."

"But why do you guys want it?"

"Well, the doctor just wants to check and make sure everything is going okay inside you. He wants to know why you had the accident you had today."

"You can find all of that out by looking in my blood?"

"Yep. Sure can," she says, placing the tube on the table beside them; then, she carefully removes the needle. "Okay, little buddy, that's it. Curl your arm for me to keep that cotton ball in place. Then I'll get you a wrap and send you off with Dad. How's that sound?"

"Good."

"And after that bleeding stops, how about a nice colorful Band-Aid?" She looks in her Tupperware box. "I have Batman, Spiderman and...hmm. That looks like it. I have to get some more. I swore I had more than this, but—well, which will it be?"

"Spiderman. He's a good one."

"Batman is good too. Don't you think?"

"No. He doesn't have real powers and stuff."

She hands him the Band-Aid.

"Thank you."

"You are very welcome, sir," she smiles. "Well, his money and smarts give him powers. And he's a real person, like you and me." She sits beside him once more. "Alright, give me your arm one last time so I can wrap you up." She says, as she begins wrapping the bright-green CoFlex bandage around the cotton ball. "There ya go. All wrapped up. Ya ready to go?

"That's a cool color."

"I thought you'd like that."

"I'm really, really tired."

"I know, sweetie. You've been through a lot today. Time to go home and get some rest. Do you want help down?"

"No. I can do it."

🦋 🦋 🦋 🦋

The nurse escorts Jacob out through double doors. Just outside, his father is standing in front of Kat, in a heated conversation, with his hands on his hips. The more Kat speaks, the more frustrated his expression becomes—until he notices Jacob approaching.

He quickly steps around Kat to him. "Jacob," he caresses his face, then looks up to the nurse. "Is he okay to come home with me?"

"Yes, Mr. Mosley, he certainly is. He's all wrapped up and ready to go." She says, brushing his curls with her fingertips.

"Thank you so much." Owen says, taking Jacob's hand.

Kyra approaches with Jacob's coat.

As Owen places it on him and zips him up, Kat observes silently from behind them. She then watches as the nurse disappears back behind the double doors.

"I'll be in touch with you, Mr. Mosley." She says sternly.

Owen throws her a frown as she walks off toward the exit.

CHAPTER 12

BAD KITTY

(4:35 PM, Friday)

Gently, Kyra pinches the corner of the moist paper towel and peels back a layer, until her white monarch butterfly is fully revealed. She places a flat piece of Styrofoam, covered with tracing paper, in front of her; she uses forceps, and carefully places her butterfly in the center. In her mind, she replays the steps and techniques her mother taught her when spreading the wings of a butterfly specimen.

She hears the home phone ring downstairs just as she places her first pin through the paper—precisely around the wing.

"Hello," says Owen, answering.

"What's up, big brother?" Marley says on the other side. "What you got going on? How's little man doing?"

"Hey. Just taking care of things around the house," he wipes his face with the bottom of his t-shirt before leaning against the wall. "Jacob is doing good. Been sleeping a lot though since the mall. But the doctor says to let him rest as much as possible. So that pretty much sums up what I'm doing. What about you? I haven't heard from you in a little while."

"Just been busy myself, man. Trying to do things to earn some money; but I think I got it figured out."

Owen smiles, preparing himself for what he knows was coming next. Asking the inevitable question. "And what's that?"

"A sugar momma."

Owen rolls his eyes and chuckles.

"What chu laughing for? I'm serious." Marley also laughs. "I tried to go out the other weekend by myself, but I felt like a stalker or serial killer; sitting all by myself and smiling at bitches like a creep."

"Ain't nothing wrong with going to the bar by yourself. People do it all the time."

Marley quietly pours himself a drink. "Have you ever done it?"

With raised eyebrows, Owen hesitates.

"Yeah, I can hear the look on your face. That's what I thought," Marley takes a sip. "You wouldn't step foot in a club alone. But you'd probably pull a couple ladies, looking like a broke-ass Idris Elba. But me, I look like a high-ass Mike Epps."

Owen bursts out laughing.

"I'm glad you find that funny," He swirls his drink in the glass. "You need to step out with me. We haven't hung out in a while and you need a break from all this drama you dealing with."

"No—No, I have to stay here. I need to take care of a couple things. Besides, I need to keep an eye on Jacob."

"Man, Jacob is fine. The place I want to go too is less than a mile from your house, so if anything happens, you can always get home quick."

"I don't know man."

"It's happy hour and you'd be home before seven," there's a pause. "Drinks are on me." Still no answer. "Come on, Bruh. You owe me for helping you move at no cost. We will call it even."

"Alright, man, alright! But I can't be out late."

"Yes!" Marley raises his glass. "I'll be there in about an hour. I have a car we can use, 'cause we are *not*, I repeat *not*, under any circumstance, getting caught trying to pick up women in that broke-down, mobile billboard you're driving."

"Yeah, let me be clear. I am not going out to pick up any women. I'll leave that up to you. But I will have a drink with my brother."

"Sounds like a plan. I'll be there soon, hurry up and get out of that nasty shirt and take a shower. I know you stank. No pullovers and ball caps either."

Owen smells one of his underarms.

🦋 🦋 🦋 🦋

Kyra proudly places her butterfly neatly on the corner of her desk, the beginning of her new specimen display since the fire. She admires it for a moment when, suddenly, there is a knock on her door.

"What?" She answers.

The door creeks open and Owen pops his head in.

"Hey. I'm gonna go with your Uncle Marley for a couple of hours, but I won't be gone long okay?"

She doesn't make eye contact; she just admires how well she set her butterfly up. "You leaving us alone again?"

"Sweetie, I won't be gone very long. And I'll be less than a mile away. If you need anything, just call me or Uncle Marley on our phones."

She leers back at him. "Can I have a sleepover? For my birthday?"

Owen's eyes widen slowly, like a tarsier lemur. His expression is that of a little boy who is caught with his hands in the proverbial cookie jar.

"Yeah, you didn't forget that my birthday was next week, did you?" She squints.

He shakes his expression, "No, sweetie, I didn't. I'll agree to a sleepover. But we will talk later about who gets to come."

A smile spreads across Kyra's face. "Just some of the girls from school. That's all."

"You know, you have a lot of your uncle in you," he smiles, but she doesn't return the gesture. "We will talk later or tomorrow about this. But for now, I need to get ready. Also, do me a quick favor, and check on your brother?"

"For what? He's asleep."

"Just do it, please. I don't want him sleeping too long. He'll be up all night if he does."

🦋 🦋 🦋 🦋

"You wanna sit at the bar, or a table," asks Owen.

"There's only a couple of chairs at the bar," Marley looks over the crowded bar, with more people piling in behind them. "Let's grab that spot over there."

"We don't need four chairs, man."

"It'll be alright. Just grab it and stop being difficult," he pushes Owen by the shoulder. "You know I don't like being shoulder-to-shoulder at a bar anyways."

"Since when?"

"Since now."

Owen proceeds to the open table, his suspicion arising.

A waitress approaches, balancing a large, round drink tray—empty glasses and bottles balance atop. With her other hand, she discreetly pulls up at the center of her top to show a little less cleavage.

"Can I get you guys anything? Kitchen is open, too." She asks, placing a bowl of peanuts in front of them.

Marley raises an eyebrow. "I'll take a crown and coke."

She then looks to Owen.

"Do you have Guinness?"

"We certainly do."

Marley makes a face, as though he's going to hurl all over the table. "Guinness? For real? Are you sure you're black?"

"What? A lot of black people drink that, man. And even if they don't. Don't be trying to put me in no box." He laughs.

"Okay, so one Crown and Coke, and one Guinness?" She asks.

"Yes please—and some of those pickle thangs?" Says Marley.

"You mean fried pickles?"

Marley points at her. "Yep, those thangs. Thank you!"

"Okay, boys. I'll get that right out to you."

As she walks off, Marley nudges Owen and squints as if he had just sucked down the sourest of lemon juice, his upper lip practically turned up into his nose.

"Really," says Owen, "fake boobs, skinny and no booty?" They both turn to watch her walk away to the bar. "Nothing but gristle."

"Right."

"Don't touch them peanuts though." Owen pushes them away. "You see she got them off that table she was cleaning when we got here. They ain't fresh."

❦ ❦ ❦ ❦

Sitting in a corner booth, near the bathroom, and wearing a black fedora hat, Kat Dillon sips her beverage—a small cup of Irish coffee. Having enough of the conversation between the two women she is accompanied by—each one-upping the other on whose husband shows them the most attention—her eyes wander about the bar. To her surprise, Owen is in her direct line of sight.

The women with her are so involved in their conversation, they don't notice their colleague's detective-like gaze toward the two gentlemen across the bar. She casually pics up her cell phone and aims it at Owen and Marley, snapping multiple photos.

❦ ❦ ❦ ❦

"So, do I have to keep on asking you to put me up for a job with your company, big brother?" Asks Marley.

Owen shakes his head. "You just refuse to let up on that don't you? If I had the work, and the money to pay you, I'd—"

Two stunning middle-eastern women—both with long, dark, shoulder length hair, and dressed in form fitting jeans to accentuate their best curves—approach the table, throwing Owen off of his thoughts.

Owen's cheerful expression drops to the floor, as his brother spins around to address them, seemingly unsurprised at their beauty and sudden presence.

"Hey, ladies! What's up?" Marley throws his arm around one of them, as the other drapes her jacket over the back of the chair next to Owen, pitching a pearly white smile to him that he doesn't return. This is my older brother, Owen. Marley squeezes the woman under his arm, "Owen, this is Adira," then he points a presenting hand to the other woman, "and that's Zabrina."

They both smile to greet him, but Zabrina extends a limp wrist, smiling, with a hint of seduction, at Owen.

Owen grabs her hand firmly, taking her by surprise, then shakes it as if he were finishing a job interview at a construction site. "Hey—Hey, yeah, nice to meet you."

Zabrina's eyebrows raise as she looks over to Adira, smirking and shrugging her right shoulder.

"Excuse me, ladies," says Owen, "I don't mean to be rude, just need to head to the bathroom really quick. I'll be right back."

He squints his eyes at Marley before stepping away.

Approaching the bathroom, he smiles at the two ladies in the corner booth—both comparing wedding rings and the amount of carats their diamonds are.

❦ ❦ ❦ ❦

At, just under, eight miles per hour, Kat drives her car past the Mosley residence, hoping to catch a glimpse inside. Nothing but a bedroom light upstairs is on—Kyra's room—and the rest of the home is dark. She makes a U-turn down the street and parks, keeping the home in her view.

She removes her phone from her briefcase and takes another photo, making sure to get the house, and the street in front, with Owen's utility truck in view.

❦ ❦ ❦ ❦

"...just started having fun, the edibles kicked in, we were dancing and all," says Adira, then points at Zabrina, "then this bitch gets the great idea to call for an Uber early, so we can beat the New Year's traffic. Fucking ride shows up at 11:30, so she starts yelling for us to 'come on'."

"Well, that's cool, right?" Says Owen.

"What!? We didn't even get to yell 'Happy New Year'! Screwed up the whole experience. All that money for VIP and drinks. We missed the most important part of the night. No, not cool!"

"Okay—Okay," says Zabrina, "I apologized a billion times for that. Besides, I made up for it. So, shut up."

"Oh, *yeah*, she made up for it." Adira laughs.

"What? What did she do to make up for that?" Asks Marley.

The two women look at each other and laugh.

"Okay, that sounds like another story we need to hear. But before that we need another round." Says Marley, waiving over the waitress.

"So, are you from here, Owen?" Asks Zabrina.

"Not from Harrisburg, but, like Marley, I was born and raised in Goldsboro."

"Oh, yeah? What brought you out here?" Says Adira.

Owen hesitates. Then looks over to Marley. "Just some things. It's really a long story."

Marly clears his throat, "he hasn't been here long. Just moved up the street and around the corner from here."

Adira looks surprised. "Me too. Not too far from this bar, actually."

"I'm in the old house on Brookshire Lane. My kids and me."

"Oh? you have kids? How old are they?" Asks Zabrina.

Adira perks up. "Wait, are you in that old Burgess place?"

Owen looks puzzled. "Yeah. Lloyd Burgess left it to me."

"Wow! Is it creepy there? Hear any weird things?

"Well, a little. It makes some noises. Needs some work. But it's a pretty decent old house. A lot of room for my kids and me," he looks over to Zabrina, who seems just as puzzled at her inquisitive friend, then back to Adira. "Do you know something I should?"

"I just heard stories, is all," she sips her drink.

Owen sits back in his chair and folds his arms. "You got my attention. Mind sharing?"

"Oh, it's just stories. There's a few stories floating around about that house," She stirs her drink with the thin plastic straw then smiles, "how much money you got? I'll tell ya. But I don't know if they are true or not."

Zabrina gasps, "Adira—"

"Are you serious?" Owen snakes his arms tighter around his body. "You're gonna make me pay to hear this story?"

"I'm *kidding*, I'm kidding," she laughs. "Okay. Just your typical haunted house stories, you know. Folks saying they've seen people staring for long periods of time out of the windows, dark figures, lights flickering off and on in random rooms inside. No one owned the house then. No one was even living there.

"Squatters could've broken in and been messing around, maybe?" Says Marley.

She shrugs her shoulders, "The lights would flicker so much, that some of the locals thought the same thing. Maybe people were coming over, sneaking in to see if they could find something valuable inside. They sent a cop over to investigate the disturbing lights and found nothing. Nothing. Just an empty, dark and dusty home," she shakes her glass gently, swirling the ice cubes, then takes another sip. "So, they killed the power, assuming there were some possible electrical issues. But days later, the lights flickered. Eventually someone broke in and removed all the lightbulbs in the house. Must've gotten really annoying for them to do that."

Marley looks over to Owen. "Well, that explains that."

"Explains what?" Asks Adira.

"When he moved in, we had to go to the store and buy more lightbulbs. Not a bulb in the entire place."

"Well, sounds like there's some truth to my story then," she nods her head. "Creepy. Hell, just driving past that place at night gives me the creeps."

Zabrina sucks her teeth, "come on girl. Don't be mean."

Owen raises his index finger from the fold in his arm, "Wait, I want to hear more. Seems like you're not finished."

"Eh, just more bullshit. Some people have even gone so far as to say there's goodies inside. Hidden treasure or something like that."

Both Owen and Marley laugh.

"I call bullshit." Says Marley.

"Like what? A treasure chest?" Owen chuckles. "Golden goblets with rubies and diamonds on them?"

Adira frowns and sips her drink some more. "Come on fellas. I'm just telling you what I've heard. The man who owned it before, his name was," she hangs her head and snaps her fingers to trigger her memory, "I wanna say, Cliff, but I forget. But anyways, whatever the hell his name was, was a jack of all trades. Carpenter, locksmith, mechanic, and I think masonry. He even served in the military. I can't remember what branch or what his job was, but he *was* in the service.

"You were gonna charge me for all this and you can't even remember most of it?" Owen laughs.

"I *did* say I was kidding," she makes Owen jump, playfully motioning as if she were going to toss her drink on him. "Like I was saying, but long story short... somehow, he got a hold of some valuables while he was overseas, then hid them, for whatever reason. People say they think it's still somewhere in the house."

"How long ago was this supposed to have happened?" Asks Marley.

"Sometime in the early seventies."

"Shit, with all that time—if there was any treasure—I'm sure someone would have found it by now." Says Marley.

232

Owen leans in. "So, what ever happened to Cliff?"

"Nobody knows. He just disappeared. The next thing you know the house was up for sale. Who knows? Some here don't take kindly to people of color. Maybe one of these white folks did something to him when they found out he had all that loot." She takes another sip and wipes the corner of her mouth with her wrist. "Anyways, Lloyd was eager to buy that house. And he did for a fairly-good amount of money. But nothing near as much as what that loot could be worth if he found it."

"Do you believe that?" Asks Marley. "That there's gold there? Sounds like one of them rumors that gets bigger and bigger as it's told."

Owen nods his head.

Adira sucks her teeth, then with a raised eyebrow, drives her long, white fingernails into the bowl of unshelled peanuts in front of her. "You don't have to believe me," she says, tossing a couple onto her tongue, and chewing with her mouth open, "it's just a story. I don't even know if I believe it—and couldn't care less. I'm simply curious if your brother heard any spooky shit going on in there since he moved in. But you both are acting like I'm the one who's crazy, and all I'm doing is telling you the story."

Zabrina takes notice to Adira's attitude and grabs her purse. "Ugh, umm, I need to go to the lady's room. Come on, girl. You know I don't go by myself."

Without looking at the men, Adira shoves more peanuts in her mouth, clicks her nails together over the bowl—to shake off the excess salt and peelings—then follows behind her friend.

"Bro," says Owen, "I thought it was just gonna be us. Why?"

"They just wanted to have a drink. Relax. I didn't ask them to come out to set you up on a date, King-O. Just some friendly conversation with some lovely ladies is all."

"If you say so," Owen laughs, "yo girl got attitude, though. Didn't take much to piss her off."

"You see, she was tearing into those peanuts," Marley laughs, "I was gonna say something, but it was too late."

"You wrong, man." Owen chuckles.

❦ ❦ ❦ ❦

Kat can hardly take her eyes off the eerie appearance of the house, dark and silhouetted against the dusk sky, when the downstairs light comes on—then the kitchen light. Kat removes a small pair of binoculars from her glove compartment and aims them to the living room window. She can see nothing from the angle in which she's parked. But she knows if she parks any closer, she would run the risk of neighbors becoming curious, or the possibility of Owen arriving home early and discovering her.

Her curiosity, and desire for the evidence needed, is overwhelming. So, she steps out of her car.

❦ ❦ ❦ ❦

Moments before Kat arrived and positioned herself to survey the home, Kyra admires her white butterfly, perfectly displayed in the center of the case her grandfather had given her. She holds it up next to the desk lamp, tilting it at different angles, when the reflection of the glass catches her brother standing behind her.

She hastily spins around, nearly dropping the display case to the floor. "Oh, my gawd, Jacob! What's wrong with you? Why don't you ever knock, damn it!?" she says, gulping her heart back down into her chest.

"Sorry! Your door was open anways, so I just came in."

Jinx comes trotting in behind him and curls up on the floor next to her.

"No—No it wasn't. I always keep it closed," she shrieks. "What do you want?"

"Can I have a PB and J? I'm hungry."

She shakes her head. "I don't care, but you have to make it yourself. And don't make a mess 'cause I'm not cleaning it up."

"Kay," Jacob takes off running down the hall.

"And don't eat any cookies," she yells, "you already had some, you little butt, so the rest of the Oreos are mine."

Jacob makes it to the top of the stairs and flicks on the downstairs light before climbing down. When he makes it to the bottom, he holds tight to the banister's acorn shaped newel cap and swings himself around it, then slides across the finished wood floor in his soft, white socks. He flips on the kitchen light, climbs on the counter, and begins raiding the cabinets like a hungry racoon.

❦ ❦ ❦ ❦

Kyra leans her small display against the wall of her shelf, beside the picture of her mother. She takes a deep breath and, with gentle hands, removes the picture from its place on the shelf. With her thumb, she caresses the glass over her mother's face, then lightly kisses it, before returning it.

There's a noise behind the wall... a dragging, scraping noise.

Unsure of what she is hearing, she leans in. Scratching. Faint scratching in the wall behind the shelving, that grew louder by the second, shaking it gently. She peeks around the side of the shelf, pulling it a few inches from the wall.

The scratching stops. She places her ear against the wall, but the growling furnace in the basement, along with the sound of air pushing through the empty space between the wall panels, is all she can hear.

Something swipes at the wall, from the other side, where her face was pressed. She steps back in sudden shock, wide-eyed, as she listens to what sounds like tiny claws scurrying away in the wall toward her closet.

Jinx pops up, ears rotating like sonars, as the scurrying of a few, develops in to many, rising louder—not only in sound—but in numbers. The walls tremble all around them, the noise racing up-and-down, between the panels, like a flock of tiny, confused birds, then stops abruptly by the closet.

The closet door shudders briefly.

Jinx approaches the door, her head low, as she cautiously sniffs the opening at the bottom.

"Come here, girl." Kyra whispers.

Jinx stands on her hind legs, sniffing all around the door, and tracing back down to the bottom, once again.

Terrified, yet curious, Kyra wipes her sweaty palms on her pants, then approaches carefully. She grabs ahold of the vintage, diamond-cut glass knob, and takes another deep breath before twisting it, easing the door open. It grinds on its hinges. The light from her room inches inside the dark closet, until it finally shines on a white doll face with sad blue eyes, seemingly, looking back up at her.

A chill races up her back.

※ ※ ※ ※

Slowly, Jacob peels back the seal of the Oreo cookie package, while still chewing the last bite of his peanut butter sandwich. Then, with the carefulness and precision of a game of *Operation*, he removes a cookie. He cringes as the noise from the thin plastic tray crackles. Before swallowing his sandwich, he shoves the crisp, creamy delight into his partially full mouth, then hops down from the counter.

Raised on his toes, he removes a cup from the clean dish rack, and pours himself a full glass of milk to wash down the thick, mushy, crunchy, sweet muck of cookie and peanut butter sandwich filling his mouth. As he gulps it down, he has the feeling he is being watched—and slowly looks behind him to the kitchen window. Nothing. He then checks the living room, which is also empty.

Confident that it was just his imagination, he retrieves another cookie and shoves it in his mouth but is suddenly startled by something hitting the back window.

He smiles, making his way up on the sink, and peers out of the window to the backyard. To his surprise, his red army men are lined up on a log close to the tree line.

Smiling even bigger, he jumps down, grabbing a few more cookies, before rushing outside to investigate.

🦋 🦋 🦋 🦋

Near a single, untrimmed bush in the backyard of the Mosely residence, Kat sneaks a peek through the kitchen with her binoculars. The light from above the backdoor is far enough away where she can hide in the shadows of the bush.

The back door pops a binding spring. She drops lower.

Gradually, the screen creaks open a few inches, then a little more. Jacob emerges slowly, panning the backyard—like a raccoon checking its surroundings before leaping into a dumpster. He darted through the yard and toward the log.

He picks up one army man, then another. All of them pointing their weapons in the direction of the treehouse.

"Dennis?" He whispers. "Hey Dennis, are you in there?"

Kat notices something catch Jacob's attention, as he spins to the right, then takes off, without hesitation, into the darkness of the forest.

"Jacob Mosley, no." She mutters.

Immediately, she follows, stopping at the edge of the trees, when she hears giggling children, chased by the sound of rustling leaves. She ventures in even further, feeling about the ground with her toes and examining her dark surroundings. Unable to see clearly, she removes her phone from her pocket, then swipes the screen for the flashlight icon. The sound of Jacob's giggling echoes through the trees above her.

"Jacob. You shouldn't be out here." She says, just louder than a whisper.

She waits. A cool—slightly harder than gentle—breeze blows through, giving her the chills. It's the only response she is going to get. She presses the icon while blindly stepping forward, brightening the scene, and catches a glimpse of the large hole in front of her, before losing her footing and falling inside. She lets out a short scream before her plump, round body ricochets forcefully off the dirt-hole wall, loosening the soil that comes crashing down with her.

Jinx watches from the window of Jacob's room.

❦ ❦ ❦ ❦

(8:17 PM)

Jinx, still staring at the hole from Jacob's window, is alerted of Owen's return home, by the sound of his keys hitting the wood console in the foyer.

Owen picks up a small piece of paper with a note written on it.

"*We definitely have rats in my room.*"

He tosses it back onto the foyer table, startled by Jinx stepping in front of him—sniffing his hands, pants, and crotch area.

"What the..." Owen reaches to pet her, but she ducks from his touch, as if it were an aggressive, low-flying bat.

Puzzled, and with a little bit of liquor in his system, he steps passed her to the living room, where Kyra and Jacob are watching a movie while sharing a small bag of jellybeans. Neither of them acknowledges his presence and maintain their focus on the television.

240

"Well, damn, 'hi' to ya'll, too." He says, with a hint of slur, but focusing more on Jacob than Kyra. "Jacob?"

Jacob gives the slightest of waves, raising his pinky as he inserts a green jellybean into his mouth.

"Did you see my note?" Says Kyra.

"Yes, I have," he removes his jacket and tosses it on a wood chair. "What makes you think you have rats, Kyra?"

"I heard them in the walls," she finally looks at him, but with a scowl. "A lot of them. We have to call an exterminator; 'cause I'm not sleeping up there again until we do."

She returns her attention to the television and snatches a jellybean from her fingers with her lips. For a moment, he gets the silent treatment as he stands near the television, watching them as they intentionally ignore his presence.

Owen folds his arms in front of him, "what the hell is going on here? Did I do something to you guys? Is there a reason why I'm being treated like this?"

"Nothing, Dad!" She snatches the bag of candy from Jacob, who is unphased by her aggression. "We just had to eat jellybeans for dinner is all. Or did you forget you had to feed your kids?"

Owen throws his hands on his face, loudly inhaling as if he were smelling his palms. "Oh my God," he says through his parted fingers, then drops his hands to the side. "I can't believe I forgot to set dinner out. I'm so sorry, kids. Jesus!"

"At least Jacob had a sandwich and *my* cookies!" She frowns.

"Kyra, baby, I'm sorry. I'll go get you something now."

"I'm not hungry anymore. Besides, you smell like alcohol and probably shouldn't be driving."

"I'm not drunk, young lady," he removes his shoes and places them by the door. "Where did you hear this noise, or rats in the wall?"

"In the wall by the closet. And someone placed that creepy-ass doll in there again."

"What?" He looks to Jacob—robotically placing jellybeans in his mouth, still. "Jacob, are you doing that?"

"I know he didn't because he was downstairs eating when it happened."

"That's not to say he couldn't have done it before."

"Well, he didn't. Can you please just go check, Dad." She snaps.

Owen is puzzled at Jacob's behavior. He understands that the kids are upset with him because of dinner, but something—something was not right with his youngest. "Jacob, are you okay?"

Jacob turns to him, cheeks puffy and with an empty expression in his dark eyes. A long line of thick drool drips from his lips. Then he slowly, creepily smiles exposing a mouth full of jellybeans crammed in his teeth.

❀ ❀ ❀ ❀

The dirt crumbles from the wall and falls to Kat's face, bringing her to consciousness. Coughing and spitting, she claws at the thick dirt to stand in her jagged surroundings, when a sharp pain shoots up her leg. It was as if someone had run a dull knife through it. She screams, falling back to the ground, causing more dirt to fall onto her. With every bit of strength she could muster, she manages to sit up to painfully inspect her wound. She screams again, grabbing her thigh, when she notices her foot is twisted one hundred and eighty degrees in the opposite direction.

Her short-of-breath cries and screams for help are muffled by the soft dirt surrounding her. She tries to calm herself, looking around for anything that will help her stand up on her good leg, but the pain is excruciating, and her escape is nearly eight feet above.

Tears of desperation fill her eyes, when she notices, at the edge of the hole, a figure of a small child looking back down at her.

"Hey—Hey, young man!" She panics, grabbing at the muddy sides, causing more sticks and dirt to fall, "Please, please get help," She cries up to him. "My leg is broken. I can't get up. Go get your mommy and daddy."

He doesn't respond, standing above like a dark statue before a starlit night sky.

"Hurry!" She yells, failing at sitting up and falling to her back, quickly throwing up her forearm to block more falling debris. Even bigger chunks of clay and mud clumps fall. She suddenly realizes, with the level of dirt growing around her, she doesn't have much time before she will be buried alive. She closes her eyes and screams toward the sky with all she has, her hands clutching and digging into the mud.

When she opens her eyes again, the child is gone.

More tears well in her eyes; the warm, salty liquid streams down the sides of her dirty face, dripping onto the dirt that is now near her shoulders.

She sobs, letting out one more whimpering sigh for help, before the loose ground above finally fails, and collapses down onto her.

🦋 🦋 🦋 🦋

A younger, white gentleman descends the staircase, wearing an all-white jumpsuit with the words *Jake's Pest Control* in big, bold black letters on the back. His flashlight is still on and dangling from his tool belt.

"Welp, I don't see no rat turds, gnawed holes, nests er fur," He says to the waiting Mosley family in the living room. "I used my scope around dem walls all over and didn't hear nutt'n either. No smell." He scratches his head. "You sure you heard right, young lady? 'Cause I don't think you got no infestation. Just a dang hole in the wall."

Kyra rolls her eyes and doesn't answer.

"She said she heard it. And I believe her," says Owen, "is there anything else you can do to check?"

He scrunches his face, as he scratches his head even harder. "Welp. I don't know. Ain't too much else you *can* do Mr. Mosley. I mean, I can lay a couple traps for ya and see what ya get. Probably be cheaper for you to get them and lay 'em yourself. I charge a little more for that service."

"Okay, I'll take your advice on that. Thank you!"

"Yes, sir. And oh—" he digs into his pocket. "Found this here in that hole," he opens his hand and dumps a rusted, crushed piece of metal in Owen's palm. "Looks like an old crumpled up police whistle. I thought it was kinda cool."

Owen inspects it, then encloses it in his hand. "Thank you, again."

"Yep."

There is a moment of silence, as Owen waits for him to say something else. But the man smooths down his hair at the base of his neck and smiles. "Um, that will be fifty dollars, Mr. Mosley."

"Oh shit, yeah. I'm sorry. You do take checks?"

"Welp," he says, giving the shabby surroundings a quick once over, "I'd prefer cash if ya have it. I can get you a receipt. Been having a real problem with bounced checks lately. I'm sure you understand."

"I understand. But I don't have any cash on me at the moment. I can place a little extra on it if you could. Maybe, ten dollars?"

The man ponders the suggestion for a moment, then shakes his head as if he couldn't believe what he was about to say. "Okay, you got yourself a deal. Just make it out to Jake's Pest Control. I'm Jake, by the way. I own the company." Owen nods his head as he fishes his checkbook from the console drawer. "You got pests, I'll put them to rest. That's my slogan." Owen keeps writing in his checkbook. "I was gonna get it on the back of my jumpsuit, but the little girl that was designing them wanted an arm and a leg for the additional words, but I—"

"Here you go," Owen says, then leads him to the door. "I really appreciate your help."

"No problem, sir. If you hear anything else, feel free to give me a call and I'll be right over."

"I will definitely do that." Owen says, ready to close the door.

"Now, I'm gonna deposit this check right away. You sure the funds are available?"

"You see the name of my bank on the check. Just go to that bank and they will cash it right there. Have a good day, Jake."

Before he could respond, Owen gently closes the door.

CHAPTER 13

GIRLS, GIRLS, GIRLS

(4:35 PM Friday)

A five by five-inch piece of plywood and four nails seals the hole in Kyra's closet. Owen taps the four corners of it to make sure its set, as Kyra watches from on top of her bed.

Outside she hears the sound of a vehicle come to a stop in front of their house. A car horn blows twice.

Kyra perks up with excitement. "They're here!" She yells, jumping down from her bed and throwing aside her bedroom curtain. "Yes!" Wasting not one moment, she sprints through the hall, down the stairs then through the foyer, bursting through the front door.

Owen dusts himself off and peeks through her curtain just as Kyra embraces one of her old neighborhood friends, Nekia, aside a burgundy minivan, nearly knocking the girl's glasses from her face.

The side door slides open and out jumps two more of her squealing companions.

Jessica, the tallest at five feet eleven inches and slimmest of them all, with long blonde hair to her elbows, blue eyes and pearly white teeth. Alexis who was near the spitting image of a modern-day Velma from the cartoon Scooby Doo. Then Mariah who exited the other side of the van into the street. The biggest of the girls who did not join in on the squealing and carrying on. Instead, she checked her reflection in the side window, pulling her dark brown hair around her chubby face.

Besides Mariah, making her way to the rear of the van to open it, they all entomb Kyra in a circle of hugs, giggling screams and Happy Birthdays.

"Here we go." Owen mutters to himself in Kyra's room. "I hope you're ready for this Mr. Mosely." He closes the curtain and takes in a deep breath.

The driver, Pauline and also Mariah's mother, removes quite a few small overnight bags from the back of the van and places them on the curb when Owen approaches.

"Thanks for picking them up for me. I don't think I could've fit them all in my truck. And with these bags," He looks down at the growing colorful mound of smaller luggage. "You ladies do plan on staying for just *one* night, right?"

The girls look at each other and giggle some more. Owen shakes his head before joining Pauline at the rear of the van to talk.

Kyra forces her way between Nekia and Alexis. "Hey Mariah!" She smiles throwing her arms around her. Mariah notices the devious smirk on Nekia's face as she turns to the other girls and whispers. Jessica laughs, but Alexis's curled lips shows she disapproved of what she said.

Kyra grabs Mariah by the hand then turns to the other girls. "Oh my God, I'm so happy to see you guys!"

"I know," Says Alexis. "It's not the same since you've moved."

"Yeah, trust me, I wish I were back. You guys have changed so much in the little time since I've last seen you. Nekia what's up with the butch look."

Nekia flicks Kyra's shoulder with her finger and laughs. "It's not butch just cause I shaved the sides. I think it makes me look badass."

"I think it makes you look badass too." Says Jessica.

"It does. It's just butchie badass." Says Alexis, smiling.

Nekia's mouth drops open. "Okay already, enough about my hair. We've all changed okay. Let's get it over with; I got a haircut, Jessica got a tattoo, Mariah gained weight and Alexis has a boyfriend and no longer a virgin."

"God Nekia! Shut up much!?" exclaims Jessica.

"Ladies—Ladies, I think I've heard enough already. Can you please take that conversation inside?" Orders Owen.

"Yes, Mr. Mosley." Nekia says with a flirtatious smile.

"Thank you."

She leans in and whispers to Kyra. "Your Dad is still so—"

Kyra grunts. "Stop, just stop now!"

"I'm just saying. Older men are *umph*, sexy."

"Yeah, well you're only seventeen. All you'd be doing with any older man is start trouble." Snaps Kyra.

"She'll be legal next year." Says Alexis

"Oh yes I will!" She straightens her glasses and gazes up at the top floor. "This is so much more different than your old house. It's kinda creepy looking though. But kinda cool creepy."

"Tell me about it. I don't know about the cool part though." Says Kyra

As the girls disappear inside, Owen begins gathering the bags.

"Typical teenage girls." Pauline says now in the driver's seat.

"Yeah, I'm starting to regret this already."

"I feel for ya Owen," She laughs starting the van. "I'll be back tomorrow around noon if that's ok."

"That was the plan."

Pauline speeds off, leaving Owen at the curb next to the small mountain of assorted bags.

"Hey neighbor." Lorna says from across the street.

"Shit." Owen whispers with stiff lips as he watches her cross the street. He forces a smile and waves.

"Well hey there, new neighbor." She laughs. "Did I startle you?"

"No! Not at all."

"I was just out front getting my mail when I heard all the commotion and giggling. Thought I'd come say hi—so, hi!" She twiddles her fingers.

"How you doing, Lorna?" He says strapping a bag across his shoulder.

"Oh, I'm fine—let me get some of those for ya. Looks like ya got your hands full here."

"Thank you."

"I don't mind helping at all," She looks to the upstairs window as she helps with the last bag. "Got a little slumber party going on tonight, do ya?"

"It's my daughter, Kyra's birthday. She wanted it." He can see Jacob standing on the other side of the screen door, staring at his finger as he scraps his nail hard across the plastic wire mesh. His eyes nearly crossed. "Hey, open the door for us, man."

Jacob stops his scraping and turns a blank gaze to Lorna, quickly locks the door latch and steps back.

"Jacob Mosley, get back here and unlock this damn screen!"

He does not respond; just glances at him, then turns his attention back to Lorna. He narrows his lips, scrunches his nose and lowers his brow, staring at her in a way that sends chills over her shoulders.

Owen jabs the frame of the screen with his elbow to get his attention, but instead Jacob races off, up the stairs behind him and to his room.

"Hey!" He yells, dropping the bags to the porch. "Damn it! I'm sorry Lorna, would you mind staying here while I run around to the back?"

"Not at all."

Owen leaps from the top step to the lawn and jogs around the home to the back, catching a glimpse of Jacob looking down at him from his bedroom window before losing sight of him under the backdoor's awning. He takes a couple of steps back for a second look, but he was no longer there.

With Owen gone, Lorna becomes curious, looking inside the home through the screen. She can barely see with the bright sunlight shining against the wire mesh, so she gets closer, pressing her face against it until the inside becomes clearer. The muffled sound of the girl's conversation upstairs echoes through, down to the empty living room, then startles her when they all suddenly scream in the upstairs bathroom.

🦋 🦋 🦋 🦋

Nekia flicks on the bathroom light laughing. "Oh my God, this is gonna be so much fun. You guys are *so* easily scared."

"Damn it Nekia," Says Jessica "We literally just got here and you're so damn obnoxious."

With a confused frown, "Have you ever known me *not* to be?" They all pause for a moment with raised brows, then laugh. "That's what I thought."

"Okay, but can we do no more of *that*," Says Kyra "This house already freaks me out as it is."

"I'll agree, but can't promise," She playfully crosses her fingers behind her back. "Can we go to your room?"

🦋 🦋 🦋 🦋

Lorna waits patiently on the front porch, growing more curious as to why it was taking so long for Owen to return. She takes another look inside through the screen. There is a noise coming from the kitchen, a ticking, but she can't quite make out what it is. She places her ear against the screen just as it stops.

"Owen?"

She peers inside. Her nose barely touching the screen when something violently swipes across it. She jolts her head back. Black dust floats from the wire mesh and settles around the bottom of the screen frame.

Owen grabs the door handle and unlocks it. "Sorry. I had to jimmy the lock in the back too. Not sure how that one got locked.

"My goodness. Just all sorts of bad luck." She says wiping the bridge of her nose.

"Seems like it."

They begin setting bags against the wall just inside the door. Lorna places her hand on top of Owen's before he could release the handle of a small light blue travel bag.

"If you'd like some help, I'd be more than happy to help you with the girls tonight. You may need a woman's touch and guidance."

"I know these girls all too well, believe me." He gently touches her hand before pulling away. Then grabs another bag from outside. "No, I really do appreciate it, but I think I can handle a few ladies."

"I bet you could." She mumbles with a faint smirk and subtly raised eyebrow.

"What?"

"I was saying, if you need any of my help to just let me know. Oh, do you have that dish from the cake I brought you?"

254

"Oh-oh, yes I do," He leaves her to head towards the kitchen. "I was gonna send Kyra over to drop it off. I've been meaning to for a while now, but there's been so much going on. I'm sorry."

She follows behind him but stops at the kitchen entrance.

"Well I can see you've already done some work around here."

"Just a little paint to the kitchen cabinets. Nothing really all that special."

"It still looks nice."

Owen wipes the cake dish with a dry towel. "Here you go. All nice and clean."

"You didn't have to go through the trouble of cleaning it. I could've done that. Gives me something to do over there you know," She cradles the dish in her palms close to her chest. "When my husband passed things got real dull. Taking care of him was all I had, sadly."

"Man, I'm sorry to here that, Lorna. It's a shitty hand we are dealt."

"That it is," She shrugs her shoulders. "Well, guess I better get going. My show's coming on in—" As she spins around to the door, she gasps loudly as if she had been without oxygen for over a minute, dropping the glass cake plate to the floor with a loud crash. She backs into Owen as Jinx runs passed her and onto the couch.

"What!? What happened?" He grabs her by the shoulders from behind, then rushes over to pick up the big pieces of glass.

She grabs her chest and calms herself, "Jesus Christ, that beast is gonna give me a heart attack. She was standing right there, staring when I turned around." She kneels next to Owen, then sucks her teeth. "Oh my. This was my favorite." She mutters sadly.

"I'd say I'd get you another one, but this looks pretty expensive," He drags the trashcan close. "I don't have much but can help pay for it."

"No, don't bother at all," She smiles "It was bound to break like everything else in my life. Just a matter of when."

"I'll make it up to you. If you need something fixed or taken care of, it's on me."

"Okay, I'll take you up on that. I got a lot that needs fixing." She laughs.

Owen tries to disguise his disgust with forced laughter, carefully dropping one piece after another into the trash. He waited for her to offer help, but she just stood above him, watching, smiling.

"Go ahead, I'll clean this up, Lorna. I know you mentioned that show you wanna catch. I can handle this."

"Oh, thanks for reminding me."

She steps passed him and over the shattered fragments, twinkling against the hardwood floor. She quickly notices the girls all looking down at her from the top of the stairs.

"Hi ladies," She smiles and twiddles her fingers. "Sorry for the commotion. We just had a little accident here is all." Upon approaching the front door, she notices Jinx also watching her from the couch. She loses her smile and clears her throat. "I'll be seeing you, Owen."

"Goodbye, Lorna. Thanks for your help."

Jessica, standing between all the girls at the landing of the staircase, twiddles her fingers mockingly.

Lorna hesitates before closing the door, hearing the faint giggles inside when she hits the bottom of the porch stairs.

🦋 🦋 🦋 🦋

(6:15 PM)

Owen clears the table of birthday cake crumbs and pizza crust to the sound of Jacob's loud toy sirens, blaring in the living room. He places the plastic cover over the store-bought cake and shoves it at the bottom of the refrigerator. He discovers a couple slices of cheese pizza left in one of the three boxes.

"Jacob? You want any more pizza, man?"

"No."

Owen tosses one slice onto a plate and holds the other in his mouth as he gathers and stacks the pizza boxes before heading out of the front door.

He forces the boxes into the already full trash bin with all his weight, then finally takes a bite out of the slice dangling from his teeth.

Kyra's bedroom light flashes on and off repeatedly, catching his attention.

🦋 🦋 🦋 🦋

"If my Dad sees you playing with that light switch, he's gonna have a damn fit, Jessica. Stop!"

"But it's so ancient. I've never seen buttons for a light switch before," Jessica laughs. "Look how when one is pushed in, the other pops out."

"It's like old *Leave it to Beaver* era Tech." Says Nekia, dragging her fingers across the carved butterflies on the bed. "I can see why you picked this room. Did you start your new butterfly collection yet?"

"Just the one over there on the wall so far.

Jessica and Alexis begin to build their overnight nests on the floor, taking up most of the little bit of space they had. Mariah and Nekia both notice the empty spot near the window by the closet. Nekia grabs her belongings, beating Mariah to the opportunity.

"There's enough room up here for someone. Bed's long enough. We can sleep feet to feet." Says Kyra climbing up.

Mariah seizes the opportunity, following behind her and positioning herself on the other end of the bed.

Nekia's jaw drops. "Ugh, Mariah. Are you seriously gonna climb up there?"

"What's wrong with that?" Says Mariah

"What's wrong with it is we don't want any fatalities below you, if you happen to roll off your cloud."

"Okay, you're going way overboard," snaps Kyra

"I'm just saying. With your weight combined with hers, you guys may break through and seriously hurt someone down here. More your weight than, Kyra's"

Alexis snickers.

Kyra narrowed her lips and glared at Nekia. "Then you should take the spot directly under Mariah."

Embarrassed, Mariah drops her head and climbs down.

"No Mariah, you can stay. She's just being a jerk. This bed is sturdy as hell. You'd have to be the weight of a cow to break through."

Nekia and Alexis suddenly look at each other and laugh, covering their mouths with their hands.

Mariah looks up at Kyra with disbelief as if she had been betrayed. "No, it's totally okay. I prefer to be on the floor anyway."

"What?" says a confused Kyra. "Did I say something wrong?"

No one answers.

Satisfied, and with a smile showing nearly every tooth in her mouth, Nekia grabs her pillow and climbs up to replace her.

Kyra watches as she fluffs her pillow. "Can you ever do anything without offending or pissing people off?"

"I tried that once." She lies down looking up at the ceiling as if she were deep in thought. "I just pissed myself off."

🦋 🦋 🦋 🦋

Owen drips a drop of dish soap in the middle of his palm and washes his hands in the kitchen sink. The smell of burning leaves blows through the window in front of him from his neighbors' yard. He scrunches his nose and covers it with his sleeve while looking out into his dark and empty backyard. With damp hands he grabs the top of the window, but it will not budge. He dries his hands and tries again, applying most of his body weight to the top of the frame, yet it still will not give.

The noise from Jacob's battery powered toys is continuous from the living room. Laser fire and sirens seemed to get louder by the minute.

"Jacob it's about time for you to take a bath," Owen says, then pounds gently at the top of the window with his fist. The playful noise continues despite his direction. "Jacob, you hear?"

He tosses the towel onto the counter and heads to the living room expecting to see Jacob at play. As he enters the noise of loud toys abruptly stops.

He then steps around the small table where they had previously placed Kyra's gifts, now covered with ripped wrapping paper, confetti, and an assortment of balloons with colorful happy birthday lettering. Pink balloons and a shiny metallic purple monkey with wide cartoon eyes and a Cheshire grin float above them.

No Jacob, just the toys.

He makes his way upstairs and peels open the bathroom door assuming maybe Jacob had followed his instructions to prepare for his bath.

No Jacob.

He crosses the hallway to his room. Empty.

"Jacob!?"

He gives the bedroom a once over as he makes his way to the window, kicking scattered toys from his path. As he leans into the window, he discovers his son, standing at the tree line and staring into the woods.

"Damn it, boy!"

Owen quickly skips down the steps and into the kitchen where the water is running from the faucet full blast. Confused, he grabs the faucet handle, when the once stuck kitchen window slams shut, splitting the glass in the corner. He draws back his hand and for a moment, was paralyzed with shock.

Looking out of the cracked window he could see Jacob disappearing into the woods. He immediately shuts off the water and bursts through the screen door to the backyard.

"Get back here now!" He stops in the middle of his lawm. "Jacob! Come here now!"

Behind him, the screen door creaks open. When he looks back, Jacob is coming out; rubbing his eyes as if he had just awakened.

CHAPTER 14

LET THE GAMES BEGIN

(9:04 PM)

After taping the light-blue gift bag shut, with a glittery decorated rainbow on the front and back, Owen shakes off the loose glitter that fell on his sheets. The last thing he has to do is sign the card, which he does quickly, with a Sharpie pen and a satisfied smile on his face.

Carefully, and as quietly as he could—with the old wood floor popping beneath his feet—he approaches Kyra's room while holding the bag in his fingertips. The card slips from the string that tied it to the bag, and fell to the floor; so, he bends to retrieve it.

The girls are inside, nearly quiet; with the exception of Kyra, all the girls are swiping their screens and texting.

Mariah notices the movement in the narrow opening, seeing Kyra's father. She soon ignores it and continues on her phone. Nekia also takes notice—having a better view from her high-up angle—of Owen fiddling with something.

Nekia, with her cell phone in tow, scoots closer to Kyra and laughs. "Oh my God, look at this video some girl posted." When Kyra leans in to watch, Nekia looks up to the door, once again.

Kyra laughs hysterically. "That's crazy. Play it again." She reaches in to press the play button.

"Why don't you have your own phone by now?" Asks Nekia.

Owen had just finished attaching the card's string back on to the bag, when he overhears the conversation.

Kyra drops her smile. "Because my dad sucks, that's why." She swipes more through Nekia's phone. "You would think with me turning sixteen, that I would have had a sweet-sixteen party, but..." she shakes her head. "I don't even want to talk about it. Oh, but have you seen this video?"

Owen drops his head and places the gift bag in front of her door, when the doorbell rings.

❀ ❀ ❀ ❀

Through the glass of the front door, Owen can see two figures standing in front of orange and white flashing lights in the background. He checks his watch.

"Yes?" He yells a few feet from the door.

"Mr. Mosley? My name is Detective Hayward. I was wondering if we could ask you a couple questions, sir."

Every possible scenario, of why a detective could be at his door, races through his mind. He hesitates for a moment to open it, but eventually flips the latch, gently pulling the door open.

A young, attractive Hispanic woman stood before him, professionally dressed in a gray suit, and dons an access badge—with her picture—draped around her neck. An older gentleman next to her pulls his unzipped, black Columbia jacket to one side, flashing his detective badge.

"Good evening, Mr. Mosley—sorry to bug you this evening. But Ms. Delgado and I have a few questions for you, if you have a moment." He removes a pen from his jacket. "Ms. Delgado is with Child Protective Services."

Owen rolls his eyes. "Here we go. Yeah... no, I don't mind. But my daughter is having a slumber party. I don't have to go anywhere do I?"

"No, sir."

They back up, as Owen steps out onto the porch. Down the street, he sees a familiar car being loaded onto a tow truck.

"What's this all about?"

"You're familiar with Kat Dillon, correct?" Detective Hayward asks.

"Yes. She's the social worker that came by my house some time ago."

"Okay."

"Well, you probably don't recognize the vehicle down the street, but that's the issued vehicle she uses to visit her cases."

"No, now that you mention it. I do remember her driving that car when she came. Is something wrong?"

The Detective and Social worker glance at each other, then back to Owen.

"Kat hasn't returned to the office. Her car is abandoned here. And you're her only case within a five-mile radius." Ms. Delgado snaps.

"Wait, hold on. You think I have something to do with her being gone?"

"No-No, Mr. Mosley. I'm strictly here to ask a few questions... not accuse you of anything."

Ms. Delgado grimaced after Owen's response. "If you don't mind, I'm going to handle the paperwork with the tow truck driver. He looks like he's all finished over there."

"Okay, I'll be right there." Says Detective Hayward. He turns back to Owen, scribbling in his notebook. "So, she hasn't come by here at all?"

266

"Not that I know of. I haven't spoken with her at all. Neither have my kids."

"How do you know?"

"Well, I'm sure they would've told me if she showed back up and I wasn't here. My kids don't keep secrets like that from me."

"Yeah. But you never know Mr. Mosely." He continues writing.

❀ ❀ ❀ ❀

"I don't know." Says Kyra.

"Come on. You have to pick, everyone else did." Orders Nekia.

"Jesus, Okay—Okay," She looks to the ceiling. "Umm, how about, Justin Bieber?"

"Oh my God, he's gross now, no!" Says Alexis, "he was cuter when he was a kid."

"Well, he's my choice. And I picked so..."

They all sit in silence for a moment, looking at each other to see who was going to break the awkward silence.

Alexis sits up. "Did you see the new boy who—"

"Wait, are we seriously gonna sit here and talk about boys like the typical, little teenage girls you see on TV?" Says Nekia. "Let's do something else."

Kyra tucks her pillow in her lap. "Something else, like what?"

Mariah, who was quiet most of their conversation, finishes slipping on her fuzzy, black and peach color, two-piece pajama set, complete with teddy bear ears on the hood.

Nekia raises her eyebrow and bites her lips to hold in her laughter.

Mariah sits up on her knees. "Can I use your bathroom?"

"Yeah. You know where it is. The door sticks sometimes, so you may have to pull a little harder to get out if you close the door too tight."

Nekia watches Mariah leave, then leans to Kyra's ear. "Why on earth did you invite *Moo*riah to the sleep over?"

"What? Why are you calling her that?"

"That's what everyone's been calling her since she gained all that weight," the other girls nod their heads agreeing.

"Doesn't mean that it's right, or that *we* should." Says Jessica.

"Did you see the look on her face when you made that comment about being as heavy as a cow?"

Kyra's jaw drops. "Holy shit."

Nekia nods her head, "yep, classic. You punched her in the gut and didn't even know it."

Jessica frowned. "It's not like she meant to, Nekia."

"Well, people wouldn't be so mean to her if she would stand up for herself. She's always crying about something, allergic to everything. She's such a fucking misfit sometimes. I bet you, she'll end up calling her Mom in the middle of the night to come and pick her up."

Mariah, all sad-eyed and head-hanging, steps halfway back into the bedroom door, locking her eyes on the pink, paisley-print sleeping bag at her bare feet. She spit out a short, disgusted laugh and shook her head. The girls instantly clam-up, knowing she couldn't have possibly gone to the bathroom that fast. The look on her face confirmed to them, that she had been listening the entire time.

"You know, maybe I do eat a lot. You'd think that when you look at how much I've changed, right," she nervously clenches and releases her dominant fist over and over, as if squeezing an invisible stress ball. "I have a lot going on. More than you know. I thought eating was the reason I was getting bigger, but I don't eat any different than before. Well, I found out I may have what Grandma had before she passed." She sniffles. "And on top of all the allergies I have, and other issues, my mom accuses me of sneaking food. She says it's 'cause I'm 'stressing out about stuff, and I'm using it as a coping mechanism.'" She shoves her hands behind her back, to hide their nervous twitching. She glances up to Nekia. "Like, always trying to be funny all of the time, to take the attention off yourself; or teasing people. Or shaving your head to hide the pain of your parent's divorce. Smoking, too."

Nekia digs her fingers into her pillow, scrunching her face into a painful frown. Every bit of that truth being told, begins to surface on her face. "You have no idea what you're talking about, so, shut the fuck up." She snaps.

"I know more than you realize. I know the reason for the divorce, too. If you don't stop talking crap about me, everyone else will, too." She finally looks from the floor to Nekia. "Kyra, can I talk to you for a second, please? In the hallway?"

Kyra scoots past an angry, yet silent, Nekia, then steps down the ladder and out into the hallway with Mariah. Kyra looks at her, amazed, and chuckles under her cupped hand over her mouth.

"Where did that come from?" she laughs more.

"I'm sorry. I just got tired of her shit. I gained weight, I'm not stupid. I just want to have fun and she's wrecking it for everyone."

"I know, I'm sorry. I know we all are good friends. We all have problems."

"It's okay. I feel better now." She smiles, then points to the floor behind Kyra.

Kyra turns around to the rainbow bag, twinkling on the floor next to the door.

"I knew I saw your dad at the door doing something. Wasn't sure what." She picks up the bag for Kyra, standing there and staring as if she didn't know what to do, then hands it to her. "It was at the same time Nekia asked you about your dad, and you said he sucked."

270

Kyra accepts the gift with mixed emotions—cradling it in one hand and running her fingers on the glittered spectrum.

"Okay, I'll leave you here to stare at the bag because I gotta pee. But you probably should open it." She thunders down the hall like a chubby speed-walker, then enters the bathroom, closing the door tightly.

As Kyra reenters the room, popping open the tape sealing the bag; she notices a familiar box on the inside. A flicker of a smile short-circuits and disappears as quickly as it happened. She opens the small card dangling from a fragile string. Horror strikes her face. She drops the bag, as if it had sent an electrical shock into her palms, then storms over to her desk—dropping hard into her chair.

"What? What's wrong?" Jessica asks.

Kyra just buries her face in her palms, without an answer.

Jessica crawls over and grabs the gift bag, then reads the card.

From: Mom and Dad

"Oh shit!" Jessica snatches the card from the bag and tucks it in her pocket. She pulls out the gift. A brand new and latest in cell phone models. The one Kyra had seen on television. Jessica slowly approaches her and places the box on the desk in front of her. "I'm sure he didn't mean to hurt you, sweetie. He probably signed it like that out of habit. My dad would have never given me a phone like this."

"What is it?" Asks Nekia, peeking down from above.

"Your dad must really think you like shiny stuff," says Alexis, "bag all glittery... cell phone case all sparkly."

Kyra removes her hands from her face, as Alexis turns over her new phone case—with a large sparkling white butterfly in the middle.

"Okay, I have to say something," says Jessica, "I didn't come over here to be depressed or start some soap opera bullshit. I came over to celebrate my girl's birthday, who I missed so much!" She gently hugs Kyra, bringing her, somewhat, out of her funk. "Are we done bitching and fighting, please? Can we please have some fun tonight?"

"Like what?" Asks Alexis.

"Do you have any games, Kyra?"

"Not anything new. They all got burned up in the accident."

Jessica, biting her bottom lip, looks around the room curiously. The girls watch as she crawls, over the blankets on the floor, to the bedroom door. Her bottom lip pops out from her mouth as she grins widely, looking down the dark, dimly lit hallway.

"I know what we can do?" She says, sitting down in front of them.

"What?" Alexis and Kyra say, simultaneously.

"The perfect game, for the perfect house."

"Okay, what?" Orders Nekia.

"Before I explain. Please tell me you have a radio."

❦ ❦ ❦ ❦

"Thank you, again, for your time, Mr. Mosley." Detective Hayward extends his hand. "We will be in touch if we have any other questions for you."

Owen shakes his hand firmly. "I wish I could help more, and I hope you find her."

Ms. Delgado—finally not distracted by the tow truck, and able to give Owen her undivided attention—takes one step up to respectfully shake his hand, however, emits a doubtful expression meanwhile. "Yeah, I'm sure you do."

"Oh, before we leave, sir, would you mind if we take a look around your property?"

A sudden chill hugged Owen from behind, followed by the feeling of someone—or something—behind him. He checks, but it's just an empty foyer and unoccupied stairway.

"Is everything okay, Mr. Mosley?" Asks the detective.

Owen spins back around. "Yeah. Umm, no, be my guest if you want to look around. I'll be here if you need me."

"Thank you, sir," says the detective, casually saluting with a limp wrist and two fingers. "Have a great night. And good luck with the slumber party."

Owen nods his head and closes the door slowly as he watches the two step-down off his porch and proceed around his home.

He backs away from the door, nearly tripping over Jacob standing behind him. He is just looking at the floor, hugging himself as if he were freezing. His skin cold and slightly drained of color.

"Daddy, I don't feel so hot."

🦋 🦋 🦋 🦋

Mariah, staring into her own eyes in the bathroom mirror, pokes at her soft, chubby, round cheeks with her finger. Her pupils sink into welling tears, until the warm tickle of the salty liquid trickles down the side of her nose and seeps into the corner of her lips.

She rolls her eyes upward and chokes down the desire to cry, aggressively wiping both sides of her face with her hands.

Slowly, she peels her pajama bottoms off and takes a seat, gasping when her bare skin touches the cool surface of the toilet. The girl's distant mutters from the bedroom down the hall are drowned out by her hissing stream of relief. She did not know why Nekia is being so mean to her, when before, they were the best of friends. *I got enough problems to deal with.*

The door jolts open a couple inches. She nearly pees on the seat to get away, but immediately remembers the tricky door Kyra told her of but could not remember for sure what the instructions were.

As she calmed herself, and continued her business, she reached for the partially opened door to close it. *Her brother may come by and see the cracked open door and think it is empty, then come bursting in with me on the toilet.*

She could hardly reach. The door only waivered back and forth with her fingertips only grazing the side. She leans in to reach a little further when a hand darts in shutting off the light switch.

She screams dropping back to her seat and breaking one of the seat bolts securing the toilet lid to the toilet.

"Jesus! Do you ever stop jacking around, Nekia?"

She grabs the toilet scrubber behind her, then uses the extension to flip the light switch. A short, blinding flicker of blue electricity from the failed bulb sends her back into darkness, but not before revealing to her, what looked like, a shadow in the corner near the tub.

"Hogh!" She claps her hand over her mouth, her eyes wide and heart shifting into overdrive.

It was only her, a sliver a light from the door, and whatever it was standing in the corner. She couldn't see much. But she could feel the change in the room's energy. Something was wrong. Without moving her eyes from the corner, she dries herself and gently pulls up her bottoms, then reaches for the door—when it snatches away from her grip, and slams shut.

She screams as loud as she can, but the air feels dense. Her scream did not travel. It was as if the sound was shoved back down her throat.

The sun had already fallen a while ago and the gap at the base of the door provides little light. With her back against the bathroom door, she twists the nob with all the strength she can muster.

She can hear herself breathing heavily. Every breath thundered in her head, like a swimmer with waterlogged ears.

The clear shower curtain gradually opens with a creepy slowness. The rings drag and squeal across the partially-rusted shower curtain rod like tiny, dull knives. It stops nearly halfway. Although she could not hear it, she could see the water, silently pouring from the bathtub's faucet.

"Hello?" She tried to whisper; except she could not hear herself speaking.

She continues tugging at the door and attempting to yell through it. Yet, there was no play in the locks or hinges. It was shut solid. The more she pounded, the heavier and thicker the door feels; it's dense, like the thick brick walls of a basement. She couldn't help but wonder if this was all a dream, with no escape.

The short, high-pitched squeal of the faucet handle turning echoes behind her. She spins around just as the last couple of droplets, drip from the faucet and into the shallow bath. The steam rises from inside the tub like a ghostly mist.

She closes her eyes—wishing it away, like she had seen in so many movies—hoping this, bad dream, will all just disappear when she opens them; then she could escape this soundproof prison.

She mashes her eyelids even tighter, breathing heavily through clinched teeth, her back and hands pressed flat against the door.

Hints of sound gradually returns around her. She could now hear the water gently sloshing inside of the tub. *It worked.* Her eyes stretch open wide. To her horror, the curtain is now fully open. Then, something speaks from it, in a faint, raspy, and shaken voice.

So Koh...Kohuk...

The words were choked and gargled.

She slams her eyes shut again. "Go-away, Go-away, Go-away." She chants, yanking, and twisting at the doorknob behind her. The water continues to splash, with the faint sounds of pounding in the tub that grows louder by the second—as though something or someone were thrashing about inside of it. "Go away!" She yells.

Abruptly, the room falls silent beside her rapid breathing. Her eyelids flutter, hesitating before opening fully. She's horrified when she realizes, she's now standing beside the tub—a tub not filled with clear water as she thought—but with, what seemed like, black...

Before she could think, gasp, or scream, two hands—with fingers thin, narrow, and completely covered with the black goo—spring up from the dark pool, instantaneously grabbing her wrists. She tries to pull away, but its strength is too much, yanking her inside of the bathtub, headfirst. She kicks frantically, while slumped over the side of the tub, with her head fully submerged in the thick muck. The black liquid travels up her neck and back, in a veiny, web-like fashion. She gradually gives up the battle as her arms and legs weaken, then fall limp to the floor.

CHAPTER 15

KILLER IN THE DARK

(9:42 PM)

"I'll let you sleep down here for tonight. You probably won't get much sleep upstairs with all the girls anyways," Owen says, tucking Jacob under a blanket on the couch. "Sick or not, I better not come downstairs to you-know-what playing on the television. You hear?"

"I won't." Jacob snuggles against the back of the couch. "Can I have the fan on."

"I'll put it on low for you. But no higher." Owen grabs a clear, acrylic cup with a lid and hard plastic straw—packed with ice and filled with water—and places it on the end table next to him. "Here you go. Should be nice and cold for you later, if you need a drink."

"Kay."

"Dad's gonna go upstairs and hide for a bit. If you need anything, come and get your sister or me." He kisses Jacob's forehead and gently strokes his head-full of soft curls. "Goodnight."

"Dad?" Jacob points to the balloons.

"What? You want one of the balloons, too?"

Jacob smiles. "The shiny-purple monkey one."

"You want that creepy looking thing?"

He nods.

"Okay," he begins untying it, "just don't be mad if your sister decides she wants it. But by the looks of this thing, I'm quite sure she won't mind." He places the balloon string, with a book posing as an anchor, on the floor. "Anymore requests?"

Jacob shakes his head 'no', while looking up at the balloon—twirling in slow circles from the gentle breeze of the fan. Its large, toothy, cartoon grin reminds him of the Cheshire Cat, from Alice in Wonderland, as it spins like a rotating sign above.

🦋 🦋 🦋 🦋

Owen stops at Kyra's door, listening to the muttered conversation behind it. With the gift bag gone from where he had placed it, his heart grows heavy, disappointed that he did not get to witness her joy, or even receive the slightest 'thank you' for his financial sacrifice. A deep breath holds in his pain and tears, as he lumbers to his bedroom.

"Okay, you only have three minutes. So, when the music stops, your time is up," says Jessica.

Kyra's door bursts open just as Owen shuts his. Jessica, Kyra, and Nekia thunder down the hallway, leaving Alexis kneeling in a corner while covering her eyes with both hands.

"six-seven-eight..." She counts aloud.

The girls giggle and scramble, shutting off the hall light—drenching themselves in darkness. Nekia quickly enters Jacob's room, while the other two run downstairs. She immediately scans the room to locate her hiding spot, then shuts off the lights.

"...twenty, twenty-one, twenty-two..."

Nekia hears Alexis counting louder, a sign that her time is running short. She desperately jams her body under the bed, pushing through a barricade of toys, misplaced socks, and loose shoes.

"...twenty-eight, twenty-nine, *thirty*!"

Nekia freezes in place and fixes her eyes on the partially opened door.

Alexis uncovers her eyes and presses the play button on her cell phone—linked by Bluetooth, to a large, portable, wireless speaker. The music from the slasher movie *Halloween,* plays loudly through its speakers, telling the hidden players to beware, the killer is on the move.

Alexis wastes not a second of her two-minute time limit to locate as many players as she can. Barely able to make out her path in the dark, she feels her way to Jacob's room.

Nekia's eyes had already adjusted to the darkness under the bed, and winces when Alexis appears, her light-colored ankles and house shoes stand out in the dark.

Alexis steps in, feels her way around the room as quickly as possible, nearly tripping and rolling her ankle on one of the race cars in her path. She stops at the foot of the bed, her toes stop just short of Nekia's forearm. She feels her way down the frame of the bed and prepares to search underneath it.

Downstairs, Jacob whimpers in his sleep, beads of sweat glisten on his forehead. He rolls over, throwing his arms over the arm of the couch and accidentally knocks his cup of water to the floor.

Alexis hears the thud, and quickly hustles through the door and to the stairwell. Nekia conceals her giggle by burying her face in the stuffed animal in front of her, immediately cringing from the smell of stinky feet.

Satisfied that Alexis will not have enough time to find her after searching for the others, she relaxes, then begins clearing a path to crawl out into the open, when the door creaks open, yet again. Like a startled rabbit, she ducks behind the toys, peeking over the stinky koala bear that reeks of little boys' feet. Then, just using her upper body strength, she pushes herself back underneath the bed, slow and easy.

❦ ❦ ❦ ❦

Alexis's noisy drumming down the stairs—and dragging her hand along the banister, like a child eager to see her gifts on Christmas morning—does not wake Jacob. Nor does the sound of her clumsily tripping over the cord of the fan and ripping it from the wall socket, despite her advantage of having the television light aid her search. If she is to win this game of *Killer in the Dark,* she had to be quick. She had to find them all.

She ignores the accident, peeking behind the couch, then jerking the window curtains open to merely a dark view of the backyard.

The fan blades gradually stop, causing the grinning-monkey balloon to slow from rotating next to Jacob.

Alexis looks around the room. Jessica, crouched next to the bookshelf behind a plastic-potted Silver King houseplant, covers her mouth with both hands, as Alexis passes only inches in front of her. If the eager killer had only slowed—just for a moment— she would have seen the soft television glow against Jessica's light skin in her dark hiding space.

Assuming she had heard something from the dining room, Alexis hurriedly races in that direction, catching the balloon string with her arm. She snatches away from it, loosening the string from

283

its literary anchor. Oddly, it twirls only once and stops abruptly when it faces Jacob, as if some force were holding it in front of his sweating, whimpering face.

🦋 🦋 🦋 🦋

Ugh, why did she come back here? Nekia does not take her eyes off the feet at the door; however, something was different about Alexis's feet. She could only see from the shins down, pale skin and with black stuff dripping to her ankles and floor, streaming down her shins and between chubby toes. *Who the hell, is that? That's definitely not Alexis.*

Nekia prepares to reveal herself, but then stops when the girl takes a step inside, switching the light on... then off again. Nekia can hear her choke during a giggle, spitting black stuff onto the floor at her feet. She does it again, turning the lights off and on, but this time quicker, building up speed like a strobe light until she stops in the off position.

When Nekia's eyes adjust again, the girl is gone. She can no longer see the feet in front of her, but notices wet, black footprints leading to the side of the bed.

Frightened, and with her eyes bucked open, she looks toward the direction the footprints lead. Her nostrils flare with each slow, heavy breath. Nothing is there that she can see, and nothing to the other side of her. The only thing behind her is the wall, which she feels with her feet. She holds her breath to listen

284

for any movement; the only auditory stimulation being the gentle wind blowing against the window. The silence is interrupted by a pop and some giggling downstairs.

❦ ❦ ❦ ❦

"We want what's ours, boy!" A thunderously deep voice of a man yells in Jacob's dream.

Jacob rounds the corner into their upstairs hallway in a full sprint—yet moving in slow motion. With a look of terror in his eyes, he glances back to see if his pursuers were close behind. The hall and staircase glow with an orange flickering light behind him. He falls to the floor in front of the bathroom, then scrambles his way inside, on all fours, and backs away in fear, as the orange light grows closer toward him, from the hall.

He attempts to stand, but is held firmly in place, as if he were glued to the floor. When he looks down, his butt and feet are sinking in some sort of black liquid, pulling him in like quicksand. He reaches for the sink, but some unseen force grabs his arms, then pins him back—laying him flat in the black pool. He can feel a force pushing on his chest as he sinks down inside. The light comes through the door, followed by heavy footsteps that approach as he sinks deeper. The orange light flickers against the walls and ceiling, just as he is fully submerged into the oily liquid— where he panics—choking and gasping for air.

Suddenly, he can breathe again, and all becomes well while he floats silently in the calm, oily blackness. His stomach tickles as if he were falling, then he lands on his back upon a hard, wooden surface. Four white strips of light tear through the darkness above him, evenly spaced apart, like wood panels and illuminate his face. The second strip from the right has an odd shape—broken and jagged—while the other three were identical. The sound of something heavy dragging across the floor, echoes around him. The white strips of light gradually disappear, as if whatever is being dragged, blocks the light shining through on his face. Feeling trapped, he pounds his fist above him, screaming, but not a sound leaves his lips.

On the couch, Jacob acts out his dream, waving his arms and hitting the monkey balloon next to him. It floats freely toward Jessica, who's still hiding behind the plant. The grinning face grows closer and closer to her. The sight of it gave her the chills, yet she still reaches out to grab it, but it slows, stopping just beyond her reach. She leans out a little further, but then is startled by a shadow suddenly passing in front of the television. She pulls back a little and waits. Nothing. *What the hell was that?* The monkey balloon gazes at her without movement. She tries grabbing it again, reaching out even further for the balloon.

"Dead!" Alexis yells, lunging out from behind the couch and grabbing Jessica's wrist.

Jessica screams, the balloon pops, and Jacob's eyes jolt open. Both are cue ball white.

The slasher music stops, ending Alexis's three-minute killing spree.

286

The girls are so busy giggling from the scare of the balloon, that they don't notice Jacob's current state when they retreat to the stairs, nor do they see Kyra crawling out from under the dining room table and creeping up the stairs behind them.

"Rah!" She screams.

Alexis and Jessica scream again, running up the stairs away from her.

❀ ❀ ❀ ❀

Hearing the commotion downstairs, Nekia reaches out and pulls herself from underneath the bed. *Did she slip out without me seeing her?* She pans the room chuckling at her own fear, when her arm is grabbed and yanked with such strength and force, she slides across the floor toward the closet and hits the wall. She scrambles to her feet.

Between her and her only escape, stands a black curvy figure—hunched over, choking and spitting, with black goo hanging thick and long from her lips. Nekia could barely see her face, but she realized who it was in front of her.

Nekia rolls her eyes. "Very funny *Moo*riah. I know it's you!" She walks past Mariah to the light switch and swipes upward, flicking it on with the ridge of her hand. She spins around to address her, "You're not even–" She pauses... she's horrified when she discovers, she is in the room alone. Just a toy-cluttered room and a messy empty bed. "Mariah?" She says shakenly, and for the first time pronouncing her name the way it was meant to be.

It was so quiet, that she could hear her heart pumping through her chest, like a small fist jabbing out a rhythm from within. She trembles, licking her lips as she carefully takes a step back toward the door.

Laughter cracks the silence as Jessica, Kyra and Alexis run past to Kyra's room.

Startled, Nekia whirls around, gasping with tense, stretched-out lips and raised eyebrows. The door slams closed in front of her. She lunges for the doorknob twisting and pulling, when the closet door creaks open in the far corner. She turns her head to see something stepping out, when the light flickers out.

🦋 🦋 🦋 🦋

The girls are all standing by the portable speaker in the hallway.

"Let's do it again. That was awesome," says Alexis. "I know a perfect hiding spot."

Kyra shakes her head. "No way. That was kinda creepy—and this house creeps me out enough as it is sometimes." She looks down the hall and turns on the light. "Where's Nekia? Or Mariah?"

288

The girls all look at each other. "Mariah had to go to the bathroom before we started, remember? Thought she had to go number one, but she's probably blowing things up in there."

"Gross." Kyra laughs. "Then where's Nekia?"

Jessica shrugs her shoulders. "Let her stay hidden. Who cares?" She laughs.

"Shh—Shh," Kyra stops them and listens. "You here that?"

They all stop, holding extremely still and rigid in place; the girls all stay silent so they can hear exactly what Kyra had heard. Suddenly, Kyra takes off down the hallway to her brother's room, and the girls curiously follow. As they get closer, they can hear pounding from the other side of the bedroom door.

Kyra pushes at it, but it will not open. Soon, the girls join her in the attempt, slamming their bodies into the wood structure, repeatedly.

"Open it!" Yells Kyra.

Owen rips open his door. "What the hell is going on, ladies? I can get past your music for that game, but this—"

"Dad—Dad, it's Nekia! She's stuck in the room and we can't get the door open! Hurry, something's wrong with her!"

Owen, wearing shorts and tank top, rushes down the hall and hastily nudges the girls to one side. With all of his strength, he strains against the door; he frantically pushes, twists, and yanks the doorknob. It will not budge. With the girls standing behind him as feeble witnesses, he slams his entire weight, shoulder first, into it, until it finally breaks free.

Nekia comes rushing out—as if a wild, hungry animal is on her tail—pushing past everyone, and nearly falling when Kyra catches her by the shoulders. Nekia pulls away from her, deflecting her hands; her eyes are wide while taking deep, quick, hyperventilating breaths.

"Hey—hey! What—" says Kyra, confused, her arms outreaching for Nekia.

"She—She..." Nekia trembles, choking out her words in between bursts of rapid breaths, then pointing a quivering finger toward the room.

Owen looks inside of the room.

Nekia's eyes jolt open. She presses her back against the wall in fear, as if something were going to jump out when Owen opened the door. Her hands shake violently as she covers her face.

Owen can see nothing horrifying... unless she feared the stench and clutter of a little boy's room. He steps inside, kicking a few things with his toes.

Kyra notices a cut on Owen's shoulder, and immediately grabs one of Jacob's dirty shirts from the floor—leaving Alexis and Jessica staring at the, once, strong-spirited girl, now folded and crying on the hallway floor.

Kyra surprises Owen from behind, as she presses the inside of the shirt to his cut. He soon realizes her intentions when she shows him the blood-stained shirt. *Oh shit.* Immediately, he heads to the main bathroom.

"What's wrong?" Says Jessica, turning her attention to Nekia.

"Mariah, she was—"

Suddenly, Mariah appears from the bathroom, nearly running into Owen when he reaches for the doorknob.

"I was what?" She says, rubbing her eyes. "You guys have any pizza left? I'm hungry."

🦋 🦋 🦋 🦋

(10:45 PM)

A car speeds off, with a petrified Nekia inside—staring through the back window at the girls, then looking up to the house behind them.

They all watch as the taillights disappear in the distance.

Owen turns to the girls. "Can I ask what it was you guys were doing?"

"Playing *Killer in the Dark.*" Alexis blurts out with a smile.

"Okay, in the house, ladies." He shakes his head, and tucks in his lips to avoid smiling. "Well, I'm gonna suggest no more of that for tonight. Couldn't you guys play dress up or something?

Maybe do each other's nails." He smooths down the sticky side of the two Band-Aids on his shoulder.

"That's so *lame*, Mr. Mosley." Says Jessica. "Maybe if we were like, living in the 1950's, or something."

CHAPTER 16

PLAYTIME IS OVER

(1:47 AM)

Jacob is sound asleep, dreaming of running through an endless field of grass while chasing an unusually-large, white butterfly. With every leap, he almost has it within his grasp. It seemed to be taunting him. Allowing him to get close enough to think he has a chance, but the faster he runs, the further in front it leads. Every bound made the grass grow taller. What once started out as ankle-high blades of uncut grass, now reaches above his head like some strange weed. He picks up speed and leaps in the air, trying to fly like he felt he could, and he almost does—when he stumbles over a rock sticking out from the dirt. He fell, for what seemed like forever, through the ground and beyond, until he hit the bottom of darkness.

As Jacob lifted his head from his dream, he felt a cool breeze travel over his moist skin. He rubbed his eyes and realized... he was in the forest—under the night sky—however, not just anywhere in the woods. He was under the treehouse, still sporting his blue pajamas. *This doesn't feel like a dream.*

He touched and rolled the dirt below him between his fingers. It was cool and moist. Like mud should be. But if he can feel it, then he definitely is not dreaming. *Oh no. Dad's gonna be mad.*

He sits on his knees, dusting off the dirt and debris from his hands while gazing up at the treehouse.

"Dennis?" He yells. *Maybe he's home.*

Getting no response, he makes his way to the ladder and hesitates, before ascending into the dark, square hole above him.

When he enters, he reaches in his pocket and removes the tiny flashlight he'd taken from his father's toolbox. Jacob never saw him using it and was always fascinated by the brightness of the twelve little, led UV bulbs inside. And with all the dark corners in his room, he made sure to keep it on him at all times. The narrow, bright beam disintegrates every bit of darkness in its path, as he holds it in front of himself like a tiny light saber.

Slowly, he enters the room he and Dennis played in previously, when a loud screech, just outside the window next to him, tore through the silence. Startled, he loses his balance and falls back, landing against the wooden toy chest behind him. He fumbles with the flashlight, before aiming it toward the window and sees the ghostly-face of a large barn owl, perched on a branch—staring back at him. One more screech is conjured, and the owl quickly spins its head in the opposite direction—then subsequently, flies off into the night. Jacob drops his arms limply and lays back, taking in a few deep breaths of relief.

After calming his heart, he gathers himself. The flashlight catches the corner of the toybox. *Something's different.* It was not the box that looked well taken care of before. It had lost its finished gleam, is dustier, and a bit aged and chipped.

Jacob kneels to open it. The hinges moan like an old treasure chest being opened for the first time. He looks inside. It is just as dusty and empty as his surroundings—not full of the bright, colorful toys he had seen and played with. It's now just an old dusty box.

Just then, a feeling comes over him, as if he were not alone and his every move is being watched. He spins around, aiming his flashlight around the room and in every corner.

"Hey..." He whispers.

He waits for a moment. Seeing nor hearing anything, he reaches to close the box, when he notices the gaps between the wood panels. The second gap had an odd, familiar shape from the rest. He shines his light on them, feeling the groves in the wood. A part of his recent dream flashes through his mind. The blackness and strips of light that appeared above him in an instant. The jagged hole in the middle. *It's the same hole. Like the one in my dream.*

Inside the box—near the far end—is what looks like a tan piece of rope, lumped and wrapped around a piece of metal bar. He inspects it a little more and finds the rope leads down, beneath the box, tied to the handle inside with a cow hitch. Jacob knew this type of knot, from seeing his grandmother wrap the long strap of her purse around the back of her seat when they went to restaurants, or places where there were a lot of people.

Grandpa would say, *"there you go again; cow hitching your* damn *purse to the back of your* damn *chair. Ain't nobody gonna steal your precious belongings here. Why didn't you leave it in the car; not like ya paying for the food anyways."* He'd chuckle. Grandma would just leer at him. *"If they try and take my purse, they'll take me with it."*

Jacob fishes the end of the rope out with his finger and pulls it inside. It doesn't have much length on it… maybe two-inches at the most. The end is frayed, not cut. He knocks on the wood twice. A hollow bottom. He tries aiming his flashlight into the hole he fished the rope from, but the thick knot is in the way. Even with his bright light shining into the jagged hole, between the spaced panels, could not reveal anything to him.

Curious, he looks around the box, inspecting the sides and discovers drag marks on the opposite end—drag marks that seemed to be caused by the repeated dragging of the heavy toybox.

Using the totality of strength his small body could muster, he tries to push the box along the direction of the previous drag marks, but it won't budge. He tries again. His soiled, muddy feet slide under him, unable to gain traction.

Jacob checks the front of the box, then behind it, discovering an old, wood plank—part of the wall of the treehouse—wedged behind the box and the wall. He yanks on the lodged, dusty piece of wood, until freeing it.

Satisfied, he tries again, pressing his feet on the side this time, and forcing the box with his legs. It slides easily, as he stretches out his legs as far as he can, until the box is halfway over the hole that was beneath it. While both excited, and in fear of what lies in the dark hole, he accidentally drops his light into it, where the sudden jolt causes the light to shut off completely. *Crap!*

With a touch of curiosity—nevertheless, even more fear—he sits on the side of the hole, takes a deep breath, and reaches inside to fish out the tiny light. His fingertips locate it, and he rolls it toward himself, getting it within his grasp.

Jacob cradles the flashlight to his chest, and looks down into the dark hole. He hesitates, worrying about what he would find beneath the toybox once he got his light working again. *Maybe I should just go home and tell Dad. I'll be in big trouble for sure.*

His sense of adventure and curiosity overrides his fear. He taps the flashlight on the floor and twists the top. A bright beam shines up to his face, but also on the face of Dennis—who is now quietly standing close behind him.

Jacob closes his eyes, and aims the beam down into the shallow pit, then opens them slowly. *Whew.* Relieved nothing jumped out at him, he moves his light up to the middle of the hole, stopping when the tops of a pair of old, blue and white tennis shoes become visible. His heart beats heavily through his tiny chest; his hands shake, making his beam quiver on its target. Slowly, he moves the light further up, revealing the decayed remains of a child with a small, dirty, white ball beside him.

He scrambles back on one hand, while holding his flashlight tight in his grip, tucked tight to his chest, with the other. His heart beats even harder, thumping against the flashlight shining up beneath his chin—pointing up at the bottom of his face, as if he were a narrator, preparing to tell a creepy campfire story.

His first thought is to get out of there as fast as he can, without looking back. But then, it suddenly hit him. The clothes the child had on. There is something about the clothes. Cautiously, he crawls back to the hole, ignoring every drop of his intuition, and snubbing the little voice in his head that tells him to run.

He lay on his belly, pulling himself close enough to the edge to peer over the side, and aims his light on the decayed body, once again. Something around its neck, hanging down into the ribcage, shimmers against the light.

A noise quickly approaches—shuffling feet that come to a stop behind him. He spins around with his flashlight. It's Dennis; he's staring at Jacob coldly, and his demeanor is a little darker than it was before. He seemed angry, staring at Jacob trembling on his knees in front of him.

"He—Hey, Dennis. You scared me."

He doesn't answer him. He doesn't blink.

Jacob aims at him with his beam. Dennis does not flinch, nor do his eyes wince, despite the sudden brightness. Instead, they roll upward with a wet, sticky sound. His mouth stretches open, long and narrow, before letting out the deafening sound of a high-pitched whistle.

Jacob covers his ears and quickly runs past him, toward the exit, climbing down as fast as he could. He only looks up once to see if Dennis is behind him. And he is. Staring down from the blackness inside. His virtually-pale face fades away in the surrounding darkness.

Just then, Jacob loses his grip. His right leg slips through the rungs of the ladder as he falls, doing a half-summersault before hitting the ground below.

🦋 🦋 🦋 🦋

With his elbows on his knees, and chin dragging up and down the length of his index fingers—that are pressed together, and pointed upwards, like two pistols under his face—Owen sits in deep thought and concern. A nurse, on the way to radiology whilst pushing an older, male patient in a wheelchair, nearly runs over Owen's feet.

Just then, Rose and Edmond emerge from the room Jacob is in. Owen dips around a corner before they can see him; he waits, before peeking out to see if they had left. He can see Rose searching the ER for him, as she walks out with her husband. She nearly catches a glimpse of him, but he drops his head, slipping out of her sight and around the corner again. *I cannot take much more of this. I can't.*

Moments later, he straightens his t-shirt, pulling it down from the bottom, as he stands. Then, makes his way into Jacob's room.

"Hey, Daddy, I thought you'd left." Says Jacob, lying in bed with his leg wrapped tightly in bandages. A small bruise shows on his jaw line.

"No, man. I just couldn't be in here with your grandparents. You don't need to hear all what your grandmother has to say about me." He looks over to the cup next to Jacob. "How come you haven't drank any of your juice? You asked for it."

"Tastes like medicine," he says licking his lips. "Everything tastes like medicine."

Owen notices that he hadn't tied his own shoes before taking Jacob to the hospital. He bends down, almost from Jacob's sight, to tie them.

"Sorry, Dad."

"What? Why are you sorry?"

"I kinda screwed things up, huh?"

"No," he sits up and touches his hand gently, "it's not your fault. Not yours at all." He hangs his head, breaking eye contact.

"I'm starting to think I'm not such a good father." He squeezes his hand gently.

"Why? You're a good dad."

"They're right, your grandparents. I should've been there. I should've been watching you. Your Mom was..." he pulls his hand away to wipe a streaming tear from his left eye. "...she was so much better at this than I am. I wish—"

He takes in a deep breath and lets it out slowly.

"Me too, Dad," Owen looks at him. "But it's just 'cause I miss Mommy. Not cause you're not doing a good job as a Dad. It's not your fault."

Owen looks at him with deep regret in his eyes, then clasps his hands between his knees.

For a moment, they both sit in silence. Jacob looks through the window next to him, and his father still periodically gazes up at him, unsure of what to say.

"Daddy, I hafta tell you something."

"Okay, what?"

"I saw something, when I broke my leg; and I don't know how I got in the forest."

"You were sleep walking, maybe. If you don't remember, that's the only way, son."

"No, Dad." He turns to look at him. "I saw something in the treehouse."

"Jacob, not now, son," he places his hands on the side rails of the bed, "I don't want to hear anything about that damn treehouse. It's the reason why we are here tonight. Because you can't stay away from it."

"But, Dad, there's something—"

The nurse bursts in the door and their conversation comes to a halt.

"Someone should be resting and not chit-chatting." The nurse looks to Owen. "Dad should be letting you rest." She hands Jacob a little white cup with a pill inside. "Here, take this. It should help you with the pain and help you sleep a little."

"Thank you, nurse." Says Owen.

She gives Jacob a cup of water. "You hit your head pretty hard, mister. Doctor says he's fine and needs to rest, though. I don't mind you being here, Mr. Mosely. But I'm gonna tuck this little guy in." She places the sheets over him and checks the connections to his monitor. "And here's the remote for you, in case you need it, sir."

"Thank you." Owen sits in a nearby chair.

"If all is well, you should be able to leave in a few hours. Extra blankets for you are over there in the chair. So, rest, *please*, and the time here will go by much faster."

Owen nods.

302

"Goodnight, fellas. I'll be by to check on you periodically, Jacob."

"Kay."

Owen grabs a blanket and takes a seat.

"Dad?"

"Jacob, you heard her."

"What's peri*do*colly mean?"

Owen smiles. "Periodically. It means from time-to-time. Now go to sleep, son."

Jacob tilts his head back after drinking the rest of the water, as Owen removes his cell phone from his pocket.

CHAPTER 17

SNEAKY SUSPICION

(3:01 AM)

With the slumber party guests upstairs and asleep, Lorna sits in the living room, watching an episode of *The Walking Dead* on Netflix, when she receives a text.

"Thank you, again. I hope the girls weren't much trouble. It looks like we will be here a little while longer. For the rest of the night, I'm sure. Possibly returning around eight or nine in the morning. Please make yourself at home. Jinx should be okay in my room for now. She has everything she needs, so no need to let her out."

"Thank God." Mutters Lorna, then replies: *"Not a problem. I've got this. You just take care of your little one."*

She locks her phone and looks towards the upstairs.

🦋 🦋 🦋 🦋

The door to Kyra's room opens gently with a soft creak from the hinges. Lorna pokes her head inside. The room lighting is a dim soft-pink from the red cloth draped over the desk lamp. The girls are wrapped deep inside their sleeping bags on the floor, while Kyra and Mariah are foot-to-foot in the bed above.

Satisfied that the girls are in a deep sleep, she closes the door and approaches Owen's room. It's quiet inside, it seems. She places her ear to his door and leans against it. Jinx's paw lunges out from the gap under the door and snags the soft cloth of Lorna's house shoe, with one of her sharp nails. She screams, then immediately covers her mouth, pulling her bare foot away. Jinx, furiously attacks the shoe, yanking at it from under the door—clawing and ripping apart tiny pieces of cloth from it.

Lorna, being careful not to be caught by Jinx's razor-sharp fury, reaches in to quickly retrieve the, now frayed, shoe and places it back on her foot. She backs away from the door, shaken from the sound of the low growl coming from underneath.

🦋 🦋 🦋 🦋

Lorna reaches into her purse and removes a small, silver flashlight, flicking it on and off, while pointing the beam to the ceiling. Pleased, she then turns her attention to the closed basement door.

She peels the door open, staring down into the dark void. Then, points her flashlight. The light switch at the top of the staircase turns on the hanging bulb over a work bench.

She wastes no time climbing down; once there, she begins whipping her flashlight about as if she were looking for something in the darker corners of the room. Dragging her fingers along the dirty and dusty brick wall, she stops at a few points and scrapes at the surface with her fingernail, ending in her disappointment. She shines her light under the work bench, pulling out boxes and shelving from its position to check the walls behind them. *It's gotta be here. It has to.*

She then notices a heavy looking, gray, vintage steel tanker desk, and drags it from the wall. Its metal legs scrape against the concrete surface, squealing, just before she stops. She peers behind it with her light, immediately spotting a loose brick— slightly protruding from the wall.

A quick search, and some shuffling through Owen's workstation, and she finally locates a flathead screwdriver; then, commences to digging and scraping around the brick.

Positive she has found what she was looking for, she aggressively works the screwdriver to free the clue from the wall— unaware of the basement door slowly closing above. She turns off her flashlight, and puts her bodyweight into the screwdriver. The tool slips and jams her finger into the bricks.

"Fucking son-of-a-bitch!" She yells, dropping the screwdriver and proceeds to caress her hand.

306

She doesn't waste any more time dwelling on her bruised finger; she switches the screwdriver to the other hand to wiggle the rest of the brick, finally freeing and sliding it straight out. Her excitement turns to confusion, as she examines the front side of the brick. Three symbols are deeply engraved in the face. The first to the left is a triangle—with each of its three points rounded in a semi-circle. To the far right is a square with all of the corners rounded in the same fashion. Both are decorated inside with a golden, abstract design of some sort. But in the center, was merely a hole. She holds it in the direction of the workstation light, and notices that each symbol had a tiny hole in the center—the size of a thin nail—completely through the brick.

With Lorna still pinned between the desk and the wall, she places the brick and her flashlight on the desk, then struggles to stand while using her good hand; she bumps into the desk and causes her light to roll off the side. It falls onto the floor, and rolls under a shelf nearby. *Damn it!*

She shivers from a cool breeze that brushes past her face, prompting her breath to suddenly appear before her. The top step creaks as the main light above the workstation flickers; subsequently thereafter, she is plunged into complete darkness.

As quietly as she can, she kneels, feeling around for the flashlight on the floor, when the second step creaks. Her searching-hand pauses—fingers sprawled out, like an angry spider, on the floor—as she freezes in place. The flashlight rolls gently up against her pinky. She grabs it quickly and turns it on, immediately aiming the reborn beam towards the steps. Nothing.

Just shadows of inanimate objects against the walls and dark corners, created by the light.

The desk is heavy. Trying to move it with one hand seemed impossible, but with a few twists of her hips and using the wall behind her for leverage, she eventually makes her way out from behind it.

Curious, she aims her flashlight to the stairwell, again, and notices the door is no longer open. *I don't remember closing that. But why would...* She sighs. *Get back to business, girl. And hurry.*

Sudden, extremely heavy footsteps race down the stairs. She lets out a frightened whimper before aiming her flashlight like a loaded gun. This time, her beam catches the reflection of dust and dirt swirling and settling from the disturbed structure.

She whips her beam about the room.

"Hey. Who's there?" She says, just above a whisper. "Kyra? Owen?"

The energy in the room was not the same. She could feel that she was absolutely *not* alone.

A cold chill creeps across her back, like icy fingertips dragging up her skin, followed by a gentle breath that floats a few strands of her hair on her neck. The faint sound of chattering teeth by her ear sends her heart racing and drains the color from her face.

Unexpected fear locks every limb in place, her mouth wide open, afraid to let out the deep breath she had gasped in terror.

308

Adrenaline kicks in, and her body reacts. Grabbing nothing she had just uncovered, and without looking back, she cradles her flashlight to her chest and quickly makes her way around the shop desk, then briskly to the bottom of the stairs. Still, she hears the chattering teeth in the background. She bolts up the stairs and bursts through the door. Both terror, and the lack of oxygen, have her dizzy and drives her to drag her right shoulder against the wall, as she makes her way down the hallway and through the foyer, where she staggers out of the front door.

Close to tears, she reaches the bottom step of the front porch, where she slows her pace, however, continues her trek. She stops in the middle of the road and looks back. No one was behind her, yet the glimmer from the glass door, shows it is closing... ever so gently.

Up in the window of Kyra's room the curtain gradually pulls to one side. Mariah looks down at Lorna with a sinister gaze and a partial grin. She twiddles her fingers slowly, as if she were mocking her.

Lorna aims her light to the window, just as the curtain closes.

Walking backwards, she stumbles over the curb on her side of the street, then sprints off to her front door.

🦋 🦋 🦋 🦋

Owen's phone is blaring on his chest, startling him from his sleep. Quickly, he cancels the ringing before it wakes Jacob and checks the message.

"I'm so sorry. Something came up and I have to go home." Says Lorna.

"What? What's wrong?" He replies.

Owen waits. He can see the notification that indicates the message had been read, and even a dancing ellipsis pops up as if she were going to reply—but then it disappeared, and even after a few minutes, nothing was sent in response to Owen.

Scrolling through his contacts, he hits the call icon for Marley.

He answers, just before the last ring.

"Aye, bro." Marley mumbles, with his mouth barely raised above the pillow.

"Look, I'm sorry, but I need your help."

"Wassup."

"Jacob messed up his leg and hit his head pretty hard. We can't leave the hospital until morning. The lady across the street was helping out but took off, suddenly. Said something came up. Can you—"

"I'm there, bro—no worries."

Owen breathes a sigh of relief. "Damn, thanks, Mar!"

"I got you. Do I need to get the keys from her, or you want me to swing through there before I go?"

"Either way. Actually, just come get my key. She may have taken off or whatever since she ain't answering."

"Got it."

"See you soon."

They both hang up.

Marley rolls over to a woman, naked and submerged in silk sheets. "Aye—Aye!" He nudges her.

She growls back at him, for disturbing her sleep.

"Let me get your keys."

She turns to look at him. "Keys to what?"

"Your car. My brother needs me. My nephew is in the hospital."

"Uh-uh, nah. You ain't driving my brand-new car. You better get on the bus or call Uber."

Marley folds his lip in, refraining from calling her a name his mother said a man should never call a woman. "First of all, the bus ain't running. Second, after all that money I spent tonight, so we can have a good time, you won't even let me—" He sucks his teeth. "Never mind. I'll call an Uber. I'm not gonna leave family hanging like that. But that also means you have to leave."

"What? Really?" She turns to look at him. "In the middle of the night, Marley? For real?"

"You don't trust me with your car. So why should I trust you to stay in my place while I'm gone?"

She rips the covers off of herself, revealing it all. Every chocolate-brown, tattooed curve, nipple, and shaved midsection disrupted his concerns for just a moment. She storms over to her purse and removes her car keys, then throws the linked, twirling projectiles at his bare chest—generating the autonomic response in him to cringe—as the hard, key fob makes a *thunk!* against his sternum.

Marley grimaces from the pain.

"You better not fuck up my car, Marley. And don't be leaving me here all morning."

Marley rubs the middle of his chest with two fingers and shows a visibly painful expression on his face. "I promise. I'll be back before eight o'clock. Damn, you aggressive!"

🦋 🦋 🦋 🦋

After checking on the girls, Marley rummages through the kitchen cabinet for snacks—settling for a bologna sandwich, with extra bologna, cheese, and mayo. Soon after, he takes his place under a warm blanket on the sofa. He flips through virtually every channel with the remote, before stopping on a televised fight in an octagon—a rerun of a mixed martial arts match between two women, who were all bloody and sweaty at this point in the broadcast.

He raises his eyebrows with perverse interest. "Mmm, I'd love to get in the middle of *that* fight. *Please* whoop my ass." He mutters to himself.

After finishing his meal, and before the fight was over, Marley drifts off to sleep. His body sinks, comfortable and heavy, in a bed of gray corduroy cushions.

Moments later, the television mimics his previous channel surfing, cycling through stations at two-times the physical capabilities of a remote. The flickering television lit up the room, like a glass box filled with bolts of electricity, that is trying to escape, until it stops abruptly on a black screen. Not a second later, there is a thump from the back of the couch that rocks him slightly. However, Marley does not open his eyes. Instead, he adjusts himself and turns over—now facing the back of the couch.

Thump!

This time, it was hard enough to shift him from his comfortable position.

He peels his eyes open and props himself up on his elbow, looking above the back of the couch. He can see nothing but the window, with the curtains wide-open, facing the backyard.

"Sa—So cold." Someone said, with a whispering, wheezing, quivering voice, just on the other side of the couch.

Marley's eyes jolt open fully, and he pops up completely.

"I can't feel them anymore." It continues, its last word sounded as if it faded off a cliff.

A chill raced up Marley's back. He didn't dare look over the back of the couch. Wrapped like a burrito in the blankets, all he could do was slide onto the floor. He kicks and squirms, until he wiggles himself free of his cocoon, then stands and backs away, without hesitation.

The basement door unlatches, slowly opening thereafter, but then closes abruptly with tremendous force.

Marley jumps, almost tripping backwards with his feet tangled in the bundle of blankets on the floor. His eyes are wide and alert, searching his surroundings, as he backs up to the base of the stairs. Once there, he bounds up them without looking back, as if there were a rabid dog on his heels.

❀ ❀ ❀ ❀

(8:12 AM)

The deadbolt, to the front door of the Mosley residence, flips open. The single, cylinder deadbolt slides up. The doorknob turns, and Owen quietly enters, immediately looking upstairs.

It is silent.

He opens the door wide, then steps back outside, reentering shortly thereafter, with Jacob—who's smiling, while hobbling and teetering on small, silver crutches. Owen is behind him coaching, as if Jacob is riding his bike with no training wheels, for the first time.

"Okay, take it easy. Take it slow."

"I got it, Dad." The bottom of the crutch catches the rug by the door, Jacob nearly stumbles, but recovers instantly. "Whoa," he laughs. Owen swiftly assists, grabbing him by the waist. "Dad, I got it—let go."

"Outward. Not straight up and down under your arms like that, son. Do it the way the doctor said, or your gonna hurt your leg more, before you get your cast-on tomorrow."

"*Okay.*" He makes his way to the kitchen.

"No. Come on over here in the living room. You need to prop that leg up, so come sit on the couch."

Jacob obeys. Owen delicately places his son's leg up onto the couch, then props up his crutches next to him.

Owen frowns at the mess his brother left, then removes the pile of blankets from the floor, along with a spilled plate of breadcrumbs. *Damn, Marley.*

"You need anything? I'm gonna head upstairs to make sure everyone's alive."

"No. I'm okay."

"Try and lie down and get some rest."

As Owen disappears up the stairs, Jacob uses one of his crutches to drag the remote, from the other side of the couch, closer.

Owen first checks Jacob's room, to see if his brother had made his bed there for the night, but the room is in the same condition as it was before going to the hospital. He then checks the bathroom prior to inspecting his own room; both are empty, besides Jinx—sitting up in the middle of his bed.

"Marley?" Owen whispers, as he walks into his master bathroom. No Marley. *Where the hell is he? I know he wouldn't just leave the kids like this.*

He gently opens the door to Kyra's room and peeks his head in. Jessica is sitting up, swiping away at her phone through some online videos. She gives him a quick wave with a straight finger, and he smiles with a nod.

"Where's Marley," he whispers, "Kyra's uncle."

She looks over to the back corner of the room, points with her phone in hand, and grins.

Wrapped in one of Kyra's blankets—as though he were twisted in pink taffy—a large manly, hairy foot sticks out from under one end; from the other end, a gentle snoring ensues.

❦ ❦ ❦ ❦

Owen waves to Jessica—the last girl to be picked up by her parents—as she takes off down the road. He angrily turns to his brother; however, he decides he will wait to address Marley until Kyra reenters the house. After seeing the last of her friends set off, she makes her blasé ascent up the stairs and disappears through the front door.

316

"You're lucky, man. You better hope none of them little girls say anything about your grown-ass sleeping in the room with them," he shakes his head. "What were you thinking, man? A bunch of teenage girls, and a grown man."

"Bro—trust me. It's not what you think."

"You weren't drunk, and decided to pass out in there, did you?"

Marley drops his head in his hands. "Low-blow, bro." He says, then walks around Owen to the front door. "Are you really gonna put me in that category? You know I wouldn't do anything like that... coming over here drunk and all. I may have had a drink before bed, but my brother called me at the last moment needing my help. So here I am."

"Don't get me wrong, Marley. I really appreciate you coming at the last minute. But couldn't you find somewhere else to sleep? You had the couch, my room, and Jacob's—"

Marley turns around, just as he reaches the door; he steps in front of Owen, preventing him from entering the house. "You and I need to talk about something."

"You gonna tell me you're a pedophile now?"

"Damn, man. Just stop for a minute and listen to me. In all seriousness, okay?"

Owen folds his arms in front of himself and waits.

"Okay. Have you ever had anything happen to you in this house? Any incidents, or accidents?"

"No."

"No weird shit or freaky shit happening to you or the kids?"

Owen hesitates with his response, looking into his brother's frightened, bloodshot eyes. "I said, 'No'. And you're starting to sound like your friends at the bar from the other night."

"Don't lie to me, man. I can tell by how you hesitated; you're not telling me the truth." He looks around to see if anyone is listening. "I've only been in this house a few hours, and I can tell you... ain't no way in hell I'm spending another night here." He points down the street, in the direction the girl's parents had gone, "that little—big girl, Mariah," he shakes his head, "I don't know what was up with her, but she was creeping around the house last night. All up and down the upstairs hallway; mumbling to herself 'n shit."

"So, she sleepwalks?"

"When the girls got up, I heard her apologizing to them for sleeping through the whole party. Man, she didn't fall asleep until that fucking sun came up. You saw how drained she looked. You had to see it for yourself. It was beyond weird."

"Mariah has always been a little on the odd-side, man."

"Listen, last night, I had the freakiest shit happen to me, while laying on your couch. Shit bumping the furniture, but no one around. The television came on. Scared the hell out of me. So yeah I—"

318

"So, you hid in the bedroom with a bunch of little girls?" Owen laughs.

"Cut me some slack, King-O. The shit was legit scary." He wipes his face with his palm. "To be honest, I thought I was high or tripping on something. I was with this girl when you called, and thought maybe she spiked my drink with something. And maybe the shit didn't kick in until I got to your place. But that wasn't it."

Owen does not respond, yet his disgusted expression is replaced with a look of slight concern and a touch of fear.

"And judging by the look on your face, you don't seem at all surprised at what I'm telling you, huh?"

Owen sits down, then slumps backward into the weathered, Adirondack chair on the porch, he inhales a deep breath.

"I can help. I know a sensitive."

"A what?"

"Someone who specializes in shit like this."

Owen shakes his head. "No, no that's not happening."

"You need to do something. What if things get worse? What about the kids? Have you asked them if they've been seeing things?"

"You actually believe in ghosts? Seriously?"

"I *was* a little skeptical at first. But after last night..." Marley shakes his head.

"Okay, stop!" Owen snaps, standing from the chair. "Stop with your bullshit schemes, man. I ain't paying some scam artist to come in my house so you can get a cut. I have enough problems, and I'm just trying to put them all behind me."

"Bullshit schemes?" Marley turns away from him, hesitating before stepping off toward his borrowed vehicle.

"If you need money, just say so. Then I can tell you no, 'cause I don't have any myself."

Marley angrily rips the keys from his jacket pocket without a word. Owen starts after him.

"Marley! Marley!"

"I'm done, bro. I understand I did some shit in the past, but I'm tired of your disrespect, King-O," he raises the key fob and hits the unlock button—it chirps once. "I'm out!"

Owen turns up his palms. "Marley!"

He can barely hear the sleek, black luxury car when it starts. It gleams as it passes, speeding off down the road.

CHAPTER 18

GROUND FLOOR

The Next Day (3:37 PM)

Owen takes a sip from his piping-hot coffee he had grabbed before leaving the doctor's office, with Jacob. After a long night—from the previous day—he is still struggling tremendously with his sleep.

Jacob, quietly sitting in the backseat, drags his fingers over the words: "*My Wounded Warrior, Love Dad*", written in big, bold black letters on his brand-new leg cast.

He firmly knocks on the hard plaster surface with his knuckles. "Is it concrete?" He asks.

"No. And stop banging on it so hard, man. You have to give it some time to set, since it's still new."

"If I had one on each leg and arm, I'd be like a Juggernaut. Or even Iron man, huh?"

"Yeah, you could, I guess."

"I'd be strong." He strokes the bumpy surface of the cast. "When I get older, I'm gonna be a doctor and make these out of metal. Not concrete."

"It's plaster, son. Not concrete."

Jacob pauses. "If they were metal, I'd probably be strong enough to fight that man."

Owen looks in the rearview puzzled. "What man?"

"The man. The man I told you about before. With the clickety teeth. I feel sick when I see him, and I get tired, too. Not sleepy tired. But like when I get done running around the backyard all day, and I feel like I can't move tired."

"You mean you felt weak?" He becomes more concerned as he watches Jacob, digging his finger into a soft part of the cast. "Jacob! Leave it!" He snaps.

Jacob wipes the tiny bits of plaster from his fingernail onto his pants. "You think Kyra will sign it, too?"

"If you're nice to her, I'm sure she will."

Just then, a text message comes through on his phone—notifying Owen by a simple whistle sound that he set up when programming Kyra's new number into his phone.

"*It's cold.*" She says.

Owen responds, "*The heat was on seventy-five. Turn it up if you need to, but not too much.*"

"Dad, you're not supposed to text and drive." Orders Jacob.

"Right—Right, okay." He says, placing the phone back in the holder on the dash.

The ellipses pops up under his response.

"*It's cold.*" She says again.

"Okay, Kyra." He mutters, locking the screen.

🦋 🦋 🦋 🦋

At home, Kyra walks into the kitchen and heads over to the cupboard for a clean drinking glass. She rubs her growling belly while removing a carton of milk from the, near empty, refrigerator, then pours a tall glass—filling it to the top. She opens the cabinet and smiles when she discovers the package of cookies in front of her, but then curses when she feels the light weight of the empty plastic cookie tray. *Jacob, you little shit!*

She searches the cabinet for something else to snack on, when she feels the handle of the cabinet, and the floor beneath her feet, vibrate from an impact in the other room. Something seems to be pounding under the floor with a steady rhythm. Her glass of milk ripples from the vibrations that grow heavier with each blow—so heavy that it shakes the foundation, pulsing the glass across the counter.

Kyra covers her ears as she moves toward the foyer where it is the loudest. A simultaneous symphony of clanging dishes, rattling furniture, and slamming doors flood her ears as she enters the front room. The nearer she got to the front door, the harder the thumping feels through her feet. The pounding abruptly stops when the glass of milk crashes to the floor in the kitchen.

All of a sudden, the wood flexes under her feet as it weakens and cracks, bubbling up from a constant pressure below the surface, then it quickly relaxes. Abruptly, it flexed again, with an enormous, punching force, lifting her from the floor as though she is bouncing on a trampoline; the sudden jolt throws her off balance, where she falls to her hands and knees. Kyra rolls to her back just when the floor splinters out—long, jagged pieces of wood jackknife upward, like sharp, pointed, interlaced fingers. Something is coming through the floor from beneath.

She scurries away, crab walking backwards until her head and shoulders slam against the front door. Taking in tiny, rapid, high-pitched breaths, she watches as the broken pieces of floor are pulled below, snapping one-by-one as if something were trying to break free from underneath the house.

Then she saw it... the long and dark fingers of an oily, decayed hand, slowly rising from the rubble like tiny, rigid serpents. The hand grabs a piece of broken floor panel, then snatches it down below, snapping the board with ease, like a toothpick.

Kyra had seen enough; she jumps to her feet and unlocks the deadbolt, but before she could release the next lock, the deadbolt reengaged itself. She frantically unlocks it again, but the cylinder lock she had just opened reengages as well. Meanwhile, the floorboards are being ripped apart by whatever it was trying to get through behind her.

Back-and-forth she races against each lock with sweating hands, anxiously whining while yanking at the door, unable to escape.

The noise behind her suddenly stops. She can feel the presence of something near her. With quivering breaths, she slowly turns her head, but before she can see behind her, the sound of chattering teeth, accompanied by a cool breeze, is at the back of her neck. She turns back towards the door, afraid to look, but catches the reflection, in the glass of the door, of a dark figure standing closely.

She gasps and spins around—wide-eyed, screaming, with her back pressed against the door—to nothing. The foyer is as it was before. The floor, unbroken. Kyra's quick and heavy breathing slows, but her hands are trembling violently.

❦ ❦ ❦ ❦

The phone lights up again from a message preview, with yet another text from Kyra.

"It's cold."

He snatches his phone from the dashboard stand. Another message comes through, then another, spamming his phone with multiple text messages reading the same thing.

"*It's cold. It's cold. It's cold...*"

"Dad!" Jacob yells.

Owen returns his attention to the road and nearly runs into the guardrail of a sharp turn. He jerks the wheel, leaning the truck hard into the curve and squealing the tires. The sound of his tools shift loudly to one side of the bed. The backend fishtails, swerving back-and-forth on the straighter road, until he regains control.

Shaken, and with both hands death-gripping the steering wheel, he looks back to Jacob, eyes wide and in shock, breathing heavily and clenching the sides of his booster seat.

"You okay back there?"

It takes Jacob a moment to respond, slowing his breath and swallowing deep. "Yeah. Can we not do that again? Please."

❦ ❦ ❦ ❦

Owen pulls up slowly at the front of his home; he notices Kyra sitting outside on the bottom front step. Her entire body is curled in a ball, with her knees pulled to her chest. She looks up from her knees with a distraught expression across her face.

"Oh, shit. What now?" He mutters.

Owen gets out, mentally preparing himself for what was about to come. The look on Kyra's face is all too familiar to him. He doesn't address her right away; instead, he helps Jacob out and onto his little crutches. Meanwhile, Kyra approaches them from behind.

"What's going on?" Owen asks. "Why are you just sitting outside like that? Something wrong?"

"I don't know. I don't know what's wrong!?" She says, trembling. "I don't know if I'm going crazy, or if it's this damn house you moved us into, Dad!"

"Watch your mouth, Kyra!" He demands.

"No! I feel like I'm gonna die in this house. Something's not right."

"What? Die?" He stops to look back at her for a moment. "Why would you feel like you're going to die?"

Kyra stops at the base of the steps while Jacob and Owen make it to the top of the porch. "I—I don't know. This house is weird and creepy. I hate being here by myself, and I won't stay here alone anymore. And it's always cold."

"I know—I know. I got your texts."

Kyra frowns. "What? What texts? I didn't send you any text messages."

"You did. I got about thirty, or more, messages all saying the same thing. Your send button must have gotten stuck or something."

"Ugh, *no*, I didn't! I didn't even take the phone out of the box yet, *Dad*." She snaps. "It's still in the bag from the other night."

Confused, Owen stops, but Jacob keeps going into the house. "What? All of the trouble I went through for that thing and you haven't even opened it yet?" He could see the rage building in her eyes. "Is it the wrong phone or something? It's the latest—"

"You signed *Mom* on the card, Dad!" She yells. "Why would you do that!? Why would you sign Mom's name on the card when she's dead!?"

Owen feels as if he was blindsided by a car. He knew what she said was true, being he would always be the one to sign the holiday or birthday cards. He never thought the habit of signing 'Mom' in the '*From*' section would come back at him like this. He drops his head.

She takes a short, quick breath and with sad, tearful eyes looks up to him at the top of the stairs. "Do you even miss Mom?" She says gently.

The pain in her eyes... her trembling hands... even though the question angered him a touch, he knows that the slightest display of anger will set her off in a direction that he did not want to go.

"Of course I miss your Mother. I miss her dearly."

"Yeah, right." She snaps.

"Stop it, Kyra!" Jacob yells, turning around inside the door.

"Where is all this coming from, suddenly?" Owen asks.

Her eye contact is intense and her breathing, heavy. Her sadness quickly flips to anger. She looks as if she is going to explode from her emotions... and she does.

"Grandma told me!" She screams. "She told me! And it's all *your* fault that Mom is dead!" Her breaths studder through her quivering jaw.

Owen's heart sinks and his jaw drops slightly.

"What?" Says Jacob. "What's she talking about, Dad? Kyra stop being mean to Dad!" He yells, with a shaking voice.

Owen looks around to see if the neighbors are watching. "In the house. Both of you, please!" He orders.

When they all enter, Kyra pushes past Owen—and storms upstairs to her room.

"What's wrong with her, Dad? Why did she say that stuff?"

Owen throws his hands on his head. "I'm gonna go find out. Do you want to go up to your room or sit on the couch?"

"My room."

Owen carries Jacob up the long flight of stairs. He can hear Kyra's muffled sobbing, down the hall, through her partially opened door. His heart grows heavy listening to her, realizing the pain and confusion she must be feeling at her age.

"Maybe you should go talk to her?" Says Jacob, sitting on his bed.

Owen knows his six-year-old is right. He knows he should've had a talk with her for a long time now. But it was a conversation he hoped to put off for a while... maybe never even have the conversation at all. However, if the conversation does take place, he at least wants to have it occur when things got better for them. But, he feels if he doesn't speak to her now—after her outburst—there will never be any peace in the house.

"Okay. Is your leg okay? Do you need anything before I go?"

"No. I'm good."

"Alright, keep your crutches close by in case you need them."

Owen takes a deep breath, preparing himself for some crying and yelling, before stepping into the hallway. Even though Kyra's bedroom door is clear down the hallway, it seems closer than he had wanted. The sobbing stops for a brief moment and is replaced by sniffles and light coughing.

Jinx emerges from Owen's room and sits in the middle of the hallway, directly in his path. Owen stops as the large cat's eyes catch the light reflecting their individual colors.

Jinx spins around and slips into Kyra's room through the narrow opening, the gap is barely large enough for her sleek body to fit. The door slams solidly behind her.

Unsure of what to make of what just happened, Owen proceeds to her room. He knocks lightly and grabs the door handle. Locked. He knocks again, a little firmer this time. "Kyra?"

No answer.

"Baby, please open the door," He gently twists and jiggles the doorknob. "We need to have a talk."

"Can you, please, just go away!" She exclaims. "There's nothing to talk about anymore."

"You know there is," He sighs. "Your Grandmother gave you a partial truth... only a piece of what she *thinks* happened," he leans his head against the door. "Just give me a chance and I'll tell you everything that happened. At least you'll hate me for the truth."

He waits for a response. Nothing. Nothing but sniffles and a muffled grown into her pillow. He reaches for the doorknob again, but changes his mind, thinking of abandoning any more attempts to resolve the matter.

He backs away from the door, staring at the doorknob as if he were trying to will it to open. It clicks. Owen lunges for it, opening it immediately before she changes her mind. To his amazement, she is already lying back in her bed, looking down at him—just as surprised and confused as he is. Jinx is lying in a corner on top of some blankets left by the slumber party girls the night before.

Owen's mouth drops open, but he cannot find the words to say.

Kyra turns toward the wall to avoid looking at him, resting her head on the tear-soaked pillow.

🦋 🦋 🦋 🦋

Jacob, with his leg propped up on the bed, is sketching away on his cast with a pen. He is midway through a drawing of his toy robot, that's propped up against the wall next to him in a victory pose. He brushes away the small pieces of plaster that had been chiseled away by his pen, then compares his art to the real thing with a satisfied smile.

Tick.

Startled, he drops his pen to the bed, then gradually looks up to the window. *Maybe it was a big bug or something that blew around in the wind.* He pauses for a moment, waiting to see if it would happen again. He feels for his pen that had rolled under his cast, then returns his attention to his picture, shading in a square portion of his robot's leg.

Tick.

Jacob jumps, and his heart flips to a faster beat. He leans to his left to see the window better, noticing, in the bottom corner of the glass, a small, dusty, impact mark. He sits in place, his pen hand trembling. *Go away! Leave me alone.*

Crack.

Another rock, larger this time, hits the glass. Jacob nearly leaps from his skin. Instantly, he goes for his crutches next to his bed, then positions them on the floor to climb on. His metal crutches creak as he shifts his full weight onto them, creating a duet of sounds with the groaning floorboards, as he travels to the other side of the room to the window.

With the speed of the slowest sloth, he leans into the corner of the glass, peering out, only to see Dennis standing in the tree line—smiling with his mouth but not his eyes.

"Go away!" Jacob whispers, fogging the glass.

Dennis gestures for Jacob to come out, but Jacob rejects him by slowly shaking his head.

Dennis's false smile quickly disappears, matching the true expression in his eyes. He gestures again with a bit of impatience, but gets the same response from Jacob, who nervously turns away from the window and begins crutching back to his bed.

Crash!

A large rock, the size of his fist, smashes through the window, narrowly missing his head, and splinters the corner of his dresser. Jacob falls to the floor. His crutches slide away from him.

🦋 🦋 🦋 🦋

With a calming breath, Owen begins looking around her room. First to the butterfly display on her vanity, then to the picture of his wife next to it. He takes a seat on the red cushion bench in front of it, directly under Kyra's bed. He turns the picture toward himself with the tip of his index finger, then closes his eyes.

"Your mother meant the world to me," he grabs the picture to bring it closer, "I know you don't believe me, but she did, and still does."

Kyra snatches the blanket over her head.

"We had our problems; God only knows that. Problems that you won't understand until you are a little older. Some people still don't get it as adults, so I don't expect you to. But I would like for you to listen to me, like you did your grandmother." His eyes well with tears as he places the picture back—exactly as she had it. "We had grown distant. Being married for so long, and not doing anything together, like couples are supposed to, we ended up growing apart. We still loved each other, but the kisses turned into stiff-lipped pecks on the mouth, and a quick exit to work. Her sitting on one side of the couch and me on the other. Our money became a priority, so that's all we talked about. The magic was gone, sweetie. I'm not blaming her 'cause it was both of our fault. It's just what happened." He takes a deep breath. "Our conversations lacked love. It was replaced by bitterness and lack of patience. When I asked her what was the matter, she just

334

passed it off as if I was trying to create problems or start a fight. Eventually I took your mother's distancing as if she just wasn't attracted to me anymore. We had gone a long time without showing any love or affection towards one another, so it became normal. Our relationship was more of a daily routine, rather than the adventure it used to be. You may have even noticed, I don't know."

Kyra's intense eyes calm just a touch. She wipes a fallen tear with the corner of her pillowcase.

"I was doing a job for a customer one day. After some long conversation, I confided in her. She informed me that she had gone through the same thing. She had me thoroughly convinced that your mom, not only lost love for me, but she had another man and was possibly cheating. To me, it was so clear. That had to be it. What else could it have been?" Owen sighs. "Well, that customer called me back for another job..." he drops his head and clenches both of his fists so hard they shook. Tears began to pour from his eyes. "And..." he shakes his head, "I felt justified being with this woman, but wrong at the same time." He wipes his tears aggressively with his wrist, but even more follow. "I had forgotten what affection felt like, and I felt I couldn't control myself."

For a moment, Owen cried without being able to speak another word. He pounds his fist on the vanity, startling Kyra.

"I don't know. But for whatever reason... things suddenly changed between your mother and me. I don't know what happened, but she kissed me. I mean *really* kissed me—like she hadn't in years. She then sat me down and explained why she was acting the way she was. She was feeling depressed about the weight she had gained after having your brother. She didn't feel attractive anymore and felt I was only forcing affection toward her out of pity. She was concerned about my new business. It stressed her out since she had to pay the bills until I started getting regular customers. I was so damn busy trying to get it together that I didn't consider what she was going through." He pounds the vanity again. "Damn it, if I had known..." he throws his hands on his face. "I didn't *know*. I didn't."

Kyra's tears had dried. Her expression somewhat deadpan as she waits for the rest of the story.

"I hugged her so tight. So close. The look in her eyes melted me. She hadn't looked at me like that in..." Owen sobs. "We were together for the first time, in a long time. Spent the night holding each other. After that night I thought everything was going to be okay. I saw promise, so I couldn't tell her what I had done. I would've taken that secret to my grave." He sniffles. "Then I got a text message about two weeks later. It... it was from that woman; she wanted to talk to me. I told her I couldn't, and we shouldn't see each other anymore. I had nothing to say to her. She told me that it wasn't the reason for the text, and I should call her immediately. Not even a few hours had passed, and she text back in large letters, "MY DOCTOR CONFIRMED I HAVE HIV, YOU MAY WANNA GET CHECKED!" He chuckles through a sob. "I thought it was just some angry way of getting back at me for not wanting to be with her, you know. Some desperate attempt to get a rise out of me. But it wasn't. I have it. And I passed it to your mother that night we were together."

Kyra's eyes began leaking once more, tears ran down the crease between her fingers her face rested on.

"Your mother cursed me every day. She would sometimes tell me how we could get through this, treatments, and all. But then, I could see the anger, the rage in her eyes. She would never forgive me." He used the bottom of his shirt to wipe his face. "I woke one morning for work. She was asleep so I kissed her on her cheek gently, so I wouldn't wake her, then jumped in the shower. From inside the bathroom, I could hear the giggling from her phone. It was her alarm going off. It just kept going and going nonstop. I rinsed quickly and turned off the water, then called her name. But she didn't answer. It was always a little darker on her side of the bedroom, so I had to feel my way to her side with my feet. I felt these little bumps on the floor. I turned off the alarm and tapped her. '*Babe, you need to wake up.*' I said."

Owen's anger began to increase. He began to act out his story more than telling. His intense tone began to frighten Kyra.

"'*Babe! You have to get up!*' I hit the switch to the lamp on the nightstand and..." Owen stood, nearly hitting his head on the bed above. He looks down in tears, explaining with his knife hands pointing at the floor. "There was a bottle of liquor, half empty. Her depression meds were spilled next to it. When the paramedics got there, it was too late. She was long gone before I even woke up that morning." His hands clinch to fists, flexing his jaw muscles while holding back his emotions, then drops back down to his seat. "It was my fault!" He pounds his fist on the vanity. "I could've saved her. I was so selfish." He slams his fist again and again, before throwing his hands over his face, finally letting go of the pain in his heart through sobbing and tears.

But the pounding does not stop. The house vibrates from a distant, steady thumping from downstairs. Owen raises his head and so does Kyra.

When Owen opens the door, Jacob, obviously frightened, is already crutching his way toward him from down the hall. Kyra climbs down from her bed.

"That's that pounding I heard before!" She says.

Owen moves down the hall with two terrified children close behind. He stops at the top of the stairs. The pounding grows, echoing through the house, with such incredible force that he could see the floor shaking below.

He puts his arm around Jacob, trembling with fear.

"What's happening, Dad?" Jacob asks, terrified.

Kyra moves in closer to them both, nearly under her father's arm.

CHAPTER 19

YELLOW

The Next Day (4:46 PM)

The door opens wide. Marley is standing in the doorway as if he wants to be anywhere else but where he is. Owen welcomes him with open arms, embracing him tightly yet the gesture is not returned. Marley's arms hang to his sides, clearly still upset about their last conversation.

"I'm sorry about the other day, Mar. Thank you for coming." Says Owen.

Marley shakes his head. "When are you going to start trusting me, bruh?"

"I'll start now."

Marley frowns with disbelief.

"No, I promise, man. I'll be a better brother." He looks over Marley's shoulder. "Did you bring your friend?"

"Man," he shakes his head, "you just love me for my resources. But then you put down the fact that I have resources. Yes, I did bring her. But before you meet her, I have to let you know a few things, okay?"

"Okay."

"First, she's not the typical woman I date. I know you're used to me showing up with these model-like chicks, but—"

Owen shakes his head. "No, I... umm no..."

"Anyways, she's just not the typical chick I date, okay. Honestly, the woman kinda freaks me out a little. She told me she was sensitive and all. So, I thought maybe that meant, you know." he points down to his crotch, "down there. Or maybe her feelings or something." He shakes his head. "No. I wasn't even close man. I mean I think she knows what I be thinking sometimes. Or what I like. Like, for example, the sex is off the chain. She does things right when I be thinking of it. Like, I sho wish she would take my—"

"Marley, I get your point, man. Can we move on?"

"Look, all I'm saying is be careful what you thinking."

The car door to an older model, but mint condition, 1960 canary-yellow Volkswagen Bug, slams shut.

Marley clams up quickly, shushing his brother before stepping to the side.

Rounding the front of the car, is a shapely black woman with shoulder-length, blonde dreadlocks pulled back into a ponytail. The pale hair color glowed against her dark skin. Her choice of hairstyle exposed her high cheekbones and full, thick lips. An assortment of silver and copper bracelets slide down her forearm, as she clutches a bag that matches the theme of her transportation. Her confident demeanor is briefly interrupted as she threw a glance to the upstairs window.

"This is Danika. Danika, this is my brother I told you about."

"Yes. It's nice to finally meet you." She says, with a touch of a South African accent.

"Finally?" Owen says curiously.

"Uh, like I told you. He's having some issues in the house. He—"

"Eish! Bokkie!" She exclaims in her foreign language. "I told you already, not to explain to me his situation. I told you, hey? Absolutely nothing."

Marley steps back, eyebrows raised and his hands up as if surrendering. "And she bossy, too."

Owen takes notice that they did not arrive alone. In the back seat of the car, a little boy peeks out through the backseat window.

"Looks like you have someone else with you. Who's your friend in the backseat?" Asks Owen, while nodding his head in the direction of the boy.

"That is my son, Chandu. He will wait in the car."

"Chandu? That's an interesting name.

"I think so," she says looking back to her son, "it's East African."

"Maybe you should show her around," says Marley. "I'll keep an eye on the little one from over here."

"Why doesn't your son just come inside. He can play with my son. They look about the same age. He's got toys and other things they can do."

"Not now, please." She says. "Maybe later."

Owen escorts Danika inside.

When they enter, Marley wastes no time removing a pack of cigarettes from his inside coat pocket. He places one in the corner of his mouth and looks to Chandu staring back at him, then places his index finger across his lips. "Shhh."

Chandu shakes his head, then leans further out of the window, glaring up at the upstairs window, above Marley.

🦋 🦋 🦋 🦋

Danika slowly makes her way into the living room, looking all around, from the floor to the ceiling. Owen follows close behind, nearly on her heels, watching and waiting for the slightest change in her facial expression—the simplest twist in her lips or raise of her brow. He has seen his share of horror movies, so it prompts him to wait for the cliché signs most psychics show when they come across paranormal energy. The horrified gasp from touching an object, the fear of entering a certain part of a room, or the eyes rolling to the back of her head. Owen waits.

Danika glances back at him over her shoulder and chuckles, "Would you mind if I have a glass of water?"

"S-Sure. You want ice?"

"Yes, please. Lots of ice if you don't mind." She asks, dragging her fingertips across the ledge of the fireplace, then stopping at the candle, while Owen rushes off to the kitchen. She strokes the brass base of the candle holder, then slowly turns her attention toward the upstairs, where Jinx, with her head protruding between the balusters, is looking back down at Danika. "Well, aren't you just beautiful." She mutters.

"What?" Owen yells over the sound of the running water from the kitchen.

"I said your cat... She's beautiful."

"Oh, thank you! Her name is Jinx. She used to belong to my late wife."

She smiles at Jinx, then turns to the back window. For a moment she stares through the thin, sheer-white curtains to the tree line out back, then parts them gently. She focuses on the trees and the dark path that leads into them, when she feels an energy behind her, swelling—an energy filled with both anger and worry, climbing up her back and wrapping around her. She turns around, noticing the basement door is now halfway open. It was not before.

She approaches the basement, feeling the energy increase the closer she came to it. She stops, just a step or two away, hesitating and rubbing her palms together, just before reaching for the doorknob.

"Here you go!" Owen says, startling her and holding a large glass jar-with the pickle label still attached-full of water.

She attempts to play off her rattled state when she turns to address him.

"Still working on getting some new dishes, so I apologize for the jar." He says. "It's the only clean one I have at the moment."

"Oh, no it's fine. But would you mind if I had a little more ice, please?"

Owen inspects the jar, turning to the clear part that wasn't covered with a dark green label, it's nearly packed with ice. "I put—"

"Please," she bats her eyes. "I like a lot; I mean *a lot* of ice."

With a raised eyebrow, Owen agrees, and takes off to the kitchen once more.

Wasting no time, Danika turns to the basement door... now closed. She pauses for a moment, then sweeps her fingers around the frame near the doorknob. She wraps her thick fingers around the brass handle and opens it slowly.

Her descent into the inky-black abyss is slow; moreover, she is seemingly without concern, as she leaves the lights off. Danika takes one step at a time, bringing her feet closely together on each step, while holding on tightly to the rail.

Owen rinses off his fingers and shoves a few more ice cubes into the jar. He inspects it while heading toward the basement, shaking the jar and rattling the cubes inside. *Ain't no way in hell you gettin more in there.*

"Danika?" He says, looking down into the pitch-dark basement.

She doesn't answer.

He flips the light switch and thunders down the steps, stopping halfway after noticing Danika, with a disapproving and irritated expression apparent in her eyes, standing near the workbench. "I have your extra ice."

She takes a deep breath and clasps her hands in front of her. "Owen, could you please, please..." She sighs again. "Would you mind turning that light back off?"

"Yeah, I can do that." He says, puzzled.

"And if you wouldn't mind leaving me alone for a moment. It's not your fault, but your energy is really clouding and disruptive."

"I'm sorry. I didn't want to interrupt. Just wanted to be of assistance if you needed it." He reaches out to hand her the ice water.

"Thank you, Owen. Would you mind holding onto it for me."

"Yeah, I guess so."

She watches him disappear up the steps; but then discovers a dark silhouette, standing near the wall on the opposite side of the room, just before Owen submerges her back into darkness.

❦ ❦ ❦ ❦

Marley is standing out front, puffing away on his cigarette, when Owen steps out from the front door.

Marley smiles. "She give you the boot?"

"I guess," he says, jogging down the three steps and standing beside his brother. "She was on me about getting her some water and packing it with ice."

Marley laughs, spitting out a stream of smoke through puckered lips.

"What?" Asks Owen.

"She does shit like that to me when she wants me to leave her alone. Would have you really thinking she needs all that damn ice. Then don't even drink it."

"Fo real?"

"Yes." Marley turns with his back to the street. "Hey, I've been trying not to look, but is that boy still staring at me?"

Owen leans enough to the left that he can see over his brother's shoulder. "Yeah."

Marley shakes his head. "Man, that boy creeps me out, too. He always be staring at me like he wants something." He lights up another cigarette. "One time, in the morning, he was staring me when I was coming out of the room, standing in the hallway by the bathroom. I was like, what? You want some cereal or something? A cookie? Some video games?" But he didn't answer. Just staring and shit. Like he didn't know how to blink."

Owen looks again. "That's crazy. But he doesn't seem to be really staring at you, man. It seems like he's staring at the front porch, or the door."

They both look at the porch.

Danika emerges from the front door, cradling a brick in her palm.

Startled, Marley quickly extinguishes his cigarette under his foot and holds it there, blowing the smoke through the puckered corner of his mouth.

"What's that?" Asks Owen.

"Well, I was hoping maybe *you* could tell *me*." She drags her fingers across the three symbols. "It's odd. I found it on the floor by the wall. There was a hole in the wall above it where it looked like someone had pulled it from. I feel a connection from it… to something in the house, but I don't understand it." She hands it to Owen. The sunlight catches the movement of the front door across the street, the glare off the glass snags Danika's attention. "Who's your neighbor?"

Owen rolls his eyes upon noticing Lorna, watching them from her front porch. "Oh, that's Ms. Michaels." He whispers. "Lorna Michaels. She's been watching me since we've moved in."

Both men inspect the brick, passing it back and forth.

Danika keeps her eyes on Lorna, as the nosey neighbor slips goes back inside, shutting the door behind her. But a single slat from the living room blinds slowly lifts.

Danika discreetly shakes her head and chuckles, then looks over to her vehicle and smiles. "It's time." She says, taking a short, but deep breath.

"Time for what?" Asks Owen.

"Owen, I can only feel the energy in your house. If the energy is negative, positive, harmless, or maybe even a possible threat to you and your family." She steps closer to him. "But I can't interact with it. I can sometimes see things and I rarely hear anything."

"So, what do you feel? I know there is definitely something going on in my house."

"Owen, you have mixed energies in your home. In order for me to fully understand what is happening we need someone who can reach out to all three realities."

"What? Three realities?" Owen chuckles. "Are you for real? What, like different dimensions or something?"

"For the most part, yes."

"I'm really gonna need you to explain, please."

"Okay, but first you need to open your mind and rid yourself of the sarcasm and doubt. This is real. Whether you choose to believe it, or not." Owen wipes the smile from his face and nods. "If you didn't believe in something, you wouldn't have requested that I come here, correct?" She smiles. "Picture and understand that everything is made up of energy. *Everything.* Everything you touch, everything you see and even everything you hear is made up of some composition of energy. Now, you have the world as we know it and exist in. All of that energy, every *bit* of energy starts here. It's created in this reality. The buildings, cars, houses the clothes you're wearing, even the cigarette pressed under your brother's foot all originate here."

Owen laughs at his unsurprised brother shaking his head.

"Your body is made up of positive and negative energy. When it dies, your flesh, your soul-energy is released. Now, listen carefully. If your soul is at peace, that is positive energy and merges with that huge light everyone, with near death experiences, claims to see." She raises her hands to the sky. "It's real, that light. Bright and white like the sun. It powers all life, and all life is drawn to it. Bugs are little particles of that life-light

349

energy. It's why you see them dancing about a streetlight in the dark night—or gather, dying inside of your living room lamp. They are drawn to merge with the living light once again."

"Oh, well that's interesting." Marley says.

Danika flashes him an impatient eye, then continues.

"Now, if the soul-energy released is not at peace, it connects with energies of a negative type. They aren't drawn to the positive powers above. They just remain here to dwell. Souls that have died hateful, angry, insane, damaged, or just plain evil remain here until they have changed. If they choose too."

"Like a hell on earth?" Asks Owen.

"Yes. Exactly what it is."

Owen drifts into thoughts of Theresa.

Danika grabs his hand firmly.

"Now, some like it here. In *that* negative reality. Some are doomed to replay their death or torment over-and-over like a broken record. Some even look to remain and spread fear and chaos, as they did when they were alive." She pauses. "But there are few that seek help. They give signs and clues, yet still fueled with anger and hate for what occurred. The longer their pain goes undiscovered by the one they are communicating with, the angrier they become. The more they manifest themselves, drawing power from their surroundings. Flickering lights, televisions, even the warmth around us is energy."

350

"Is that why it gets cold when you feel a presence?" Marley asks.

Danika nods her head.

"We hear ghost stories about apparitions walking through walls and falling through floors," she continues, "they pass through doors and all, as if they didn't even matter. But in their reality, it is there. And just as solid as the ground you're walking on. If a door is closed, they must open it, just like you, to pass through. But it takes energy."

"So where do we go from here?" Asks Owen. His eyes glistening and bloodshot.

She looks to her car and nods her head. "Like I said before explaining all of this. You need someone who is powerful enough to do it all."

Her son exits the car and gently closes the door. He looks down at his shoes as he began his approach. Danika says something in her native tongue, firmly, and he immediately raises his head. His dangling black dreads nearly cover his face, but the worried look in his young-eyes is very evident. He brushes his dreads to the side, then hooks his thumbs on the straps of his Army-green backpack.

CHAPTER 20

THE OCTOPUS

Kyra and Jacob listen quietly through her opened window above, glancing at each other periodically, as they listen to shocking lectures on spiritual energies by Danika. They lean into the window to get a better view of the little boy approaching the adults.

Danika puts her arm around him. "I've always made it a point to enter a home before Chandu. Son, say 'hi'."

He begins kicking a large stone sticking up from the ground below him. His dreads drop down, covering his face again, like cord-curtains that sway with his movement. "Hi."

"Nice to meet you, Chandu." Owen fumbles the pronunciation slightly.

"No. It's Chandu, like Shawn—Do," the boy says in a sweet, but firm, manner.

"I apologize." Owen says, shaking his hand. "So, Danika, what do you mean because I'm confused. You go in before him? Why?"

"I apologize for being so partial with my explanation—"

"That, you definitely weren't." Marley interrupts.

She flashes him another impatient glance. Meanwhile, Chandu is paying close attention to the base of the porch, peeking through his swaying dreads at the woodchipped opening, and into the emptiness below the structure.

"My son has abilities far beyond mine, let alone most psychic mediums."

Chandu looks up to her. "Mom you said you wouldn't call it that."

"I'm sorry, sweetie. I mean *sensitives.* He hates the "P" word." She brushes the dreads from his face.

"When he was born his name was Zane. No particular reason, I just liked the name. Then, when he was a few years older, I discovered his ability to see. Touching things that may have energy, knowing where it came from, who owned it, and its history. I don't even think he knew what he was doing. It just came naturally to him, and he spoke about it, always smiling, as if he were describing a cartoon scene on television. One night, I heard him talking in a room at his friend's home we were visiting. You would have sworn there was a person right there in front of him. No one was there, no explanation of an imaginary friend or anything. Later, my friends told us of some little things that would happen around the house. Things moving, doors closing, and cold spots in the very room Chandu was in." She rests her hand on his shoulder. "He truly has a gift. So, I made the choice to legally change his name to, Chandu. It means Octopus in my native language." She smiles and caresses his face. "He is still only seven years old and not able to handle some of the dangers his abilities expose him to," she looks up to Owen, "So, I go in first to make sure he will be safe."

"So, I guess that's a good thing, you bringing him and all?" Marley says.

Chandu returns his gaze to the hole beneath the porch.

Marley hugs himself and shivers, "Alright ya'll, I'm cold so..."

"Oh, ya. I'm sorry, we can take this inside." Owen says, escorting them in.

Kyra races—and Jacob crutches—quietly, yet as fast as they can, to the upstairs landing, looking over the banister and down into the foyer. As the adults talk, Chandu looks up to them, greeting them with a gaze of his own.

"So, what's next?" Asks Owen. Chandu slips away from them to head toward the back window. "Do we burn some sage or candles? Do we join hands and close our eyes?"

Marley notices as Chandu parts the curtains, and his discreet waist-high wave, while staring into the backyard.

"No. None of that. No high-tech gadgets or equipment. No séance or chants in the dark. We just watch and listen, is all. Remember, there's a reason these spirits are here. Once we figure that out, we solve everyone's problem." She looks up to Jacob. "For now, let's just introduce the boys, and let them play, while we try and figure out the mystery of the brick Marley is holding."

Owen takes the brick from his brother, then places it in the center of the kitchen table in front of them.

❀ ❀ ❀ ❀

(Thirty Minutes Later)

Kyra is upstairs with the boys, in Jacob's room, programming her new phone and surfing the internet at the same time.

Jacob and Chandu are on the floor playing with his Army action figures. More Jacob playing than his new playmate, who watches curiously, while Jacob makes machinegun noises with his lips. As always, he has the green men shooting at the red.

Jacob impatiently looks to Chandu. "Are you gonna play?" He scoots the red men toward Chandu. "Here, you can play with the red guys, if you want."

"Okay." He says, scooting closer to the tiny war display.

"What do I do with them?"

Jacob sighs. "Haven't you ever played Army before?"

"No."

Jacob frowns with skepticism. "Okay, well. See the guns they are holding? You have to set up your men and position them to aim at the enemy." Jacob hands him one of the red Army men that's holding a long rifle.

Chandu rubs his finger on the tip of the rifle, wiggling the thin, loose, plastic barrel. He then sets it down—ever so gently—pointing the rifle toward the bedroom door. Just then, the screen on Kyra's phone fizzles; a split second later, it functions as normal. She nearly drops her phone from the odd malfunction. Instead, she taps it on the side with the palm of her hand and continues as if nothing happened.

Chandu sets an Army man in position, then another—and another—until all the red Army men are set up in a tactical one-hundred-and-eighty-degree formation, facing the empty doorway. Overlooking the complete opposite direction of Jacob's green Army men.

Jacob sucks his teeth. "No, you're doing it wrong." He reaches to rearrange Chandu's Army men.

Chandu keeps his focus at the entrance, looking upward. The floor suddenly groans, as if weight is shifting on the floorboards in front of him. It creaks again, entering the room, now getting closer.

One of the red Army men is suddenly flicked from formation. Before Jacob could grab it from the floor, it's flicked again, narrowly missing his face, and lands on the bed. Jacob draws his hand back, startled at the sound of the floor creaking in front of Chandu, accompanied by the frightened look on his face.

Chandu scoots back and moves closer to Jacob.

"What's wrong?"

He doesn't answer in the midst of his recoil—knocking over all the Army men behind him during his retreat—from what he can see, but others can't.

"What is it?" Asks Jacob. "You see something?"

Kyra is so engulfed in her phone, that she is entirely oblivious to what is going on around her.

"The man from under your porch?" Chandu says, suddenly turning his attention to Kyra, then back to the intruder.

The Army men are crushed, flattened under an unseen force heading in Kyra's direction.

🦋 🦋 🦋 🦋

Marley is in a corner of the basement with a flashlight, tracing the wall with his fingers, while Owen and Danika are inspecting the brick she found. Owen flips the brick over a few times when it slips from his grasp, and forcibly falls to the wood surface. A small piece falls off the side, exposing a smoother, less-jagged surface.

With the heavy backside of his flashlight, he gently taps, chipping away the armor of the brick, subsequently making it smaller than what it once was. Eventually, with the outer shell of the brick broken away, small, straight grooves are exposed on the outer edges. He grabs an old paint brush, and the brushes away the rest of the dust and cement-mortar chips.

Marley pushes an antiquated wooden-shelf to the side, stretching and separating the old, dusty cobwebs from the wall that are attached to it. He fans and dusts himself free of the falling dirt and debris, when he notices a brick, slightly discolored from the rest, sitting in the center of a clean spot on the wall, where the shelf was sitting.

Owen digs his fingernails into the grooves on the sides of the brick. "Looks like this whole thing may fit into something." He examines it some more. "Maybe that's what they are for. It's some piece to a puzzle, I bet."

"Yeah, but *what* puzzle." Danika says.

Marley chips away, with a screwdriver, at what he discovers is a fake brick, hollow on the inside. "Maybe this one?" He suggests, holding his light over a hole in the shape of a brick. "Bring that over here."

As they approach, Marley dusts out the remaining debris inside the hollowed-out brick opening. He points his beam inside of it, illuminating three pipe-like stems, evenly spaced apart, and grooves matching the outside of the brick Owen is holding.

Marley grabs the brick from Owen and inspects it. "Look." He says, flashing the light on the brick, and showing the three holes where the tiny stems could match.

He quickly places the brick up to the hole, but it won't fit. He tries to force it, but the puzzle piece will not slide into place. "Get me a hammer."

"Stop—Stop—Stop, Marley," He takes the brick before his aggressive brother does any damage, "Here, look at the bottom of it. See the grooves?"

They both look inside the opening and notice the grooves were mismatched with the way Marley was placing them. Owen flips the brick and inserts it halfway, then turns to look at them. All of their eyes are open wide, anticipating what is to come.

Owen pushes. It's a rough fit, but with a few extremely-gentle taps to the side with the flashlight, it clicks into place. Owen immediately draws back his hand and waits for something to happen—as though it is a scene in a Tomb Raider movie.

"What's wrong?" Asks Marley.

"Nothing," Owen looks up at the ceiling, then around the basement, "You hear anything?"

"No, I don't hear shit." Says Marley. "What, you think some secret door was gonna open. A magic scroll fall from the wall or from a portal from another dimension." He laughs "There's symbols in the bricks and I'm willing to bet they are part of a key, or something." He flashes his light on the symbols. "You see anything around here that looks like these?"

Screams from upstairs, and thundering stomps across the floor, startle the three. They drop everything to race upstairs to see what the matter is, when the basement door bursts open, and Kyra comes rushing down the steps in front of them.

"Suhh—Something is in the room!" She screams. "Jacob's room! It came after us!" She begins pulling at her uncle's wrist.

Owen steps in front, "What? Where are the boys, Kyra?"

They all begin pushing their way up the stairs.

"Where are they, Kyra!?" Owen yells. "You left them!?"

By the time they get to the base of the foyer staircase, Jacob is already halfway down the steps, nearly falling over his crutches, clearly shaken and on the verge of crying.

"Jacob, what happened? Where's Chandu!?" Yells Marley.

Danika pushes past them all and runs up the stairs.

"I don't know," Jacob stammers, "I couldn't see it. He could. But we couldn't."

"What?" Yells Owen, grabbing Jacob's arms.

"I don't know. It was big and came into the room, but I couldn't see it. Then, that boy started talking to himself, all weird."

"I'm gonna call Grandma, I'm gonna call!" Kyra cries, ripping her phone from her back pocket. "I can't take it..." She whimpers, fumbling to unlock her phone, but it slips from her hands and tumbles end-over-end, down the steps, and lands at the bottom near the front door.

Kyra wastes no time racing back down to retrieve the phone, when it abruptly slides away from her, as if she'd kicked it—but she hadn't. It begins spinning clockwise in the middle of the foyer's floor, and builds up speed until it is a circular pink-blur. Kyra steps back, looking at the adults who are mesmerized. The spinning phone moves slowly across the floor toward Kyra. The screen lights up and it chimes, as if messages were being received, then it slows to a stop.

Kyra, accompanied by her father standing behind her, hesitates to pick up the, seemingly, possessed device, but gathers the courage. Numerous notification banners show messages from an unknown sender... all repeating, "*So cold. So very cold.*"

Danika returns to the top of the stairs. "We need to gather. Jacob's room, please."

CHAPTER 21

NO STRINGS

"While we were out fiddling with that brick in the basement, the kids had an encounter—from which Chandu had his first communication with the entity in your home." Says Danika. "He's particularly protective over certain spots in this home—this room being one of them. Chandu felt his anger was focused mostly on your daughter, for being in here."

Kyra perks up. "What? Me? Why me?"

"Who is *he*?" Asks Owen.

"I have no idea. But he's terribly angry and in tremendous pain. Or, at least when he died, his pain was so incredible that he feels it in the afterlife." She turns to her son.

"He... he showed himself," Chandu says, looking at the floor. "His fingers were black and had pieces missing, like something chewed at them. His face, too. His clothes were dirty and caked with mud. His teeth clicked together so hard and fast I thought they'd break." He looks up at Owen. "His anger won't let him move on, so he stays here. I felt his pain. And he won't find peace until he finds what he's lost."

"Lost? What did he lose?" Asks Owen.

"Maybe that brick has something to do with that story we heard at the bar that night?" Says Marley.

"About the gold?" Owen laughs.

Marley hunches his shoulders. "Explain the brick, then. The symbols in it?"

"What are you two talking about?" Asks Danika.

"Nonsense." Owen barks.

"Is that what this is all about, Chandu?" Ask Marley. "Gold?"

"No."

"See. No gold." Owen smirks. "But, if that's not it. Then, what is it? Or do you know?"

Chandu looks back to the floor. "Why haven't you told your dad?" He then turns his attention to Jacob.

They all look toward Jacob, puzzled.

"I..." Jacob hesitates, taking a step back on his crutches. His face shifts from surprise, to blank and expressionless.

Danika takes notice to something strange near Jacob's temple. She leans in to look closer.

"Tell me what, Chandu?" Asks Owen.

"You found something and didn't tell your dad. Why?" Danika presses. "What's stopping you?"

He stares at her intently; yet, he doesn't answer.

She continues her gaze and smiles. "I was gonna wait to give you your gift, Jacob. But I think now is just as good a time as any. Don't you think?" She sits back, removing a bracelet from her wrist. "Do you like gifts?"

Jacob still does not answer; but something within him smiles at the thought of a gift.

She grabs his arm and places the U-shaped, shoddy-made bracelet, constructed of tan and silver twisted metal, onto his wrist. She sits back and watches him, as if she just hit the power button on an old, floor model television and is waiting for the picture to appear.

Everyone is confused, with the exception of Chandu, who is playing with an almost-exact replica of the bracelet presented to Jacob, on his own wrist.

Jacob takes her committed observation as impatience; as though she is waiting for a little bit of gratitude, in which his dad taught him to always show when given something.

"Thank you?" He recites in appreciation.

Danika smiles; portraying a smile where the corners of the lips curve, but the eyes are not involved—a quick, half-second flash of a smile. Then, she continues to watch.

"What was he supposed to tell me?" Asks Owen, redirecting the situation back to what he feels needs answered more promptly.

"There is a lot going on here," She says keeping her eyes on Jacob, "But in order for us to understand everything fully, we have to rid ourselves of any obstructions or mental blocks. Any types of interference that would cloud our thinking and manipulate us.

Suddenly horrified, Kyra's eyes widen. "Oh my God, Jacob, your face!"

Just under the skin of Jacob's temple, something thin and narrow squirms about like a worm. The leading end of the worm-like object slithers around to his cheek, then up, disappearing just under his bottom-right eyelid. His eye rolls upward, tearing up, and loses the color of the pupil, promptly fading it to white.

Owen stands to his aid.

"No! Owen don't touch him. Your son has an intruder we need to rid him of."

Owen obeys, only to jump back up again when Jacob falls backward onto his bed and starts to mildly convulse.

Danika intercepts Owen, standing in between Jacob and his father, as Jacob squirms around in front of her. She grabs his wrist with one hand, then the bracelet with the other and slides it up his forearm until it's tight against his skin.

Owen is being gently restrained, by Marley, as he watches in shock.

"I know this has to be hard to watch, but you have to trust me right now." Danika insists, fitting the bracelet even tighter up his arm. The more-snug to his arm the bracelet is, the more-violently he convulses.

"What the hell are you doing to him!?" Owen yells.

The worm-like creature appears in his forearm, appearing just below the bracelet, squirming aggressively as though it is fighting against the touch of the metal.

Danika seizes the opportunity and slides the bracelet back down his arm. The more she did so, the more the worm avoided it, retreating down toward his hand, where it bunches around itself at his wrist.

She slides it down even further, slowly. The head of the creature pokes at the skin from within, pushing through his fragile skin like a tiny needle. The surrounding veins near it turn black.

"Quick, Owen, do you still have that glass of water I asked you for?"

366

"What? No, it's downstairs on the table."

"Hurry! Someone get that glass, or another, please! But I need it now, please!" She orders rapidly.

Marley accepts the responsibility, stepping over Chandu and pushing past Kyra and rushes out of the bedroom door.

Danika pinches the exposed tip of the worm and pulls. It thrashes its body about under his skin, then tries to retreat, attempting to reverse into his arm. She holds it firmly, but she can feel it slipping.

"Quickly!" She yells in a stern manner.

Marley enters in a hurry, snatching small handfuls of ice from the overflowing jar.

Owen grabs it from him, and positions himself next to Jacob, as Danika prepares to pull the rest of the struggling creature from his arm. He holds the glass next to her. His shaking hands can hardly contain the water inside.

"Steady, Owen... steady." She calmly says.

He grabs the glass with both hands and holds on securely.

Danika pulls the remaining length of it from his arm and drops in into the jar, where it fizzles like acid, then sinks to the bottom.

Kyra gasps. "It looks like that string he was playing with."

Immediately, Owen hands her the glass and tends to his son, who is exhausted, breathing heavily, and has his eyes tightly shut.

Danika holds the glass up and examines the inside. The water grows black; starting from the bottom and working its way up to the top, the string emits an inky-blackness, mixing with the clear water. She promptly opens the window and dumps the contents out to the grass below.

"What was that?" Owen pleads. "And why was it *in* my son?"

Jinx enters the room and leaps onto the bed next to Jacob. She gently places a paw on his chest, sniffs his face and nuzzles his cheek. She locks eyes with Owen, then looks to Chandu.

"I'm not sure. But it was a form of possession or control. A way to keep Jacob quiet until whatever it was, that gave it to him, finished what it was doing."

Jinx jumps down from the bed and leaves the room.

They all have their eyes on Jacob, with the exception of Chandu, who follows behind Jinx.

"This bracelet. Is it magic or something?"

"It's an amulet from Northern Ghana, charged up with magical powers by an Earth priest."

"What kind of powers?" Asks Owen.

"Whatever it is you provide the craftsman with when it's being created... versus the Earth priest, or soothsayer, putting their own choice of power in the jewelry; but to speak about what it specifically does, can compromise its power."

"I think I'm gonna need one of those, asap!" Says Marley.

"If only it were that easy." She retorts.

Kyra notices Chandu is missing. She steps out into the hallway to look for him. The bathroom door is open, and the lights are off, but she looks inside regardless. Nothing. She suddenly hears whispering down the hall, coming from her room's opening. The light is on inside. She remembers leaving it off earlier, when she and Jacob wanted to remain unseen while looking down on their new visitors in the front yard.

The whispers become clearer the closer she gets to her room; she continues hugging the wall to stay away from the weaker, groaning floorboards in the center. She stands on the outside of the door against the wall, to continue listening.

"Uh huh. Uh huh. I can do that if you want." Chandu says.

Everyone else is in Jacob's room. Who could he be talking to? She decides to push the door open further and step inside. Chandu has his back to her, sitting on the floor near the far corner of the room. He suddenly goes silent.

"Who are you talking to?" Kyra asks.

"He needs you."

"What? What did you say?"

He still has his back to her, "I—I didn't say it. I'm just helping."

"Helping what?" She steps around him.

Jinx is sitting in front of him, very attentive and her ears perked high.

"Cats have a special ability, too." He turns to address her. "Did you know that?" He sits up on his knees. "My mom says they always have one foot in hell and the other here."

"Oh, okay. So..."

"Do you know how your mom died?"

She grimaces from his question. "What business is it of yours? You should learn not to ask rude questions like that."

"It's really not rude. It is reality and I'm just trying to get you to see that he needs you."

"Why do you keep saying that?" She exclaims.

"I told you, I didn't say it. I'm just—"

"What? You just did. It came out of *your* mouth. What's wrong with you?"

"Well, I said it, but *I* didn't say it."

"Then, if you didn't say it, who did?" Kyra shrieks. "And who is he?"

Chandu looks over to Jinx, and smiles. "Your mom did."

❦ ❦ ❦ ❦

As they are all watching over Jacob, none of the adults notice the absence of the other children. Owen holds onto his resting son's hand, watching as the small wound and black veins on his arm fade away... healing without a trace.

Danika removes the bracelet and hovers it over his body, first, running it up his arm once again, then across his chest and down the length of both his legs, finally returning it to his wrist.

"Is he okay now?" Asks Owen.

"Seems to be. Let's just let him regain his energy. He was being drained, for quite some time, by the looks of how black that water is." She looks behind her, "Chandu, can..." Startled, she then looks to Marley who hunches his shoulders.

"Where are the children?" She asks.

Marley looks to his right where they were previously sitting. "I don't know, they were just right here a minute ago." He gets up and heads for the bedroom door.

"Wait. I'll go look for them. Stay here with your brother and help watch over Jacob." She directs.

Marley nods, stepping to the side for her, as she walks out.

Hearing the commotion down the hallway, it does not take her long to locate them. Kyra is crying and yelling, cornering Chandu with her finger pointed in his face. "It's not true. It's not true. You shouldn't say stuff like that to people!"

"Hey—Hey what's going on!?" Yells Danika, gently grabbing Kyra's wrist and wedging herself between them.

Jinx lays by the closet door.

"He's playing mind games. He was talking about my mom, and she's dead!"

"Hold on. Back up for a minute." Orders Danika, trying to understand the cause of the heated situation.

"I wasn't playing games." Says Chandu.

Kyra snatches her hand away from Danika's grasp. "He says my mom is in your *negative realm*. Which pretty much means he's saying my mom is in *Hell!* I heard you talking about it."

"Kyra, sweetie. Listen." She touches Kyra's shoulder. "And I want you to *really* listen to me on this, okay?"

Kyra takes a deep breath and sits down.

"There is something you should understand. My son has a great deal of contact with things that he has never come across before. Things he has yet to understand." Danika kneels in front of her and takes her wrist. "Chandu doesn't know you, correct? Whatever it is he says... sometimes, just comes out without acknowledging what it is he's saying. And it could come out as rude and raw. But he has no reason to lie to you. He just says what it is he sees. He means you no harm, nor disrespect."

"He—He said my mom is talking through our cat!"

Owen appears at the door. "What's going on?"

Kyra rolls her teary-eyes. "Oh, God."

"I would love to explain. But before I go any further, as painful as it may be... could you explain to me how your wife passed?"

❦ ❦ ❦ ❦

Marley sits on the bed next to Jacob, patting him lightly on the wrist, as he looks around the room.

He can hear the muttered conversation down the hall, and taps his foot impatiently, as he waits for them to return.

He stops moving for a moment, thinking he heard something. There is nothing to be heard right away, but then it happened again—a soft scratching noise coming from Jacob's bedroom closet. Squinting his eyes, he looks toward the sound's origin. The setting sun gives the room a burnt-orange lighting but makes the inside of the closet appear even darker.

Something small moves at the base of the door, then disappears back inside the closet. He rests Jacob's arm onto the bed so he can investigate further.

As Marley gets closer, he can hear the scratching more distinctly. He grabs the doorknob and swiftly yanks the door open wide. With the exception of Jacob's clothes, there is nothing visible besides a pair of small tennis shoes, shoved to the left, and a football to the right—leaving a clear, empty space in the middle, under his clothes. He leans in, kicking the football to the side, and pulls the string overhead for the light.

"Damn. Ya'll got rats?" He mutters stepping back.

"Uncle Marley."

He nearly lost all bodily functions, startled by his little nephew standing behind him, leaning on one crutch and rubbing his eyes.

"Damn, Jacob. You trying to send your Uncle Marley to an early grave." He guides him back to the bed. "You need to rest, little man." He pauses for a moment, hearing something behind him. He turns slowly, only to witness the closet light flickering out and the door creaking closed—stopping at its partially-open position.

❧ ❧ ❧ ❧

Kyra is crying uncontrollably after having to hear the story from her father, once again. Tears stream from her bloodshot eyes.

Owen is trying to maintain his strength, but after hearing his daughter's pain, he can't help but weaken, burying his face in his palms and letting the tears flow.

Danika hangs her head, "She's not at peace. And because she isn't, her spirit remains in that negative reality. I'm sorry."

Kyra wipes her eyes. "I can't believe she's there. She's a good person. Why would God put a good woman there? She didn't do anything wrong," she looks to her father, "*He* should be in Hell, not *her*!"

If it was any quieter, Owen's heart shattering into pieces would have been audible to everyone in the room. The expression on his face could not be any more painful; the rage in Kyra's eyes can't be any more evident.

Danika places her hand on Kyra's shoulder, again. "Sweetie, your mother can be saved. The negative reality isn't a permanent place, unless the entity wants it to be. But you must listen and clear your mind. The hate and anger you show for your father is like candy to the negative. And the sadness, guilt, and regret your father has does the same." She stands. "They can use energy from televisions, radios, lights—just about anything that has a positive charge to it. But negative mental energy... that's powerful stuff."

Owen wipes his tears and leans against the door frame.

"Now. We can solve your problems, hopefully. It will only lessen some of the events going on in your home; however, I'm sure what you'd like to do is get rid of all the issues, so they won't return. And everyone is happy." She looks over to Jinx, who's lashing her tail back and forth. "I have a feeling your mother would want that."

Marley, still wide-eyed and in shock, quickly pops in the room with the others, holding Jacob high on his hip while dangling Pupuka between his thumb and forefinger, as though it is a soiled diaper. He tosses the dusty toy to the floor.

"Where'd you get that?" Asks Owen.

"It was in the closet. In Jacob's room."

Owen nudges it with his toe. "So why did you bring it in here?"

"Because when I checked the closet before, it wasn't in there."

"That's Jinx's toy, Pupuka." Says Kyra, wiping her face with her sleeve. "We found it here when we moved in. She's been dropping it in random places all over the house ever since she got it."

Danika bends down to retrieve it. "Boy, it's an ugly thing, isn't it?" She grips the arms of it tightly and closes her eyes; then, soon reopens them with surprise. She immediately begins pulling the seam at the back of the doll, ripping and pulling until its yellow stuffing is revealed.

"What the Hell are you doing?" Kyra blurts out.

She continues tearing out the fluffy, square, yellow foam insides and tosses it on the floor, when something small and metallic falls to her feet. The room falls silent. She places the violated doll on Kyra's desk to retrieve the mechanical-looking piece of metal.

It seems to be made of brass and is the shape of a pyramid. A gold stem sticks out from the bottom, looking like a triangle-shaped, metal lollipop. Beautiful, intricate designs are engraved on all four sides.

"What is it?" Asks Marley. "If I didn't know any better, I'd say it's a dreidel... but I have a feeling there wouldn't be a dreidel hidden in a toy. So, you got any guesses?"

"Your guess is as good as mine." Says Danika. "But it looks and feels like we may be onto something."

Danika spins the object by the stem between her fingertips. "The doll has told us it's secret. Now I think it's time for Jacob to tell us his."

CHAPTER 22

THE TRUTH SHALL SET YOU FREE

"If there is a dead body of a child in that treehouse, don't you think we should get the police involved?" Owen asks.

"No!" Exclaims Danika "The police will only bring their usual questions and create more chaos. Besides... I don't trust them. We have to take care of the matter, if your home is going to be at peace. That's first and foremost. There's something here we need to solve. I can feel it. Just trust me."

"So then, what do we do next?"

"I think you and I need to visit that treehouse." Says Danika. "Marley can stay back and watch the kids."

"Why am I the babysitter all of a sudden?" He sneers. "My stomach hurts just *being* in this house."

Neither Danika nor Owen acknowledges his question or concern and leave the room without further hesitation.

Disappointed, Marley takes a seat; he looks over at Chandu, standing next to the window, as he stares back at Marley.

"Don't you start with that." Marley orders.

🦋 🦋 🦋 🦋

Owen leads the way into the forest with Danika awfully close behind him—being he has the only light shining on their path of dead leaves and sticks. Her open-toed shoes allow her the undesired touch of the moist debris below and walks as if the trail is riddled with piles of doggie-waste landmines.

Owen peeks back at her, "You doing okay?"

"I'll be fine. Just didn't come dressed for this part, is all."

"We are close." He says, stopping and pointing his light up to the treehouse. "See, wasn't far at all."

Danika stands behind him, looking up at the large treehouse in awe. "You let your son play up there?"

"Not exactly." He takes a deep breath. "Okay, let's get this over with."

Owen peeks his head up into the darkness of the treehouse through the floor opening. He draws his flashlight above himself, clumsily bumping it against the frame of the floor-drop before fumbling it to the floor. Coughing from the burst of raised dust, he quickly recovers it and climbs the rest of the way in, followed by Danika, who reaches for his assistance with her one free hand.

"I can't believe I made it up into this thang," she looks down at her exit, "Now I don't know how in the heck I'm supposed to get back down."

After helping her, Owen pans the area with his bright-white beam. His teeth are gritty from the dirt he nearly swallowed, so he gathers the saliva and shoots a big gob of dirt-filled spit to the floor.

"Disgusting," says Danika. "You are definitely Marley's brother."

The floorboards whine in the dark room ahead. Owen quickly aims his light in that direction. Nothing. He takes long, quick strides toward the sound, in hopes to catch whatever made the noise, but the room is empty.

"What's that?" Asks Danika. "Aim your light over here?"

He does, shining on Danika—kneeling in front of the opening in the floor beside a toybox. He kneels beside her, shining his light inside.

Danika covers her mouth, her eyes wide and filled with horror. "Oh, my dear God."

Owen looks away briefly, covering his mouth with the backside of his wrist, then hesitates before illuminating the remains of the child again. He, then, places the flashlight on the floor, aiming it at the toybox. "Give me a hand?" He asks, placing his palms on the toybox. Danika does the same, both lean their bodyweight into it and push the box the rest of the way across the floor.

The entire hiding space beneath it is revealed. A funnel-web spider—that found its home in the skeletal chest cavity—retreats into its hole.

Owen sits back to look, but notices Danika had not released her grasp, her eyes closed and squinting. Her hands still tightly grip the wooden box. It takes him a moment to realize what is happening, so he waits, unsure of what he should do next.

She flinches as if electrical current is being pulsed through her hands. The thoughts in her mind race, like the forward/skip button on a DVD player, cutting through portions of the critical events that led to the child's demise.

A view through Dennis's eyes... seeing everything from his perspective, playing in the kitchen and tossing a white ball around in, what is now, the Mosley residence.

The cold wind from the below-zero winter howled through the cracks of the kitchen window. He is suddenly startled by a loud, crashing sound at the front door and commotion in the living room. An argument erupts between his father and some other men who had entered the home. Dennis scrambles under the kitchen table, catching a glimpse of his father leading the men—three white men—into the basement.

Moments later, his father emerges from the basement.

"Dennis—Dennis?" He anxiously whispers. Immediately locating him under the table, part of his father's face is covered with blood. After snatching a kitchen chair and jamming it under the handle of the basement door, he grabs Dennis, nearly dragging him to the backdoor before he could get his feet underneath himself to stand.

Once outside, he tosses Dennis over his shoulder and races through the bitter cold to the tree line, then drops him to the ground. He kisses him on the forehead and pushes him away. "Go—Go!" He nervously looks back to the rear door of the house. "And don't come out until you hear my whistle! Remember?"

Dennis nods.

"Do you have yours?"

Dennis pats his chest and pinches the whistle underneath his shirt, then nods his head again.

The sound of a shotgun blast, from inside, startles them both. He points to the woods. "Hurry, now!"

Confused, Dennis obeys and runs into the forest with his ball under his arm. He looks back only once to see his father running back to the home, only to be greeted by the angry men coming outside.

Dennis crouches down, shivering and peeking through the leafless trees and bushes as one of the men strikes his father to the ground with a backfist.

382

Dennis clutches a branch with his free hand and screams silently, then runs off into the forest.

Quickly, he climbs the ladder to the treehouse, but stumbles in the hallway and drops his white ball—which rolls across the floor. He pushes the heavy toybox to the side, and climbs into his hiding spot, immediately yanking at the rope beside him. The rope is attached to the box, which aids in sliding it back over him, guided by metal tracks underneath it. Before he is totally concealed, the white ball ricochets off the wall and falls inside, finding its resting spot alongside him.

Above, something heavy falls beside the box. When he pulled the rope to open it, pressing his feet against the sides for more leverage, the rope snapped and fell limp in his hands. He's trapped and in the dark. The toybox refuses to budge regardless of how much he tried.

Hours passed and Dennis grew colder, stuffing himself in the corner of the small compartment in a desperate attempt to preserve body heat. For hours, he pounds away at the bottom of the box with his tiny fists and blows the whistle that hangs around his neck—but no one comes to his rescue, leaving him alone until hunger, fear, and the freezing cold take him away.

She releases the box, and looks over to Owen, tears falling from her saddened eyes.

"What?" He asks, "What did you see?"

She reaches down into the hole below, and gently lifts the tarnished necklace from around his neck. The object hanging from it gets stuck for a moment, but with a little wiggle she is able to free it from his chest cavity. What looks like an old infantry or police whistle solidifies what Danika already knows... Dennis.

CHAPTER 23

WARMER

(9:51 PM)

Marley and Kyra inspect the mechanical object that was ripped from Pupuka's insides.

Marley places it under Kyra's magnifying glass on her desk. "Looks like it may be part of a machine. But why was it in the doll. Not like it had some mechanical parts in it."

"Obviously, someone was trying to hide it, Uncle Marley. Can I see it?" Asks Kyra.

He drops it in her palm.

After a moment of fiddling, she twists the stem at the base and the pyramid fans out and opens with a *click*, revealing the remainder of the stem hidden within it.

"Interesting," Marley says, watching her slowly twirl it, like a fan, by the stem. His eyes suddenly jolt open wide. "Shit! I think I know." He grabs Kyra by the wrist and quickly leads her out of the room.

❦ ❦ ❦ ❦

"You saw all of that, in that short amount of time?" Asks Owen.

"It's a rush of visual information." She hands him the necklace with the old police whistle dangling from it. "And, believe it or not, sometimes it hurts. I can't do it all the time, only when there is a tremendous amount of energy attached to an object."

He holds the whistle, noticing right away that it is much colder than he had expected the piece of metal to be. On the side is engraved with a single name, *Dennis.* Along the length of the whistle are thick, straight, tarnished lines—also engraved into the metal—with tiny tribal markings within them.

"What are we gonna do with this?"

"Hold onto it tight," she folds his fingers over it, "Don't lose it. After what I saw I'm sure it's important."

❦ ❦ ❦ ❦

Moments later, Owen and Danika exit the forest in strides.

386

"Don't you think we need to call the police?" Asks Owen. "I mean, we got a dead child in a treehouse in the back forest."

"No! No police until we figure out what we need to know. The police could cause more problems. They have a way of flipping things around and making *you* the criminal. *No* police. We can handle this without them."

Owen snatches open the screen door in a hurry, but is stopped by the locked door.

He yanks and twists at the doorknob. "Damn it!" He exclaims.

"Wasn't it just unlocked before we left."

"Yeah," He looks through the kitchen window. "Stay here, I'll run around to the front and unlock it."

"But why do I need..."

Before she can finish her question, Owen already made his way around to the side of the house. She sighs, tossing her hands up in front of herself in resignation.

Owen leaps from the front walkway to the second porch step, suddenly smashing through the rotted wood. As he attempts to free himself, grabbing the rail and using his other leg for leverage, his other foot finishes off the steps, crushing through.

"Shit!" He exclaims, turning his body to reach for the railing again, when his ankles are grabbed from beneath and he is yanked below. His arms and neck scrape against the jagged pieces of wood as he falls to the dirt underneath the porch. He sits up quickly, frantically kicking up dirt while scrambling back on his hands.

Unable to see his attacker in the darkness, along with the dust and dirt he had kicked up, he sits motionless. The moonlight shines through the broken opening he was pulled through, yet doesn't provide him enough light. His eyes stay fixed on the pitch-blackness straight ahead, as his fingers find the smooth cylinder of his flashlight. His heart punches against his ribs, beating heavily, as he held his breath to listen to his surroundings.

Owen remains still, moving only his hand, as he activates his flashlight—when something rushes him, knocking the flashlight away and dragging him by his ankles further underneath the house. He rolls to his stomach, screaming for help while clawing and digging at the cold, loose dirt he is being drug through. He tries to work his feet free, but it feels as if his ankles are bound tightly by large strong hands.

The flashlight rolls into a dip in the dirt, fortunately aiming in his direction, and reveals his scuffle is with nothing but the air around him.

With his feet disentangled from whatever force was binding them a split second before, he scurries toward his flashlight. He snatches it from the ground and aims the beam of light in the direction of his attacker. Just dirt, cobwebs and debris is visible, directly underneath what Owen believes is the floor of the foyer. He covers his mouth, being careful not to inhale the floating dust with his heavy, panicked breathing. He isn't able to see much, due to the flashlight reflecting off the dust particles, but as it settles, his heart flutters from what he discovers, sitting against the wall.

A decayed corpse of a man, sitting on the ground with his back against the wall and his head slumped forward. His skull is black and brown, with some gray, curly hairs still attached to his chin and head. The man's red, flannel shirt is a brighter red at the bottom than around the shoulders and head, and looks like small holes had been chewed through it in multiple places. *Rats?*

Owen keeps his light trained on him while grabbing for a piece of broken two-by-four with his free hand. He stays low in the tight space, having only a little-less than four feet of space to maneuver. He shuffles his feet towards the body with the light and weapon in front of himself. He reaches forward with the jagged, broken end of the wood being conscious of maintaining his distance; he then pokes its foot a few times before pulling back. He coughs from the floating dust, daring to get a little closer. He pokes the corpse around the head and shoulders. The glint of something on the man's decayed right hand, catches his eye.

He positions himself in front of the body, gathering the nerve to cautiously and slowly reach over to inspect the jewelry on the hand. Then, he hears a sound—like hundreds of wet, slimy and slithering worms —behind the man's body. He crawls around to his right and looks behind the corpse's shoulder. To his horror, the back seemed to be glued to the wall by an oily substance. When he pulls the man's shoulder from the wall, it sounded like wet Velcro peeling apart. The substance seems to move-about with a mind of its own and has the familiar scent of motor oil. Owen quickly releases the shoulder in disgust. When he did, the oil reaches out from the wall with tiny tentacles, reattaching to his shoulder and pulling it slowly, returning the corpse securely to the wall.

Nearby, he can hear Danika calling his name. He gently removes a ring from the decayed finger and scrambles away on his hands and knees to the exit. He looks back once more, before leaving, flashing his light in the corpse's direction. His head is no longer slumped forward... it's turned, as if it were watching Owen.

❦ ❦ ❦ ❦

Marley inspects the brick they had placed in the hole in the basement, dusting a section with his index finger. Kyra curiously watches from behind her uncle, as he aims the fanned-out pyramid piece, ever so carefully, into the triangle carving on the left of the brick. He inserts the gold stem, pushing it in until the three corners of metal are flush with the carving. Then, he stands back.

"Is it supposed to do something?" Asks Kyra.

"Shit, I don't know. Not like I've done this before."

Kyra reaches in and fidgets with the stem, then, with her thumb, she pushes it the rest of the way in, until it is flush to the fanned pyramid key and brick, with no metal protruding at all. They hear a more solid *clank,* deep within the wall.

Marley jumps. "You sure *you* haven't done this before?"

A grinding noise behind the wall vibrates the brick, causing it to chatter in the slot. Then, abruptly, it stops.

Marley stands back. "Okay? What was that?"

They wait for a moment to see if anything else was going to happen.

"There's two more symbols. Maybe we have to find the other keys in order to unlock whatever this is?"

"Yeah, good point. I just hope this ain't no *Hell Raiser* crap or something out of Jumanji. We got enough bad shit going on."

Unknown to them, a thick, black liquid oozes from the bricks and up the wall at the far end of the basement behind them, defying gravity while pooling and spreading on the ceiling.

❦ ❦ ❦ ❦

"Owen?" Danika says, peeking down into the new hole in the porch. "You down there?" She hears Owen's coughing and leans into the hole.

He nearly scratches her face when he lunges out and grabs the frame of the porch to climb free. She jumps back, panicked, but then, realizing it was him, reaches out to aid.

Out of breath and covered in dirt, Owen opens his clenched fist in front of her, revealing a gold square-shaped ring. She reaches for it, but he pulls his hand away.

"You sure you want to do that?" He asks.

"Are you sure you want to know what's going on in your house?"

Owen hesitates, but then hands it to her carefully.

She takes a seat on what is left of the front steps, then closes her eyes, grasping the ring tightly in her palm.

A first-person view of military men in front of a house, wearing tactical, camouflage uniforms, rush into a building. He passes a mirror in the hallway, showing the rank and name patch on his uniform, Corporal Hill. Their weapons are at the ready as multiple men yell "Clear!" while entering and exiting different rooms.

A black chest is being opened, filled with small gold bars, then another to the right. The soldier next to him, the name and rank on his uniform Sergeant Michaels, rests his weapon to his side with a huge greedy smile crossing his face, and rubs his dry palms together.

The view changes again to Sergeant Michaels in civilian clothing, with an inebriated look in his eyes and pointing his finger to Corporal Hills's forehead. "You better not screw us on this either, boy." As he slams another shot, two other white men behind him nod their heads in agreement. He frowns, holding the shot glass to his lips as the liquor burns its way down his

throat. "Ehm, we got eyes, boy. We got eyes on you, best you believe that."

�

Another soldier sits before him. His skin dark and flawless, with the name and rank of Sergeant Burgess on his uniform patch. His expression is unsure, as if he could not believe what he had just heard. He points his thumb behind himself discreetly, looking over toward the three men as they sit with their trays of chow, in the far part of the mess tent. "You better be careful dealing with them racist, white motha-fuckas. They'd kill you before letting you have any part of that gold. You listen to old Lloyd Burgess. And I'm telling you, you just a fucking mule nigga!" He sits back in his chair and crosses his legs. "Wake the hell up, brotha. Use that money for your son's operation. All they gonna do is add to their arsenal of guns and create more uniforms for that racist White Wolves bullshit they support."

✻

The front door of the house is kicked open and three men enter wearing ski masks. The one in front has his arms out wide and the two behind him are armed, one wielding a shotgun and the other a hunting rifle.

"Well, hey there Corporal Clifford Hill. How's business?"

The view changes abruptly to the man on top, pounding his fists into Clifford's face again and again. He then raises his ski mask. Sergeant Michaels. He takes a deep breath and looks down at Clifford, wide-eyed and fierce. Michaels notices a silver necklace around Clifford's neck and rips it off, a polished, nickel-

plated metropolitan whistle hangs from it. "What's this? So you can call your mute?" He tosses the whistle on the floor and his goon smashes it with the butt of his rifle. He raises his fist once more to strike.

Clifford throws his hands up. "Wait—wait, okay. I'll show you where it is. Wait! Just wait!"

Michaels bites his bottom lip and shakes his head. "Well, that's all I wanted, boy." He climbs off him. "Look here. Every bit of that gold better be here. Hear? Not one bar missing." He looks around the room. "Or I'll string that little mute nigger son of yours to a tree in the back woods there."

Clifford leads them down the stairs and to the basement. His eyes wide and shifting as if he were waiting for the right moment. "There, behind the desk." He says, pointing.

As they all turn their backs to him, he races up the stairs, then slams the basement door shut.

"Dennis—Dennis," he anxiously whispers, immediately locating him under the table, and noticing the terrified look on his son's face. He snatches a kitchen chair and jams it under the doorknob of the basement, then grabs his son.

Clifford shudders from the bitter cold hitting his face and entering his lungs, while sprinting through the backyard with Dennis draped over his shoulder, until he reaches the tree line. He kisses him on the forehead and pushes him away. "Go—Go!" He nervously looks back to the backdoor. "And don't come out *until you hear my whistle! Remember?" Dennis nods. The sound of a shotgun blast from inside startles them both. He points into the woods. "Hurry, now!"*

He is met by the men at the backdoor and backhanded to the ground by a heavy fist.

❦

Shortly he comes to his senses, but surrounded by the white porcelain of his tub, his legs hung over the side and held by one of Michaels boys. Still a bit dazed, he attempts to sit up but is struck in the forehead by the butt of a rifle. "You stay right there, boy. Get up again and you gon feel the action from the other end of this rifle." Says Michaels, appearing at the side of the tub with a large bottle of motor oil. His other goon grabs his wrists and pins his arms down above his head. "Now," Michaels twists off the cap, "I asked you politely and you didn't seem to respond to it too well. But you gon talk." He hangs the bottle over Clifford's head. "Where the fuck, is the gold." He pours the oil directly into his nose. When his mouth opens for air, he pours it there. When his mouth closes, he goes back to the nose.

After nearly forty seconds of the mechanic's version of waterboarding, he stops. Clifford tilts his head to the side, gagging, choking and spitting up motor oil. The men's loud laughter is gurgled from the thick oil poured in his ears. Clifford could feel the man's hands slipping from his wrist, the oil causing him to lose his grip as he chuckled. He waited for the right moment, slipping one hand free and striking the man, that was holding his wrists, in the jaw, then kicking the man holding his feet in the face.

Startled, Michaels drops the motor oil and lunges for the shotgun but slips on the oily floor surface. Clifford scrambles from the tub and hops away toward the bathroom door—when a shotgun blast tore through his side.

He stumbles to the floor but painfully scrambles back to his feet, still fleeing, while holding his side. Clifford clumsily makes his way down the stairs, then out the front door into the howling, freezing-cold wind. He presses on a wood panel in the porch and climbs through an inconspicuous opening on the side, leading beneath the porch.

His jaw quivers. The stomping above him echoes in his hollow surroundings, as the men run up and down the stairs in their search for him. He could hear the muffled, raging directions barked by Michaels to his two goons to 'hurry and find him'.

The bright lights of a car, stopping in front of his home, catches his attention. Suddenly, the front door bursts open and a man thunders across the porch sending dust down on top of him. Clifford leans in, peeking between a gap in the wood, barely able to see who it was with the wind blowing through. His teeth chattering from the bitter cold.

Michaels approaches the car as the window rolls down. A woman turns to address him.

His hand grew cool and moist with his own blood seeping through his thick flannel clothing. He grit his teeth and bore the pain as he drug himself toward an opening at the base of the house.

Danika's vision fades. With a surprised look on her face, she turns to the house across the street. "Lorna Michaels." She mutters.

"What?" Owen asks, feeling confused. "What about her?"

"Your neighbor. She has something to do with this. He bled to death, cold and alone. The dead man you found under the stairs."

"How did you—" He frowns. "You lost me."

"It's the boy's father. The boy we found in the treehouse. His father is the owner of this ring."

🦋 🦋 🦋 🦋

Kyra screams, looking up to the ceiling as Marley lays flat against it, sinking into the blackness of some thick liquid that formed above him. His arms and legs are bound by several black, whip-like tentacles that begin slithering about his face, wrists and thighs.

In a desperate attempt, he manages to free an arm as his body is nearly submerged. He thrusts his hand out, reaching for Kyra. She stretches out for him, but barely grazes his fingertips with her own.

"Uncle Marley!" She begins carefully climbing and unstable vintage shelf next to her, reaching out again for his hand. His face sinks into the dark muck when the shelf gives, falling over and closing the distance between their hands. She grabs it firmly. The weight of her fall yanks Marley free. They all fall to the floor, when the shelf, and another beside it, crash down on top of them. The black muck seeps slowly into the cracks of the ceiling, disappearing until there's no trace of it.

Dazed, Kyra crawls free from under the toppled furniture and backs against a wall. "Uncle Marley?" She whispers, her heart pounding. Her bruised and abraded skin burns on her hands and forehead.

With shaking hands, she bends down to grip the side of a shelf. Then stops. The faint sound of chattering teeth echoes before her. An unseen force grabs her by the neck and forces her back against the wall. The basement light flickers, suddenly showing flashes of the entity holding her. Tall and dark. Its breath cold, damp, and musty.

It leans forward, mere inches from her open mouth and inhales deeply.

Kyra's eyes jolt open as she feels her life force being pulled from her stomach, out of her mouth and into the entity's. The more he takes in, the stronger his grip tightens, and the more solid his appearance becomes. His face connects with hers by a thin, glowing, blue layer of vapor flowing rapidly into his mouth.

She can hear the upstairs door booming, as someone kicked and yanked at the doorknob, but she cannot scream. Her eyes roll upward as she falls limp and weak in the entity's grasp.

A bracelet of twisted metal is suddenly launched in from under the basement door, ricocheting off the wall, and cutting through the entity with precision. Its appearance fades, dropping Kyra to the floor.

The door bursts open, Chandu showing himself at the middle of the staircase, is holding and aiming a thick rubber band and another bracelet like a slingshot, ready to fire. Jacob crutches down behind him. Both boys watch as Kyra catches her breath, coughing and wheezing on all fours.

Owen races down the steps with Danika following closely behind him. "What—What happened." He asks, dropping down beside Kyra.

"Help Uncle Marley!" Kyra orders, looking over and pointing to the fallen shelves.

Owen wastes no time, immediately lifting the top shelf with everything he has, then the other, freeing Marley's legs.

Danika quickly checks his pulse. "He's ok. Just unconscious."

Both Owen and Kyra breathe a sigh of relief as the strong woman roles him to his back, then cradles him over her lap. She looks down at him, gently caressing his face.

"You have something that can help him? To bring him to?" Says Owen, crouching beside her.

Without a word she continues caressing, stroking the edge of his jawline with her fingers, then smacks Marley firmly on the cheek twice. His eyes jolt open wide—as if he had awakened from a nightmare—kicking his legs, and throwing his hands up in defense.

His sits up, confused, looking to the ceiling then back to Danika. "What'd you do that for? What happened?" He says holding his face.

"That always works." Says Danika as she flashes a smile. "Come on. All of you. Gather yourselves quickly upstairs. There's something I need to explain."

CHAPTER 24

WHISTLE IN THE DARK

"There's something we all need to do, but I must explain what is going on first." Says Danika, placing the tip of her prayer hands to her lips before continuing. "The spirit of Clifford Hill is attached to this house. And when I say attached, I mean his corpse is literally attached to this house, which makes him strong. The same way the child in the treehouse is attached to that."

"Wait. Let me get this straight," Says Marley. "I've been getting my ass kicked by a spirit named *Clifford*?"

"Marley! Stop," Orders Danika. "This is a father and his son, separated during a home invasion. I could go into a long explanation about what happened, but all you need to know now is that all the father wants is his son to return home. The spirit of the child in the treehouse needs to be reunited here with his father."

"And how do we accomplish that?" Asks Marley.

"I believe the whistle has to be blown from inside the house or the backyard, signaling the boy it is safe to come home. Remember what I said about a spirit being bound by his last ordeal before death? This is theirs."

"What whistle?" Asks Kyra.

"With the whistle Owen has. We got it from the treehouse. Something happened to the father's whistle, but I believe it's the same. And as long as we use it here. In the home. I think it will work."

"So, what are we talking about it for? Let's do it now." Says Marley.

Owen begins searching his pockets and jacket.

"Where is the whistle?" Asks Danika.

"Shit! I must've dropped it near the porch, or up under the house. I don't know." Owen says.

"You went under there? The porch?" Asks Chandu.

"Yes."

"But that's where *he* is. The angry man."

"Trust me, I know that now."

"I have a toy whistle." Says Jacob.

402

"No, sweetie," says Danika, "This whistle has a distinct sound. It needs to be the one the father had or the boy's."

"You have to go back and get it." Says Danika.

"The Hell I do! There's no way I'm going back under that porch with the dad still sitting down there sucking on the house with his back."

"Well, it's the only way you're going to get any peace around here and have this home for yourselves. You have to save a few troubled souls to find that peace." Says Danika.

"Few?" Frowns Owen.

Marley notices the ring Owen is fiddling with between his fingers while deciding his next move. "What's that?" Marley points.

Owen hands him the ring. "It was on the father's hand."

"Looks like the same design as that metal piece we found in that doll earlier." He hands it to Kyra. "Do that thing you did before when you opened that key."

Kyra curiously takes it in her palm, then gently twists the inner loop of the ring. A small stem emerges from a tiny hole that is centered on one of the sides; along with tiny teeth arising along the four edges of the ring—making it look like an odd-shaped gear. The more she turns the inner portion, the further the stem protrudes; then, it finally stops, locking the stem and teeth in place.

Kyra smiles and hands the newly transformed ring back to Marley.

He sucks his teeth. "Looks like we may have the second key here," he holds it out to Owen, "But I'm not going back down there by myself unless you guys are coming with me."

"We do what we need to first, Marley. We don't have time for any puzzles."

"We all have something to do. I think all this ties into something, for sure," he puts the ring on his pinky. "Okay, you go down there with me, and I'll go with you to get the whistle, King-O. How about that?"

🦋 🦋 🦋 🦋

Marley carefully places the square piece into its corresponding shape in the brick, aligning the stem with the centered hole, like Kyra did with the other. He looks back to the others standing behind him, then presses the stem firmly inside. The brick vibrates again, like before, but clicks twice this time before becoming silent.

"One more piece." Marley says.

"Don't get your hopes up. We aren't even sure what this does or what's behind this wall, if anything. This could be a trap, for all we know."

404

The lights flicker and buzz, followed by a sudden chill in the air.

"Uh-Oh." Chandu says quietly, grabbing his mother's hand. "We have to forget this for now. Maybe hurry and find that whistle."

"Upstairs, now please!" Orders Danika. "We should go to the front yard where it is safe."

The children go first, and the others follow, with Owen in the back.

As they burst out from the basement door, and spill into the hallway. They all stop, both in horror and in awe, before entering the foyer.

"What's wrong?" Owen curiously asks, forcing his way through them to a pile of his furniture, couch, love seat, and coffee table all jammed-up against the door—blocking their front exit. Owen steps closer to the barricade.

Jacob scans the room, crutching his way over to the window behind him. A clear night allows him to see directly to the tree line out back... something moves, just under his skin near his temple, then disappears.

"Can I get a hand over here?" Owen asks, preparing himself to shift the furniture away from the door.

Marley assists as Danika and Kyra watch in concern. The two men struggle with the heavy sofa, then the table—pushing it all to the side to clear a path to the door. Danika clasps her hands in front of her chest.

Kyra shakes with fear, her body trembling as if she might explode. "Please—please—please can I just go to Grandma's. I don't wanna be here! We can just go. All of us!"

Owen shoves the table to the side. "We have to deal with this. Together. All of us, Kyra." He turns to face her. "You and your brother—" he looks over her shoulder to where Jacob was previously standing. "Where's your brother?"

Something pops upstairs and Jinx comes racing down the steps. Without hesitation, Owen and Marley take-off up the stairs. Danika joins them, gently pushing past Kyra—who stops at the third step.

"Where are you guys going!?" She yells, "How could he be up there or gotten past us." No one replies.

She catches some movement from the corner of her eye and watches silently as the back screen-door comes to a close. She runs to the kitchen window for a full view of the backyard, arriving just in time to see Chandu about five paces behind Jacob, following him into the forest. She pounds on the window to get their attention. Chandu looks back briefly, but continues behind Jacob until they disappear into the darkness.

The adults continually yell, searching for the boys upstairs. Danika, near Jacob's bedroom window, sees Kyra running through the backyard and into the forest.

Owen starts down the hall. "Jacob? Ja—" His wrist is swiftly caught from behind by Danika.

"Go get the whistle, Owen. I already know where the boys are." Orders Danika.

Marley comes out of Kyra's room.

She releases Owen's wrist. "Marley go with your brother. We need to end this quickly."

"Where are they!?" Owen yells frantically.

"Trust me, please. Just go! Now!" She orders, leaving the other two standing in the hallway.

"Wait—Wait!" yells Marley. "Can we get a bracelet or two before we go down there to that thing?"

"It doesn't work how you think it does." She says.

"Just give me one. It will make me feel better about going down there."

She huffs while removing a bracelet from her wrist and tosses it to him, before descending the front stairs.

🦋 🦋 🦋 🦋

Owen and Marley stand just outside the caved-in steps of the porch. Despite the moonlight above, it shines no light underneath the porch; which is pitch-black and seeped out a stale odor. Owen aims his flashlight inside, but the bright beam has no effect on the darkness inside the hole. It's as though it is inviting them to come closer.

"You gotta get closer. I can't see shit." Orders Marley.

"You have a flashlight, too. Why don't *you* get closer?" Owen glances back at him, turning up his lip, then gets closer to the hole.

Marley takes a deep breath and slips on a bracelet.

"Why do *you* get to wear it?"

"Cause I'm the one who asked for it." He smirks.

"Well, then you have no problem going first."

"Oh no, fuck that! You go, King-O. You already been down there so you know where to go. Besides, this is your house, not mine."

"Damn, Marley," Owen shakes his head, "I thought I could count on you."

"You can count on me being right here behind you," Marley smiles, "You can count on me not going in first. You can count on me getting the fuck out of there if I see something wrong. You can count on me if—"

"Alright, damn. I got your point."

With his brother behind him, Owen steps down inside the porch, this time, on his own free will. They begin feeling around on all fours in the soft soil and broken pieces of wood, shining their lights around the darkness—their light beams shining like tiny spotlights.

Rather than staying focused on the mission on hand and searching the ground for the whistle, Marley's light flashes about every corner in paranoia.

"Let's hurry up and get out of here," says Marley, "Where did you see that thing? The dad's body."

Owen points his light to the opening at the base of the house. "In there."

Marley leans to the right on all fours in order to see inside the opening without getting any closer. "Shit! Seriously, bro? Do we *really* need that whistle?" He whispers, scooting back a tad.

"Your girlfriend says we do. And she's the expert."

"First, she ain't my girlfriend. Second, you definitely going first."

Owen dips down slightly to crawl into the space, with Marley lighting his way behind him. His light catches the skeletal remains Owen spoke about, sending chills up the back of his neck.

"Ugh—my God!" He says, dropping his light from the sight of it.

🦋 🦋 🦋 🦋

Nearly stumbling and rolling her ankle in her shoes from sticks and dead leaves under her feet, Danika searches the forest for the children while heading in the direction of the treehouse.

The sound of cracking wood and Kyra's scream sends Danika sprinting to her destination, soon arriving at the base of the treehouse where Kyra lay, nearly in tears, from a fall. Danika notices the collapsed ladder next to her.

"Are you okay, sweetie?"

Squinting her eyes in pain, Kyra holds her right knee with both hands and nods her head. "I'll be okay."

"Where are the boys? Did you see them?"

Hissing through her teeth from the pain. "Yeah, up there. They went up there." Still holding her leg, she points with her pinky. "I was behind your son when the ladder fell. Something, ugh, somethings wrong with my brother though."

"Why do you say that?"

"He's acting weird. Like a zombie or under a spell or something. He wouldn't look back or respond no matter how much I yelled."

"Oh, my. I was afraid of that."

"What?"

"I didn't get rid of all of it. I should've double checked."

"What do we do? What's happening to my little brother?"

"It's Dennis. The boy your brother has been playing with. Your brother is in danger and we must hurry. Can you get up?"

"Yeah." Kyra hobbles for a moment on her feet favoring her left leg.

❀ ❀ ❀ ❀

Jacob is motionless, standing in the middle of the moonlit treehouse room with his back to Chandu. He is staring at the wall as if he is watching something, or someone.

Chandu can feel the other presence but cannot yet see it. The room grows colder when fear, loneliness and anger strike him at once, resonating from the wall Jacob was fixed on. As he moves closer behind Jacob, his eyes trained on the dark portion of the wall, he could feel something staring back at him. Then, he could hear scraping, like nails against a chalkboard, growing higher in pitch the closer he became.

Jacob spins around smiling eerily at Chandu. Then, something squirmed in his temple underneath the skin. Jacob shoves Chandu back with one hand causing him to stumble back and fall into the empty toybox behind him. Chandu tries to sit up but the top slams shut, hitting him in the head—rendering him unconscious.

Danika and Kyra can hear the commotion in the treehouse, while they frantically struggle with the remains of the wooden ladder.

❀ ❀ ❀ ❀

After searching, digging, and sifting around the dirt, they nearly give up. Owen sits back, next to Marley who had already given up minutes ago, aiming the flashlight in the direction they were avoiding the most.

Marley leans back against the wall. "There's only one other place to check," he says, "And that's *right there* next to ya boy."

"We ain't gonna find it just sitting here." Owen snaps.

"Well get to it. I'll provide the light."

"Man, you are a chicken-shit." He shakes his head, then crawls in the dead man's direction.

"Chicken? Did you see what just happened to me in your basement? You're lucky I'm still here. And when all of this is done, we gonna start going to church like Momma told us."

"Just hold the light." He orders, as he sifts around the surface of the dirt. The closer he got to the remains, the colder the chill gets, feeling it sweep over his skin. He checks around it, then toward the right side of the corpse—next to his hand. He stopped, suddenly. His eyes slowly widen with fear and disbelief. He looks back to his brother.

"What?"

Owen does not answer. Instead, he turns his attention back to the hand of the corps, clutching the chain with the whistle Owen just had earlier.

Without a word, he reaches for it... slowly. His hand trembles as his fingers stretch out for the gold chain. He draws his hand back quickly, then turns his gaze to the skull, staring into the dark, empty holes its eyes once were. He takes in a deep breath, gathering the courage, and finally snatching the whistle quickly, ripping the chain from its boney grasp.

"I got it," he says, out of breath as if he had just sprinted an entire block, "Let's go!"

Marley drops his light, sighing with relief, then leans against the wall next to Owen. Suddenly, the wall gives out and he falls backwards into it, struggling as he falls to the concrete floor of the basement.

"Marley!" Owen places the chain around his neck and slides down on the dirt after him.

Marley is already crawling to his feet when his brother tumbles in beside him, dirt and rocks spilling down thereafter.

CHAPTER 25

A SPIRITUAL MONSOON

Jacob continues staring in the dark, empty corner of the treehouse. A dead-entranced expression is plastered on his face. The wood floor groans in front of him and Dennis slowly emerges, as if he is gliding across the floor. He approaches Jacob, moving slowly through the moonbeam shining through the window; he floats back into the darkness, standing like a shadow before Jacob.

Jacob's eyelids flutter and his pupils fade to white. Oozing from his left tear duct, like toothpaste being squeezed from a tube, a small piece of white string, the length of his finger, extends out. It falls to the floor, turning black and sizzling upon touching the wood.

Weakened to his core, Jacob collapses to the floor. The color returns to his eyes, and Dennis suddenly straddles him, pinning Jacob's elbows to the floor with his knees. He removes his chalkboard from behind himself and shows Jacob what was prewritten in his shaky, child-like handwriting. "Don't you wanna be friends? Friends forever?"

Jacob looks up at him while struggling to get free, but he is too weak to fight.

Dennis smiles when he feels Jacob's body go limp, then waits for a response. Jacob closes his eyes and rests his head back onto the floor. Dennis becomes furious, grabbing his chalkboard again and forcing it in Jacob's face, tapping the board repeatedly with his fingernails. Jacob only opens his eyes for a moment, then closes them again, shaking his head.

When Jacob finally opens his eyes, he looks up to Dennis, who is staring back down at him. "Let me go, Dennis." He says calmly. "Please."

Dennis frowns, balling a fist with his free hand.

Chandu comes out of his unconscious state and immediately begins pounding on the lid of the toybox.

He screams as loud as he can. "Mom!"

But the heavy, nearly airtight container muffles his cries for help. He strikes the sides with his elbows and kicks the lid, but the wood is too strong. He then stomps his feet on the bottom, over-and-over.

❦ ❦ ❦ ❦

Danika could hear the pounding on the floor above her, as they finally lay what is left of the wooden ladder against the tree.

"Chandu!" She yells.

The pounding on the floor is louder and she can hear his faint, muffled cries for her.

Danika wastes no time climbing, but then turns back toward Kyra—still standing at the bottom. "Go back! Tell your father to blow the whistle when they find it. Don't waste any time. Tell him to blow it while he is in the backyard! Hurry!"

Kyra runs off, leaving Danika to climb with no held support from the bottom of the shaky ladder. She takes every step with care, nevertheless as quickly as possible.

"Hold on, baby." She mutters, looking up toward the window.

❦ ❦ ❦ ❦

Owen finishes dusting himself off.

"I hope this little whistle is worth all the trouble we going through for it." Says Marley.

"I know," Owen tucks the whistle in his shirt, "Let's go find the others, quick!"

Before Owen takes a step, he is tripped at the ankle and falls to his face. His flashlight skips across the floor and under some broken furniture.

"...the fuck. Are you alright?" Asks Marley.

Owen coughs, raising the dust from the floor in front of his face. "Yeah." He rolls over and pulls his feet toward himself; abruptly, the dangling light bulb near Marley brightens, then explodes, plunging them into darkness.

Marley flinches away from it. "What in the Hell, was that?"

Marley taps the button to his flashlight. The first few clicks did nothing, then suddenly a flash of light illuminates from it, aiming through the wood planks of the steps. Owen sees something dark lurking underneath them just before the flashlight shuts off again.

"Marley?" Owen says, rising to his feet and moving back toward his brother.

"Hold on, King-O," he says, while focusing on removing the batteries from his flashlight and placing them back in. "I think I got it." He taps the bottom, sending another quick flash of light to the corner of the basement, catching a glimpse of where the dark figured is now standing.

"We need to go!" Owen says.

Marley shakes the light, jiggling the batteries inside—still having hope that it'll work—when it comes on again, staying lit this time. Owen snatches the light from Marley and aims it in the corner. Nothing but an illuminated, dusty brick wall is before them.

Marley shivers from a sudden chill running up his side, followed promptly by a cool breeze against his neck. He turns to see where it's coming from, and is horrified by a thin, white vapor spitting out like a cold breath next to him. He gasps. But before he could react entirely, he's thrown against Owen's workbench with immense force, then falls to the floor.

Owen barely opens his mouth to speak, before the necklace he's wearing is grabbed from behind and pulled tight, creating a make-shift ligature around his neck. He drops the flashlight and desperately claws at the chain that's digging into his neck, the whistle's tip presses hard against his Adam's apple.

🦋 🦋 🦋 🦋

Danika, finally making it up to the treehouse window, peers inside to see Dennis on top of Jacob. His back is to her, but she knows that Dennis is aware of her presence. He calmly sits up, placing the chalkboard to the side. His head slowly turns nearly one hundred and eighty degrees in order to lock eyes with hers.

She feels his anger. His emptiness. His loneliness.

Chandu continues pounding away at the inside of the toy chest. Hearing him, she throws herself onto the window ledge, pulling herself over to get inside. Dennis grabs the chalkboard and throws it like a frisbee, grazing her cheek. Stunned, she falls back from the window out of sight.

Dennis smiles from the sound of the wood ladder crashing to pieces below.

❦ ❦ ❦ ❦

"Dad—Dad!" Kyra yells as she rushes in through the back door and into the kitchen. It's empty and quiet. She makes her way into the hallway, running into Jinx—sitting in the middle of the floor, with her ears perked and tail thrashing back-and-forth. She yowls deep and long, barely opening her mouth.

Kyra jumps from the sound of a loud crash in the basement. She rushes to the door, twisting and turning the knob, but it's closed solid. With no lock on the door, she knows it has to be something else keeping it closed.

She presses her face to the crack between the door and doorframe. "Dad, you down there!?"

"Kyra, don't come down here! Run!" Marley yells, while knocking broken pieces of a wood table off his legs to stand.

Marley runs to aid Owen who is lifted from the floor and pinned against the wall by a smokey, black apparition. It floats in front of him—mimicking the movement of ink swirling in a glass of water. Marley watches in horror as Owen's energy is drained from his lips and into the manifestation of the entity's mouth. As Owen is further drained of his energy, the apparition subduing him becomes more solid and well-defined in appearance.

Marley grabs a broken table leg, maneuvering it like a baseball bat, and charges, swinging through the apparition and falls to the floor. With the sound of Kyra pounding at the door in the background, he makes another attempt to save his brother. He grabs Owen by the wrist and pulls, but the entity has grown stronger from his stolen energy, and holds Owen firmly in place, despite Marley's efforts.

The house trembles. Dust falls on top of them, but it doesn't stop Marley from pulling on his brother as hard as he can, pressing his foot against the wall and baring his teeth.

Upstairs, Jinx is calm, even with the floor beneath her shaking and the walls around her vibrating. Pictures swing on the single nail supporting them, knick-knacks vibrate off the kitchen counters and fireplace ledge—smashing them to the floor.

Kyra steps back from the door in the sudden chaos, looking around her surroundings that feel as though they will cave down around her at any moment. She notices Jinx's calm demeanor, staring as she whips her tail about the floor even faster. The lightbulbs in the house furthest from them begin to explode, one after the other—down the upstairs hall, the light at the back door through the kitchen, the foyer... all the lightbulbs burst, with the exception of the last light that flickers above her and Jinx.

Kyra drops to her knees, plugging her ears while anticipating more loud noises to come. But all the chaos abruptly stops. The light above her shines bright, then returns to its normal, sixty-watt glow.

420

Marley struggles, feeling helpless as he watches his brother's life being sucked from his body. He screams and grunts, but it is of no use.

Kyra's rapid breathing begins to slow. She drops her hands from her ears, looking to Jinx, still motionless and staring down at Kyra. Both of her eyes return to the familiar green they once were.

A glint of movement behind Jinx catches Kyra's attention. One lonely, white butterfly floats through the foyer, and past the hallway they are standing in. It flips it's wings in a little dance then disappears into the living room. Curious, Kyra follows it, watching as it lands on the back-window curtain, then slips behind it, out of view.

She looks back nervously to Jinx, yowling repeatedly— deeper and longer than she ever heard her do before. Kyra approaches the window, hearing the fluttering against the glass, then pulls back the curtains with one big jerk.

Her eyes widen with amazement as she watches the one butterfly in the center of the window, flipping its wings, yet on the other side... thousands more, identical to it, flutter against the glass violently. Kyra slowly backs away, tripping over a raised corner of the carpet, and falls to the floor. She's locked in awe, watching and listening to the humming against the glass, before it cracks.

❦ ❦ ❦ ❦

Danika dangles from the base of the treehouse, the thick fabric of her top hooked onto the head of an exposed nail, and her fingertips grip the ledge. It was a long drop down for her. If she let go, she knows she would definitely break both of her legs... or worse.

She spots a stub of the tree, from a broken-off branch; she kicks off her decorative shoes and reaches for it with her right foot, gripping it with her toes for support. It is a struggle with all her weight on her toes, but she manages to pull herself high enough up to grab the ledge of the broken-out window again.

Dennis is still standing over Jacob when she peers inside. He grabs Jacob by the ankle, dragging him toward the square opening in the floor.

❦ ❦ ❦ ❦

Marley screams.

Hearing his desperation, Kyra comes to her feet. But before she could get to the basement door, the window cracks further, then relents—bursting and spilling in thousands of white butterflies, entering like a plague of locusts. She collapses back to the floor just as they reach her.

They move like a swarm of bees over her, then down the hall. Part of the swarm completely cover the basement door, while another group slips underneath, through the gap. The door pops open slowly, and like a triggered hive of bees, all the butterflies take flight through the opening. Down the stairs they go, immediately attacking the entity pinning, Owen, now white-eyed, to the wall. The color fades from his face as they swarm around the apparition like a tornado of confetti, trapping it and pulling it away from him. Owen collapses to the floor.

Marley covers his face with his forearm as he makes his way through the blinding madness to his fallen brother. Owen's body is cold when he grabs him under the arms, dragging him to the stairwell. He could barely hear Kyra, crouched down at the top of the stairs, yelling to him through the deafening sound of fluttering wings around them.

She hurries down beside them to help.

"We have to hurry!" She yells.

"Help me get him upstairs!"

Deep moaning from the struggling entity below gives them both the chills as they finally make it up the rest of the stairs, and through the basement door. Kyra kicks the door closed.

"I got Dad," She orders, removing the whistle from around his neck, "You have to go out back and blow the whistle. You have to do it *now*, Uncle Marley!"

The basement door shakes vigorously—as if something is pushing against it—bowing out from the pressure.

Marley takes the necklace and places it around his neck, leaving Kyra, cradling her father's head, in the hallway.

❧ ❧ ❧ ❧

Dennis raises Jacob by the ankle with tremendous strength, dangling him over the hole.

Danika falls inside the treehouse through the window. "No, Dennis!" She yells, crawling over to open the toybox that Chandu is still pounding away at. "Dennis, stop this now!" She yells, turning to him. "You have to go home. Your father is waiting for you."

Jacob reaches for the edge of the hole, but Dennis raises him higher, then smiles.

"Oh, my God, what is taking them so long!?" Danika mutters. "Blow it!" She screams toward the window.

Dennis looks at her curiously.

A distant, majestic tone of a whistle reverberates through the forest. Its sounds seemed to touch everything around it and travels high-up, where it fades into the sky.

Dennis looks to the window. He drops Jacob safely to the floor, then makes his way toward it. Once there, he smiles faintly, looking back to Danika, before fading away like a gray mist in the wind.

Chandu explodes from inside the toy chest as if whatever force holding him in was released. Danika wastes no time running to him, snatching him from the box and holding him tightly.

❀ ❀ ❀ ❀

As dawn approaches, Marley lowers the whistle after one last blow, looking out into the forest and waiting for something to happen. The trees rustle and the wind kicks up a gentle breeze before him, swirling through the grass and bushes as it approaches. He spins around to the sound of the screen door opening behind him, then groaning closed.

"Help!" Danika shouts.

Marley hears her in the distance and takes off into the woods.

The breeze flows inside the house, passing over Kyra and her father—still sitting on the hallway floor. As the breeze brushes Owen's head, cradled in Kyra's arms, the color rushes back through his skin and his eyes open, glistening the deep brown they should be.

The breeze travels under the basement door, dragging bits of dirt from the floor along with it.

Kyra sits up, suddenly hearing sobbing coming from under the basement door. It wasn't a sad sound. It was familiar to her. She'd heard it before when her father came looking for her at the state fair. She was only six years old, and somehow slipped from his and her mother's view. She remembers how strong her father's arms were when he found her, on her tip toes in front of a cotton candy stand while holding a dollar bill to the cashier. He held her so tightly and cried with the same emotion.

She had only been missing for a few minutes, but to them it felt like hours. A tear runs down her cheek.

CHAPTER 26

OH, BEFORE I GO...

(8:33 AM)

Kyra is in her room, cleaning up the mess of things that have fallen from her shelves and desktop. The picture of her mother is among the first items she returns to the shelf, the single crack across the glass shows when she adjusts it to a proper angle. She lifts her desk chair, finding her butterfly display case, then smiles when she discovers the case is empty. She sat back on her knees, unable to hold back her flowing tears.

Owen stands in the middle of the living room, the broken pieces of—what used to be—his back window crunch under his steel-toed boots. The sun peeks over the trees and shines into the living room, warming his face. He closes his eyes and takes a deep breath.

Danika walks in behind him.

"The boys are asleep," she says, "It's a much-needed nap for them.

"Yeah. It was a long night." Says Owen. He turns to her and smiles.

She returns the gesture. "They are gone, you know. It doesn't feel like you have anything to worry about here. Not anymore."

Marley and Kyra walk in from upstairs.

"Thank you!" Says Owen, taking Danika's hands in his own. "Thank you so much for your help. If it wasn't for you and your son..." He takes a deep breath and tilts his head back.

"No need to thank me. It was all of us. We helped set a tortured father and his son free." She smiles again.

Jinx comes running down the stairs and stops next to Kyra with the beat-up stuffed animal, Pupuka, in her mouth.

Kyra kneels next to her. "I see you found Pupuka. Sorry we practically destroyed her. I can fix her right up." She says, taking the doll from the large cat's mouth.

"So why do you call it Pupuka?" Asks Marley.

"I saw it online. Means ugly in Hawaiian."

"What a fitting name." Danika chuckles.

428

Kyra looks into Jinx's eyes. Hoping to see two different colors returned like before. "Mom?" She mutters.

Hearing her, they all look to each other.

"Is she still with us?" Kyra asks.

"No, sweetie," says Danika, "She had to move on."

"She saved Dad." She says, tears welling in her eyes again.

Danika looks up at Owen. "Yes, she did. She truly forgave your father. That is why she is no longer with us."

"She... she moved on?" Kyra's eyes drain, the tears curving down her cheeks and dripping from her chin. Then, without a word, she drops Pupuka to the floor and storms out the back door.

Danika looks to Owen. "Go."

Owen quickly follows behind Kyra. She's standing in the middle of the backyard with her fists clenched tight. He doesn't know what to say, so he approaches her cautiously. He is sure she may hold him at fault, but he had to do something.

With his left hand, he grabs her fist from behind and holds it firmly. She keeps it clenched and turns to him, sobbing.

"I did it..." She says.

"Did what?"

"I called social services." Her fist clenches tighter as more tears flow. "I'm sorry." Her breaths are short and shuddery as she tries to hold strong and keep back any sobbing.

Owen squeezes her fist tighter, but gently. "I don't care. I love you." He smiles. "I just hope one day you can forgive me."

As Kyra is about to drop her head, a white monarch butterfly, unknown to Owen, catches her attention and lands on his shoulder. She smiles at it, watching as it slowly fans its wings.

Owen notices her gaze and sudden change in mood.

"What?" He looks over his shoulder.

"You don't see it?"

"See what?" He looks again but sees nothing.

"The..." She smiles again, then giggles as it flies off into the dawning sky. She releases her tight fists and grabs her father's hand firmly. "Never mind." She quickly hugs him around the waist.

Owen's heart thumped heavily against her cheek as he embraced her even tighter.

🦋 🦋 🦋 🦋

(Later that afternoon)

Owen and Marley are standing, deep in the forest, over two shallow graves; sticks tied into crosses are at the head of each. Owen tosses the last of the dirt with his shovel onto the father's grave.

"Not sure why we are doing this." Says Marley.

430

"We need to keep this between all of us. Can you imagine the explanation we would have to give to the police? The house would be crawling with cops and detectives searching through everything. Hell, they may even try and take the house, and maybe the kids," he tosses the shovel over his shoulder, "It's best that we lay them to rest here. Together."

Marley jabs at the dirt with his shovel. "Should we say anything?"

"Oh, I didn't think about that."

"We have to say something. Can't just leave them here without a word or two."

They look at each other, then bow their heads.

"Umm," mutters Owen, "May your journey be safe and peaceful. Rest in peace. Amen."

Both pause, waiting to see if one another has anything else to say.

Marley raises his head. "That's good enough for me." He throws his shovel over his shoulder as well.

"Me too."

As they make their way back to Owen's house, Marley peeks at his older brother through the corners of his eyes. "So, what now? 'Cause you know, I think we make a fairly good team and all. Not sure why you haven't hired me yet. And I know you could use the help."

"Mar, trust me, if I had the money to pay you to be on my team, I would. I just don't have the means right now. And I have all the repairs to the house to worry about, too. It's gonna be rough."

"Okay. Well, just so you know, I can do *rough,* King-O. No worries there. I need your help just as much as you need mine now. We can get this fixed right up. But don't ask me to move in with you 'cause... well..." He laughs. "So, you're not gonna move after all of this?"

Owen laughs. "Hell no. I got nowhere else to go."

🦋 🦋 🦋 🦋

(6:57 AM)

The next morning—after they all have had a much-needed night's rest, while sleeping in the living room like a slumber party—Danika awakens early with Kyra to cook breakfast. Kyra opens the kitchen curtains to let in the rays of the rising sun. She closes her eyes as it warms her face.

The smell of pancakes and eggs saturate the noses of the sleeping men and boys, who slowly rise like mummies from a long slumber.

Owen sits up from his nest of blankets, rubbing his eyes. He smiles, taking in the new energy in their home, and the aroma he hadn't smelled in so long. Danika, scraping the eggs from the

432

skillet into a large bowl, feels his energy, and flashes the faintest of smiles.

🦋 🦋 🦋 🦋

After breakfast, Danika and Chandu gather their things and head out the front door. Kyra is on the porch stroking Jinx's fur when they come out.

Danika turns to her and smiles. "It was a pleasure meeting you, young lady." She leans over to hug her tightly. "Maybe someday we can meet under a much more pleasant situation."

Kyra returns the hug. "Thank you." She squeezes her even more snug. "Thank you for everything."

Jacob bursts outside, juggling the screen door with his crutches, startling them, followed by Owen, finally holding the door for him, then Marley.

"Are you ready?" Asks Marley.

"Oh, yeah, I'm ready." She laughs.

Owen watches from the top of the entryway stairs, as Marley leads them to Danika's car. "So, you're for sure it's gone? You didn't feel anything?"

"Yeah. I'm sure," she turns to him, "I know you felt the difference this morning. No need to worry." She then looks across the street to Lorna's home. "Like I said before... entities only stay if they have some unresolved issues."

Jacob removes the whistle tucked in his shirt, still caked with dirt and mud from under the house. He places it to his lips, and Owen quickly catches his hand.

"You may wanna clean that off before putting that to your lips, son."

Jacob crutches back into the house making his way to the kitchen sink.

Owen notices Danika and Marley standing a little closer to each other than before. He steps off the porch. "Hey. You guys have something you wanna tell me?" He insinuates, pointing back and forth between the two of them with a smile.

"Nothing you haven't already noticed or suspected." Says Danika with a wink.

Marley bares his bottom teeth over his top lip with a frown. Owen laughs.

🦋 🦋 🦋 🦋

Jacob holds the whistle under the warm water, using his fingers to loosen the hardened dirt on the outside. As he continues removing more of the dirt coating, he can make out more ridges and designs, engraved on the outside shaft, that weren't evident before.

"Kyra!" He yells, wiping it down with the dry cloth hanging from the faucet. "Kyra!"

She comes running in beside him. "Dang, what?"

"Look," he holds up the whistle near her nose, "What's this stuff on it?"

"That's weird." She says, taking it from him. Her eyes widen. "Come on!"

🦋 🦋 🦋 🦋

"I'll be back this weekend to help you clean up." Says Marley while standing outside the car door.

"Sounds good. I'll let you know as soon as we get a job. We could definitely use the money, now."

"Yeah. Maybe we can get separate trucks and do some advertising," Marley's eyes gleam, "Maybe we can change the name to *Two Handymen Two Mosley's?*"

"Yeah, probably not." He laughs.

Marley waves, then gets in the passenger side of the bright-yellow Volkswagen Bug. He rolls down his window. "Love you King-O!"

Danika speeds off—with the metallic whirring-sound from the exhaust that only a VW Bug can make.

Owen waves back. "Love you too, little bro." He mutters.

❦ ❦ ❦ ❦

Lorna enters her back door, dirty from working in her garden. She hears the conversation between the two brothers across the street and approaches her front window to eavesdrop, like she always does, pulling the curtain back gently. As the VW Bug drives off, she sucks her teeth and pulls the curtains completely closed, then heads off to her bedroom to undress. When she enters, she passes a picture on the dresser of her late husband, Sergeant Michaels, in his military uniform. There's a smaller picture jammed in the corner of the frame—one of him and a few of his friends, standing in front of a Confederate flag, clutching their cans of beer, and raising them in a toast.

She peels off her gloves, heading into her master bathroom, then tosses them into the dirty clothes hamper; suddenly, her bedroom lights flicker off behind her. She pauses for a moment and looks back curiously to her dark bedroom. She approaches the doorway slowly, peeking into the room and flipping the switch by the door multiple times, but no light comes on. *What in the Hell.* She could easily open her thick curtains for light, but instead, she closes the bathroom door, creeped out by the darkness in her bedroom.

After undressing, she places a robe on her weathered body when the lights go out completely and the house grows silent.

She pauses once more, holding her breath as she listens carefully. It's quiet, as if the power has been shut off entirely.

She suddenly has the feeling of being watched. Someone, or something, is definitely in the house with her.

The hinges of the bathroom door pop and grind, opening behind her. She gasps, seeing a tall silhouette standing in the partially-opened door, and the faint sound of chattering teeth.

"It's you," she whispers, "I know it's—"

The door slams shut, as a souped-up, heavy-duty, pickup truck barrels down the street with a loud muffler, drowning out her screams from her upstairs bedroom.

🦋 🦋 🦋 🦋

Kyra finishes moving some fallen furniture from in front of the mysterious brick with the two keys already inserted. She looks down at Jacob, who is too short to reach the brick, and extends out her hand for the whistle.

"What are you going to do with it?" Jacob asks, handing it to her.

"I don't know. But this looks like it would fit in that middle one. Me and Uncle Marley put the other two keys there."

"What's it supposed to do?"

"I guess there's only one way to find out, right?"

Slowly, she reaches up, and carefully places the front of the whistle inside the middle hole. She pushes it in the rest of the way, with her thumb, until she hears the click, then pulls away promptly.

437

The basement door opens.

"Kyra? Jacob?" Owen says.

"Down here." Says Jacob.

Owen joins them by their sides. "What are you two doing?"

"Kyra put the whistle in that hole. Now it's making noise."

After a series of grinds and clicks, one large brick pops out, halfway from the rest surrounding it.

Unsure of what to do next, the kids look to their father.

At first, Owen hesitates, but subsequently reaches for the exposed brick, wiggling it, and pulling it free. The weight of it was unlike any brick he'd ever lifted. He gently set it down on the floor in order to inspect it more thoroughly.

"It's all scratched up." Jacob says skeptically, kneeling next to Owen.

Owen runs his fingers across the scratches—that appear to have a dusty, golden sheen within the groves.

A loose brick that was above it, slips from its position and smashes to the floor. Kyra rushes over to it. Its fake, rock-like, cement shell crumbles as she lifts it up, exposing a large, shimmering, golden nugget inside. She taps it on the floor, removing the rest of the phony covering.

"Dad! It's…" she holds it up "I think…"

438

Owen can't believe what he is seeing. Clumps of melted gold hidden within it. He looks down at the brick in front of him and smashes it to the floor. It, too, crumbled in his hands, showing an oddly-shaped nugget, the size of a fist. He turns it over to a smooth side and rubs it clean, polishing it with his shirt.

"Dad..." Jacob murmurs in amazement.

Owen's surprised and unbelieving expression, mirrored in the golden reflection, becomes instantly blurred from his falling tears.

THE END

Made in the USA
Middletown, DE
01 October 2021

48938105R00262